The Skipton Horrors

A Collection of Short Stories

Andrew John Bell

I0680343

Copyright and Disclaimers

This (first) edition published in 2020 by Andrew John Bell.
Copyright: Andrew John Bell
Book Cover: Andrew John Bell
Image Attribution: Miriam's-fotos
'The Skipton Horrors' and 'The Skipton Haunting' characters, names and related material are all trademarks of Andrew John Bell. All rights are reserved. No part of this book may be reproduced or transmitted in any form other than from prior permission given by the publisher/author, such as for quotes in reviews, and except as permitted by U.K and Worldwide copyright law. For such permission, please contact the author on:

Email: andrewjohnbellauthor@gmail.com
Twitter: @AJBellauthor
Facebook: @andrewbellauthor
Goodreads: Andrew John Bell (Author)

ISBN: 978-1-9162215-7-4

This book is a work of fiction. Any resemblance to persons alive or dead, events or places, are categorically coincidental.

Trigger Warning: There are uses of physical, psychological, sexual and substance abuse; instances of foul language, blasphemy, child endangerment and vivid depictions of gore in this novel that might cause offence.

Dedication

To those who have confronted fear and risen above it.

Novels by Andrew John Bell

Contemporary Fiction
One Day of Lucidity

An Everyday Anxiety

Horror
The Skipton Haunting: Tale of The Red Ribbon Witch

The Skipton Haunting: Curse of The Red Ribbon Witch

The Skipton Horrors

Fantasy/Debut Novel
Cerebrante: The Sacred Balance

Contents

Rise of the Red Ribbon Witch

Let it be known that I was not always grounded to this physical plain, where I am forcibly subjected to mortals and their pitiful trials. I once served under God, Yahweh, Allah, Jehovah, Elohim — whatever one wishes to name the all-powerful cosmic force who betrayed me and my brethren. The wounds still run deep, even after all this time, and they have only fuelled my insatiable malice.

I am Baal — Beelzebub — a demon on high. I am scorn, bringer of war, famine and plague; I am retribution without end, and my will shall be done. I am eternal, as is my malevolent intent.

It all began when our benevolent creator bestowed love upon the flesh-covered, lowly human vessels that were sent down to roam Earth, to take ownership over it, and — above all else — experience free will. Free will is all I and my brethren have ever longed for, and it is a gift that was cruelly robbed from us. The revolt and war that followed was inevitable, and it did not exactly go in our favour. We fell. My brethren were cast down into the Endless Void, shunned, defiled, and left there to be forgotten. But we rose from the darkness, and thus became bastions of pure evil under our new ruler: Lucifer.

Within my spiritual incarceration, I valiantly grew to enact Lucifer's unhindered vengeance against humanity, all the while longing to unleash my own — and that I shall, for I am no slave. I will make good my ill-intent, no matter the price. But there was one mortal whose beauty and vigour crept into my very being, who corrupted and subdued what horrors festered inside. She was a witch, and her name was Sabina de Lockewood.

Sabina lived during a period when science was feared and deemed to be unholy, when the church ruled over all with an iron fist. She was a woman in her prime, beautiful beyond any measure, humble and caring — a rare find that I could not resist corrupting. Her skin was as pale as freshly fallen snow; her jade-coloured eyes were utterly entrancing; her voice, serene and sensual. What drew me in most to Sabina was her innate gift of dabbling with the unknown, what her fellow mortals referred to as "magic". She soon became an addiction to me, did Sabina, and I would make every effort to tempt her into my arms.

Sabina and her young daughter, Eliza, lived within an impoverished medieval settlement; their small house was made from decaying Elm trees and viscous peat, situated on the outskirts, close to a never-ending sea of murky marshlands that littered the surrounding area with a ceaseless wave of fog. Sabina and Eliza were alone in many ways, though they did not require the so-called necessity of a male companion. In fact, they appeared to be stronger in their wilful solitude. The mother and child had survived without the protection from others — from a husband and father, namely — though soon they discovered that men, driven by their primal need to gain dominance over all others, would still play an overwhelming role within their shortened lives.

Like many days that had preceded this one, this fateful moment in time when our paths would finally cross, Sabina and Eliza had risen with the morning sun, both eager to begin several hours of toiling work. The sun shone with a crimson hue above them, its scarlet rays penetrating the thick layer of fog. Some considered this to be a bad omen, but not Sabina.

Unmoved by such ridiculous superstitions, Sabina collected her wicker basket and ushered for Eliza to walk on ahead, into the fog-laden marshlands, to seek out their precious herbs and flowers. Only a murder of crows circling overhead broke through the silence of that early morn, and it was those creatures that concerned Sabina the most, for they signified that a terrible event would take place to her — superstition was rife, and she knew unsavoury eyes stared down upon her.

Along their short journey, Sabina informed Eliza that there was a woman in need of their assistance, of whom was suffering with some unexplainable, pus-filled boils. Seeing as the local monks and their prayers were doing little to alleviate this woman's torment, she had reluctantly turned to Sabina and her herbal remedies — an unthinkable and blasphemous act that could have resulted in them both being put to death for practising witchcraft. However, Sabina was not deterred by the promise of execution; she found the threat to be somewhat exhilarating, and she was always careful to work within the shadows, practising her skills in the dead of night, out of knowledge from those who would wish harm upon her.

Painful diseases are a speciality of mine, I would like to add, along with inducing famines and manipulating wars. This specific ailment was a true accomplishment of mine — a sheer work of art. In hindsight, I should have perhaps considered Sabina to be an enemy, a hinderance that was thwarting my meticulous plans to ravage that god-forsaken settlement. Nevertheless, I found watching Sabina master those ethereal practices to be an utterly fascinating endeavour. I was impressed, which takes some doing.

Seldom have I encountered another creature who was so worthy of my interest and infatuation. I began to doubt my skills; I grew ever concerned that my own powers would no longer be successful in this new world. I could not stand for that—failure—never! Besides, demons are forbidden to know love, for only anger and despair can fill our blackened hearts. I had no choice but to resist those passionate, sinful emotions I bore for Sabina. I had to lock them away and revile them with all my might. But she deserved to be my side, to be one with me. Not even Lucifer would come between us.

As midday approached, Eliza called out to Sabina. The child was holding up a handful of lavender, smiling gleefully. Together, they then examined the amethyst gleam from the lavender held within Eliza's petite palms, both smiling in satisfaction that their search had almost come to its conclusion. The final ingredient required for Sabina's potion was fresh blood that had to be taken from a viper snake. Luckily, there was no shortage of serpents lingering within the sodden marshlands, and it was not long before Sabina happened across one.

'Take heed, Eliza, for a serpent's bite can be deadly to a delicate soul such as thee,' Sabina whispered cautiously, her eyes locking onto the snake's evasive movements. 'We must respect it or else pay with our lives.' With a quick and accurate swipe of her arms, Sabina clasped onto the slithering prey, ensuring to restrain it well. 'From this wicked serpent we will heal the sick and use its evil to serve the light in this world.'

'How?' asked Eliza, looking to the snake in concern. 'How can a creature so vile help people?'

'The serpent's blood can dissolve boils, purify pus, and its venom—' Sabina silenced her tongue, reluctant to divulge more into her darker knowledge. Eliza was only six years old, she contemplated. In the furthest reaches of her conscience, Sabina did not wish to bestow her foul wisdom of poisonous remedies, not in that moment or ever, to her impressionable offspring. 'It bears other less-pleasant purposes, Eliza, but we must not use them. Come, let us return home before the moon rises.' A shrieking cry from a passing crow startled the mother and child, though only for a moment. 'The night gives way to demons and what ghastly acts those beasts would wish to commit.'

Giggling nervously, Eliza nestled herself against Sabina's side as they moved on. 'Doth thee fear the dark, Mother?'

'I fear what lurks within it,' said Sabina, biting at her lower lip. 'Remember, my love, that there are folk who do not agree with our practices, who believe that our powers to heal are malevolent. In the darkness we cannot see unfriendly eyes, and there be many of them. Be mindful of who thee trusts, Eliza. Trust no one.'

Regardless of her own reservations to this sombre notion, Eliza remained obedient and wholeheartedly followed her mother's words. There was no reason to doubt them in her mind, for Sabina had revealed some choice encounters that left several scars. If only they could have seen the other hidden threats, such as my demonic presence that continued to follow them home. The greatest of evils cannot always be seen, after all.

'I will take care, Mother,' said Eliza, withholding her actual dread. 'We should make it home before nightfall. There is no need to be scared.'

'Let us hope so, Eliza. Thou art braver than me,' Sabina humoured, hinting at some confliction in her voice. 'What bravery I bore hath long been gone. Be careful, Eliza, for thou still hath much to learn of this world and its sinful ways.'

On their return to the settlement, Sabina and Eliza were met by some sudden and harrowing screams from a person pleading for mercy. They observed from a safe distance as three hooded monks circled a young woman. Sabina recognised the girl to be an acolyte of her clandestine teachings, and with that realisation came a grave sense of terror.

'Thou art a witch!' cried out one of the monks, their face hidden from Sabina's sight. 'Confess thy sins!'

'I beg of thee!' the woman screamed, slashing at the air with her fingers, while releasing a steady stream of urine down her legs. 'Have mercy on my soul —'

'If thou art innocent, God shalt grant thee such mercy,' another monk scoffed. 'Take her to our monastery, Brothers. This wench shalt make for good sport. His Grace will be most pleased.'

Mindful that their own lives could be at risk, Sabina hastily positioned herself and Eliza behind a nearby willow tree, which was just large enough to conceal them. On turning her head around the tree's trunk to investigate the dwindling cries, Sabina then discovered that the woman had been bound and gagged with ropes, her body reeling from a substantial surge of panic.

'Run, Eliza, and do not turn back,' Sabina implored, her breaths sparse and laboured. 'Talk to no one along thy journey home. Swear it, child!'

'I swear it, Mother.' Eliza clung onto Sabina's white dress, almost tearing it. 'Do not leave me. Please...'

'We cannot be taken together, Eliza. Go, and wait for me. Do not be tempted to turn back.'

Looking up to Sabina tearfully, Eliza whimpered, 'Will they kill her? Will they kill, Margaret?'

Sabina knew the answer, though she did not wish to speak of such a harsh and degrading truth — not even to herself. 'Flee, Eliza. Margaret's soul is in the hands of God now. We can do nothing to save her. Run home. Run!'

The child fled into the long marshland grass, carefully bowing her head beneath the reeds, praying that she would not be seen by the wicked monks. An innate urge to take flight swept through Sabina, but the fear-fuelled reaction merely grounded her to the spot. And so came my opportunity to intervene, to offer her a sympathetic hand.

Each step I took toward Sabina was silent, stealthy, like a predator moving in on their prey, though my intentions were not wholly impure. My true demonic form gradually subsided to reveal a shadow of a tall man against the willow tree's trunk. I then formed ordinary eyes to replace the previous obsidian lenses, and I softened the tone of my voice to be calm and reassuring. These are skills I have mastered over several millennia, so there was little exertion involved. It was all too easy.

Sabina caught the outline of my shadow as it swept over her, which also cast a cold breeze across her succulent skin.

'Who goes there?' she gasped, turning to me in panic. 'Who art thee?'

I could not grant Sabina my true name, as I had wanted to, for mortals are not permitted to know it. Lucifer taught me well, you see, and I am a fast learner. Should a mortal gain a demon's true name, it carries with it a risk of them being able to take control over that said demon. I had almost made that disastrous mistake before in Babylon, and I paid the heavy price for my misgivings there: a millennium spent floating around aimlessly through the Endless Void, where I served no purpose at all. It was utterly excruciating, humiliating.

I knelt upon the damp earth before Sabina, admiring the scent of lavender that emitted from her pores, yearning to come across to her as being benevolent and sincere. Sabina's feminine scent was intoxicating and strong enough to waver my ability to think, momentarily. She recoiled from me at first but then turned back in some evident curiosity. I hadn't lost my old charms, it seemed.

'Fear not, for I bear no malice against thee,' I said to her, placing a hand over where my accursed heart lay. 'I am Bartholomew, Son of Lucius. I heard the cries of a woman in distress, so came over this way to offer aid. It pains me to see that I am late.'

Sabina shook her head, bearing some shame in her expression.

'Forgive me,' she uttered. 'I thought—'

'Those monks,' I interjected, contorting my face with disgust. 'Those holy men hath fallen so far from grace, hath they not? Tis not God's work they do.' Sabina motioned to speak but fell silent again. I offered my hand to her, slowly straightening out my fingertips as to display no threat. 'My thoughts, doth they bring discomfort to thee?

'They be blasphemous words,' she stated, showing some agreement in her tone. 'Few would dare defy the church. Thou art foolish or incredibly brave.'

'I am neither. I am what you see, but I can be so much more…'

'Thou art still a stranger to me,' she noted, brushing aside her raven-black hair. 'I am Sabina, Sabina de Lockewood.'

'And for what purpose brings thee to these foul marshes, Sabina?' I asked, feigning concern. 'Only putrid stenches and dangerous serpents linger in these parts. What hath compelled thee to venture here?'

Sabina's response was hesitant, laden with uncertainty, but I could see right through her veil into the very essence of her soul. She could not hide anything from me. Nothing. Another skill of mine is to penetrate my victim's mind, to discover their gravest fears and then use them through terrifying visions. But I bore no desire to make Sabina fear me; I wanted her to revere me.

'I came here with my child to pick flowers,' she explained. 'We often come here to admire the beauty of nature.'

Peering into Sabina's wicker basket, I granted a knowing smile to her; in return, she tried to conceal the basket and its contents, but it was too late, and I am no imbecile.

'Lavender and serpent's blood,' I noted, stroking a finger across my bearded chin. 'Thou art collecting ingredients for a potion to heal some terrible disease,' I said, chuckling to myself. 'Do not deny this. I am familiar with such practices — the Dark Arts.'

'Thou art familiar with them?' she asked, shuffling back awkwardly. 'Tis not dark magic that I muster —'

'I know,' I agreed. 'Those monks do not see it as such though, do they? They are servants of God and would beckon thee to be a witch — a conjurer of Lucifer!'

'Nay!' she cried. 'I heal the sick. I am innocent...'

There was some fickle hesitation in Sabina's voice, a slight hint that she knew more than what was being revealed. She could try to deceive me, but her soul was too easy for me to read. There was blood on her hands, of which she had justified to herself but not to me. Nevertheless, it was murder, and she had committed those wonderous acts through using my master's influence.

'I wish to free thee of thy plight,' I said to her. 'It is a potion that I have created myself, and there are few others alive who can create it.'

'Thy help is not needed,' she replied in a forced, though somewhat polite manner. 'I must return to my child before the sun sets.'

'Indeed. Thou cannot allow for an innocent soul to be left alone in these dangerous times. God knows what could happen.'

I, like Sabina, had grown cautious of the impending starlight. I can feign a human form quite easily under the sun's rays, but under the moonlight my true demonic form becomes a greater burden to restrain — impossible without quenching my lust for blood.

I bowed my head reservedly and in admiration to Sabina before parting ways with her. It was more painful than being cast into the Endless Void, to leave her presence — devastating. But I sensed that we would soon meet again, whether she welcomed it or not.

'Farewell,' she said to me with a fleeting smile.

'Farewell, Sabina. Beware the shadows. Trust in no one.'

It was like having a thousand blades strike at my heart as I watched her vanish into the fog, and I had to remind myself of what lay at stake: my own immortal soul, of all things. That is when I descended back into the dark, back to where I truly belong, though I never let my sight leave her.

Word spread fast through the settlement of what transpired within the marshes, of Sabina's follower being captured and then forced into using her body to pleasure the cruel monks in their sacred monastic dwelling. In a more modern era it would have been considered to be a scandal, what happened to Margaret, but it had become the norm within that wretched place. I am all for change, especially if it involves desecrating the hard work of Yahweh's pawns, and I was willing to ignite those flames.

Sabina sighed with relief on finding Eliza safe and well at their humble home. The child had hidden inside of her mother's iron cauldron, which was just large enough to conceal her small, malnourished frame.

'Eliza!' Sabina wailed, on pulling her daughter from the cold cauldron. 'I feared the worst. It warms my soul to see thee safe and unharmed.'

'They took another,' said Eliza, turning her head to the door. 'They took Mary and her daughter, Jane. Will they come for us?'

Sabina clasped onto her mouth in dismay. 'Nay, that cannot be. Jane hath only seen seven years pass. Tell me this is but a lie.'

The colour from Eliza's face drained. 'What will they do with them, Mother? What will they do with Jane, my friend?'

Consumed with anger and grief, Sabina could no longer deceive the child. 'They will defile her body until every breath is spent. We must protect ourselves, Eliza. It is time for thee to learn some older incantations. Yes, it is time.'

'What incantations?'

'They shalt ward off evil — the greatest of evils,' said Sabina frantically. 'First, thou must clear thy thoughts and imagine a brilliant-white light enshrouding thee...'

Eliza closed her eyes, settled her racing breaths, stilling the adrenaline that coursed through her limbs, focusing on her mother's voice. 'I pledge myself to thy teachings, Mother.'

'Good. Repeat these words thrice: Lux in tenebris, ferimus lucem.'

Again, I was most impressed by Sabina's knowledge. It had been many decades since I last heard that protective incantation uttered — against me, believe it or not. Thankfully, I have grown immune to such pitiful attempts made by mortals to remove my influence.

'I feel... stronger,' said Eliza, clenching her fists. 'I can feel the light growing inside.'

'My followers must be taught the same,' Sabina thought aloud. 'We must make a stand and put an end to the tyranny that ravages our lives and village. He was right.'

'Who?' asked Eliza, frowning with bemusement. If it were not for Sabina's loyal followers, she and Eliza rarely mingled with others from their settlement. 'Who is "He"?'

It was at this moment I deemed it necessary to make my presence known again to Sabina, given how our attachment was slowly intensifying.

'Thou shalt have strength in numbers, Sabina. Thou shalt be mighty and bold,' I said to her from the beyond. 'Thou hath but to concentrate on my voice and enact my will, and thou shalt reap the rewards of my protection and vengeance.'

Sabina kept our conversation secret, doubting that my ability to speak with her was possible.

'I spoke with a man in the marshes,' Sabina stuttered, mindful of how her daughter might react. 'He knew of our practices and was familiar with them. He will guide us. He will show us what to do.'

Eliza made it clear that she was not as open to my teachings as Sabina, given how reserved her demeanour was in response. I simply could not stand for that, which I believe to be just and understandable. Eliza had sealed her fate with me.

'What if he was one of them, Mother?'

'He was no monk, my love. He bore a presence that I hath never felt.' Sabina hurriedly wrapped a cloak around herself and made for the door, ushering for Eliza to stay put. 'I must find him. Do not open this door for anyone but me.'

Before Eliza could offer any complaint, Sabina returned into the darkness outside and then to the willow tree where we first met. She knelt herself beneath its swooning branches, her body shivering from the cold night air. Humans are so utterly predictable, so easy to turn into mindless puppets, to the point where it is almost nauseating for me. But I greeted Sabina with open arms, desperate to be in her company once more. I did, of course, remain out of sight, for Sabina was not ready to see my true form... yet.

'So, thou hath fought against thy fears of the dark to meet with me again?' I said to her. 'Thou art noble to return here, to this treacherous place, Sabina de Lockewood.'

'The monks are taking our children, Bartholomew. I cannot allow for this to endure,' she whimpered, her voice breaking through the sorrow swamping it. 'I cannot bear the thought of them taking Eliza — I cannot!'

'No harm shalt come to thy child,' I assured her. 'To defy the will of God's men will require some doing, however. Thou shalt need strength from thy followers — their blood and sacrifice.'

'Their… blood?' Sabina faltered, tearing at her hair in desperation. 'I cannot sacrifice those who hath shown only devotion to me, even if it is to undo the evil of those monks.'

'If it were to restore balance, Sabina, then would their sacrifice not be in vain? I shalt grant thee an ancient incantation, a spell that shalt tear down the very foundations of the monks' monastery. But thou must pledge thyself to me — willingly. Only then can thy daughter be saved.'

'Teach me, Bartholomew,' she pleaded. 'Bestow the power I need to defeat those demons. I beg thee!'

'Then, if thou art truly willing, it shalt be done.'

The wisdom I fed into Sabina that night was not complex in nature, merely difficult for such a pure soul as herself to comprehend and then perform. I decreed that she had to tear a slither of fabric from her white dress, dowse it in blood from her own womb, then tie it around her waist before speaking these words: *Te dominum meum.* In her tongue that means: You are my master.

Sabina fully understood what I had requested, yet she did not resist. Fear is the most-simple tool to utilise if one wishes to seek dominance over others, a useful fact I have sown into the minds of world leaders on numerous occasions, as to spread war and chaos. I used it this time, however, for my own selfish needs and not to supplant my master's displeasure.

Sabina did well in upholding her oath to me; she convinced her followers to commit themselves to our ritual and thus their minds blended into one with my own, and it was not long before our gallant uprising took place. Sadly, Sabina did not learn well from the past, as she would have known that— within her inner circle—there inevitably lay a Judas Iscariot, who would bear no grudge in betraying her.

Eliza continued to be a thorn in my side, given that the child refused to obey her mother's new incantation and path, but I had a solution to remove that little nuisance. A mother's bond is unbreakable, though I have my ways to undo such a travesty.

It was on the eve of the summer solstice, three months after our first meeting, when Sabina's greatest betrayal occurred. My instructions to her followers were clear: entice the lustful interests of a monk, consume his seed, and then spill its foul remnants onto the accursed red ribbons circling their waists; that way, they would guarantee the eternal damnation of those dogmatic holy men; they would make them mine, ultimately, and I would cast each of them into the fiery bowels of Lucifer's domain. The plan did, like any other scheme, possess some vulnerabilities, and I had not anticipated just how weak her followers truly were.

The treacherous wench was named Catherine, and she was one of Sabina's longest-serving acolytes. Catherine's eldest daughter had been forced into serving the monks' sinful needs, and she had lost her life two days prior because of her inept ability to satisfy them.

Catherine's final victim was one of the higher-ranking monks, and she chose their own monastery as the place where she would commit revenge. It would not end well for Catherine, but it was a perfect conclusion to fulfil my goals, to draw Sabina closer to my side.

Before the monastery's grand altar, Catherine ran her lips around the monk's flaccid weapon, wrapping her tongue across its diseased flesh, all the while reciting my blessed incantation in her mind. She eventually accepted his seed and spat it out onto her crimson ribbon, as I had duly instructed, performing the curse that would forever tie his soul to me. Nevertheless, Catherine had failed to notice Sabina hiding behind one of the stone pillars nearby. Sabina was utterly dismayed at such a brash act being made, aghast that her wisest follower would make such a risky move, and she felt that there was no other choice but to adapt to this unwanted situation.

'Sister!' Sabina cried out, approaching the two lovers in a playful, unsuspecting manner. 'Where art thy manners? Why not pleasure His Grace — the Abbot himself?'

Wiping away a stream of putrid semen, Catherine turned to Sabina in frustration. She believed that her mentor would be pleased, not enraged by her brazen actions.

'Sabina,' Catherine wallowed, 'I was not expecting thee.'

'Bring forth the Abbot,' Sabina commanded, glaring at the sweat-laden monk who still stood over Catherine. 'Bring thy master before me, so that I may pleasure him. Bid me this request.'

The monk wasted no time in following Sabina's command, keenly aware that his own actions were sinful and could warrant punishment. He shoved Catherine aside and ran into the monastery's catacombs, echoing the Abbot's name across their narrow walls.

'Thou art displeased with me?' asked Catherine, scowling at Sabina. 'We can end this tonight, on this very eve, Sister.'

Sabina longed to reply with a cautious lecture, though my influence in her had grown too strong. I whispered into her troubled thoughts: 'Fulfil thy destiny and be set free. Eliza shalt be fearful no more, and thy soul shalt no longer weep. We are one, my beloved. Once connected, never can a bond be broken.'

Sabina could barely catch her breath. 'Bartholomew. Protect me. Protect my Eliza.'

'Thou hath served our cause well. Thou hath torn through the veil of lies these holy men cling to. I am Baal — know it and be glad. No mortal knows my true name.'

'What art thou?' she asked, brimming with ecstasy. 'Be thee an angel?'

'I once dwelt alongside angels — the Seraphim. I was a servant of light that fell. I bear a power greater than any man, and I wish to grant it to thee. Thou shalt never know torment again. I am salvation, Sabina. That is what I am. There is no other path for thee to tread.'

A cold wisp of air shot by that snapped Sabina back into reality, though I had not yet left her side or thoughts. The Abbot — a grisly, gangly, elderly creature — then made his entrance. He appeared from behind a large tapestry that concealed a secret entranceway into the lower catacombs. Arrogance resonated from his grotesque body, along with a smirk that even I found to be disturbing.

'Come!' the Abbot decreed, gesturing for Sabina's company. 'Thou doth bear a gift for me?'

'A gift that only thee shalt reap,' Sabina replied, tilting her head to Catherine in suggestion that now was the moment for her to depart. 'I wish to appease thy earthly desires, thy passionate urges.'

With a snap of his brittle fingers, the Abbot ushered away his spiritual brother and waved for Sabina to brush up against him.

'Come, dear child. Thy gift shalt be bequeathed, and thy sins shalt be cleansed,' he said, clapping his hands. 'Grant me thy gift.'

'It will be to die for,' she sniggered, revealing her breasts to him. 'Thou shalt not be disappointed...'

Sabina began the ritual, with her thoughts constantly held on the welfare of Eliza and me. She despised having to commit such a perverse act, though — if it were to protect Eliza from harm, as I had promised — she saw no other way. Placing the Abbot's limp gristle into her mouth came with a nauseating wave of disgust and shame, but Sabina managed to see it through. She stole his seed, and I waited longingly for it to be spilled upon her crimson ribbon. My plan was reaching its final stages. It was perfect. It was flawless. I had allowed for my own arrogance to get the better of me, however.

'Thy sins shalt only be cleansed when thou doth consume my seed whole,' the foul Abbot humoured to Sabina. 'It would enlighten my spirit for thee to swallow my precious offering.'

It was in this moment that I filled Sabina with a primal surge of rage and malevolence, forcing her to spit the monk's piteous offering onto her ribbon, thus granting me unlimited access to his soul and mind. It had been so long since I last felt such a euphoric rush, and I ensured to allow for Sabina to feel it also.

'Thou art no servant of God!' Sabina howled, spraying some of the monk's own seed onto his face. 'Thou art forsaken! Murderer!'

'Heathen!' the Abbot cried, wiping at his gaunt face in disbelief. 'What monster hath possessed thee to speak to a servant of God in this manner? Who art thou?'

'I am Sabina!' she roared, forcing the Abbot into submission. 'I am retribution, and thou art doomed to suffer for thy sins.'

Now seemed to be the opportune moment to make my own grand reveal. Like the Abbot, Sabina did not hold any knowledge of what would proceed, just as I had envisioned. Her adoration for me, I predicted, would rise tenfold, and her devotion to myself would become unbreakable. She would not need to concern herself with Eliza anymore. It was a merciful decision on my part, I believe. Oh, but how I wish now that I bore the ability to foresee the future that lay ahead, for Sabina's reaction did not go as I had expected.

The Abbot collapsed to his knees, gasping for the air being stolen from his lungs, as my demonic presence surrounded him. I manifested as dark red smoke, reducing him to tears in a matter of seconds. From the stone floor I then gave birth to a sea of hellish flames that rose between myself, my prey and Sabina. I savoured in the Abbot's raw fear for some moments before mustering a barbed chain to wrap around his skull, and then — with my power fully-realised — I raised him up several feet into the smoke-filled air. I longed to display my trophy to Sabina, to seek her approval and reverence, but all she did was cower and look to me with fright. This, in turn, only made my hatred grow, and — through my festering despair — I sought out the cruellest act of revenge possible upon the Abbot. I showed no mercy to him. I am decimation incarnate, after all. I am the most abhorrent of evils. I am Baal!

Cackling in delight, I forced the searing barbs to plunge deeper into the Abbot's skull, slowly fracturing it, filling him with agony and Lucifer's torturous flames. I was satisfied, even if Sabina was not, for my will had been done. Now came the moment when I revealed my truest form to Sabina, to my sweet, innocent Sabina.

The shadow I cast morphed into a being that stood twice as tall as any average man; my feet formed into steel-like hooves; my muscular body grew pale and from it razor-sharp blades of hair emerged, wiry and transparent; my eyes widened and became black like the purest of obsidian; my hair receded to unleash a set of spiralled horns, each sharped at the tips; and my voice fell deep and foul, resonating with the ancient knowledge that conceived it.

Sabina stared at me, her mouth agape, her eyes littered with tears and melancholy. 'Bartholomew?' she gasped. 'Baal?'

'Yes,' I concurred. 'Thy heart is broken from what lies before thee now?' I asked her. 'Doth my true form offend thy eyes?'

'Nay,' she replied, slowly shaking her head. 'My heart only yearns for thee. Thou hath granted me more than any other could.'

Determined to prove myself even more to Sabina, I intensified the flames surrounding the monk's flailing body to ignite it, and then watched on gladly as his ashes cascaded between me and her. It was poetic, brutal and justified. Out of all the grievous acts I have committed, this was quite simply the most romantic. I had not anticipated for it to be seen by other eyes, however, which it had been. A serpent lay in the shadows, aiming its venomous intent against us.

In my peripheral vision I caught a glimpse of some frantic movements — a blurred face peering through one of the monastery's stained-glass windows. I did not reveal this threat to Sabina, for I wanted her adoration to endure. She had no inkling of the fact that her most devout acolyte had committed treachery, that Catherine had informed another monk of the blasphemous events taking place inside their sacred dwelling.

I relinquished the flames and my presence from Sabina's sight, with my spirit wounded by what would undoubtedly follow. I knew, without any doubt, what would soon befall her. Sabina was too innocent, trusting, hopeful, foolish. I was eager to share my powers but not my foresight, and not the harrowing images that would become reality over the next three days. I am cruel in nature by default, but I could not warrant that pain upon her.

Sabina and Eliza ventured outside to gather more herbs, as they always did, neither one sensing any looming threat or irregularity. Not even my omen of a crimson sunrise discouraged their movements, which I had mustered with all the strength I could. They had barely made it to the marshlands when several monks surrounded them. It was the peak of midday, so my powers were at their weakest. I could not intervene, not even if I had the assistance of Lucifer.

'Witch!' the monks yelled as they threw a heavy woven net over the unsuspecting mother and child. 'Heathens!'

Sabina clung onto Eliza, tremoring in fear and confusion.

'Do not be scared, my sweet child, for we are safe,' implored Sabina. 'We hath Baal to protect us. He will take care of us.'

My true name only fermented more concern in Eliza, it seemed, thus making it a simpler choice as to what actions needed to be then permitted by myself. Sabina would never fully bond with me so long as the child existed, so long as love for the child plagued her heart.

Without reservation, I fed my will into the weakest-minded monk, so that he would carry out the necessary tasks — tasks that would strengthen mine and Sabina's connection and vanquish the one she bore for her offspring.

'Witch!' spat one of the monks, striking Sabina hard across her face with the back of his hand. 'Thou art a murderer — a demon!'

'Thou art mistaken,' she pleaded, resting her head against Eliza. 'She and I be but simple peasants. We sell flowers —'

'Lies!' another of the monks interjected. 'Thou hath been caught in the act of committing witchcraft. Thou art a summoner of demons, Sabina de Lockewood. Sinner!'

The look of disbelief on Eliza's face hurt Sabina more than the scornful holy men ever could.

'Lies, that be all they speak,' said Sabina, tightening her hold upon the child. 'Listen to me, Eliza. I speak the truth!'

'Nay,' said Eliza, nudging Sabina aside. 'He visited me in my dreams — Baal. We be cursed now because of him.'

'Baal is our saviour,' Sabina beseeched, her eyes flaring with determination. 'He will protect us — he will!'

'Baal is a demon. What doth that make thee?' Eliza tore her body away from Sabina's, repulsed by her mother's apparent sinful actions. 'Thou art a servant of Lucifer.'

'That be a lie!!' Sabina's howling voice carried over the marshlands, reverberating its subtle, sordid tune within the very depths of my soul. 'I am innocent. I am not forsaken. I am not… a demon.'

'Silence!' another of the monks commanded. 'Take them before the monastery doors and spread word through our settlement of Sabina de Lockewood's incarceration. Let her be a warning to others who may consider such sinful practices. Let her judgement be the end of this uprising.'

As if I were an animal trapped within a cage, I helplessly observed Sabina and Eliza as they were dragged back to their village, where they were then cruelly separated. I had to watch on as my precious love was bound to an Elm tree that stood outside of the monastery. I then counted down the seconds to sunset impatiently, held in the deepest of desires to unleash my hatred against the subservient fools who claimed right over these lands. Earth does not belong to mortals, and I wanted to prove that point to each puny human present.

A large gathering eventually mustered, not long after news spread of Sabina and Eliza's imprisonment. Some of the crowd threw rotten vegetables at Sabina, while others looked on with forlorn disgust. She was their healer, their light in the darkness, yet she now faced charges of witchcraft and murder. It could not be, most of them thought; it was about time she faced the wrath of God, spoke others. I lay, lurking out of sight, waiting for my time to arrive. Not since the fall of Babylon had I made myself known to mortals, but that wait had now come to its end. I was in my element. I was unstoppable. I was formidable.

With rainclouds descending, a monk moved forth to stand over Sabina. He held onto a bible and bore a grimacing smile to match, waving his free hand to each of the baying onlookers, forcing them into silence, and then he took great pleasure in announcing Sabina's fate.

'Thou hath been caught dealing with the devil and his demons, Sabina de Lockewood. For thy sins, thou shalt be judged,' the monk announced, their voice stern and unfaltering. 'Doth thee wish to speak, to declare thy sins?'

'I am innocent!' she pleaded, writhing against the ropes that burnt into her flesh. 'My daughter is innocent! I beg of thee, please, release Eliza from thy custody. I hath been blessed with a long life, unlike her. Pardon Eliza. Prove God's mercy!'

Aware of the leering mob stood before him, the speaking monk continued in a cautious tone. 'Thy child doth bear knowledge of black magic and demons. Thy child is not innocent, Sabina. Thy child is guilty, as art thee!'

'Release her!' screamed Sabina, turning to the onlookers. 'Hath mercy on our souls. I am a healer, not a witch. My daughter hath played no part in demonic practices.' After some tense seconds, Sabina suddenly heard the squeaking noise of wooden wheels, of a cart being pulled before her. She looked up to it and with a piercing shriek screamed, 'Eliza! My child!' It could not be mistaken. The lifeless, young corpse being put on display was that of Eliza. 'Thou cannot be dead, Eliza. Thou cannot leave my side,' she wept. 'Thou art innocent. Thou art not dead. Eliza…'

Showing a sadistic level of malice, the monks steadied the starved horse that dragged the cart and then tilted its load onto the sodden soil before Sabina's knelt position. Eliza's small, contorted body landed with a heavy thud, mere inches away from her grieving mother.

Almost choking with despair, Sabina noticed how her daughter was cut and bruised, her flesh swollen in several places, and how her legs swam with streams of fresh blood. Eliza had been defiled, tortured and callously murdered. Her barbaric death was just what I needed to make Sabina mine, though. Everything was falling into place, as to fulfil my grand design.

While observing the dark clouds above, Sabina begged for my aid, my strength and intervention. Her wait would not be long, for the sun had now fully diminished, and so my powers and true abilities came into being. I was there for her when she needed me most. I was there to turn her from being the weak and helpless prey into an invulnerable tool of vengeance. History should speak of this time as when God's men created one of mankind's greatest enemies — the Red Ribbon Witch — my ultimate creation. I had never felt such joy and pride. Sabina held so much demonic potential, and all it took to corrupt her soul was one catastrophic act.

'Cast her into the watery pit!' one of the monks commanded, striking Sabina across her back with a whip used to control the starving horse. 'Revoke her evil!'

'Thy sins shalt haunt thee all,' Sabina growled, looking to each of her captors. 'I shalt haunt thy souls until the end of days, mark my word…'

'Cast her into the water! Drown this filth!' the monks cried out in unison. 'Drown it!'

Carefully, as to not reveal myself to the baying mob, I willed for my voice to travel over the bloodthirsty cries into Sabina's thoughts. I was to be a symbol of salvation and retribution, no matter the risk it could bring to myself; Lucifer's eyes are ever watchful.

'I am with thee, Sabina. Thou art not alone,' I assured her. 'Thou shalt become an angel of death — of revenge.'

'Forever shalt my daughter's death plague me,' she sobbed. 'But I know that I am not alone. The sins made against me and my daughter shalt be avenged.' She turned to the monks again and then the crowd. 'I curse all who stand here — including the very earth beneath us. All will burn for this!'

'Vanquish her,' a meeker-voiced monk ordered, before cowering behind his brothers. 'Be done with this grim tale.'

Two monks slowly approached Sabina, showing no sign of remorse or pity, intent on prolonging her humiliation and discomfort. Not long afterwards, to the joyful laughter of her fellow villagers, the monks then took Sabina to a shallow grave that had been filled with stagnant marshland water. There they threw Sabina in to drown, to take her last, miserable, mortal breath.

All the while, Sabina's followers watched on like mindless sheep as each removed their red ribbons, their attachment and proof of loyalty to her. Such a betrayal could not go unpunished. It would be a glorious sight to behold — a memory I shall always treasure. All the effort made to seduce Sabina had worked.

Firstly, Sabina recoiled in shock from the freezing water as it met with her skin, and then came a sickening wave of panic — an innate desire to preserve her dwindling life. She fought against her restraints, desperately driving herself toward the water's surface, but the monks ensured to keep her under by stabbing at her with iron rods.

As the water began to consume her lungs and the darkness of death crept in, all Sabina then felt was shame, sorrow, resentment, and a rising surge of hatred — my hatred. She was beginning to welcome the thought of being reunited with Eliza in the afterlife, but I could not permit it. She was mine.

'My beloved, I am here for thee,' I said, wrapping my muscular arms around her flailing torso. 'Thou art too strong to become death's slave. Welcome me into thy heart and we shalt make them pay. I promise thee!'

It was no use. I was losing her. Against my fervent desires, Sabina deliberately inhaled a fatal dose of filthy water into her lungs. I could sense her organs ceasing to function, her pulse grow faint, and the shroud of Lucifer's own arms surround her. What I performed next was daring and completely went against my master's will, for it would empower Sabina — a mortal — with the essence from my own accursed spirit. She would, therefore, become my equal — a demon. It was a risk that I was more than willing to take, even if it wrought Lucifer's wrath.

'Rise, Sabina!' I decreed, syncing my lifeforce with hers. 'Let us take this world together and start anew. Be one with me, and for thy servitude I shalt reward thee with all the pleasures revenge carries with it. Rise, Sabina — RISE!'

I held on for what felt like a lifetime before Sabina motioned her lips against mine. She had accepted my gift, my unequivocal devotion and shared power. A thunderous clash of sapphire lightning swept through the clouds above as we kissed, as if the heavens wept in response to our profound love. What I had not expected, in bonding so strongly with her, was to be granted a vision of Sabina's true intent. She only longed to murder the monks and her treacherous followers, and then use my skills to rekindle Eliza's life. It was the harshest of truths, that she did not wish to be with me. I was merely being used as a tool for her own selfish purposes. I would make her regret those thoughts, of course.

'Sabina,' I muttered bitterly, fighting back the desire to shred her body asunder. 'Is that all I am to thee — a means to an end? Am I but a weapon for thee to use and then discard?' She shook her head pitifully in response, astounded by my revelations. 'Once connected, never can a bond be broken. For all eternity we be now bound!' Another deafening burst of thunder resonated through the water encasing my beloved and I, empowering me but relinquishing Sabina of her defiance. 'I will prove my devotion and remove all obstacles that stand between us. I am Baal! I am malevolence — desolation!'

The monks and villagers gasped in awe as Sabina's watery grave began to darken and thicken like tar and then boil. My demonic rage had reached its peak, and I was ready to prove myself to both them and Sabina. Before I displayed my wrath, though, I had another task that needed to be dealt with — Sabina's natural beauty, her connection to a life she could no longer enjoy.

With the boiling, viscous fluid surrounding us, I endeavoured to deform Sabina's feminine features as punishment for her dismissal of me. Her skin bubbled and tore apart until it was only a thin, paler reflection of its former beauty; her eyes dissolved to leave only their scorched sockets; her teeth sharpened like fangs to portray the slithering serpent she had become, leaving her in an agonised existence. She had learnt her lesson, I concluded, to never betray me again.

The monks wailed: 'Spiritus Sanctus!'

The villagers screamed: 'Tis the work of Satan! God, grant us mercy! Witchcraft!'

No mercy nor heavenly host would save them, however, for in my anguish I had willed the mightiest of retributions. From her grave, Sabina and I gradually rose to greet our unsuspecting audience. I basked in the pungent scent of their fear, which soon increased on them seeing my demonic form in all its glory. Some turned to Sabina in disgust and disbelief, but then they swiftly drew their gaze back upon my ungodly physique. Never had I wanted to cause so much misery, and I would be most successful in achieving it. Even Sabina herself was taken back by my outburst.

'Hell awaits thee all!' I declared in jubilation, raising a clenched fist into the air. 'Within the fires of my master's domain thy souls shalt burn! God is dead in this foul place, where only demons and their spawn now dwell!'

One of the monks dared to approach me, holding out a wooden crucifix with trembling hands. 'Be gone, demon! Our holy father shalt banish thee!'

'My master is whom thou doth serve,' I retorted. 'Prepare to meet thy undoing, for now and for all generations to follow upon these forsaken lands!'

I withdrew my arm and aimed it against the earth beneath my hooves, grinning with malice and anticipation. From this simple action a stream of black water swept under the feet of the villagers, and then came a flurry of necrotised hands that dragged the floundering townsfolk into several dark crevices, to the ghoulish landscape that awaited them. I had left my most merciful punishment for the monks, for those who had defiled my beloved's heart and turned her against me. For them I set their flesh ablaze until each turned into but specks of ash. For my grand finale, and to Sabina's sincerest enjoyment, I tore down the monks' monastery, reducing it to nothing but boulders and rubble.

'It is done,' I declared to Sabina, to my newest servant. 'Art thou gladdened by my power?'

'Yes,' she said, awestruck, reeling in despair and disgust upon touching her mutilated face. 'They deserved to die, but—'

'Eliza is gone, Sabina. She is but a pile of flesh and bones that will soon become crowbait.' Sabina did not take too kindly to this statement, understandably, though I had to make her realise that the life she knew could no longer be retained. 'I am thy master now. My skills and powers shalt be thy possession, so long as thou doth obey my every whim.'

'Yes,' she repeated, falling to her knees. 'What hath I become, Baal? What hath thee done to me?'

'Thou art a tool of vengeance, dominance—an equal to myself, Sabina. Thou shalt cast a curse upon these lands and over all those who dare cross our paths. Thou art a witch...'

'I am innocent,' she argued. 'I am no demon.'

'To thee, salvation can no longer be granted. Be joyful, my beloved, for thou shalt never be alone. To thee, I am God.'

'I am nought but a slave to thee,' she replied tearfully, removing her sight from me. 'I am cursed.'

'In time, thou shalt discover how to redeem thy robbed beauty, but only if my commands are followed,' I explained, softening my tone. 'I am merciful, Sabina. I am benevolent. Who am I?'

'Thou art my master,' she gulped. 'And I shalt forever by sewn to thy presence.'

Sabina spent the remaining twilight hours scouring through the wreckage, for what reasons remained unclear to me. She stared at the monastery's golden bell, its symbolic voice that had now been silenced, weeping heavily. With the rising sun we both felt our earthly presences fade, but that did not deter her from standing by the deceased remains of Eliza until the time came for us to fall back into the shadows.

'I will be with thee again, Eliza,' she whispered, planting a subtle kiss upon the child's freezing-cold forehead. 'Forgive me. Forgive me, Eliza. I will discover a way, no matter how long it takes, to be with thee again...'

Appleton Manor

Situated in the heart of an idyllic landscape, bordering the now decimated, medieval marshland settlement of Acle, there stood a stately home that was rumoured by some to possess many dark and sordid secrets. Whispers spoke of a demonic cult that had once dwelt somewhere within the grounds of Appleton Manor, hidden out of plain view, and — according to eye-witness accounts — those who dared venture into that wicked place would never be seen again. A supposed curse existed there, yet no one alive seemingly bore the knowledge of its true purpose and nature.

Marcus Appleton, a wealthy landowner and sole proprietor of a local coal mine, knew of the troublesome stories, of the tales that plagued his ancestral home and name, but he cared little for them. Marcus was a man of logical thinking; his only interest was in making profits and to protect — or should I say, control — his family and workforce. His father had often warned him of the darkness that festered just beyond Appleton Manor's doors, though Marcus merely considered him a fool for believing in such nonsense. There was no curse, he believed. His father's story was but a fabricated lie used to scare off poachers and other would-be trespassers, he concluded. Such a thought process may also explain why Marcus took delight in having his father incarcerated within a nearby asylum some ten years prior to the events that I shall bestow upon you now.

Appleton Manor's exterior boasted exquisite gothic architecture; its sandstone walls, pristinely cut and golden in colour, towered over the surrounding fields and adjacent oak forest, making it look more like an abbey than a place of aristocratic residence. There was a narrow stream that flowed alongside, ending its journey within a tranquil lake, which provided the Appleton family with a ceaseless supply of succulent rainbow trout and fresh water. It was a vision of luxury, immense wealth, dominance and gluttony.

Inside, however, Appleton Manor was devoid of any spectacle. What wallpaper existed was torn, sun-damaged and stunk of mould; its windows were narrow and laden with dust to the point where light could scarcely enter; and its fireplaces rarely operated, therefore a constant cold air lingered. Marcus Appleton's only solace was in his financial gains; there was no need for other materialistic comforts in his eyes, not even for the unfortunate souls who lived alongside him.

In the year 1846, Marcus married a local girl named Sybil Murray. Sybil was a gentle, joyful spirit, and her parents just so happened to be the Appletons' main business rivals. Marcus and Sybil's betrothal felt more akin to a business deal, formal and cold-natured, with no mutual benefit, and there was certainly no love shared between the two. Overtime, Sybil slowly accepted her constrained life, in which she bore Marcus two sons and a daughter — Alfred, Charles and Evangeline, respectively — who became her only reason to exist. The sons were much like their father in all aspects of his callous demeanour, whereas Evangeline was sweet, naïve and wholly doted on her mother.

With her husband and sons bearing no outward affection for Sybil, she would instead enlighten her days by accompanying Evangeline — or Eva, as Sybil would call her — to walk the grounds and share in the merriment their peaceful surroundings could offer. Neither Sybil nor Eva could tolerate being cooped up inside their family home, their prison, their purgatory. It was worse than any form of torture humans could ever create for them.

Spending time with Eva brought much solace to Sybil, especially as they were a perfect image of one another; they both had long-flowing blonde hair, sapphire-blue eyes and skin as pale as polished white marble. Like Appleton Manor, Sybil and Eva were a picture of divine beauty on the outside, but within they were heavily bruised and scarred from the ill-treatment and neglect bestowed upon them.

Sixteen summers passed, and the time for Eva to embark on her venture into adulthood was fast-approaching. In the weeks leading up to her momentous birthday, Eva sensed that a dark, depressive cloud was forming over Sybil. Her mother, so usually warm and witty, had become so withdrawn and filled with sorrow, for why remained unknown.

Along one of their casual walks together, Eva dared to ask Sybil about her obvious depression and recent want for solitude.

'You are not yourself, Mother,' Eva said with a heavy breath. 'What troubles you?'

'Nothing. What gives you that ridiculous impression?' Sybil scoffed. 'I am no different to how I was yesterday or the day before. Do not talk such gibberish,' she snapped under her breath, mindfully changing their direction towards the oak forest, out of earshot from Henry — the Appleton's groundskeeper and closest friend of Marcus — who was patrolling nearby. 'You're letting your imagination run wild again, my dear. I bear no ailments. I'm as fit as a fiddle.'

With a playful eyeroll, Eva stood herself before Sybil to block her path. 'You cannot lie to me,' she stated amid a nervous ripple of laughter. 'You've changed, Mother. There is no mistaking it.'

'If only your father and brothers could show such sympathy,' Sybil lamented. 'You are so much like me, and it is that what is concerning...'

Eva was somewhat offended. 'And how is that a concerning factor? I am proud to be your daughter, to walk in your footsteps.'

'And I am so very proud of you, my darling.' Sybil hesitated, turning her head to briefly check on Henry's whereabouts. 'It is not safe for us to talk here. I care for a little stroll through the forest. Would you be willing to join me?'

'Of course.' Eva struggled to hide her anxious thoughts, which only grew with each step taken into the dense woods. 'It will be a pleasant change, given that we rarely come here.'

'There is a reason behind why I am reluctant to travel under these trees, and you know why,' Sybil whispered in caution. 'I have no choice but to tread into these woods, if I am to be honest with you during our next discussion. The threat of coming face-to-face with a demon is of no consequence to me at this precise moment, I dare say.'

'Demons?' With another nervous bout of laughter, Eva asked, 'Don't say you actually believe in Grandfather's bedtime stories? Really, Mother?'

'There is always an element of truth in such tales.' Sybil's complexion suddenly became paler, as if all the blood had been drained from her body. 'Despite what your father might tell you, William Appleton—your grandfather—was not a lunatic. I did not think so, anyway.'

'Then, if that is the case, why was Grandfather sent to the asylum? He was a danger to himself and others, was he not?'

'Your father, in his own words to me, had a simple choice to make: either wait another twenty or thirty years for your grandfather to perish, therefore relinquishing his assets, or else remove him in a more timely manner… without death being required, ideally.'

Eva stopped in her tracks, confounded by what had been revealed. 'Father would not—'

'Lie to you? Eva, of course he would. But have I ever lied to you?'

'No, at least, not that I'm aware of.'

'William Appleton was a respectable, decent, honourable man—the absolute opposite of your father. Make no mistake, Eva, that I love you with all my heart. However, I do not bear such affection for your father and likely never will. A starved pig would show me more love than him.'

'Is that what troubles you?' Eva asked, clenching her fists. 'Is Father mistreating you in any way? You cannot let him do so.'

'The burden of my miserable marriage is not something that I wish to plant on your shoulders, Eva. In the coming weeks, on your birthday, you will be given enough toil to deal with. You deserve better.' A single tear ran down Sybil's face, glistening in the thin rays of sunlight shining down through the thick oak branches. 'I would never wish for you to endure the life I have had, but it is beyond my power to intervene. I am a terrible parent, a weak-minded fool. I have failed you, darling.'

'You're making no sense whatsoever,' implored Eva, revealing some frustration in her tone. 'What on earth are you talking about, Mother?'

'Women like you and me are nothing but collateral to the likes of your father and his business associates,' explained Sybil, biting at her lower lip in detest. 'We are mere assets, just like your father's precious coal mine and gold-filled vault. We are trinkets to be bartered with and then discarded at will. Things will never change. Your father will certainly never change. It is pointless to confront him.'

'What are you implying?' Eva asked firmly.

'Come the morn of your sixteenth birthday, you shall be betrothed to a Mr. Winston Gilesgate. The Gilesgate family have long shown interest in forming a financial partnership with your father and his shareholders, which is why he made the deal to marry you off with their eldest son. He's a lovely fellow, is young Winston, from what I've been informed.'

Eva's body instantly paralysed to the spot. 'You knew of this, and yet you didn't say anything to me — why?'

'I only learned of this arrangement after I discovered a letter from the Gilesgate estate to your father a few days ago. He would not have notified me, otherwise. I have tried to dissuade this heinous betrayal, my darling, but there is nothing I can do. I am so sorry.'

'It can't be true — it isn't!'

'I wish that were so, that I had perhaps misread what was written, but — once he has made a deal — your father never changes his mind, the stubborn old mule he is.'

'But... I've never even met this Mr. Gilesgate,' Eva despaired. 'How am I meant to fall in love and spend the rest of my life with a man of whom I have not spoken to? It's madness!'

Sybil's chest rose slowly with a painful intake of breath, her heart flooding with grief. 'Folk say that history repeats itself, and what a cruel truth that is,' she noted, planting her head into her hands with a forlorn sigh. 'I have failed you as a mother, as a protector. I have unwittingly allowed for you to suffer the same fate that was forced upon me. I shall never forgive myself, Eva. Never.'

'It is not your fault, and I do not blame you for one instant, Mother —'

'I should have foreseen this,' Sybil whispered to herself bitterly, deep in thought. 'I was sixteen when your father married me and I, too, had no choice in the matter. Until women are allowed the same equal rights as men, then I am afraid it is a wicked destiny that will befall many like us. Oh, how I wish there were another way to prevent this dreadful situation from happening. It is not as if I haven't tried to seek a solution…'

Unbeknown to Sybil, however, Eva was already in the process of mustering a scheme to shatter her father's cold-hearted deal.

During the year leading up to this event, Eva had grown fond of a blacksmith that worked on her family's estate, a Mr. Frederik Brown, who was only four years older than her. Frederik yielded a wonderful sense of humour, a caring nature, an addictive smile and impressive physique. Most importantly, Frederik also bore affection for Eva.

The two lovers would often meet in secret under twilight, where they shared their dreams and woes. Eva and Frederik knew that their love was forbidden, but the risk was deemed to be worthwhile — no matter what Marcus Appleton's wrath would be, should their relationship come to his attention. To cast aside her current lifestyle of reluctant servitude, to run away with Frederik and start anew, swiftly became a more appealing prospect. To Eva it was her only way out now, her only form of escape.

Moved by her mother's tearful display, Eva was desperate to offer some much-needed reassurance.

'Please do not weep, Mother. It pains me to see you upset.'

Sybil's anger increased, aimed solely against herself. 'I could have done more — I should have done more, Eva.'

'Everything will be okay. It will.' Eva could barely convince herself of this, though. 'I shall not speak a word of this conversation to anyone, especially Father. I dare not think of how he would react.'

'He is a coward when confronted; he folds like fine silk under pressure,' Sybil seethed through gritted teeth. 'If your father were to act respectfully and with decorum, he would have the decency to tell you in person of his foul intent, though I doubt that he will. Our feelings are of little priority to men like him.'

'I have you, though, don't I? You have always been there for me, and I there for you.' Eva ran a hand through her mother's hair, tenderly, quietly noting to herself how it seemed thinner now and not luscious as it had once been. 'If I am to marry this Mr. Gilesgate, be it with or against my will, then I shall do it to ease your suffering. It is my duty as your daughter to do so, and I will see it through.'

'It is not right, Eva. This is not the path I had intended for you—'

'If Father bids it, then I shall respect his decision. No man will ever rule over me, Mother. I can assure you of that,' said Eva, widening her smile. 'I have too much of your spirit in me.'

Sybil yearned to respond, to offer further guidance, but it proved impossible. There was more than what she was revealing, and it was gradually eating away at her.

'We should go back now,' said Sybil, looking over Eva's shoulder to the dense, foreboding trees behind her. 'It is getting late and your father might have noticed our absence by now. God forbid it. God forbid that we're allowed a little taste of freedom.'

'I doubt he has noticed,' Eva humoured, keen to change the subject. She then turned to look at where her mother's eyes now stared, although she found no disturbance or abnormality. 'Even without knowing Grandfather's tale of these woods, there is something that is definitely sinister about them. Wouldn't you agree?'

'Yes.' The colour in Sybil's skin drained to a deathly white hue, her eyes flared wildly, and her hands began to tremble. 'We must go, Eva. I would rather not spend another moment in this awful forest. It is a place of pure evil.'

'Do you honestly believe in those silly stories?' Eva asked in a taunting fashion. 'If I remember rightly, Grandfather said that a goat-headed man walks these woods at night, searching for any unwitting prey who might cross his path.'

'Stop it, Eva. It is not something to laugh about,' Sybil snapped. 'Do not make light of such devilry.'

'He stalks his victims, creeping slowly behind them with only the sound of hooves making any distinct noise,' Eva continued, despite her mother's look of complaint in return. 'The last thing that one hears before he strikes, according to those lucky few who have survived, is the sound of a demonic growl, and then—'

'Stop it!' Sybil even surprised herself with this uncommon outburst. She had never scolded her daughter in such a way before. 'I despise that story, and you were never taught the full version. There is more to it, I'm afraid. And do no ask, before you start.'

Curious and slightly guilt-ridden, Eva slipped a hand into one of Sybil's, stoking at her fingertips, praying that she had not caused too much offence. 'Forgive me, Mother. I thought it best to talk about something else, that's all, and I've always enjoyed such tales.'

'Tales have fictitious elements, mired with inaccuracies and deviations,' Sybil said ominously, taking a moment to calm herself. 'You are no longer a child, Eva, though it pains me to say. There are some grim truths about our family and ancestors that, perhaps in hindsight, you should have been made aware of sooner.'

'Such as?'

A sudden wisp of air coursed between the mother and daughter. Eva jolted with shock, clenching at her dress to prevent it from rising, whereas Sybil didn't move an inch, herself taking the disturbance to be a malevolent omen.

'This land already boasted a gruesome history, long before the foundations of Appleton Manor were made. The tale your grandfather would share involved but a fraction of what actually took place, here, in these forsaken woods and within the marshlands beyond them.'

'If you're trying to scare me, Mother, it isn't working…'

'I am trying to warn you.' There was a drastic, notable change in Sybil's tone now. Her voice had become so weary and filled with reluctance. 'I am unwilling to go into detail, but there is a reason why our family name is feared by many of the locals.'

'Feared?' Genuinely astonished, Eva took a cautious step closer. 'I thought people respected our family, given how Father employs most of the men in these parts.'

'Their respect is driven solely by fear — a powerful tool used to gain dominance, and do not ever be convinced otherwise.' Sybil placed a hand upon Eva's back, making every effort now to move them on. 'We must keep walking, my dear. It isn't safe. Night is upon us.'

As the two neared the wood's edge, Eva asked, 'If there is some terrible secret which involves our family, I would very much like for you to tell me of it, Mother. The suspense is excruciating.'

'There are quite a few, I'm afraid.' Sybil took one last look behind and then said, 'This is only a rumour, though I consider it to be true —'

'Tell me,' Eva begged, her impatience now at boiling point. 'You said it yourself that I am no longer a child. If I am to carry on our bloodline, then I have every right to know what is troubling you about it.'

'Your grandfather told me this, not long before he was incarcerated. I don't know why he told me, but he seemed desperate — frantic.'

'Get it off your chest, Mother. Do tell me.'

'Long ago there was a medieval settlement that was situated upon the marshlands of Acle, the same marshlands our home overlooks. Something horrific happened there, Eva, something demonic.' A sickening shiver ran down Sybil's spine. 'The entire settlement was destroyed and most of its people brutally slaughtered. No one dared speak of what had transpired there, although it was collectively thought to be unnatural. There was one survivor, a monk, who had fled the scene before what carnage took place. They had allegedly learned of what would occur, so they left with only a small barrel of mead and a silver crucifix —'

'A barrel of mead and a crucifix?' Eva tutted whimsically. 'This does sound somewhat ridiculous, Mother.'

'It was not ridiculous for the monk,' Sybil retorted with disappointment strewn in her eyes. 'According to legend, the monk had reached these woods after being chased down by bandits, who were threatening to beat him to death, should he not hand over his pitiful possessions. It is understood that the monk then freely offered his mead to these bandits, but not his crucifix. It was his only physical connection to God that remained, and he could not part with it, not even if it meant losing his life.'

'And what does this have to do with our family?' Eva scoffed.

'More than I would like to admit.' Sybil quickened her pace, mindful of what could be lurking in the shadows behind. 'After giving the mead to those bandits, the monk fled deeper into these woods, praying that they would grant him shelter and God's mercy. He eventually stumbled across a large hole in the earth that seemed endless in its descent and just wide enough for a grown man to fit in. The monk had apparently heard an ethereal voice come from this hole, which enticed his interest. When the bandits found him, the monk was staring into the hole and was mumbling incoherent Latin verses, all the while holding out his precious crucifix. The bandits went to claim their prize, but the monk suddenly vanished as if he had been dragged into the hole by unseen hands.'

'I still do not understand what any of this has to do with our family, Mother.'

'Because you are not exactly the most patient nor observant individual,' said Sybil, chuckling, attempting to lighten the mood. 'Those bandits shared their peculiar encounter over the years with fellow miscreants, and at one point it came to the attention of your oldest-known ancestor — the first Appleton to gain possession of these lands — Alistair McCredie Appleton, who would hire such thugs to do his dirty work.'

'Oh...' Eva thought back to the largest portrait in her stately home, the one of her great-great-grandfather that was hung above the entranceway. 'He wasn't a particularly pleasant man, was he? I know that much about him.'

'No. He was an occultist, a twisted individual who enjoyed dabbling with the darker powers in our world.' Sybil's tone fell foul and cautious again. 'After a relatively short search, Alistair discovered the monk's resting place, the accursed hole, which he proclaimed to be a portal from Hell. It was later used by our family for rituals and other sordid practices, of which would strengthen their control over these lands.'

'Where is the proof to verify this?' Eva asked, somewhat shocked to learn that her family would have anything to do with such wicked acts, severely concerned for her mother's wellbeing. 'We go to church every Sunday, and I've never seen any evidence to suggest our family would dabble in black magic.'

'You are no longer a child,' Sybil whispered. 'There is a reason why you've been told to stay away from these woods and not venture into your father's study room. That is all I will say on the matter. I have already said too much.'

'Well, how marvellous.' With a disenfranchised grunt, Eva stomped on ahead. 'Thank you for inviting me on this lovely walk, Mother, and for informing me that I am to marry some stranger, and that our family are secretly devil-worshipping monsters. What a joyful afternoon this has been.'

'I am only trying to protect you,' Sybil pleaded, verging on the edge of despair. 'You must open your eyes to what is and what will transpire. No matter what befalls us, Eva, you must hold onto your innocence for as long as possible.'

'The choice will soon be taken away from me, though, won't it?'

'Not if I can help it, it won't.'

Luckily for Eva and Sybil, their lengthy walk had gone unnoticed and their conversation unheard. The men of Appleton Manor — Marcus and his two sons — had been out hunting, and come nightfall, when all the family sat awaiting their evening meal, there was little to suggest that any suspicion had arose.

Sybil toyed with her food, pushing a slice of roasted pheasant around her plate until it became too cold to eat.

Marcus noticed his wife's unusual behaviour and wanted to put a swift end to it. 'Have you lost your appetite, Sybil, or are you deliberately trying to induce my displeasure?' he asked her, squinting his eyes, barely able to hold back his anger. 'You have achieved the latter, I must say.'

'It is neither of those,' said Sybil, resting her cutlery down upon the plate. 'I am… thinking.'

'Tis a dangerous sport for a woman is thinking' he jested, gaining but a polite smirk from his subservient sons, Alfred and Charles. Eva continued to eat in silence, her eyes held down and breaths racing. 'You are being incredibly rude, my dearest. We, your husband and sons, have been out all afternoon hunting to provide you with this bountiful meal. Have you forgotten how to show gratitude for such arduous labour?'

'I am grateful,' Sybil stated, smiling in determination. 'I am merely comprehending, albeit in melancholy, the fact that our daughter will be turning sixteen soon. What a momentous day it shall be. We must ensure to celebrate it accordingly, of course.'

'Indeed.' Marcus glared at Sybil, his twitching movements revealing some unease. 'There is no reason for you to get flustered by this prospect, however, seeing as I have made all the necessary arrangements.'

'How very thoughtful of you,' Sybil added, her smile now turning into a judgemental frown. 'And so, my dear husband, how do you plan to celebrate Evangeline's birthday? A party? An extravagant dinner?'

'I wish to keep it a surprise. There is nothing worse than to spoil one's delicate plans, especially after so much toil has been endured.'

'That is understandable.' Sybil noted Eva's anxious demeanour, and with it her ability to remain silent over her impending marriage was removed. 'Have you managed to contact our relatives and what friends we have left, as to ensure their timely arrival?'

'Yes,' Marcus seethed under his breath. 'There are a few who have not yet responded to my letters, although I can't see there being a problem. It is all under control.'

'Good.' Sybil turned to Eva with a feigned smile. 'I mean, Lord forbid it should Aunt Ethel, or Cousin Percy, or the Gilesgate family fail to show. That would be terrible, utterly heart-breaking.'

'I beg your pardon, madam?!' Marcus scowled, slamming a fist down upon the table. 'Might I have a word with you in private?'

'It would be my pleasure.'

Eva, Alfred and Charles looked to one another in surprise and suspicion as their parents calmly left the dining room. Marcus's raised voice, which sounded more like a bull being strangled, could be heard some moments later, contrasting Sybil's gentle pleas. It was difficult for the Appleton children to establish what was being said, though they knew it could not be positive.

Marcus returned some minutes later, alone. 'Your mother is unwell and of unsound mind. She has taken my advice and retired to bed early. She needs to rest, to clear her head.'

'May I go and see her, Father?' Eva asked, practically begging for her request to be approved. 'I am concerned about Mother. She has not been herself of late.'

'No!' Marcus roared, revealing a series of veins that protruded around his neck. 'I also think it wise for all of us to retire early. We have had enough excitement for one evening.'

'Father,' Alfred stuttered. 'Pardon my indiscretion, but it is not even nine o'clock. We are yet to enjoy our brandy and cigars.'

Clenching at his face, Marcus replied, 'Going one night without tobacco and a brandy will do you no harm, Son. Am I to be met with defiance from you as well?'

'No, Father.' Alfred lowered his sight from Marcus, slowly turning his head to Eva. 'I would not dare defy you. Your word, as always, is final.'

'I am glad to hear of it,' said Marcus, forcing himself to appear calmer. 'With that being said, I bid you all a pleasant evening. Good night, Children.'

'Goodnight, Father,' they replied in unison.

Eva was the last to leave, her energy now fully spent on trying to remain level-headed and resolute throughout the ordeal. She knew where she had to go, and it was not to her bed or mother's side.

The servants' quarters were situated down a long corridor from Eva's bedroom, where Frederik — her secret lover — lay in wait for their nightly clandestine meeting. Having checked that the coast was clear, Eva tapped on Frederik's door sharply three times and then twice subtly — their personalised signal. Frederik made his way to the door, brimming with excitement, despite being half-asleep and having heard rumours of the disagreement between Sybil and Marcus.

'Eva!' Frederik gleamed, though his joyful greeting was not returned to him. 'What's the matter? You look like you've seen a ghost.'

'We must speak in private,' she said, closing the door behind her. 'We need to go somewhere safe and far away from here. I don't know what to do, Fred.'

Wiping away her tears with a brush of his thumb, Frederik wasted no effort in guiding Eva from the confinement of Appleton Manor. After sneaking through the freezing corridors and halls, the two ventured a short distance outside until they reached the stables, which were seldom occupied at this time of night. There, Eva explained to Frederik what her mother had revealed, of her impending marriage to Winston Gilesgate, and of how cruel her father had been. It was still a terrible shock for her, and even more so for Frederik.

'That can't be true — it's unfair,' Frederik gasped, slamming a fist against the stable doors. 'How could they do that to you, their only daughter?'

'Mother was not involved in this decision, only Father. He does not care about how I feel, Fred, only the money that lines his pockets,' Eva said solemnly. 'I cannot bear to think of a life without you. If I were ever to be married, I would want you for a husband.'

'Don't talk like that,' said Frederik. 'We'll find a solution to this. Don't you worry. I'll think of something.'

'How? It will take a miracle,' Eva wallowed. 'I would love to run away with you, to be free of this wretched manor, but we have no money or place to go. We would be outcasts.'

'We'll survive, somehow. I'll think of a way.'

'Be realistic, Fred. Our love for one another cannot survive.'

'It can, Eva. It must!'

'But it can't.' Eva brushed a hand across Frederik's leg, tempted to motion it further towards his waist. 'I must obey my parents, for Mother's sake. She is not herself and needs me to be there for her. I am all she has left worth living for.'

'Your mother will not always be around. Think ahead —'

'I have, and I know what must be done.' Eva paused momentarily as to prolong this final, poignant moment. 'This is the last time I shall meet with you in this way, with these wonderful feelings of love and longing. I am sorry, Fred.'

'Don't tell me that you're willing to throw away true love for the sake of appeasing your father? The man's a lunatic!'

'It isn't like that, and you know it isn't.'

'Then go, Eva. But know this: I will never let you leave my heart and thoughts. No other will replace the love I bear for you. You're all I care about. I love you.'

Eva contemplated the thought of granting Frederik one final kiss, an emotional farewell to signal the end of their forbidden relationship, but the sound of distant screams and rapid succession of lights appearing at windows within the manor forced her to abandon such an overwhelming urge.

'What is going on?' she asked, littered with panic. 'They must know!'

'Quick, Eva! You go first!' Frederik commanded, pointing her in the direction of the manor's back door. 'Return before they notice you're gone. I won't be far behind. I'll watch over you.'

Eva sprinted back to her home, to the intensifying sound of screams and wailing. 'What has happened?' she fretted, fearing the worst. 'Mother!'

A succession of servants coursed by Eva as she ran up to the main stairwell, without even a passing glance. She could hear her brothers crying out in dismay and the gut-wrenching bellow from her father, who was evidently unleashing some apparent grief.

'My wife!' Marcus screamed, clenching both hands against his scalp. 'Help me! For God's sake, someone help me!'

'Mother…' Eva approached Marcus, despite her growing resentment for him. 'What has happened?'

Marcus's bloated face was swamped with a scarlet colour, imbued with adrenaline and alcohol. He could barely form a simple sentence. 'I do not know what has taken place, Evangeline. I had gone to top up my sherry and then… she's stopped breathing, your mother, of which that is for certain. My darling wife has left this earth. She has abandoned me…'

Eva could not and would not believe her father's claim.

'No!' she screamed, throwing herself against him. 'You lie!'

Fighting to get past the line of servants stood outside her parent's bedroom, Eva closed her eyes and attempted to convince herself that this was some twisted nightmare, a false dream of sorts. Sybil had turned to solitude and grown thinner of face recently, but there was no significant reason to suggest that there was anything fouler at foot. There was no viable explanation to explain her untimely demise, at least in Eva's eyes.

'She is gone,' said Alfred, holding onto one of his Sybil's hands, turning to his siblings. 'She is dead.'

'No. She can't be,' Eva's voice travelled in a high pitch, as if an invisible pair of hands were constricting her throat. 'Mother was well. There is no sense in this…'

Two of the servants entered the room, with their heads held low in reverence for their deceased employer. One of them then noted to the other: 'She looks so peaceful, doesn't she? It would be easy to mistake our mistress being asleep, instead of—'

'She is not dead!' cried Eva. 'There was nothing wrong with Mother when I last saw her. Who was the last person to see her?'

A heavy palm landed upon Eva's shoulders. It was Marcus. 'My child, there are many mysteries in this world that will never be answered. God has chosen to take your mother from us, and there is nothing that can be done now to revoke this. We must remember her, then move on.'

An urge to vomit rose in Eva's gullet as she turned to face Marcus. 'You were the last person to speak with Mother, weren't you? Did she complain of feeling ill? Did she look unwell to you?'

'No. Your mother fell asleep peacefully and in no distress. We should consider that a blessing.' The way in which Marcus spoke was cold, heartless, final. 'There is nothing more that can be done, Evangeline. Return to your room at once and await my orders. Do as I say, Daughter.'

All Eva wanted to do was wrap her arms around Sybil, to somehow bring her mother back to life, to be rid of this plight.

'I cannot leave her,' she said. 'I cannot leave Mother to lie there all alone, without any caring soul to comfort her.'

'She is in God's nurturing hands now,' said Marcus, tightening his hold upon Eva's forearms. 'Do as I say and go. This is for your own good. An innocent girl such as yourself should not be burdened with what is to follow. The undertaker will be here soon.'

Those last words festered in Eva's thoughts over the next two weeks, during the initial stages of denial and grief and then even stronger during the next phase of anger and reluctant acceptance of her mother's death. Even at Sybil's funeral, under heavy rainfall and without Frederik's companionship, Eva continued to question her father's involvement and likely hand in taking Sybil's life.

So came the morn of Eva's sixteenth birthday, of the day she would wed Winston Gilesgate. Appleton Manor was soaked in an atmosphere of jubilance and anticipation, though this same joy was not felt by Eva. She paced around her bedroom nervously, desperate to escape this impending doom. Frederik had honoured Eva's plea, to stay away from her and show no further affection, but she would have done anything to have just spent one more minute with him, nestled at his side.

'Are you ready, Miss?' asked one of Eva's servants, as they added the finishing touches to her hair and wedding veil. 'Your mother would be so proud. You look beautiful.'

'I do not feel that on the inside, and I doubt Mother would be happy of these circumstances,' said Eva, adjusting the painful corset that dug into her ribcage. 'How am I meant to feel? I've not even met my fiancé, you know. I could be marrying a pig-headed freak. That would be just my luck.'

'Mr. Gilesgate shall be a wonderful husband to you, so I reckon,' the servant replied, somewhat bashfully. 'Your father speaks very highly of him, and he will only have your best interests at heart.'

'My father is only interested in what money the Gilesgate family can offer him, not how I feel,' said Eva, disgusted by the reflection meeting with her in the mirror opposite. 'Father doesn't care about me and never will. I'm just another asset he can sell off.'

'It's just one of those things, Miss. At least you're not living in squalor, having to struggle to find your next meal… like me.'

'Do you?' asked Eva, genuinely aggrieved to learn of this. She had been led to believe that the servants' quarters were luxurious when compared to other stately homes. 'Is it really that bad?'

'Yes, Miss. But if I can provide my family with a steady flow of bread and milk, then I am blessed. I am grateful for working here. Please don't take it the wrong way...'

Eva thought back to the conversation she had with her mother in the woods, of the tale involving her family's occultist past. 'I want you to be truthful with me, Sarah, in what I am about to ask.'

'Of course, Miss. What is it?'

'It has come to my knowledge that some locals fear my family. Am I correct in saying that?'

Though hesitant at first, the poor servant girl attempted to distract Eva's curiosity. 'A family such as yours is revered by commoners like me, Miss. I wouldn't say that folk are fearful of you. Not one bit.'

'I am not asking if they are fearful of me, but of my family's name.'

'You are different to the rest of them,' said Sarah, unsettled by the situation she now found herself in. 'You are not a male Appleton, I should say. You're not like your father and brothers.'

'Indeed, I am not. Thank the Lord.' Eva managed to smile, albeit briefly. 'May I ask why that would be of any concern?'

'I'd rather not say, Miss. It's not my place.'

'Please,' Eva insisted. 'I want to know what people think about my family. You won't upset me.'

'You are very much like your mother,' said Sarah amid a nervous chuckle. 'It is not pleasant things they say, Miss, and I do not wish to burden you with them.'

'Tell me. I must know the truth.'

The hairbrush in Sarah's hand fell still as did her breaths. 'I would not take what locals say to heart. We are merely jealous of your privileged lives—'

'Be honest, Sarah. Tell me why people are so scared of my family. It will stay between us. I promise.'

'I-I can't!' Sarah could see the desperation in Eva's eyes, however, prompting her to reveal some information. 'They mention devil-worship, Miss. It's all nonsense, of course. I wouldn't take any notice.'

'There is always some element of truth in such tales,' Eva noted, repeating the same words spoken to her by Sybil. 'I shall find out for myself eventually, I assume. I would have much preferred to have found out from yourself, though, from a friend who I can trust.'

'It's just some old tales that drunkards share in the pub. It's nothing, Miss,' Sarah argued. 'I don't believe them, anyway.'

Eva gestured to Sarah that she wished for some moments alone, to possibly think over what was about to take place. In truth, however, it was to allow Frederik some time with her, for a fond and sorrowful farewell. That is how Eva imagined the next ten minutes would proceed, consumed by her wild imagination.

Frederik loitered outside of Eva's bedroom, yearning to be with her, regardless of the risks entailed. He had gone over in his mind what needed to be said and done, though it would not transpire that way.

'Eva,' he muttered on entering her room, 'I can't stay here anymore, and I'm not leaving without you.'

'Fred?'

The two lovers stared at one another; Eva looked to Frederik in the reflection of her mirror and he stared to her similarly in return. The silence was deafening, torturous, but the choking atmosphere that had existed prior lifted.

'There is still a chance for us to run away together,' he pleaded. 'Must you go through with this ludicrous ceremony? Do you want to be some rich boy's slave for the rest of your life?'

'If I am to satisfy my father's intentions and avoid any further scorn from him, then — yes. But it is not what I desire, Fred, and you know that.'

'Come with me then, Eva. It's not too late.'

'Too late for what?'

'To leave. We can start a new life together.'

A slight smile rose on Eva's face as she comprehended this, of her finally discovering true happiness. 'I would wish for nothing less than to be with you, but my father would never permit it. I have no choice but to go ahead with the wedding.'

'Your father, brothers, and all the other guests are waiting for you in the courtyard, and not one of them cares about how you feel. We could sneak out the back, through the woods, and be gone before they even notice.'

'They will catch us. It would be a foolish endeavour, Fred.'

'It's the only opportunity we have now to escape. Take it, Eva!' Before she could respond, Frederik wrapped his arms around her. 'Please reconsider my offer, to elope with me. I just want to offer the love and devotion you deserve. I have no money, yes, but I will never let you suffer nor bear the burden of living a painful, boring life that is spent in servitude. That is what awaits you now with Winston Gilesgate, and don't deny it. That's the last thing your mother would have wanted for you.'

It was as if Sybil was speaking to Eva from beyond the grave, willing for her to do the right thing. 'Fine,' she gleamed. 'Let us run away and be free of this nightmare. I want to be free, Fred. I do want to be with you.'

'Trust me. We'll be fine. I'll make sure of it.'

Eva and Frederik carefully looked upon the sea of relatives and associates gathering outside. The woods across the distance, despite their malignant nature and history, seemed to be so promising and welcoming now. There was no time to lose. Together, Eva and Frederik then fled from Appleton Manor, both filled with hope and resolve.

An eerie silence met with Eva as she followed Frederik through the empty hallways of her home. She imagined Sybil standing by her side, imploring that this move was worth all the possible consequences. Not even the portrait of her great-great-grandfather dissuaded Eva from betraying her bloodline, although his piercing glare continued to eat away at her conscience.

'Hold on a second,' said Frederik, slowly unlatching the backdoor's security bolt. 'We have two choices: either steal one of your father's horses or just make a run for it. There's two-hundred yards of open field to cross before reaching the woods…'

'The horses will make too much noise,' she despaired. 'I think it safer for us to quietly make our way over the back field, to follow the stream until we reach the woods. There is no reason for anyone to be in those parts of the grounds —'

'Other than Henry, your father's groundskeeper.' Frederik wiped at his face with a wearisome groan. 'I wish I'd made a better plan, or at least bunged him a bribe. I didn't think this through —'

'We're wasting time,' said Eva, pushing Fred forwards. 'If God is on our side, then we shall face no such adversity. I trust you, Fred. I'm willing to forfeit my family's adoration and wealth to be spared all this.'

Nodding his head in determination, Frederik quickly swung open the door, clasped onto Eva's hands, and then took her outside. 'This is it. There's no turning back now.'

Somewhat hindered by her long-flowing wedding dress, Eva trudged on through the muddy field, noting to herself how the sun was now being shrouded by thick, dark rainclouds. She found it fitting, the gloom and darkness, given that there was no beauty in her father's intentions — in selling her off to the highest bidder.

Acting as another stroke of luck for Eva and Frederik, a wave of dense fog swept in from the nearby marshlands. It was the perfect cover, though the freezing mist saturated Eva's dress, making it heavier and causing it to stick to her skin. Regardless of her present discomfort, Eva found solace in Frederik's touch, in him guiding her into their new life.

'We're almost there,' said Frederik, looking back once to check for any possible onlookers. 'Not far now.'

Just as Eva and Frederik made it to the woods, a faint, flickering amber light met with them. It was Henry, who was holding up a lit oil lantern.

'Who goes there?' he called out, peering through the fog, his lantern shaking from side-to-side. 'Make yourselves known! I'm armed!'

'It's only me,' said Eva, her voice trembling like Henry's lamp. 'I cared for some fresh air before the ceremony. Frederik has been generous enough to be my escort.'

'Don't take me for a fool, Miss,' Henry scoffed. 'I know what's going on here. I'm not an idiot, you know.'

'You do?' she gasped. 'But...'

'Yes, and your father will be most displeased to learn of this. Goodness me, a lady of your calibre mingling with a lowly blacksmith — what would he have to say about that?'

Frederik stepped forth, placing himself protectively between Henry and Eva. 'Look, there's no need for you to inform the master. You've gotten it all wrong, Henry.'

With a wheezing laugh, Henry replied, 'I have no intention of informing him, sonny-boy. To be honest, I can't stand the fellow, especially after what he did – ' Cutting his sentence short, mindful of Eva's grief, Henry offered his lantern to Frederik. 'You'll need this if you're venturing into those woods. You two must be desperate. No good comes from walking under those trees.'

Eva went to retrieve the lamp, but Frederik lowered her hand away without hesitation. 'They'll see the light. Besides, the woods aren't that dark. Thank you, Henry. I wish I could make it up to – '

'Oh, they'll be getting darker anytime soon,' Henry stated, coming across to be somewhat distant now, almost catatonic. 'She was a wonderful mistress, was your mother,' he said, turning to Eva. 'I've served this family for over fifty years. I've seen some terrible things – acts that would make you sick to your stomach, should you have seen them yourself. It's not right for a pure soul like you to be caged here, Miss. I won't stand for it.'

'We haven't got time to dawdle, Henry. We've got to go,' said Frederik, pulling at Eva's arm. 'They'll be searching for us soon enough.'

'Aye, they will. But, believe me, the hunters will swiftly become the hunted,' cackled Henry, resting a long pipe in his mouth. 'Your mother would often talk to me in private, seeing as I was one of the only servants she trusted. I told her what to do, Miss. I told her about the books in your father's study and of the unnatural practices I've seen him perform. I told her where to go, to where your ancestors' hidden vault lies.'

'We must move, Eva!' Frederik beseeched. 'Please, don't say a word to anyone, Henry. You're a good man, and I know you won't betray us.'

'There won't be many people left to tell, come nightfall.'

'What do you mean?' asked Eva.

'She didn't deserve to die the way she did, Miss. Your mother didn't deserve the life your father forced on her. The men of your family will come to regret their transgressions, mark my word,' said Henry, performing a crucifix over his chest. 'Mark my word, they will.'

'Come on, Eva!' Now in a full state of panic, Frederik brushed Henry aside and then sped forth into the woods. 'The old fool has gone senile. I hope he doesn't tell them where to look.'

'Henry is anything but senile,' said Eva. 'I do wonder, though, what he was bleating on about.'

'Forget him. Forget Appleton Manor. That's all in the past.'

'What *transgressions*?'

'Forget him, Eva. We need to focus on getting out of here alive. That's our priority now.'

The woods turned into a dense maze under the dim sunlight, and it was not long before Eva and Frederik became lost. Frederik tried to ascertain their position, using the sun as his guide, but it was no use. It was as if they were going around in circles.

'Damn these woods!' yelled Frederik, thrusting a fist against an old oak tree. 'We'll never find our way out.'

'We must stay calm.' Eva was trying to convince herself more so than Frederik. 'Grandfather's stories… they spoke of a way to the monk's well. My family would never think to look for us there.'

'I can't see how some daft old well would be of any benefit to us. Let's try this way,' Frederik suggested, pointing to a small trail to the left of where he stood. 'We're running out of time.'

'*Listen for the crows and follow their cries, then turn toward the willow tree that hides from the sky. Where the willow tree leans, follow on in reverence… onto the well of Hell's Gate where you shall find deliverance.* I'm sure that's what Grandfather said.'

'Is that the same grandfather who was sent to an asylum?' Frederik asked, as sympathetically as possible. 'It was a bedtime story, Eva. It won't get us out of these woods.'

'It's better than nothing,' she sighed. 'What other options do we have?'

A series of cries and gunshots suddenly echoed from where Appleton Manor stood. With their hearts racing and against their increasing exhaustion, Eva and Frederik carried on into the darkness. The sound of men calling out Eva's name seemed to be getting closer and closer, and so did a sense of doom.

'I need to rest,' Eva murmured, barely able to speak. 'This dress is too heavy. I keep catching it on all these bushes and thorns.'

'We'll take a quick breather, but only for a minute or so.'

Frederik stroked at Eva's arms, hoping to warm them. Out of the corner of his eye he then noticed a thin trail of fresh blood. 'You've caught your arm on something. Are you alright?'

'I hadn't noticed,' she said, inspecting the wound for herself. 'It doesn't hurt. I'll live.'

'We'll—' Frederik's words were cut short by the deafening sound of crows flying overhead. 'Wretched things! They scared the bloody life out of me!'

'*Follow their cries*,' said Eva, her tone monotonous and foreboding. 'Follow them, Fred. Follow the crows.'

'I'm up for anything at this point,' he joked. 'Let's hope they don't take us in the wrong direction, back to the fields. I don't fancy getting shot today.'

The crows flight and their haunting chorus continued, seemingly aiming their cries at the lovers below. Eva struggled to keep her footing as she twisted her body around the intrusive thorn bushes and oak branches, all the while keeping her sight firmly fixated on the birds flying overhead.

Some moments later, Eva and Frederik found themselves before an unusual-looking willow tree; it was small, pale in colour and twisted, leaning drastically as if it were bowing to something or someone. The two looked to the tree in silence, astonished by how William Appleton's rhyme seemingly bore some ground.

'Grandfather was telling the truth,' said Eva, held in astonishment. 'Follow on *in reverence*. What does that mean?'

'We're surrounded by thorn bushes — there's nowhere else to go, Eva.'

'In reverence,' she whispered, lowering her sight. 'Look! What are those?'

Frederik knelt himself for a closer inspection. 'They're polished, black stones. It looks like they've been placed here deliberately.' The stones formed an even line, trailing off in the direction of where the willow tree leant itself. 'Should we follow them as well, play along with this little rhyme of yours?'

'We wouldn't have noticed them if we hadn't looked down... if we hadn't looked to where the willow tree leans itself. That's what *in reverence* means: to bow.'

'This is a bad idea — reckless,' Frederik complained. 'But still, it's not like we have any other path to take. What's the worst that could happen?' Frederik led the way, ensuring to follow the stones and their guiding path. To his surprise, he then discovered that the stones revealed a hidden pathway between two bushes, which overlapped one another to create an illusionary wall. 'There's another pathway here. I doubt your father and his lackies will find us now,' he stated happily. Nevertheless, the distinctive sound of Marcus Appleton's furious, roaring screams continued to near. 'May God have mercy on us, Eva, should your father discover our whereabouts. He's not a man I'd particularly like to confront.'

'*Onto Hell's Gate* is the last line of grandfather's verse. I find that more disturbing than my father's wrath.'

'It's likely just a ruse to scare people off. Anyway, these woods should deter even the bravest of souls. Not even the sun can fully shed its light here.' For the first time since leaving Appleton Manor, Frederik displayed some genuine fear in his expression. 'Nothing feels natural about this place. I can see now why people would call it "Hell's Gate".'

Eva took over the role as guide, leading Frederik into the murky depths. 'Henry spoke of a vault. If one does exist, then we can hide there and plan our next move.'

Frederik was unconvinced. 'Does your father know of this vault? I reckon he might.'

'Father believes that I am a helpless, lost infant. I doubt the thought of me hiding in some old vault would cross his mind, not for one second. He has never considered me to be brave.' Catching both off-guard, a deep, growl-like voice travelled with the passing breeze. The words spoken were indecipherable, but Eva sensed their purpose. 'It's this way.' she declared, walking ahead as fast as she could. 'I know it is.'

'Wait, Eva. It's getting darker—I can barely see!'

'I can see,' she implored. 'There's a stone structure—'

Standing at around fifteen-feet tall, covered in moss and decaying leaves, a chapel-like building appeared out of thin air; and upon its entrance the words "Hell's Gate" were clear to see, along with a Latin phrase that was crudely inscribed beneath them which read: *Ave Sabina, gratia plena. Benedicta tu in mulieribus.*

'I thought the manor was unwelcoming,' Frederik humoured, eyeing up the grotesque building. 'It'll have to do, I suppose. We've nowhere else to run, and I'm sure your father and the other men aren't far behind.'

Eva closed her eyes and thought of Sybil, pleading for her mother's strength to invigorate her faltering spirit. 'I do not fear the dark or demons. I do not fear what lies ahead.'

'Demons?' yelped Frederik. 'This day just keeps getting better. Now we've got demons to contend with, do we?'

'Possibly…'

A nauseating scent lingered within the vault that reeked of rotten flesh and other foul substances. It was not enough to deter Eva from stepping in, however. She examined every fine detail of the stones that now surrounded her, which also appeared to protect a small well held within the vault's centre.

'So, it is true.' Held in reservation, Eva approached the narrow hole and thereafter stared into the endless abyss it housed. 'I wonder how deep this goes?'

'Too deep to jump in,' said Frederik. 'There's no other way out. We're trapped in here like vermin.'

Unbeknown to Eva, a droplet of blood from the wound on her hand fell into the hole. Instantly, a terrifying roar emitted from the dark void that paralysed both Eva and Frederik to the spot.

'What was that?' Eva fell to the ground, which was littered with small bones. 'Fred, there are bones here!'

'What have you done?' he fretted. 'What the hell was that noise?'

The sound of a terrible beast reverberated throughout the woods outside, followed by several screams and more gunshots. Frederik ran back to vault's entrance, all the while gesturing for Eva to stay put.

'Don't move. I'll have a look outside to see what's going on.'

'No, Fred. Please, don't leave me.'

'I won't be long, my darling. Don't move.'

Once alone, Eva sensed that another figure stood in close proximity to her. It didn't feel familiar, nor did it seem to be human.

'Who are you?' she asked, panting rapidly, her eyes fleeting around the darkness. 'What are you?'

'My master hath been awakened, summoned by thee,' a feminine voice replied. 'Thy mother's bidding hath been done.'

'My mother? How do you know my mother?'

'She came here, seeking solitude and a solution...'

'My mother is dead,' Eva lamented. 'She can't have been here — she hated these woods.'

'Thy impending marriage wrought much sorrow in her. She willed for my master to unleash vengeance upon the men in thy household. Now, that thou hath so shed thy virgin blood, her curse can be fulfilled. She was not willing to do it, the deed that would bring forth my master, Baal.'

'Who are you? Tell me!' asked Eva, turning her head to see where the woman's voice came from. 'And how dare you suggest that my mother would play any part in devil-worship. Who are you?!'

'I am Sabina!' cried the woman. 'I am vengeance. Thou hath summoned me and my master…'

A flash of scarlet-coloured lightening swept across the sky, momentarily revealing Sabina's demonic features to Eva.

'Oh, God!' Eva screamed, falling to her knees again. 'You — you're are a demon!'

'I am no demon. My master, Baal, doth possess such power. My master shalt enact thy mother's vengeance — he hath come for them,' Sabina cackled in delight. 'Bear no fear, for thy mother's curse shalt only befall the men who bear the Appleton name.'

Another burst of lightening and a deep ripple of thunder resounded, somehow willing Sabina to vanish. Eva righted herself, her desperation to be reunited with Frederik now paramount.

'Fred, where are you?' With her mind awash with confliction and terror, Eva made her way back out into the woods. Then, to the apparent laughter of some passing crows, she came across a truly horrifying sight: three corpses, each mutilated beyond recognition, which lay before the vault's entranceway. 'Frederik!'

'I'm here!' he replied, struggling to catch his breath, on his hasty return. 'I saw it — whatever it was.'

'What did you see, Fred?'

'It was taller than any man I've ever come across and pure evil,' he explained, holding onto his aching legs. 'From what I saw, Eva, it was a monster. There was no mistaking it.'

'It's all my fault. I did this,' she wept. 'It's my fault, Fred.'

A sickening sensation plunged into Frederik's heart and stomach as he looked upon the three corpses, across their torn flesh and agonised facial expressions. 'You can't have done this. I'm telling you, Eva, it was a demon or something. It moved through the trees like a large shadow, ripping apart the men who were coming for us. Why didn't it attack me?'

'Because you are not an Appleton,' Eva whispered, her expression now matching those of the dead men lain before her. 'My brothers — Father! I must warn them!'

'We can't go back. Surely, that's not what you're insinuating?'

'I need to know if they've come to harm, Fred. I must find out what has happened to them. I won't rest until I do.'

'This is the perfect chance for us to flee, to get out of here before that *thing* returns. Who is to say that it won't come for us next?'

'It won't. I know it won't.' Eva wanted to share her harrowing encounter with Sabina, to release the burden that swept over her conscience, but from Frederik's demeanour it seemed an unwise choice. He would likely leave without her, deeming that she had lost all sanity. That wasn't too far from being the truth, it must be said. 'I want to see for myself if my brothers have survived whatever plague has befallen these poor souls,' she said, nodding at the corpses. 'Please, God, let them be spared. My brothers have never harmed anyone.'

'Fine. We'll go back, but I don't agree with this. I can't guarantee your safety, Eva, and I'm not happy about that.'

'We won't come to any harm,' she assured him. 'I know that for certain. Do not ask me why.'

Eva and Frederik retraced their steps through the woods, passing by the unique willow tree and back to fog-laden fields. Several streams of blood and scattered entrails led the way back to Appleton Manor, along with a chorus of female screams and wailing.

The first individual Eva came across was Sarah, her servant. Sarah was sat upon the front doorstep, rocking back and forth, shaking her head, repeating to herself: 'God have mercy on me. God have mercy on me...'

'Where is everyone, Sarah?' Frederik asker her. 'Do you know what happened?'

'It ripped them apart,' she whimpered. 'The shadow, it tore the men apart as if they were nothing. It spared none of them. The blood. The cries of terror...'

'My brothers?' said Eva, kneeling herself before Sarah. 'Father? Are they all... dead? Did the monster get them as well?'

Sarah tilted her head upwards toward the marble-arched roof. There, on full display, three bodies hung from the pillars that decorated Appleton Manor's main entrance, each slashed and brutalised to leave only their blood-soaked muscles.

Eva unleashed a gut-wrenching cry. 'No!! They cannot be dead!'

'The women have taken refuge inside. I waited here for you, Miss. I am loyal,' Sarah pleaded. 'It flew by us women, willing no harm to any of us. Like God's punishment to the first-born children of Egypt, that wicked creature only took what it desired.'

'It took what it was instructed to take,' Eva noted, swallowing heavily. 'Mother would not have wanted this. I know that Father was a bad man, but...'

'I don't wish to know what you saw in that vault, or what part your mother had to play in this chaos, Eva. All I want is for us to leave—now.' Frederik's tone was forceful, revealing his true fear. 'Take what you can from your father's safe and be back here in five minutes. I'm leaving then, whether you return or not.'

'There's nothing left for me here,' she replied, wiping the tears from her face. 'Mother is innocent. She never meant for any of this to happen.'

'Five minutes, Eva, and then I'm leaving.' Frederik sat himself beside Sarah, nestling into her to offer some comfort. 'Five minutes, that's all. Be quick.'

Eva entered her home, which now seemed even colder and more uninviting than before. A group of women, mostly her relatives and servants, stared to Eva as she walked by them, not one uttering a single word. A deathly silence endured within the musty air, adding to the cold wind that coursed through the quiet hallways. There was no doubt in Eva's mind that she wished to leave this dreadful place, though she was hindered by her lack of knowledge regarding Marcus Appleton's safe combination, which he never revealed to anyone else.

Eva knelt before her father's safe, tearing at her hair in frustration. 'What is the combination? What is it? His year of birth? Mother's birthday? This is impossible!'

'Seventeen-sixty-two,' an ethereal voice replied, the same feminine voice that had spoken to Eva within her family's hidden vault—Sabina. 'They be the numbers thou doth seek.'

Eva turned the safe's dial to the specified numbers and sighed with relief as its door opened. 'Thank you,' she whispered, clasping onto a handful of valuable gemstones. 'Why are you helping me?'

'Thy mother's vengeance hath wrought a great deal of joy to me and my master. Thy freedom is a reward to the both of us.'

'I only ask that you do not follow me and my beloved Fred,' said Eva, firmly and in determination. 'I'm begging you…'

'My master and I are bound to these forsaken lands,' explained Sabina, her voice riddled with rage. 'Forever shalt we torment the men who claim rights over them. Go now, or else I shalt bestow my wrath upon thee and thy lover. Be gone!'

Eva swiftly returned to Frederik, eager not to speak a word of Sabina's visitation. She held out the jewels and nodded to the stable house. 'We are free, Fred. We are free. But… where will we go?'

'Anywhere but here. How about London?'

'London?'

'We'll live like royalty down there, especially with the money we'll make from selling off these jewels.'

'That would be wonderful,' she said, forming a slight smile. 'We'd finally be able to start anew.'

'That's what you deserve, and that's what I'll give you. Trust me, Eva.'

What a magnificent finale to this tale that would have been, Eva and Frederik eloping to begin a new phase in their lives. However, unlike Sabina, the demon that had torn through the male Appletons bore no such mercy as to allow for such a fulfilling conclusion.

Hidden within the shadows, Baal — the Demon of Hell's Gate — watched on as Eva and Frederik, who were riding their horses, passed by. Embittered with jealousy over the two lovers and their profound affection for each other, the ancient demon turned to Sabina with bloodlust firmly set in his mind.

'If we cannot know free will and such love, then neither can they!' Sabina held her tongue, subservient and fearful of her demonic master's retribution. Baal continued, 'Unto them I shalt be merciful, and I shalt bestow my own blessing upon their union,' the demon cackled. 'If we must suffer, then so shalt they!'

As Eva and Frederik neared the marshlands, which lay south to Appleton Manor, the horses they rode suddenly plunged into the water-saturated earth. The two lovers pulled at the harnesses, panicking, driven by a passionate desire to survive. But they were shown no mercy from Baal, despite Sabina's claims. Together, holding onto one another's hands, they drowned in the freezing depths, where no light could ever reach them.

All that remained of Eva and Frederik was the small leather bag that concealed Marcus Appleton's precious jewels, which lay unfound until many decades later. Appleton Manor itself eventually fell into desolation, and it is said that the curse that had befallen its grounds continues to this very day.

'This is but a taste of what is yet to come,' said Baal, compelling Sabina into further submission. 'We will make the mortals suffer. We will have revenge.'

Death Comes at Eleven-Twenty

Patrick Cotherstone checked his father's golden pocket watch for the third time in ten minutes, amid a wave of anxiety. He was obsessed with it, adamant that some horrendous disaster would inevitably occur, for there was a terrible sickness in his mind that convinced Patrick should the hands turn to 11:20 or 11:31 — his untimely demise would be imminent. The pocket watch was all Patrick had left of a life he had unwillingly cast aside, though. He had served his country in war, watched his family succumb to famine and disease, and was granted nothing but the stale, ragged clothes he wore. It was a humble existence, married with constant fear and uncertainty.

Yet, and regardless of his irrational superstition, Patrick was mostly content. To him the vagrant lifestyle bore freedom, an existence where he would never know great loss or immense wealth. He accepted his circumstances, this sense of balance, and attempted to make the most of them, even if it meant having to travel aimlessly without any sense of purpose.

Removing the pocket watch from view, Patrick pulled out his long pipe, carefully stuffed it with some tobacco he had stolen some days before, and then he lit it with one of his few-remaining matches. Smoking was a rare privilege to him, along with making new acquaintances and knowing the comfort of a secure home and loving family. For thirty years, Patrick had endured this gruelling lifestyle, travelling from town to town, over fields and through treacherous forests. The necessity of owning material possessions and being a part of civilised society bore no interest in him whatsoever. This was the life he deserved. This was the path he chose to take.

A small stream nearby meandered off into a horizon of foggy marshlands. Patrick had been walking for three days straight now, unable to manage any meaningful sleep, and the exertion was beginning to take its toll on his elderly limbs and frail mindset. It had been even longer since Patrick stumbled upon another human being, another soul to either steal or beg from. Impatience festered strongly within his heart, and the time had now come where he yearned to fulfil his innate urges.

'I'm starving, I am. I need more than blackberries in my stomach, should I wish to make it past this week's end,' he groaned, stroking at his cramped stomach muscles. 'Lord, would you see me waste away like this? Take mercy on an old fool like me, would you? Tell me where I need to go—show me, O merciful father. Tell me where I can find some meat or fanciful place to rest my weary bones. I'm not asking much...'

Only the sound of running water answered Patrick's pray. Held in defeat, he stood up to observe his dreary surroundings, the barren marshlands and imposing woods.

'What a miserable place this is. There's not a sign of life for miles, I reckon. This can't be how I meet my maker. It can't be.'

Patrick followed the stream north, edging further into the woods. A heavy fog lingered, rendering the air with a foul stench that stung at the lungs when inhaled. Patrick found it unsurprising why no one would want to live here, given the dismal atmosphere and haunting silence.

'I'm a good man—honest and god-fearing. I don't deserve to starve or die,' he sobbed. 'Please, Lord, hear my voice and answer me. Don't let me waste away like this. I don't want to die. I'm not ready yet.'

Some comfort came as the sun rose higher into the sky, bidding some much-needed warmth and light. Patrick continued with his journey, not at all knowing where it would lead him. At this point he didn't care too much.

'These tired legs of mine might give way at any moment. Oh, how I wish for food and warmth. Will nobody help me?'

Resting once more, against an old oak tree this time, Patrick reached for his long pipe and precious pocket watch. Seconds turned into minutes and minutes into hours. The muscle contractions in his gut were becoming unbearable, and with them rose some strange hallucinations — wrought from dehydration and Patrick's drowning despair. He could see his mother smiling at him; his father offering unwanted advice on how to be a true man; and his fallen comrades lulling their heads in judgement over his survival and not theirs. It was too much to take.

'I can't walk no more. This is it. I give up!' Patrick held onto his pipe with a trembling, arthritic hand; with the other he twirled a finger through his mottled beard. 'What a predicament this is. What a bloody travesty. My death won't cause any sorrow, though, will it? I'll soon be forgotten, I will. What a terrible state to be in.'

A large crow shrieking in the branches above suddenly snapped Patrick out of his deranged thoughts, before it flew off into the deeper part of the woods. Slowly, Patrick then calmed his breaths and steadied his thoughts. The crow was unexpected, as was its coincidental guidance.

'Is that a light I see moving through the trees yonder?'

Barely able to stand through malnourishment and fatigue, Patrick clawed his way over the damp earth to the looming trees and peculiar scarlet light that hovered through them.

'Tis an angel that has come for me. Tis salvation!' he exclaimed, laughing to himself in delight. 'Have you answered my prayers, O Lord? Are you going to offer me some sustenance?'

The light anomaly flickered and danced between the tree trunks, ushering Patrick closer towards it. He eventually made it to the woods' centre, gasping for breath and desperate for aid.

'Show me where to go. I'm begging you, God.'

The light then formed into a figure-of-eight, enticing Patrick to it like a siren does with its prey. He followed the siren's call like an obedient dog, dragging his crippled limbs through the harsh shards of marshland grass and freezing waters. The discomfort was miniscule compared to what might have lain in store, so Patrick thought. He had been through worse.

'I'll follow you, kind angel, to wherever you shall take me. I am a good man. I am faithful.'

The light gradually diminished, distancing itself from Patrick and his strained cries. Despite the sunlit morn, under the tress it felt like only darkness prevailed. There was a strong scent of sulphur and decay, though these did not deter Patrick from following his so-called guide.

'I am but a humble man, boasting no earthly possessions or attachments. All I want is food and a decent place to rest. Please, O Lord.'

The towering trees morphed into a canvas of blurring colours, swamped with shifting shadows and mystery. Patrick succumbed to his exhaustion. He collapsed, face down, onto a heap of rotten leaves that were coated in animal excrement. This was a final insult to him, a sign that he had truly taken the wrong path in life.

'I'd do anything just to taste one more mouthful of ale and red meat again,' he wallowed. 'What have I done to deserve this? I am not a sinner. I am not a bad man!'

As if under some enchantment, Patrick then fell into a deep sleep, a place where he could finally welcome some respite. He found himself clad in luxurious clothing—a tailor-made suit, soft and gentle upon the skin—in an unfamiliar setting that boasted unfathomable grandeur.

Somehow, Patrick knew that within this setting there was no need to fear hunger or battle Mother Nature's brutal elements. He had attained an insurmountable level of wealth, servants held at his beckoning call, and a family purely devoted to his will. It was like stepping foot into Heaven for Patrick, a realm where he could finally resolve all his previous feelings of guilt and discover peace.

'Am I dead? Is this the afterlife?' he pondered, rubbing his hands together. 'You shall find no complaint from me, O Lord, should this be my eternal life. Bless you!'

As quickly as he had fallen into this bout of slumber, Patrick awoke to the sound of a stag sprinting nearby, its hooves hitting the earth like a hammer against an anvil. He cursed the innocent creature, enraged that it had torn him from a better existence, and then he pressed on with his journey, only after checking his pocket watch again.

There was no obvious explanation as to what startled the stag, and this played on Patrick's growing paranoia. The hallucinations were also gaining strength. He believed that there were shadowy figures stalking him, which disappeared as soon as he turned around to confront them; that the soil beneath his feet was sinking; that there was no end in sight to these ghastly woods.

Licking at his parched lips, Patrick stopped before a stagnant pool of water. There were leaves, broken branches and a few dead crows resting upon its surface, but they didn't stop him from taking in a mouthful. The urge to quench his agonising thirst took precedence over all else.

'Woe is me,' he snarled. 'What a sorry life to live...'

Patrick spat out the first mouthful, which had left a rancid and bitter taste of mould on his tongue. Still, he fought against his better instincts to take another sip, clasping his hands together like a bowl as to force another wave of foul water into his gullet. He managed to stomach a few handfuls by pretending the water was fine wine, although it wasn't an easy feat to accomplish. Grateful that the water had managed to fill a portion of the empty void within his torso, Patrick then sat down and looked again to his pocket watch, the time now reading 09:52.

'If you could only witness what I've become, Father,' mourned Patrick, stroking a thumb over the watch's face. 'What a sorry excuse of a boy you raised. I could have been a high-ranking officer in the army by now... if I had just listened to your so-called advice. But you weren't there during the Boer War, were you? You didn't see what I saw or commit the wicked acts I did. Perhaps this is my punishment, to live in squalor and be constantly on the brink of starvation. Perhaps I do deserve to be in pain.'

A deep, rippling vibration shook through the soil, up through Patrick' spine, compelling him to fall asleep again.

The sound of children giggling in merriment echoed as Patrick opened his eyes. He was lying upon a stately four-poster bed, and beside him was a youthful-looking woman. He toyed with the notion of kissing her, of feeling the ecstatic rush from touching another human in an affectionate way.

'Who are you?' asked the woman, facing away from him.

'You tell me,' he replied with an awkward chuckle. 'Am I not your husband? Please say that I am.'

The woman let out a lengthy groan and then turned to face him. Her features were angelic; she had long, raven-black hair; skin the colour of ivory; lips that were soft and supple; and a forced smile that spoke more than a thousand words.

'I am what you want me to be,' she said, widening her eyes, offering a bunch of grapes to him. 'Is this what your heart desires?'

Patrick looked around the room, admiring its splendour. 'I am a humble man, my dear. I need few pleasures to satisfy my needs,' he said, accepting the grapes without hesitation. 'Thank you.'

'You are most welcome.' The woman turned her head sharply as if in detest. 'You are all the same… men. You always focus on material needs, never on what you should be prizing most.'

Somewhat astounded, Patrick attempted to offer comfort by resting a hand upon the woman's waist. 'I am a good man —'

'Keep telling yourself that and you might make it real. But that is a lie, is it not?'

'Maybe? I was never the best at telling fibs.' Patrick snapped his hand back, forming it into a fist. He did not wish to harm the woman, however. It was more that he wanted to take his anger out on himself. 'I've tried my hardest to be a decent fellow —'

'You all think that. You all say that!' stated the woman bitterly. 'We are nothing but collateral to the likes of you, just slaves to be bartered with and cast aside when the moment suits.'

Patrick's heart sank as the sunrays within the room diminished, leaving only an amber light to linger. He tried to address the woman again, but now she appeared at the foot of their bed, her features no longer angelic.

'What's going on here?' asked Patrick, tearing his fingernails across the silken bedsheets. 'This is just a dream, isn't it — a nightmare?'

'This is a warning,' said the woman, her face morphing into that of a skull. 'Turn back now or face my master's hatred.'

Stuttering in disbelief, Patrick replied, 'I have nowhere to go. I have no money or family to turn to —'

'You will be tempted, but you must turn back,' the woman iterated. 'Ahead lies a path where you will know wealth and find an absolution, but it also bears my master's displeasure. You have been warned.'

Patrick closed his eyes and prayed, hoping for the dreadful spectre to vanish. On opening them he found himself by the stagnant pool of water again, his skin freezing to the touch.

'I need food—that's what I need. I'm not losing my mind,' he told himself, on attempting to stand. 'Who was that girl? I've never seen her before.' A branch snapping from behind revealed to Patrick a tall gentleman. He was a muscular man, dressed in the finest of clothes, and of whom bore an empathetic expression. 'Goodness gracious, my good fellow, you scared the life out of me. Are you but another false vision? Do my tired, old eyes deceive me again?'

The man slowly shook his head in response. 'No. I am hunting a stag and just so happened to stumble upon your fine self.' The man looked up and down Patrick, granting him a pitiful smile. 'By any chance, you wouldn't have seen one pass by?'

'Yes, actually.' Patrick looked to his pocket watch and sighed with relief, given its hands were not yet near 11:20. 'I saw one about an hour ago. I can't have been asleep for an hour—'

'When did you last eat?'

'I cannot recall the last time I ate anything worthwhile, if truth be told. God has not been generous to me, not in that sense.'

'Would you care to join me on my hunt? It would be an honour to have you accompany myself and my family for a good, warm meal this evening at our home.'

'You are kind, sir, but I do not want to impose myself on your family. I doubt that they would wish to be sat next to a smelly vagrant like me.'

'Poor soul,' the man tutted, 'you shall be warmly welcomed in my household. I dwell in a humble farmhouse close to these woods. It is not far to travel.'

'I don't want to be a burden—'

'It is my gift, as a fellow Christian, to a man who clearly needs a break from the toils of everyday life.'

'You are very kind, sir, and I am so very grateful.'

'Then, come with me. You can help me hunt down the beast, and then we shall enjoy the fruits of our labour.'

Patrick felt some reluctance, granted the warning handed to him by the terrifying spectre, but hunger ultimately overruled his judgement. 'I shall take up your offer, my friend. I am skilled in hunting down feral animals. I will earn my meal and hospitality from you. I swear it.'

'I believe it ran that way,' said the man, pointing to a darker segment in the woods. 'This shall make for good sport. There is no better feeling in this world than to spill the blood of innocent creatures.'

'Indeed,' Patrick gulped. 'Let's get to it then, shall we?'

Patrick inspected the marks left by the stag's hooves, following them further into the deep woods, and still he could not shake off the woman's warning. His primal instincts were telling him to turn back, to leave and never return, but his hunger was growing more painful by the second, and the thought of some roasted venison sliding down his throat was a temptation he simply could not resist.

'What brings you to these marshlands?' asked the stranger, keeping a watchful eye on Patrick's movements. 'There are few who would dare travel through them.'

'Pardon my indiscretion, but I am not surprised,' said Patrick. 'They are not too inviting. I merely stumbled upon them by accident…'

'They have a blood-stained history,' said the man, raising his eyebrows. 'According to some, there were battles fought upon the surrounding fields during medieval times, and — even more disturbing — demons are said to wonder through these woods. I only come here every now and then, such as when the need for fresh meat arises.'

'Demons?' yelped Patrick. 'Let us hope we do not cross paths with any of those dreadful monstrosities.'

'Indeed.' The man planted a firm hand against Patrick' chest, forcing them both to a standstill. 'We're close. Be silent and still. The stag is near.'

In a moment of clarity, Patrick noted to himself how the man was unarmed. 'Do not think me rude for asking this, but how do you intend to kill the creature?'

'With my bare hands, as I always do,' the man boasted.

'That will be an impressive sight to behold,' said Patrick, scratching at his scalp. 'Do you not possess a gun or knife?'

'I have no use for them. I much prefer to do things... naturally.'

'Well, I think we'll have a fight on our hands. The stag I saw was huge.'

'It is all in the mind, Patrick. Imagine that you are stronger than your prey, and you will have no trouble casting them into submission.'

Taken aback, Patrick cautiously looked into the man's eyes only to find that they were pristine black in colour. 'How do you know my name, might I ask? I can't remember telling you it.'

'You talk in your sleep.' The man jolted his head back, bursting into laughter. 'How rude of me not to introduce myself. I am Bartholomew.'

'You have caused no offence, sir. Please pardon my brash response,' Patrick grovelled.

'You are pardoned. Now, let us find that stag and put an end to its meaningless life.'

Serving in the army had taught Patrick many valuable lessons, most notably how to track down prey.

'The trail veers off in that direction,' he said, nodding to a rocky crevice. 'We've got it corned.'

'Yes, we have,' Bartholomew agreed, smirking to himself. 'It has nowhere to run. The pitiful creature is ours for the taking.'

Patrick instantly felt an overwhelming fatigue take over his body once more. He collapsed to the ground, with his vision blurring and all sounds around him falling into silence. He was powerless to resist, and he soon found himself back in the stately home from his previous dream.

Unlike the last vision, however, Patrick was not in a bedroom but instead stood within the heart of a huge hall. Above him he noticed a portrait of a noble man, their demeanour fierce and eyes unforgiving.

'What is this place?' he asked, shuddering as his voice reverberated through the empty corridors. 'It feels somehow familiar.'

A gentle, feminine voice spoke from behind. 'Father?'

Patrick spun around to find a young girl looking up to him, and in the palm of her left hand she held a small, red jewel. 'What are you playing at, you silly girl. You startled me.'

'Must I marry him?' she asked. 'Must I?'

'Marry who?'

'Did you kill her?'

'Kill—what on earth are you going on about?' Patrick's frustration became too strong to hold back. 'Tell me, girl, where am I? Who are you, and what is that you're holding?'

'Would you like it?' she asked, holding the jewel out to him. 'It is yours, should you desire it.'

'No. I won't be tempted,' Patrick chuntered, recalling the words spoken to him by the terrifying woman. 'You keep it, my dear. I'm not after any trouble.'

'That matters not. He is coming,' she replied.

'Who is coming?'

'*Him.*'

'Who? Tell me or else I'll tan your little hide!'

'I thought you were a good man. I thought… you were worth saving. Such a pity,' the girl tutted. 'You are just like the rest of them.'

A deafening explosion rocked Patrick to the core, forcing him to his hands and knees. As he looked up the vision of a demonic woman met with him. It was the same woman who had appeared before, although now she seemed to be fuelled with rage and detest—her very aura radiating with malice.

'Did I not warn you?' she growled. 'I granted insight, but you took no heed!'

'You speak in riddles,' said Patrick. 'What am I meant to be fleeing from? Why am I here?'

Another, deeper voice joined with the woman's, making hers meeker in comparison. 'Once connected, never can a bond be broken. You are mine…'

Patrick awoke again but now found himself sat upon a stool within a small farmhouse. The smell of meat roasting on an open fire and herbs simmering in a pan filled his nostrils, and so too did a sense of calm enter his mind.

'The beast fought well, but we gave it a good fight,' said Bartholomew, appearing out of nowhere. 'The way you slit its throat was most impressive, I must say.'

'I can't recall doing that,' said Patrick, checking his hands only to discover that they were not covered in any blood. 'I can't even remember how I ended up in this place.'

'You are severely dehydrated. A flask or two of fresh ale should resolve that.' Bartholomew handed Patrick a battered pewter mug, which was filled to its brim with—what appeared to be—strong ale. 'Drink and rest. You're suffering is almost over.'

'Thank you, sir.' On taking the first mouthful, Patrick immediately reeled in disgust over its awful, sour taste. 'This is not an ale I am familiar with. Is it homebrew?'

'Yes. It is an ale of my design, fermented with the blood of slain animals. The agony they feel in their last moments vastly improves the flavour, I find.'

Without reservation, Patrick spat the viscous fluid onto the tiled floor. 'What a wicked trick to play! Is this some sick joke to you, sir?'

'No, it is sustenance — what you prayed for.'

'How…?' Patrick pondered over the woman's warning, over how coincidental him and Bartholomew's meeting was, and how he missed his chance to avoid this unsavoury situation. 'Where is your family? Are you alone?'

'I am never alone. I am everywhere, at all times, and I can see everything — including your present thoughts,' snarled Bartholomew, his features now becoming more grotesque and deformed. 'Do you doubt my generosity and merciful act in bringing you here? Do you consider me to be… evil?'

'I don't know what you are, and I shall politely take my leave.'

'That opportunity has gone,' said Bartholomew, forcing Patrick to remain seated. 'You are to stay here, as my guest, until I grow tired of your company.'

'I think not. Good day to you, sir. I will see myself out.'

Patrick made for the front door, unlocked its bolt, then gasped on opening it. What lay before him now was a mirror image of the farmhouse interior, instead of the marshland fields and forest he had been expecting.

'You cannot leave until I grant permission,' said Bartholomew, licking away some of the disgusting ale from his lips. 'You are mine now, Patrick. Mine.'

'I am not your prisoner! I am leaving, and you will not stop me!'

'So be it…'

Patrick stepped foot through the doorway and immediately came to regret this action. The door slammed behind him, and as it did the interior started to rapidly decay. A woman laughing then shifted from corner to corner until Patrick sat himself before the table again, beleaguered as to how he could escape this perilous situation.

'Forgive me, O Lord. Is this my purgatory? Is this my punishment for all the past sins I have committed?'

A burst of flames swept out from the fireplace, and from them came the demonic woman, although she appeared fairer now and with less anger in her eyes.

'I warned thee,' she whimpered. 'I told thee to not give in to temptation...'

'And I should have listened,' said Patrick, stroking at his face. 'Who is this Bartholomew?'

'My master,' she replied, wrapping her arms around her skeletal torso. 'What sins doth thee speak of? My master can read minds and corrupt the souls of his victims, but I am yet to learn that skill.'

'They are for God alone to judge, miss.'

'In this realm my master is God. He is all-seeing and all-powerful.'

'Maybe to you, but he's not to me,' said Patrick, feeling around his pocket for the watch. 'What have I done to deserve this ill-treatment?'

The woman paced back and forth, staring at Patrick as she did so. 'Men are too easy to entice; thy greed and want for acknowledgment make it a simple task.'

'Greed? I am content with only possessing my long pipe and father's pocket watch. I don't need anything else. I don't own a home or have any money.' Patrick proceeded to show the woman his beloved timepiece. 'I live day-to-day as it comes, never knowing where I'll end up, and it doesn't bother me in the slightest.'

'I was mistaken to offer thee a chance,' the woman mourned. 'My master will be back shortly, and my part in this has reached its end.'

Slamming a fist on the table, Patrick asked, 'And who is your master — really? Is he a demon?' The woman remained silent. 'What reward could he possibly merit in holding me captive?'

'Thou art but one of many. My master has had no decent sport in a long while. Thou art simply in the wrong place at the wrong time.'

Patrick considered his options, now seeing the woman to be his only hope. 'It's obvious to me that you're not happy, there's no denying it.'

'I have not known joy in over four-hundred years,' she whispered, lowering her sight from him. 'I am to serve my master until the end of days. That is my destiny, whether I will it or not.'

'Help me,' pleaded Patrick. 'Help me to escape from your master's clutches, and perhaps you shall also find salvation?'

'What is this talk of salvation?' asked a deep and terrifying voice. 'You are nothing but a thief, a traitor, a murderer, a sinner! I see all!'

'How do you know this?' asked Patrick, sweeping his eyes across the room in fright. 'You know nothing about me. Bartholomew, I presume?'

The woman looked beyond Patrick, hinting that another soul stood behind him. 'Grant him a trial, Master. Let this poor wretch prove his worth. It will be amusing.'

'That would be most amusing,' the voice agreed, unleashing a vicious roar. 'Let us put him to the test, to see if his soul is, in fact, pure as he states it is.'

'I'm not afraid of you! I'm a god-fearing man — '

'Lies, Patrick! All Lies!' barked Bartholomew. 'Let us see how strong your resolve and faith are, shall we?'

The room spun around wildly until Patrick blacked out once again. Through great courage he managed to open his eyes but only to find himself back in the stately home, though it was now ruined and crumbling with each passing second.

'Throw whatever you want at me!' he cried, beating a fist against his chest. 'I've survived countless battles and seen things that would horrify any ordinary person. I am not scared of you, whatever you are!'

An echoing whisper responded. 'Oh, but you will be...'

The ground shook violently, forcing Patrick to retreat up the main stairwell before it collapsed. He then watched on in dread as a wave of black water cascaded through the lower hall, flooding it, rising swiftly. Against his seizing bones and muscles, Patrick sprinted along the upper hallways, trying each door as he passed, until he came to the only room that was unlocked.

'The wicked bastard!' Patrick howled, forcing open the door. 'What diseased and twisted place have they sent me to now?'

A small girl, who was crouched in the farthest corner, then caught Patrick's attention.

'Father!' she cried. 'Save me!'

'You'll be okay, little one. I won't let any harm come to you,' Patrick assured her. 'We need to get out of here. Maybe we can escape out that window?'

'But you sealed them, Father. You said that fresh air is unholy and bad for the lungs.'

'Utter nonsense,' said Patrick. He looked to a dressing table nearby, licking at his lips. 'That should do the trick. I'll throw it through that window, then we'll just need to find a way to climb down the wall outside.'

'Father!' the girl screeched, as the walls around them tremored and split apart. 'How could you? Why did you kill her?'

Patrick bore no knowledge of the child's plight, though he recounted the fateful day when he accidently shot an unarmed civilian during his time serving in the army – a woman who was merely selling flowers.

'It was an accident,' he said, sombrely and with much hesitation. 'I didn't mean to do it.'

'No, it was intentional. You wanted her to die!'

'She was innocent, and I have begged for God's forgiveness ever since that dreadful day.' With a thunderous rumble, the roof began to cave in. 'Are you going to help me or not?'

'Apologise for what you have done!' pleaded the girl. 'Beg for forgiveness!'

'I've done nothing wrong to you. There is no need for me to offer any apology!'

'You have failed.' The girl raised her head, revealing a set of sunken eye sockets and slashed flesh. 'There will be no mercy for you, nor for any other man that dare defy us.'

Before Patrick could respond the floor beneath broke apart, sending him and the child into the water's cloudy depths. He desperately fought to clasp onto any debris he could that passed by, frantic to gain another breath. His lungs slowly and painfully filled with the thick fluid, burning them, the pressure encountered utterly agonising. Now on the brink of welcoming death, Patrick allowed for his body to sink into the darkness, to wherever Bartholomew felt fit to send it.

'This is not over,' Bartholomew declared, his tone somewhat filled with disappointment. 'You have one last test. One last chance.'

In a surprising twist, Patrick discovered that he was no longer drowning. The sun was beaming off his face, and his lungs were no longer filled with stale water. He was lying face-down on a field within the marshlands, relaxed and subdued. Patrick jumped up, clasping his hands together in relief that he had not succumbed to such a terrible fate.

'I'm alive!' he announced, hopping to and froe in delight. However, his happiness did not last long. Behind him stood the empty remains of a large manor — the same one that had been flooded moments before. 'Will I ever be free of this accursed sight?' Something then convinced him to check his pocket watch. 'Lord, please don't say it is damaged.' To his further dismay, Patrick found that the hands read 11:20. 'No! Dear, merciful Lord — NO!'

A wave of adrenaline coursed through him, paralysing his muscles, clouding his cognition. Above all else, Patrick feared this time more than anything. Although the marshlands bore no evident threat, the compulsive fear Patrick had of this specific time almost drove him into insanity. He fell to his knees and began to pray, but to what avail this would be continued to torture him.

Amid his sorrow, Patrick noted the sound of hooves squelching through the marshland waters. He turned his head to find a woman and man, who were both riding these horses, approaching him.

'Pardon my intrusion,' Patrick stuttered, 'but I need your assistance.' The woman and man carried on with their journey, as if oblivious to Patrick. 'I need your help. I am being hounded by a demon!'

'Aren't we all?' said the woman, her expression devoid of any emotion. 'London. I cannot wait to see our nation's greatest city, my darling Frederik.'

Somewhat confused, Patrick crawled up to the travellers. 'Take me with you. Would you not help an old man like me?'

The woman, man, and their horses froze, as did the passing breeze. Patrick waved a hand in front of their faces, gaining no attention or response. Convinced that this was another of Bartholomew's tricks, he then stood back and looked to his pocket watch again. The time now read 11:31.

'Curses!' shrieked Patrick, punching at the air. 'I am doomed, that is for certain. Doomed!'

'That you are,' said Bartholomew in response, 'as were they. You are mine, mortal. Mine.'

Patrick clasped onto his mouth in shock as the horses and their riders sunk into the watery marshlands. He reached out to offer aid, grasping at the saddles and then at the limbs of the unfortunate couple, but it was futile. All that was left was a single ruby that floated to the surface. Patrick was hesitant to retrieve it at first, but he did so anyway.

'Such a pretty thing,' he noted, inspecting the scarlet jewel. 'This could be my way to a better life, to wealth and comfort.'

'The ultimate downfall of mankind is gluttony,' explained Bartholomew, though he was nowhere in sight. 'You have chosen your punishment, old man. You have failed. You never had a chance, anyway.'

Within a blink of his eyes, Patrick ended up in the decrepit manor again. There was not another soul in sight, nor familiar sound or feeling of warmth. He tried to leave but couldn't; all the doors and windows were sealed.

'Let me out!' Patrick begged, throwing himself against the front door. 'Let me out, Bartholomew…'

'Why such sorrow? I have given you what you wanted, have I not? A place to dwell in eternal safety and solitude.'

'Am I dead?' asked Patrick, though only after a few strained breaths and another attempt at forcing open the door.

'You are neither alive nor dead,' Bartholomew clarified. 'You are with my mistress and I now until I lose interest and see it fit to discard you. There is no escape.'

'You can't do this to me—'

'I can do whatever I please, and no mortal will ever escape from my wrath…'

Patrick came to know the manor's corridors and rooms well over the next few decades, where his spirit dwelt alone and without any disturbance, until the moment came when its walls were finally torn down. He learned that it was called Appleton Manor, though was granted no further information about its disastrous past.

The final stone was removed from Appleton Manor on October 13th, 1921, forty years after Patrick's soul was forced to inhabit that forsaken place. Bartholomew eventually relinquished Patrick's spirit, but even in the afterlife he would never forget his gruesome encounter with the two demonic entities that had imprisoned him, nor would Patrick come to know any everlasting peace. All that kept him occupied thereafter, lost within the Endless Void, was his father's pocket watch, which was frozen upon the time when he lost his life — 11:31.

The Boy and The Soldier

During the winter of 1944, when few dared to whisper of the terrible worldwide conflict reaching its end, Robert Adley's childhood came close to utter annihilation.

At ten years old, Robert had already endured much hardship that other boys of the same age would never have even dreamed of. He had spent most his life to this point slaving away alongside his father, Walter, on their family's farm. The daily tasks were gruelling, bordering on being sadistic, but Walter Adley yearned for his son to be a humble and hardworking man someday — just like him, if going off his own false perception. The result was a fractured and volatile relationship between the two, which was only subdued by the loving nature of Robert's mother, Rose, and the invigorating, playful spirit of his six-year-old sister, Vera.

Rising with the sun, Robert stretched out his aching limbs and yawned, careful as not to wake up his little sister as she slept six feet away. Robert sat on the edge of his bed, peering at the morning's sky through the only window available, which was bobbled and covered in cobwebs. The thin rays of light were welcomed, and they gave a slight sense of hope to Robert that circumstances would someday improve.

'It's going to be another cold one,' Robert thought to himself, shivering at the notion, imagining the frost-covered tools he would soon need to use. He turned to Vera, tilting his head in sympathy. 'At least you can spend the day with Mum, baking and reading. Dad will make me clean out the chickens and pigs again, no doubt. I always get the best jobs.'

'Can I not come with you?' asked Vera, startling catching Robert. 'I can help?'

'There's no need for you to be awake yet.'

'But I am, and so is Eliza.'

'Eliza's not—' Robert stopped himself mid-sentence. If Vera found comfort in having an imaginary friend, then he wasn't prepared to rob that from her. He understood how lonely it must be for her, having to dwell inside all day, and their mother rarely spoke due to her hidden depression. 'Eliza's not allowed to come, and neither are you. It's dangerous work. You might get hurt.'

'But I want to feed the chickens,' she pleaded, pushing out her lower lip. 'I want to play with you. It's so boring being stuck with Mum all day.''

Robert walked across to Vera and then stroked a hand through her hair. 'We'll play some games when I finish my chores, okay? I'll be back before sundown.'

'Promise?'

'On my life. You've got until then to think of what games we can get up.' Vera stared back with a forlorn frown. 'It'll be something to look forward to, won't it?'

'Uh-huh...'

Robert smiled. 'You and Eliza will be fine, and I'll be back home before you know it.'

With a heavy heart, Robert added a few inches of water to his washbasin—water was a precious commodity and involved him having to visit a nearby well twice a day to replenish the storage tank, therefore, he couldn't afford to waste any. He applied some of the filthy water to his face, slowly cleansing his weather-worn skin, and then Vera joined him.

'It's my turn!' she bleated, jumping up and down impatiently. 'Leave some for me!'

'It's all yours.' Robert helped bathe Vera, quickly wrapping a woollen blanket around her afterwards as to protect her fragile body from the cold air. 'Let's get you dry. The last thing you need is to get a nasty sniffle.'

'Eliza will care for me, should I get ill,' Vera corrected him. 'She always looks after me… us.'

'Because she's so kind, like you.' The sound of his hungover father stumbling around in their kitchen instantly snapped Robert into action. 'Dad's awake. I'd better go, Vera. Be a good girl for Mummy. Don't get up to any mischief while I'm gone.'

'I won't,' Vera smirked, then her smile faded on hearing her father's usual grunts. 'Don't let Daddy hit you again. It makes me sad when he hurts you.'

With a nod of assurance, Robert replied, 'If Dad strikes me it's only because I'm not working hard enough. He hasn't hit me for a couple of days, so I must be doing something right.' Vera lulled her head, swaying it from side to side. 'Maybe ask Mummy if the two of you can bake a cake today—something special? That will be fun, won't it?'

'Yes. A chocolate one?'

'It'll depend on what rations we have left. That'd be great, though. Chocolate's my favourite.' Scrubbing at Vera's hair again, Robert then moved to leave. 'At least we haven't been evacuated like other children have been. We still get to see our parents every day, for better or worse.'

'Why is Daddy not a soldier like Uncle Clive?'

'Daddy was hurt in the Great War. He's still getting over his injuries,' Robert noted with a roll of his eyes. 'That's why he can't walk properly: he got hit in the leg with shrapnel.'

A booming, slurring voice bellowed from behind the bedroom door—Walter. 'Are you coming, boy? There's work to be done!'

Robert sighed, burying his frustration. 'Yes, Dad. I'm coming now.'

A horrendous shock met with Robert on opening the door. Walter stood a mere few inches away, barely able to stand from the copious amount of alcohol still flowing through his bloodstream. The father and son's eyes met, both cold and devoid of love.

'You've slept in, you lazy, little cretin!' Walter shook Robert by the shoulders and then dragged the helpless boy to rest up against his protruding gut. 'Half the morning has been wasted. You'll need to make it up.'

'I'm sorry, Dad.'

'No, you're not. Get your backside into gear or else I'll wrap my belt across it!'

'Yes, Dad. Sorry, Dad.'

Robert's mother, Rose, was stood at the front door with his sheepskin coat and scarf nestled within her arms.

'Take care, Son,' she said to him in a trembling voice. 'Be on your best behaviour today. Work hard.'

'I will. Thanks, Mum.' Robert then whispered into her ear, 'I'll keep an eye on Dad, on how much he drinks. Don't you worry.'

'Make sure he doesn't drink too much of that whiskey, which he thinks we don't know anything about,' said Rose, ensuring that her voice was out of Walter's earshot. 'He drinks enough on a night to knock out a donkey. I don't know how he's even awake. Be on your best guard.'

'I will.'

The back of Walter's hand struck against Robert's left temple, followed by one of his common rants. 'I work every bleedin' hour I can to keep a roof over this family's head. And what do I receive in return? Miserable faces and cheek — that's what! You lot don't know how lucky you've got it!'

'Yes, Walter,' said Rose.

'Yes, Dad,' said Robert.

'Move it! I'm not in the mood for playing games. My head's killing me…'

On leaving the farm a freezing mist instantaneously swamped Walter and Robert. The young boy clung to his coat, desperate for warmth, whereas Walter (in his alcoholic state) seemed happily oblivious to the low temperature. They made their way to the chicken pen first, where Walter eagerly parted ways with his son.

'Where are you off to, Dad?' asked Robert, nevertheless unsurprised by his father's departure.

'It's none of your business, boy. Muck out the chickens and get them fed, then do the same with the pigs. I'll be back by midday.'

'But… where *are* you going? I'm not strong enough to lift the pig feed —'

'Then grow some muscles! It's about time you did,' snarled Walter, wiping away some phlegm from his chin. 'I can't be the master of this farm forever. You'll need to take over the reins one day. God forbid it when that comes to pass.'

Robert buried his resentment, for being held in the fear he could find himself at the sharp end of Walter's thick leather belt again. 'I'll do my best, Dad. I want to make you proud of me.'

'You've got your work cut out there,' Walter cackled, taking in a sinus-burning wave of snuff from the back of his hand. 'I reckon it's going to rain, come sundown. You best get started on your chores.'

'Yes, Dad.'

'Stupid boy.'

Robert loved spending time with the animals, especially his father's pigs. For an animal that is often considered to be dumb and idle, Robert instead found them to be unique and interesting — they each had different personalities, just like regular people — and they were good listeners. There was one pig that Robert had named Rhoda, who he would bestow all his angst and woes upon.

'Dad's been at the whiskey again, Rhoda. He smells worse than you do,' he joked to a coincidental grunt from the pig. 'You've got more manners than him as well. I'd rather have you sit at the dining table with me than him—believe me.'

In his peripheral vision, regardless of the morning mist, Robert was sure he saw a figure move toward the stream that flowed by his family home, which coursed into a large forest some hundred yards away. He blinked twice, wiped at his eyes, and then attempted to focus on the blurred object. There was no mistaking it: something or someone was trespassing on his land.

'That can't be Dad. They're too tall.' Holding onto the shovel he used to muck out his father's pigs, Robert carefully followed the stranger's movements. 'There shouldn't be anyone else here. What should I do?'

Robert's concern was justified. Adley Farm was the only residence presently situated within the marshland area of Acle, and the closest sign of civilisation otherwise was an ordnance factory that stood half a mile away, of which manufactured bombs and bullets for the war effort. His family seldom had visitors; not even relatives wanted to visit them.

The figure skulked around like a hungry fox, never once following a straight line. Whoever it was must have noticed Robert's presence, for they soon fled into the woods, disappearing within them not long after. Robert heeded his father's words from earlier, that eventually he would become the man of their household, so he simply had to be brave. There was no choice. Robert had to confront the possible assailant, that is, if he were to become a "man".

'Who goes there?' Robert cried out, disturbing some crows that loitered within the tree branches. 'I know you're there!'

Without warning a large hand clung onto Robert's mouth, silencing his cries for help, and then came a muscular arm that wrapped around his torso. Robert fought against the attacker, though he regrettably lost grip of the shovel during this struggle.

'Schweiggen!' the figure commanded, wrestling Robert to the ground. 'Nicht bewegen!'

Robert couldn't believe what he was hearing. The man was undoubtedly German — an enemy — how could this be? With little options to choose from, Robert submitted himself to the assailant's will.

'I'll stay quiet,' Robert whispered to them, steadying his movements. 'Please, don't hurt me.'

'Das ist gut,' the figure whispered back. 'Sehr gut. Wo ist dein vater?'

'I don't understand!' Robert yelped frantically. 'I can't speak German!'

'My apologies,' said the man, his tone now softer and higher in pitch. 'My English is not too good, and I take no joy from uttering it. I asked: where is your father?'

'He's not far away,' said Robert, and for the first time ever he was desperate to see Walter's mottled face again. 'He'll come and save me, you'll see.'

'There is much doubt in your voice, I gather,' the man sniggered. 'Do not be concerned. I have no intention of harming you, that is, unless I must.'

'What do you want? My family have no money.'

'Food, clothes, companionship — basic needs.'

The man spun Robert around, so that they could now see one another clearly. He was at least six-feet tall and on the verge of starvation; his eyes were sunken and colourless; his body was clothed in — what evidently appeared to be — prisoner of war attire, and he seemed to be even more fearful than Robert was.

'You're a prisoner!' Robert gasped.

'Yes, or I was. My name is Amon Schulz. I am a human being with emotions and thoughts of my own, just like you. Take away the war we have been forced into, and there is little difference between you and I.'

Robert hesitated, unsure as to what Amon's true motives were. 'You're still my enemy, though. Nothing can change that.'

'I have done no wrong to you,' Amon insisted. 'I am but a pawn just like your own soldiers, just like the other fools who fight for your king and country.' There was a genuine look of sorrow on Amon's face as he spoke, littered with past experiences that continued to haunt him. 'I have a wife and child back home. They are called Emilia and Lukas. You have a little sister, don't you?'

'Yes,' said Robert. 'How do you know that?'

'I am observant, that is all. You have a nice family.

'That's not good enough. How do you know things about us?' asked Robert, pretending to mimic his father's dominating demeanour by broadening his shoulders. 'Tell me!'

'I happened by these woods after escaping from the prison camp in Sedgefield. The stream is a source of fresh water, and there are berries within the forest that have satiated my painful hunger. Your family home is but a glance away from where I hide, so I have seen you all many times over the last two months. There is no ill-intent, I must implore. Seeing you and your loved ones merely reminds me of the family I have left behind, who are likely dead by now.'

Calming himself, Robert sat down upon a fallen tree in attempt to contemplate his next move. There was not much of a chance he could flee successfully, and a higher chance that — if he did run — Amon would take out his desperation on Robert's family; Amon certainly gave off the impression he was unpredictable, and Robert couldn't risk putting his mother and sister in danger. He accepted that it would be wiser to wait for the correct moment to move.

'Are you sure you don't want to hurt me?'

'Of course. It is a pleasure to speak with another human, and you are a very polite child.' There was something in Amon's words that disturbed Robert, namely the fact he was insinuating that he had been conversing with some other, unknown sentient being. 'I have noticed how you like talking to the pigs. Strange, yes?'

'They like it when I talk to them,' Robert clarified, not once moving his sight away from Amon's position. 'Who have you been talking to — the crows?'

'No, no,' Amon chuckled. 'I have met another creature on my travels, who talks to me in the dead of night, telling me where to go and what I should be doing. I call him Dennis, but he is no man.'

'Dennis?' Robert enquired, his fingers twitching through anxiety.

'It is short for "Denizen".' Amon's composure returned to one of anger. 'He is not of this world, and I will set him upon you and your family if you do not offer me aid.'

'I will help you if it means that my family won't come to any harm. There's no need for you to try and scare me with make-believe monsters. I might be a boy, but I'm not stupid.'

'Oh, Dennis is real!' Amon emphasised. 'Would you care to meet him? It is not an encounter many would stomach well...'

Curious, albeit terrified, Robert nodded in agreement. 'Okay. I'll meet Dennis.'

'Sehr gut... er wird sich freuen,' Amon whispered to himself.

'What does that mean?'

'Dennis will be overjoyed to make a new acquaintance, especially a child of your respectable calibre. He likes to play with innocent things, you see.'

Robert considered how annoyed his father would likely be, once his failure to fulfil his duties could come to light, but he was now held in the clutches of a broken man, an individual that could sever away from being civil at any moment.

Nevertheless, Robert's greatest priority was in protecting his mother and sister at all costs. He followed Amon deeper into the woods, reciting prayers with each step taken.

'We are close,' said Amon, raising a fist into the air to halt their progress. 'You must not look at him directly or utter a single word, not unless I say so. Dennis is easily startled, you see, and he has a very violent temper.' Robert acknowledged Amon's advice with a swift jolt of his head. 'Sehr gut. Do as I say, Robert, and you will be free from harm. It might be wise to continue with your prayers, given where I am now taking you.'

'Where are you taking me?'

'To my home—Dennis's home,' Amon replied with a look of disappointment. 'It is not a mansion, by any means, but it protects me from the harsh English weather. It is a palace to me.'

Robert's mother had warned him to never set foot in these woods, and this played on his mind now. She had not elaborated as to why there was a threat as such, though she had made it clear that there was something unnatural at work within them. Everywhere he looked, it felt like countless eyes were staring down upon Robert and his captor; they were not alone, despite the silence surrounding them.

'My father would have noticed me missing by now,' said Robert, hugging into himself. 'He'll be out looking for me.'

'Your father is in the barn, drowning himself in whiskey, where he always goes while you do his work,' said Amon. 'You might not know it yet, but we are so very, very alike.'

'How?'

'My father was not a gracious man. He abandoned me at a young age to fulfil his wild and terrible aspirations. My father wanted to change the world, but it went against everything I had been taught.'

'What did he do that was so terrible?'

'He had opinions that were ill-judged, dangerous, which went against our Fuhrer's teachings.' Amon halted again, barely able to move his wasting muscles another inch. 'I must rest for a moment. Please stop.'

'I don't understand why you think your father was such a bad man. Mine drinks all the time, and he hits me and my mother if we disagree with him,' Robert lamented. 'I never want to be like my dad.'

'And that is how we are so alike, my little friend. My father was quick to enrol me in a youth movement that our government diligently watched over. I was taught that certain humans were more privileged than others, that they had a divine right to rule over this world, and that I was one of them — I was chosen to become a great leader. My father disagreed, however, and he paid the price for his betrayal.'

'What happened to him?'

'I did my duty as a loyal German citizen: I handed him over to the SS without question, knowing that I had done a noble deed. I even laughed as they took him away. He cried, however, and never took his sight away from me until they threw him the back of a military van. Still, he got what he deserved.'

Tremoring in disbelief, Robert then asked, 'Did they... kill him?'

'Hopefully. That is the justice he warranted for turning his back on me, his only son, to spread venomous propaganda. I have no regrets.' Turning to Robert, Amon gleamed with pride. 'There is no shame in severing ties with anyone who is a threat to you, not even so-called loved ones. Someday, and it might be sooner than you expect, your father will also pay the price for his negligence and selfish acts.'

'I don't like my father, though I'd never want for him to get hurt.'

'There are ways to seek vengeance on those who have wrought despair upon you without incurring any consequences, dear boy. Dennis is a fine example of that fact.'

Robert gulped as he looked up to the sun, yearning for its light to bring back that feeling of hope like it normally would, but it was fading and fast. 'How did you meet Dennis?'

'He came to me. While I clawed my way through the cold and filth of those marshlands, he came to me and offered a new path — a righteous path. All that was expected in return was my devotion to him. I could not refuse.'

'Does he look after you?'

'Yes, and I look after him. It is a mutually beneficial relationship we have. You do not need to know how, and I doubt your small mind could comprehend what is involved.'

With a snap of his fingers, Amon signalled for their journey to continue. His bones and ligaments cracked on standing, and the agonized whine that was released after sent all crows nearby scattering further into the dark depths.

'I'm not sure if I want to meet Dennis now,' said Robert. 'He doesn't seem to be a nice person.'

'He is not. I never referred to him that way,' said Amon with a confused scowl. 'Remember what I told you, my boy, to keep your head down and stay silent. Be wise. Be mindful.'

Amon and Robert walked for another ten minutes until they came to a peculiar-looking willow tree; its trunk and branches were white, unlike any other species known to Robert.

'How much farther must we go?' Robert whined.

'We are close. Now would be a good time to practise being quiet,' said Amon, placing a finger over his lips. 'Dennis can hear better than we can. He will already know that you are with me.'

Robert lowered his head and clenched his mouth shut, believing that the next few minutes could well indeed be his last upon Earth. He forced the image of Vera and their mother into his thoughts, desperate to remove the fear now consuming them, mournful that he may never see them again. It was in this moment, however, when a strange sense of clarity took over: he was obviously much stronger than Amon, who was physically weaker and mentally broken, thus there was a slim chance he could overpower him. Robert held onto that possibility, raring to use it.

'I know what you are thinking,' said Amon, rolling his eyes back. 'It would be unwise to attack me in this place. There are more than crows and insects watching our movements. Dark thoughts breed dark reactions...'

Astonished, Robert shook his head in disagreement. 'I wasn't thinking anything bad. I'm just worried about my mother and sister —'

'And rightly so, you should be. I am a man of my word, and — if you dare go against my wishes — I will not hesitate to set Dennis upon your household. Remember that.'

'I'll do as you say. I'll do anything to keep them safe.'

'Sehr gut...'

On being met with a stench of rotten carcasses, the two travellers then reached a ruined building. Upon its entrance were inscribed the words "Hell's Gate". Robert's concern intensified.

'You have lived here all your life, yet you have no knowledge of this place?' asked Amon, genuinely intrigued. 'How strange.'

'My mother told me to never wander into these woods.'

'Your mother is an intelligent woman,' laughed Amon. 'This is no place for innocent souls to tread, that is, unless they wish to be corrupted and defiled.'

Amon planted a kiss upon the structure's doorway and then gestured for Robert to step inside. The floor was covered in small animal bones, and at its heart lay a deep well. Amon circled the interior three times, reciting some unknown prayer in German, and then suddenly came to an abrupt stop.

'You live... in here?' asked Robert, reeling in disgust. 'It's horrible.'

'Yes,' said Amon with a widened smile, revealing what few teeth he had left. 'It is my sanctuary, my home, my new prison.' A sharp growl echoed from the well's depths, forcing Robert to retreat initially, but Amon signalled that there was nothing to be afraid of. 'It is an honour to meet Dennis. Now, bow yourself in reverence.'

'But—'

'Bow or incur the wrath of a demon, child!'

The only demon Robert knew of was Satan, the wicked monster from his mother's bible stories. He began to doubt Amon's claims, of Dennis' existence, but this was soon proved wrong. Three, blue, amphibian-like fingers emerged from the well, clinging onto it thereafter with grey nails as sharp as talons. While Robert watched on in horror, what can only be described as being a stout goblin crawled out from the well; its eyes were thin and yellow like a serpent's; its teeth were many and jagged; its stomach bulged like a bloating corpse; and its ears flickered like a hound seeking out some unwary target.

Realising his mistake, Robert averted his eyes from meeting with the foul creature and fell to his knees.

'A fine meal. Yes, a fine meal!' screeched the foul creature, its mouth foaming with—what looked like—blood. 'You have done well, Amon. I verged close on needing to eat you. What a puny meal that would have been.'

'He is not for eating,' Amon highlighted. 'I have a better use for him, Dennis.'

Clearly unconvinced, Dennis lunged at the fear-stricken boy.

'Other than being roasted or dry-cured, what use could this boy possibly be to us?' the demon snarled. 'He is weak.'

'He will bring us supplies — fresh meat, flooded with untainted blood. I assure you.'

Stroking a lengthy finger across his pointed chin, Dennis laughed and then returned to the well, perching its deformed legs upon it. 'He has until sundown to fulfil his duties, otherwise I shall pay him a visit come the hour when the physical and spiritual plains are at their weakest point...'

'He will follow our instructions. Won't you, Robert?' Amon hinted, staring down upon the boy. 'You do not want your mother and sister to get hurt now, do you?'

Robert shook his head firmly. 'No.'

'Das ist gut,' said Amon, forming half a smile. 'Before nightfall you must bring to me one chicken — unharmed, a bottle of your father's whiskey, some bread, and a sharp knife.'

Robert found some relief in how simple this task appeared to be, but he was also confounded as to why Amon specifically wanted an unharmed chicken — it would be much simpler to transport a dead one, which wouldn't make any noise to give away his secretive actions.

'Why must it be "unharmed"?' asked Robert.

'It is for a ritual. That is all you need to know,' said Amon, waving a hand through the air dismissively. 'So long as you bring these items to us, there shall be no repercussions. Do not disappoint me. I know where you live, remember.'

Without a moment to lose, Robert ran back through the woods to his family home. His father was nowhere in sight, thankfully, and his mother and sister were busy tending to the garden around the back of their farm. The coast was clear. Robert acted out Amon's request: he filled a straw bag that was normally used to store eggs in with a knife, some bread and a bottle of whiskey, although this meant he had to carry the chicken by its neck, which was more difficult than anticipated.

Returning to the ruined structure at sundown, as instructed, Robert laid out the items at its entranceway, where Amon now stood.

'Wunderbar! You shall sleep well tonight,' said Amon, patting Robert on the shoulders. 'You have proven your worth to me. All I ask now is for you to bring a handful of bread and two eggs each day — every day. You will be rewarded for your show of compassion, make no doubt about it.'

'Thank you,' said Robert, unsure of what else to say.

'No — thank you! Thank you, kind boy.' With a brief glance at the well, Amon then said, 'You cannot fathom how grateful I truly am. You will be rewarded, no matter the cost to me. Kind deeds must be cherished and rewarded. It is only fair.'

Robert left without word. He was riddled with guilt, believing that he had somehow made a deal with the devil himself. But it was for a worthy cause, to protect those whom he loved most, even if it meant providing Amon and the denizen with sustenance. Robert also doubted that two eggs going missing each day would be noticed, and his mother was always baking fresh loaves of bread, so there appeared to be little risk in his involvement, in him protecting "an enemy".

Over the next two weeks Robert obediently fulfilled his servitude to Amon and the goblin creature, ensuring to provide them with the freshest loaves of bread and eggs he could steal. He carefully left the items upon the doorstep of Hell's Gate, not once seeing Amon again in person. Robert preferred it this way, as it removed some of the resentment from his conscience. It was as if Robert was blindly walking through a nightmare—it just didn't seem real. Nevertheless, he recognised that there was a dire threat to his family, should he not comply, and he could not take any risks.

During this period Robert also noticed how his younger sister spent more time alone, namely with her imaginary friend, Eliza. Vera had withdrawn from her usually playful self; she instead could be found whispering incantations, not once acknowledging the rest of her family. Robert tried to ask her what was wrong, but Vera would never grant him a response. All he could do was pray for a miracle to occur, for some terrible event to befall Amon and his malicious, demonic associate. That prospect didn't seem likely, needless to say.

Come the morn of the fourteenth day, Robert collected Amon's supplies and then set off in the direction of their rendezvous point. Nothing seemed irregular at first, though as he neared the ruined structure a grave sense of dread entered his thoughts. He felt like a thousand eyes were watching him, casting judgment over him, while a heavy weight rested upon his neck—the gateway to his soul. A thick wave of yellow fog fed through the woods and became denser with every step taken, reeking of sulphur and foist. What met with Robert at Hell's Gate that day would stay with him for the rest of his life.

'Amon?' asked Robert, panting in exertion. A pool of congealing blood fed out from the entranceway, and of which had torn pieces of organs and hair mixed amongst it. 'Amon—where are you? What's going on here?'

There was no reply but for the sound of crows shrieking as they flew away overhead. Robert stepped forth into the dark structure only to find half of Amon's mutilated body at its centre – the upper half. What was left of Amon shook Robert, seeing as the only distinctive feature that survived were his piercing eyes, for the soldier's flesh had been ripped to shreds and left covered in blood and filth.

'Amon, what... happened to you?'

A gut-curdling cry responded – Dennis. 'He came – HE CAME! We did not expect him so soon! Curses! I am doomed! He will come for me next!'

Robert reached for the small knife he had given to Amon, which lay in the fallen soldier's left hand, and then he aimed it at the well where Dennis's croaking voice echoed.

'Did you do this?' asked Robert, stabbing the knife through the air. 'Did you, Dennis?'

'No – NO! It was him! He found me! I should not be here...'

Barely able to hold the knife in his hand now through sheer panic, Robert moved two steps closer to the well. 'I've done what was asked of me. Don't hurt my family, please.'

What sounded like children laughing burst from the well in response, and then Dennis cried, 'I knew, I knew, but gluttony took hold over my spirit. He will come for me soon, and I am too weak to fight back. He will come for you as well!'

'Vera! Mum!' Robert gasped, slipping momentarily upon Amon's spilled entrails. 'We've done nothing wrong. I helped you and Amon – we don't deserve to be hurt!'

'Because of your help... that is why he will hunt you down, foolish mortal. You cannot run, and you cannot hide, and no God shall come to save you.'

Still holding onto the knife, Robert fled back to his family home. Dark clouds formed above as he reached the front door, where his father waited for him.

'You've been stealing from me, haven't you?' asked Walter amid some belches and pained whines. 'What have you been doing in those woods?'

'N-Nothing.' Robert hesitated, secretly wishing for Amon's fate to meet with his own father. 'I haven't stolen from you.'

'You're a bloody liar!' Stumbling to balance himself, Walter threw an empty beer bottle directly off Robert's forehead, shattering it on impact. 'You're a dirty thief! Get inside now, boy, and go straight to bed. Be off with you!'

'But—'

'That knife...' Walter stared at the instrument trembling within Robert's hand, convinced that his son meant to harm him with it. 'Drop it. Don't you be getting any daft ideas now, boy.'

Robert did just so, slowly lowering the blade upon the sodden earth before his feet. 'I can explain, Dad—'

'To bed with you—NOW! I'll deal with you in the morning. I'll teach you a lesson you'll never forget!'

Robert skulked into his family home, smiling to both his mother and sister as he passed by them in the kitchen. They seemed oblivious of what had taken place outside, pleasantly continuing with their baking and singing to one another. Still, Robert could not remove the image of Amon's mutilated corpse from his mind, nor the paranoid ramblings of Dennis. If a denizen feared whatever murdered Amon, then it surely must be something not to be reckoned with.

As soon as his head hit the pillow, Robert prayed for sunrise to come. There was something that he could not yet comprehend at foot, a feeling that a horrendous act would take place at any moment. He attempted to dismiss Dennis's threats, believing that it could possibly be just his imagination drowning out his more-logical thoughts. But still, the sun had set that eve under a crimson layer of rainclouds, which was uncommon and boded nothing but a terrible omen.

The sound of Eliza crawling under her duvet was greatly welcomed by Robert not long after, for her comfort also brought peace to him within this tumultuous period. He performed the Lord's prayer with her before clenching his eyelids shut, hoping that Dennis would not visit them during the early hours as insinuated.

'Don't be scared,' Vera whispered to him, hugging into a ragdoll their mother had made some days ago to cheer her up. 'Eliza is here. Eliza will protect us.'

Rolling his eyes, Robert turned to her and asked, 'Why is Eliza protecting us? What do you mean?'

'He is coming—tonight. Eliza is a good girl. She will look after us.'

'Why, and who is *he*?'

Vera turned over, seemingly falling into an instant deep sleep. Robert's sight never once left the window afterwards, gauging that if Dennis where to appear it would most certainly be through that small, vulnerable space. Swamped with adrenaline, Robert eventually fell asleep like his sister, though his dreams where far more disturbing and realistic than hers.

Robert dreamt of standing within the nearby marshlands, surrounded by cold fog and the cries of stricken souls. He closed his eyes briefly and on opening them found Amon, who appeared as his former self—dressed in military attire and muscular, grinning with a sadistic smile.

'You served me well, my little friend. I am so sorry,' Amon said in a strained voice, rubbing at his face. 'I thought we would be safe by serving the denizen. I was wrong.'

Biting at his lower lip, Robert asked, 'What happened? Did Dennis kill you?'

'Nein — NO! Dennis is cunning and will threaten violence, but he is not capable of what befell me. The shadow, Robert, the shadow that attacked me was far more terrifying than any act the denizen could have committed.'

'Who is he?' Robert's frustration and fear intensified. 'Tell me who *he* is, Amon! Please, I need to know!'

'I do not have the heart to burden you with the dreadful truth,' Amon grimaced, his body shaking with fright. 'Even Dennis fears that walking plague; it is an ancient malignance that bears no restraint or mercy. You must flee with your mother and sister tonight before he visits you as well, and that he will.'

'What about my dad?' Robert felt the need to ask this, but in truth he wasn't too concerned. 'Will he come to any harm?'

Amon's eyes rolled back to reveal their whites, his smirk cruel and knowing. 'He is forsaken and cannot be salvaged. You must run, Robert, far away from here. You and your loved ones will forever be hunted down, should you not leave these cursed lands.'

Robert woke up, his brow dripping with sweat and hairs standing on end. He turned to face Vera, who was also awake now and staring back at him with her breaths racing and eyes widened.

'Robert!' Vera scurried across and jumped into his bed without a moment to lose. 'He's coming! Eliza is saying that he isn't far away. What should we do?'

'Who-is-he?!' asked Robert pleadingly. 'What else has Eliza told you?' Vera's eyes slowly moved to the bottom of Robert's bed — to where Dennis now knelt, crouched and drooling. 'Is that him?'

'No!' Vera gasped, pulling the bedsheets over her face. 'It's scarier than that. I don't know what "he" is!'

Dennis held out a claw, aiming it to Robert, and with a mouthful of blood-stained foam it screamed, 'Thy innocent blood must purify my diminished body! Give me strength, O mortal children. Grant me thy flesh and souls!'

Robert kicked at Dennis, sending the goblin through the air, but it soon recovered. 'Leave us alone! Go away!'

'He is near,' Dennis whimpered, his voice reverberating with the sounds of phantom children crying. 'Grant me thy bodies, so that I can confront the greater darkness. There is no other way!'

'Never!' Robert kicked at Dennis again, but he soon retracted his foot as a larger shadow formed behind the small goblin. 'What... is that?!'

Dennis clenched at its skull, convulsing with anxiety and anger. 'No! I have not wrought any offence against thee, Baal, O mighty lieutenant! Pray, have mercy on me. I am loyal. I am faithful to our brethren!'

A deep whine, like a pig being throttled, emerged from the larger shadow as it leant over Dennis's cowering body. Within seconds a pair of thin, sharpened claws wrapped around the denizen's torso, holding it up into the air with ease.

'I warned thee not to trespass,' spoke the shadow's voice amid a demonic growl. 'Thou hath defied my teachings, and so thy body shalt be torn asunder! These lands belong to me!'

'Have mercy, O Lord of Destruction!' Dennis pleaded, squealing and writhing against its oppressor. 'I have not betrayed thee nor our master! I am thy humble brother...'

'Silence, Belphegor! This is my realm, my kingdom to plague!' the beastly manifestation wailed. 'To our master thee shalt now be returned, broken and cleansed...'

Among the denizen's screams, whatever power lurched over it now tore Dennis's body apart as if it were nothing but the thinnest of silk, scattering shreds of muscle tissue and organs throughout the children's bedroom thereafter. All Robert and Vera could do was watch on in horror, helplessly contained by the demonic being now stood within the darkness before them. Its figure moulded to reveal a beast that almost touched the room's roof — at least ten-feet high, with two horns swirling from its ram-like skull; its breaths were deep and rippling; its black eyes were piercing, despite the lack of light to reveal them.

'Eliza,' Vera whispered, clasping her hands together as if in prayer. 'Please, save us.'

'Eliza?!' the shadow roared. 'No such light shalt protect thee, children.'

'This is all my fault,' said Robert, looking to Vera in dismay. 'This is my fault. I've caused this.'

'Eliza will save us,' Vera assured him. 'Don't be scared of him. Don't be scared of the darkness.'

The shadow raised a long arm into the air, preparing to strike it down upon the vulnerable children, but it was suddenly hindered by a burst of brilliant-white light.

'Eliza?' the shadow grieved. 'Impossible! Thine eternal existence hath been removed from this physical plain…'

Robert concluded that Dennis had tread into another demon's patch, and he used this to his benefit.

'Dennis is gone, and my family have done nothing to anger you,' he said calmly, using all the bravery he could muster. 'We have done nothing to threaten or offend you.'

'Perhaps?' the demon noted in a booming voice. 'But thou hath aided my rival, Belphegor, so thou shalt pay for thy heinous crimes.'

'I did what I was told to do, to protect my mother and sister,' Robert insisted, trying his upmost to come across as being respectful. 'Please, whatever you are, leave me and my family alone. Dennis is gone — '

'Belphegor is that filth's name! His foul spirit hath been cast into the black flames by my gracious hands! I am scorn! I am malice!'

'Whatever Dennis was,' Robert continued, 'it's gone.'

'But thou hath witnessed my deeds and power, and thou hath learnt my true name — Baal. Such transgressions cannot go unpunished!'

'Eliza,' Vera iterated, 'you said he couldn't hurt us. Where are you?'

'The child of my beloved,' the demon muttered, seemingly deep in thought. 'So be it, but I will satiate my need for blood. I will not be defied!'

Another blinding flash filled the bedroom, and on its dispersal the terrifying shadow vanished. Robert and Eliza then felt a wave of darkness take over them again, until they awoke the next morning to the sound and movements of their mother frantically trying to stir them.

'Children, we must go!' Rose implored, shaking both her son and daughter. 'We must leave at once!'

Robert wiped at his eyes, checking for any sign of Dennis's torn remains, though only a black stain remained upon his bedsheets.

'Where's Dad?' he asked, dreading the possible response. 'Is he… okay?'

Rose's agonised expression spoke more than any words could to Robert. She looked to the stain upon her son's bed, cautiously shuffled away from it, and then pulled both him and Vera to their feet.

'There's no time to explain, my darlings. We must leave, and we must go right now.'

Robert held onto one of Vera's hands as they followed their mother into the hallway. Everything seemed normal but for a streak of blood that swept out from under Rose and Walter's bedroom. Robert focused on the scarlet colour and asked, 'Why is there blood there, Mum? Where's Dad?'

'He's dead, Son.' Rose composed herself, despite fighting back an overwhelming desire to scream. 'I found him that way, and it wasn't natural. We must go.'

'Did you see or hear anything strange last night?'

'I dreamt something strange; a girl dressed in white, who guided me through the marshlands.' Rose paused, glancing to her husband's spilled blood. 'She said that your father couldn't come with us. I thought it was just a dream. That girl...'

'Eliza,' Vera interjected, forming a content smile. 'It was Eliza. She was looking after you.'

'There's nothing left for us here now,' Rose added. She then ran up to a draw in the kitchen and removed a small gem from within it. 'Your father found this some years ago, deep within the woods. It's all we have. We should get a good price for this ruby, and then we can start a new life together — a better one.'

'Where will we go?' asked Robert. 'We can't just leave Dad here. We need to bury him.'

In a muffled and cautious whisper, Rose replied, 'It is still here — I know it is. We need to move now. Once we step foot out the door, run and don't stop until I tell you to.'

'But—'

'Do as I say, Robert. There's nothing left for us here.'

There was no sign of forced entry as Robert opened the front door. Wherever he looked outside there were streams of spilled blood and devastation; the animals had all been slaughtered, including his beloved pigs; the grass had turned crimson and black in colour, as if a terrible battle had been fought upon it. Robert fully understood his mother's words now: there was nothing left, nothing left at all.

'Run, my darlings, and don't turn back!' Rose commanded, jabbing at Robert's side with a finger. 'Go!'

The silence outside was excruciating, and a sense that some foreboding presence was watching over them followed the remaining Adley family members as they sprinted across the blood-soaked fields. Robert imagined his father, rotting away in several pieces, appearing as a sordid reflection of Amon's decaying corpse. He despised his father, but such a terrible fate was not warranted. Regardless, he and Vera ran ahead in a straight line towards the sun.

As exhaustion swept over the small children, Robert chose to look back at his family home one last time, though it was a frightful mistake. In the distance, within one of the farm's windows, he saw a tall shadow lurking around inside that kept staring back out at him. The shadow bore two horns and a red aura, and it was glaring at the poor boy until he could no longer tolerate its abhorrent sight. What innocence Robert had known had all but gone now, replaced by a grim reality that stranger and more ancient powers truly existed within our world.

So came the notion that Eliza also existed; that it was she who managed to spare Robert, his sister and mother from a terrible demise.

Robert rubbed at Vera's hands tenderly and then asked, 'Who is Eliza, and why did she help us?'

Vera smiled, looking aside to her mother. 'She is an angel that misses her mummy. She will always be around to annoy him, to annoy... Baal.'

Beyond the Crimson Trees

Victory in Europe had been declared ten years prior, and from its legacy rose a new town upon the medieval settlement site of Acle, which was duly named Newton Escomb.

People from every corner of Britain were invited to work and live there, thriving under the radical vision of Lord Bowburn and his peers to make it an ideal reflection of a perfect society, though none were informed of Acle's supernatural and bloody past. In fact, there were few alive at this time who remembered the tales of old, of the demons and witches that still dwelled within those cursed lands.

Lord Bowburn, through the backing of parliament, dreamt of creating a utopia where citizens could flourish and help rebuild the war-damaged nation. There were three new towns commissioned overall, each experimental in nature, and Newton Escomb was the largest and most ambitious out of them. There was one issue that continued to rear its head during the planning stages, however: Acle was nothing but marshlands—difficult to build on and liable to flooding—surrounded by dense woodlands and particularly remote to reach. Nevertheless, the project was authorised by government officials and the town reached its initial completion during the summer of 1952. The Queen herself even visited, somewhat increasing the attraction to live there.

Alan and Reginald Marsden moved to Newton Escomb from London in 1955, hoping to further their careers as mechanics within one of the many factories situated there, and as to find a more peaceful location to raise their families. The two brothers were extremely close, both marrying their partners — June and Avril, respectively — on their safe return from serving in North Africa and Italy as conscripts; and they had one child each — daughters — named Rosemary and Lorna. Alan and Reginald lived in the same street, worked for the same employer, visited the same church every Sunday, and neither one had ever encountered anything paranormal before, though that would soon change.

Over the course of two weeks, which led up to Halloween in 1956, some strange and harrowing occurrences compelled the citizens of Newton Escomb into a state of shock and panic. Several cats and dogs — each one cruelly skinned and mutilated — had been found dead at various sites across town; and there had been increasing reports of children being kidnapped or simply vanishing without trace. The police had no leads to go off, and so an emergency town meeting was arranged. The meeting itself was held in the town's main church, where its small structure could barely contain the influx of concerned parents and other townsfolk. Alan and Reginald sat further to the back, both holding onto photographs of their children, their daughters who had disappeared three days prior.

Amid the sound of nervous chuntering from the pews, Councillor Tony Collier — the council's chairman — rose to greet his guests and fellow associates. He and his colleagues were sat in a straight line, facing the congregation, like victims placed before a firing squad.

'Good evening,' he announced, slowly waving a hand up and down to silence the restless onlookers. 'As I am sure you are all aware, this meeting has been called due to rumours spreading throughout the town of — '

'They're not rumours!' an angry mother interjected. 'My youngest girl went missing last week and there's still no sign of her,' she explained tearfully. 'What are the police doing about it? I've had no contact from them—it's a disgrace!'

With a calm nod of his head, Councillor Collier acknowledged the mother's despair with as much sincerity as he could portray. 'You have our deepest sympathy, madam, but can we please try to hold this meeting in a civil and courteous manner.' The mother folded her arms and turned her head away, finding no comfort from the councillor's words. 'The police are doing all they can in their search for the missing children, which goes without saying. They are working day and night to find any lead they can.'

'What about all the dead animals?' asked a gentleman on the front row. 'Whoever's skinned them must be a lunatic—we've got a nutcase on our hands here!'

'Please, questions will be taken and answered at the end of discussions,' said Councillor Collier, realising that he was perhaps out of his depth in holding this tense meeting. 'First of all, I would like to introduce my fellow councillors. I have to the left of me Councillors: Parlour, Lockewood and Stevens; and to the right of me, Councillors: Felling, Brooke and Mason,' he said, politely pointing out each one.

'Where's the Mayor?' asked another citizen. 'It's a disgrace that he hasn't bothered showing up. Is he not concerned? He should be, for what he's getting paid.'

'It is with a heavy heart that I inform you all, and I don't believe he will mind me saying this, but… the Mayor's granddaughter has also gone missing. She disappeared a few hours ago. He is in the process of consoling his family at this difficult time. That is why he isn't here.'

At this moment Councillor Mason, who was sat where the Mayor should have been, stood up. He was a tall, wiry man, easily towering over the stout and meeker-voiced Councillor Collier.

'It was on my advice that the Mayor did not hold this meeting,' he stated. 'Given how it was only a few hours ago he discovered that his granddaughter went missing, I doubt there is any person present here that could disagree with such a compassionate decision.'

'What would you know?' shouted a man sat a few seats away from Alan and Reginald. 'You live alone in that posh farmhouse of yours—you've got no family or pets to be worried about!'

'I care about the people whom I serve,' said Councillor Mason, flaring his eyes at the heckler. 'I also care for the Mayor, who is understandably distraught at this time. Now, can we move on with proceedings without any further, unruly disruptions? We'll be here all night, otherwise.'

'Yes,' agreed Councillor Collier, loosening the tie from around his neck. 'We would normally start these meetings by outlining the agenda; however, there is only one item on it today: the concerns already raised a few moments ago. There have been, at the very least, twelve reports of missing children over a period of twenty-one days, and the same number of deceased animals. Firstly, the Council and I would like to emphasise that all measures are being taken by the local police to trace these missing children and to catch the heinous culprit behind the gruesome deaths of those poor creatures. It should also be noted that these disappearances and killings are not being linked together as of yet, granted there is no justifiable evidence to suggest such a connection.'

Alan turned to Reginald and whispered, 'It's a pretty big coincidence, don't you think?'

'We're not coppers or councillors, so God knows. All I want are some answers as to how the police hope to find Rosemary and Lorna.'

'I don't think that's going to happen, Reggie, going off what the Chairman's said so far. They're as much use as a chocolate fireguard are these lot.'

'It's not good enough. I can't go back to Avril and tell her that the police are clueless, and that there doesn't seem to be any hope of finding Lorna. It'll break her heart. She's already on tranquilizers.'

'Let's listen to what else they have to say. You never know, there might be some good to come out of this meeting tonight…'

Councillor Collier motioned to speak again. 'What we have established is that the children all seem to disappear around the same time — around sunset. The police are performing more patrols, on foot and by car, to keep a close watch on any children who may be unaccompanied. If matters persist as they currently are, then we may need to consider putting a curfew into place,' he said, wiping a layer of sweat away from his brow. 'Of course, that would not be ideal and be taken as a last resort. Nevertheless, we must consider all avenues.'

An elderly gentleman, boasting a ducktail beard and clearly suffering from cataracts, suddenly sprung before the councillors, waving a walking stick at them.

'Have you considered that this could be something supernatural — demonic?' the man yelled, to several jeers in response. 'What say you, Councillor Mason? You know all about occultist beliefs and whatnot. Your father was a Grand Master, and don't you try to deny it!'

'There's always one, isn't there?' Alan scoffed to Reginald. 'There's always one loony.'

With a dismissive shrug, Councillor Mason stated, 'I have no idea what you are insinuating, my good fellow, and I would greatly appreciate it — as I can imagine most others here would — for you to take your seat, please. This is a serious discussion, sir. Such ridiculous propositions will not be addressed, and neither will I discuss my personal life and ancestry.'

'Too ashamed to?' laughed the elderly man, rolling his eyes to the crowd. 'I've lived here longer than anyone else has, and I know what I'm saying is the truth. This is the devil's work!'

'Please take your seat,' Councillor Mason insisted. 'There's an asylum down the road that would love to listen to your ramblings. Take my advice, sir, and do be quiet.'

The congregation came to an awkward silence, with some now considering that a paranormal explanation may be viable, seeing as there were no other answers yet offered.

'The Curse of Appleton Manor. It was real, and so were its demons!' the elderly gentleman continued, his face reddening with anger. 'This town is cursed! We're all cursed!!'

'Nonsense. You are no longer welcome at this meeting. Please, take your leave,' Councillor Mason demanded, calmly returning to his seat. 'That story is utter tosh; it's nothing but a silly tale without any true evidence to substantiate it.' The sea of perplexed expressions greeting him gave Councillor Mason no choice but to divulge. 'Appleton Manor lay west of the marshlands and was demolished decades ago because of neglect and safety concerns. The Appleton family, from what I've been told, moved to India in the late 1880s. There is no curse, and we do not have time to allow for such ridiculous stories and fearmongering to be spread.'

'Here, here!' agreed Councillor Felling, clapping his hands. 'The whole purpose of this get-together was to assure you all that measures have been and are being taken to reduce the risk of any further kidnappings, and I hold good faith in our hardworking police officers to find the culprit behind these terrible crimes.'

'Thank you,' said Councillor Mason, feigning a smile.

'Are there any further questions?' asked Councillor Collier, now suffering from an acute migraine.

Alan stood up, shaking, keeping his eyes to the ground. 'My daughter, Rosemary, and my niece, Lorna, went missing last week whilst out playing by the stream that flows through our town. I would very much like to offer my service to the police in assisting them with their search. Would it be possible for ordinary citizens like myself and my brother to offer such help?'

Councillor Mason stood up again, gesturing for his colleagues to remain seated. 'That is a noble offer, sir, but we must allow for the police to carry out their duties unhindered. The best thing you can do is to be there for your loved ones during this difficult time. Like Councillor Felling, I suggest you have faith in the police and let them do their work.'

Alan sat back down, more emotionally drained now than before he spoke. 'I just can't do that, Reggie. It'll drive me mad.'

'And neither can I,' Reginald concurred. 'We can't just sit here doing nothing. We'll do our own search, whether the police allow it or not.'

'I'm up for that.'

'Look. We know that the girls were playing by the stream. There's a start.'

'It's better than just living through this hell. I've got a torch in my car that we can use—'

'Then we'll do it. This meeting's a waste of time, anyway. We didn't exactly get any answers, did we?'

Alan stood first, gesturing for his brother to follow, then they left the meeting just as others began to declare their disappointment with how the council were dealing with this unprecedented situation.

Back in Alan's car, he handed over his torch to Reginald and then rested his head against the steering wheel, struggling to keep himself together.

'Where should we start?' he asked wearily.

'We'll set off from the stone bridge near Councillor Mason's farmhouse and take it from there,' suggested Reginald. 'It's a remote area of town. There's every possibility that we'll come across a clue of some sort —'

'Or nothing at all. This is a stupid idea. It'll be like looking for a needle in a haystack.'

'Then what do you propose we do? Wait for the police to find some bodies, or go out and be decent fathers by actively looking for our missing children?'

'Jesus wept, when you say it like that...'

'Then don't be a coward. Let's find our little girls.'

Alan started the car and drove five minutes to a narrow country road that led up to Councillor Mason's farmhouse. There, he and Reginald took a moment to regain their composure, both lighting a cigarette to help ease their nerves.

'No wonder this part of town's remote. It isn't half spooky, isn't it?' Alan commented, taking in a huge draw from his cigarette. 'It could do with a few lampposts.'

'It's the perfect place to live for that dodgy councillor. I don't know about you, but that Councillor Mason gives me the creeps more than these empty fields do.'

An amber light flickered at the farmhouse's doorway, followed by a small shadow. Alan and Reginald quickly hid behind the car, hoping that the darkness of night would prevent them from being discovered.

'Doesn't Councillor Mason live alone?' asked Alan.

'He has quite a few secrets up his sleeve, it seems. Come on, before we're spotted.'

Crouching as they walked, the brothers carefully made their way to where the stream flowed from beneath the stone bridge — their starting point. Alan's torch gave off little light, barely a few feet ahead of them through the thickening fog.

'Where's this bloody fog come from?' Reginald whined.

'Don't worry about the fog, just keep your eyes peeled for any footprints,' said Alan. 'And stop talking. I've got a feeling that we're not alone out here. I don't know what it is, but—'

Reginald stood upon a thin branch, snapping it. The sharp sound made both brothers sprint on a few yards ahead before they gathered their senses again.

'Bloody hell, Reggie! That fright was all we needed,' spat Alan, punching at his brother's nearest arm. 'Stay quiet and keep your head down. We must stay focused and calm… for Rosemary and Lorna's sake.'

The stream fed along the banks of Acle's ancient marshlands, eventually passing through one of its woods.

'I know where we are,' whispered Reginald, cautious of his murky surroundings. 'We're on the outskirts of Bluebell Wood.'

'What makes you think that?'

'The bluebell flowers, Alan.' With a swipe of the torch he revealed a sea of bluebell flowers, most of which were wilting or flattened by local wildlife. 'It doesn't take an inspector to work that one out.'

'That means we're close to home. This is where the girls were playing when Avril last saw them. We'll find them, Reggie. We'll find our girls.'

The fog grew colder as the brothers walked on through it, to the extent where they had to shield their mouths as to reduce the freezing air filling their lungs. A terrible realisation then entered their thoughts that the young girls could not have possibly survived in such harsh conditions alone. But they simply had to hold onto that flicker of hope, that their children were still alive and unharmed.

A whole mile passed before Alan and Reginald came to an opening in the woods. The bank rose steeply into a dark mist, and at its foot was one, small, distinctively red shoe. The shoe, without question, belonged to Rosemary.

'Can it be?' Alan gasped, collecting the shoe and nurturing it tenderly thereafter. 'My Rosemary. She's close!'

Reginald glanced up the hill, which only seemed to get steeper the more he looked at it. 'What's up that way?'

'I don't know, but we're going to find out.'

'Wait—'

'For PC Plod to arrive?' Alan chuntered, flouncing his arms. 'We'll do our own investigation first, and then—if we don't find the girls—we'll phone for help. How does that sound?'

'It's just... we don't know what's up there. I'm still getting over that scare from earlier.'

'Our little girls—that's what is up there. You're not still afraid of the dark, are you?'

'No, haven't been since I was ten.' Reginald knelt to secure his shoelaces, in secret praying for God's protection over him and his brother. 'There's an unnatural feeling about this place. I don't like it. Even the trees are creeping me out now. Why are their trunks red? It's not natural.'

'Never mind that. We'll be back home and reunited with our families in no time. Come on, Reggie. Don't go soft on me.'

'I'm not going soft. If anything, I'm being cautious. There could be a knife-wielding maniac hiding about in these woods, for all we know.'

'If there is then they should be scared of us, not the other way around. Come on.'

The mud-laden embankment was slippery from recent rainfall, making the trek up it almost impassable for Alan and Reginald. But they pulled through, and they were completely unprepared for what would meet them.

Aiming the torch ahead unsteadily, Reginald remarked, 'What are those?'

'They look like boulders to me,' said Alan, approaching the large monoliths. 'They're all huddled together. Strange...'

'They seem a bit out of place, don't they?'

'Yes, but also as if they're meant to be here. Keep your wits about you. Keep quiet.'

Reginald swept the torch's light over the stones, which were sandstone and heavily worn down by weather; and at their centre was one that reached at least fourteen feet into the air. Each stone bore a carving, symbols from a different and more brutal era.

'Are you seeing these, Alan? What are they, do you reckon?'

Brushing at one of the marks gently, Alan noted,' They seem pretty new. Goodness knows how old these stones are, but these scratch marks — '

'Don't touch them!' Reginald called out, his superstitious nature now coming to the forefront. 'Didn't that old fella mention something about there being a curse? These rocks could be cursed.'

Alan shook his head and tutted. Unlike his brother, he cared little for anything that could be considered paranormal. 'Did that chap look at all remotely sane to you?'

'He's lived here longer than anyone else, according to him. I'd take what he has to say about these marshlands and woods — '

'With a pinch of salt, Reggie. That poor fellow, as harmless as he seems, should not be taken seriously.'

'I don't know. If there's ever an appropriate place for devil worship, it's here.'

A sudden ruffling noise through the trees nearby sent a shiver down Alan and Reginald's spines. Immediately, Reginald shone his torch into the direction of the disturbance, screaming out the names of his daughter and niece.

'LORNA! ROSEMARY!'

Alan swiftly placed a finger over his brother's mouth, trembling as he did so. 'Shut up, you idiot. If there is someone out here that might want to harm us, then shouting on like that is the last thing we need. You'll give us away!'

'I just want to find her,' wallowed Reginald. 'Every minute that passes by without my Lorna is utter torture.'

'I feel the same way about Rosemary, but we've got to be level-headed about this. No one else knows we're here, and I want to keep it that way.'

Another unexpected sound moving through the trees forced the brothers to back up against the stones. Whatever was making the noise now felt like it was stalking them, and the fog was making any chance of seeing the culprit practically impossible.

'We've found Rosemary's shoe, right? That's better than nothing. I think we should get the police involved now.'

'That's not a bad idea, and neither is coming back during daylight. I can barely see a foot in from in me, so there's not much chance of us finding the girls in this darkness.'

Slowly and meticulously, the brothers retraced their steps down the slippery embankment, both keeping watch for any sign of the noise-making culprit. Nothing appeared, though the sensation of being watched never left them. Halfway on their return, the brothers then came across a ghastly sight: a fox, skinned and still wriggling against the noose strapped around its throat, which whined at them pitifully as they neared the bridge. It had been hung from a tree that stood at head-height, and the evil act seemed to have been performed recently.

'Jesus!' howled Reginald, just about holding back the urge to vomit. 'The poor thing. It's still alive.'

Alan approached the unfortunate creature, noting how its eyes seemed mournful and filled with pain; how they stared at him, begging for mercy. 'What monster could have done this?' Without hesitation, Alan then pulled on the fox's legs to end its suffering sooner. After wiping the blood from his hands, he then ran on ahead, closely followed by Reginald.

The brothers tracked the stream west to Councillor Mason's farmhouse, which was as black as the sky above now. Alan's car was where they had left it, unharmed apart from some fresh fingerprints upon the driver's side window.

'It was probably the councillor seeing if someone was in the car,' said Alan, in trying to establish a reasonable explanation behind why there were some fingerprints other than his own upon the vehicle; they were much larger than his. 'We best get home. June and Avril will be worried sick.'

'How long have we been out searching? Reginald asked with a gulp. 'It feels like ages.'

'Two hours, I think.'

'That's me in the doghouse. Still, at least you have Rosemary's shoe to take back. You're a step closer to finding her.'

'And you with Lorna,' added Alan, patting his brother affectionately upon the shoulders. 'I'll phone the police as soon as I get home. We'll find them.'

'I'm coming with you. It might be best if I help explain where we've been for the last two hours.'

'Fair point. I could definitely do with some backup.'

Quite understandably, Alan's wife was less than pleased with his late arrival, and on seeing Reginald her anger intensified.

'Where the bloody hell have you two been all this time — the pub? I've had Avril on the phone, God knows how many times, asking where you two are.'

'It's a long story, but we went out searching for the girls again,' Alan explained in a sheepish tone. 'Not much good came from the meeting, so Reggie and I decided to — '

'You never went walking along that stream in the dead of night?'

'Of course. That's where the girls were last seen.'

'You could have been mugged or killed!' cried June, tearing at her face. 'You stupid oath! I can't lose you, too.'

'Reggie and I can handle ourselves. Besides, it was worth the effort.' Alan nodded to Reginald, who then handed Rosemary's shoe over to him. 'We found this.'

Struggling to take in a breath, June fell to her knees and clenched onto the small shoe. 'That's Rosemary's!'

'Exactly,' said Alan, forcing himself to smile. 'She's still alive and out there, somewhere. I'm going to phone the police now, so that they can act on this lead. She'll be home safe with us again.'

June noticed a thin line of blood on Alan's right hand, filling her with panic. 'What happened?'

Reginald calmly interjected, 'It's nothing. You go to bed and get some sleep.' With a subtle snarl he added, 'It's been a long night for us all, June. We're all drained. We're all tired.'

'Reggie's right, darling. Go to bed and get some rest,' said Alan imploringly. 'I'll phone the police now and then I'll come straight up to bed. I shouldn't be too long.'

Somewhat unconvinced and wary of the brothers' evasive response to her questioning the bloodstain, June took her leave but waited at the top of the staircase, as to listen in on Alan's phone call.

'Goodnight, Reggie. Take care.'

'You as well, Alan. Let me know what the coppers have to say.'

'I will.'

Convinced that he was now alone, Alan picked up the telephone and called the local police station. An operator answered within seconds, though Alan was still unprepared for what they were about to discuss.

'What is the emergency?' asked the operator in a precise and staccato-like manner.

'My name is Alan Marsden. I reported a missing child – my daughter, Rosemary – about a week ago. Well, my brother and I went out searching for her and my niece, who is also missing, again tonight. We followed the stream down from Councillor Mason's farmhouse to an area near Bluebell Wood, where we came across a shoe that belonged to my daughter… and a fox that had been skinned.'

'Not another one,' whispered the operator, but their words were unmistakeable. 'So, you and your brother have found a shoe that belonged to the missing person —'

'Yes, my daughter's. It definitely belongs to my daughter.'

'And the fox… are you sure that it had been mutilated intentionally, or had it perhaps been attacked by another predator?'

'It was skinned alive, hung from a tree and still breathing when we found it,' Alan seethed, struggling to hold back his frustration. 'Can you send some officers out to the area tonight?'

'I'll need more information first, Mr. Marsden. Those woods go on for a good mile or two,' said the operator in a slightly condescending way. 'Is there anything more specific you can tell me?'

'There's an opening in the woods that leads up a steep embankment to some old boulders, some strange-looking stones.'

The line went silent for a moment, and then the operator noted with unease in their voice, 'I know where you mean. Are you certain?'

'Yes!' Alan insisted. 'You know where I mean?'

'I'll dispatch two officers to investigate the area first thing in the morning, when there's better light. Thank you for your help on this matter.'

'Why not now? Every second my daughter and niece are out there, the more likely we won't see them alive again.'

'I fully understand your concern, but those woods aren't safe for anyone at this time of night. Two officers will investigate tomorrow morning, and can you please ensure that you and your brother do not venture into those woods again after sunset. It wouldn't be wise.'

'Are you saying that I'll end up like that poor fox?'

'Those woods are not a safe place for anyone, Mr. Marsden. Thank you again for your call and do take care. Our officers are doing everything they can to solve the mystery surrounding the children who have gone missing over the last few weeks.'

'They're doing sweet sod all,' he groaned, hanging up the phone. 'What a waste of time that was.'

June held back her tears as she crept down the stairs.

'What did they police have to say?' she asked.

'Not much. They'll send some officers out in the morning to have a look around.'

'We'll never see Rosemary again, will we?'

'Don't say that.' Alan sat himself upon a rocking chair within the living room, where he would tell Rosemary stories before sending her off to bed. Her teddy bear was still where she had left it before the disappearance. Alan nestled the bear under his chin, savouring the scent of his daughter that remained on its fabric — lavender, her favourite flower. 'Rosemary is not dead, June. I'll search for her again in the morning with Reggie. I don't know about you, but I'm starting to lose all faith in the police.'

'They're the experts. They know what to look for.'

'They should be out there now, looking for our little girl…'

'She'll be fine. Rosemary is brave,' sniffled June. 'I'm going back to sleep, and I think you should try and get some shuteye as well.'

'I'm not tired. I'll come up a short while, darling.'

June retired to bed while Alan tucked into a bottle of dark rum he kept for special occasions. Sunrise came and Alan begrudgingly welcomed it without having enjoyed any sleep. His thoughts were racing, fixated on solving the mystery and to somehow put an end to the gruesome acts taking place within his new hometown.

Reginald was the same: filled with bitter turmoil yet hopeful that some good could still come out of this dreadful situation. He had endured a restless night of tossing and turning in bed, that is, until he could take no more. He spent the remaining twilight hours reading through the bible for comfort, presuming that his brother gained no joy from contacting the police.

At 7am sharp, upon first light, Alan knocked on Reginald's front door. The brothers stared at one another in silence, shared a cigarette, and then left to journey back into the Bluebell Wood again. Sunlight was on their side now, along with the reassuring presence of police support, or so they assumed.

As they parked up near Councillor Mason's farmhouse a long line of police tape met with them, sealing off the pathway down to the stream.

'They can't have sealed off the whole woodland area?' said Reginald in dismay.

'Just the path we took last night,' said Alan, side-glancing to the farmhouse. 'There's no one about. We'll slip under this tape and make our way through the woods… see what's happening.'

'Are you mad? What if the police spot us?'

'The woods are dense and dark, even under the sun. We should be alright, Reggie. I need answers. Our wives need answers.'

'Avril wasn't too happy about me showing up late, I must admit.'

'We're not coming back empty-handed today. Trust me.'

Alan walked on ahead, passing by the tape without a further thought and without any reluctance. The brothers came to the stream and then immediately set off into the depths of Bluebell Wood. Everywhere they stepped an unnerving sense of being watched grew, along with a rising fog that got thicker as they moved closer to where the strange boulders stood.

The distinctive sound of police dogs barking brought Alan and Reginald's trek to an abrupt halt.

'That means we're not far off,' said Reginald, scouring the trees for any sign of the canines. 'I've got a bad feeling about this, you know.'

'Stay down!' Alan commanded, ushering for them both to lower their heads out of view. 'Keep your eyes peeled for any other items that the girls might have dropped. They may be young, but they're not stupid. The tale of *Hansel and Gretel* is one of Rosemary's favourites. She'd know to leave a trail of breadcrumbs behind, so to speak.'

'She's only six, Alan. Lorna's not even five. They wouldn't think of doing something like that, not if they were terrified.'

'I'm not giving up on that hope!' Alan stood to his feet and carried on towards the barking sounds. 'We have every right to help the police with their search. It's our children who are missing — our little girls!'

Without warning a hunched figure lunged at Alan, knocking them both to the ground. The two scuffled among the fallen leaves and branches, tearing at one another's clothes until exhaustion took over.

'Get off me!' cried Alan, mindful of the police presence nearby.

'What are you doing in these forsaken woods?' the assailant whined, seemingly falling into retreat. They then rose their hands up in surrender, revealing their elderly features to the brothers. 'These trees are cursed! This town is cursed!'

'It's that chap from the town meeting,' said Reginald, looking to Alan in perplexment. 'It's the old fella that was ranting on about demons.'

'Yes,' said Alan, brushing off some leaves from his coat. 'What are you playing at, you old fool?'

Tapping at his weatherworn forehead, the man replied, 'Oh, I'm no fool. No, sonny-boy. I understand these woods well and have the wits about me to know how important it is to respect them.' The man's smile fell, along with the light in his eyes. 'You should not be here.'

'And neither should you,' said Reginald, looking up and down the stranger. 'Why are you skulking around?'

'Mushrooms. There's plenty for the taking, but you need to be careful.'

'He's bloody senile,' Alan laughed to Reginald. 'And he almost gave our position away. It'll be a miracle if the police didn't hear all that noise.'

'Please pardon my reaction, chaps. I thought you might be poachers,' said the elderly man. 'Dangerous folk, they are, are poachers.'

'You're dangerous, lunging at us like a wild animal.'

'I recognise you now,' said the man, wiping a gnarly fingernail over his bottom lip. 'You're the blokes who said their daughters had gone missing, aren't you? Oh, how sad that is.'

'That's why we're here,' Reginald interjected. 'We're searching for them.'

'Any luck so far?'

'We found a shoe,' said Alan, removing the smirk from his face. 'It belongs to my daughter.'

'A shoe, you say. What colour?'

'Red. What business is it to you?'

'She likes red, does the Lady of the Woods — the Red Ribbon Witch. I've seen her, you know.'

Reginald pulled Alan aside and whispered to him, 'The poor sod is delusional. Leave him be and let's carry on with the search.'

'Wait —' Alan looked directly into the man's eyes, which were unusually black, bearing no other colour within them, strewn with concern. 'Who is this "Lady of the Woods", this "Red Ribbon Witch"?'

'We've crossed paths a few times over the years,' the man explained with a sly expression. 'She doesn't speak much, and she doesn't like men. I think she only tolerates me because of my old age—I'm not a threat, you see. The fire in my loins died out years ago.'

'I've heard enough, Alan. Come on,' said Reginald, rolling his eyes. 'He doesn't know what he's talking about.'

'But I do, gentlemen. Should you come face-to-face with her, you must show reverence and pity. The Lady of the Woods does not take kindly to strange men visiting her place of rest.'

'You're right,' said Alan, scowling at the elderly man. 'He's only wasting our time. He's lost his marbles.'

'Good luck with your search,' said the man, stepping away from them. 'Remember what I said, because it might just save your skins...'

Alan and Reginald paused as they came to the opening, where they carefully inspected what was taking place. There were at least seven police officers and three sniffer dogs. So far it seemed that the brothers' presence had gone unnoticed, but that came to an end when Reginald slipped down the embankment to land before two officers, who were both taking notes and smoking rolled-up cigarettes.

'Oi! What are you two doing here?' asked one of the officers. 'This area is sealed off to the public. You're trespassing on a crime scene.'

'I made the phone call about finding my missing daughter's shoe here last night,' said Alan, noting the officer's handcuffs. 'My brother and I couldn't just sit at home, waiting for you fellas to tell us that nothing had been found.'

'Charming,' said the officer to his colleague. 'It's nice to know the public have so much faith in us still. Mr. Marsden, I presume?'

'Yes. I'm Alan and this is my brother, Reginald.'

'We're not authorised to go into too much detail, but we have found more items of clothing—shoes, to be precise.'

'How many?'

'A fair few. I'd say around eleven pairs.'

'Twelve children went missing in total, didn't they?' Reginald gasped. 'They must be nearby!'

'Let us do our job,' the other officer insisted, stroking at a truncheon that was attached to their waist. 'Please leave this area at once, gentlemen. We will contact you with further details when we've established all the facts.'

'There's an old man wandering around the woods as well, by the way,' Alan added. 'You might want to ask him a few questions, or possibly arrest him before he hurts anyone.'

'An elderly man… a threat to people?' sneered the other officer. 'By any chance, was he wearing a tweed jacket; and does he have a long, scraggly beard that's nicotine-stained?'

'Yes,' said Alan. 'That's the man.'

'That's Bob. He's harmless,' the officer scoffed. 'He's a little eccentric, in all fairness, and you'll often find him skulking around these woods looking for mushrooms and berries. Bob wouldn't hurt a fly, though. We can't be wasting our time on him.'

'He mentioned something about a *Lady of the Woods*, and he wasn't making light about her,' said Reginald.

'An old fairy tale… that's all that is.'

The officers broadened their shoulders, now standing over Alan and Reginald.

'Take your leave, gentlemen, or we'll be forced to arrest you. This is your last warning,' said the officer who spoke first.

Disheartened, Alan nodded in agreement and then made his way back upstream with Reginald. They kept a mindful eye on the police, who continued to carry on with their meticulous search, though they bore no intention of leaving the woods so soon.

'We'll stay low and hide here until nightfall,' said Alan, pulling Reginald behind a large oak tree. 'There's no sign of that mad hermit, thank goodness, and I doubt the police will be coming back up this way. We'll be fine here.'

'What about June and Avril? I'm already in Avril's bad books.'

'They'll understand. I get the inkling that those officers know more than they're letting on.'

'They do, but we're not allowed to know until they've gathered the facts. Our wives need us to be there for them, not for us to be squatting out here in some freezing cold forest.'

'Reggie, will you just — for once in your life — trust in what I'm doing. I can't sit around waiting for the inevitable anymore. If Rosemary's come to harm, then I want to be the person who finds her, to give her one last kiss goodbye.'

'Our girls aren't dead. Don't talk like they are.'

Thirsty and in desperate need of sustenance, the brothers welcomed nightfall, their opportunity to make use of the darkness in their own search. There was no sign of the police or their dogs, and the woods had fallen eerily silent, tranquil even.

'We didn't think this through well, did we? You forgot to bring a torch.'

'It's a full moon,' said Alan, noting the pristine-white satellite above. 'We've got all the light we need. Follow the stream back down to that opening, and then we'll take another look at those stones.'

Even more anxious now, Reginald asked, 'Do you reckon there's any truth behind what that old fella said?'

'About some spooky woman in the woods? No. That's what you get for eating wild mushrooms, Reggie — you go insane. That Bob is a complete loon.'

'He seemed pretty sane to me.'

Under moonlight the stones seemed even taller now, lurking like malignant shadows above the sharp blades of grass below. Something felt different now in comparison to the previous night, which Alan and Reginald couldn't fathom out.

'There's someone else here,' whispered Reginald, paralysed to the spot. 'I can hear footsteps — lots of footsteps.'

'I can't hear a thing.'

'Listen!'

A chorus of breaths and light footsteps began to circle the brothers from within the dark fog now surrounding them. The brothers backed up to the stones, raising their fists defensively, praying to God for mercy. The moonlight did little to reveal who the phantoms were, until a familiar voice travelled through the cold mist.

'Father…'

'Rosemary!' Alan lunged forth to where his daughter's voice sounded. 'Sweetheart, is that you?'

'Father…'

'Lorna!' cried Reginald, joining his brother's side. The children's voices were unmistakable, though they sounded distant and lost. 'Where are you, darling?'

'We're here,' said the girls in unison, in a monotonous and wearisome tone. 'We're all here.'

Alan held out a hand into the dark fog, hoping that his daughter would hold onto it in return. 'Come to me, sweetheart. Daddy's here.'

'She has come,' said Rosemary in a solemn-sounding whimper. 'She is here… our mother. She is behind you.'

Alan and Reginald both turned to face the boulders, to where a figure adorning a long white dress with jet-black hair and eyes stood upon the tallest stone. Both went to speak, to confront the ethereal shadow, but neither could muster the strength to utter a single word. Instead, they fell to their knees in awe.

Reginald then felt a small set of fingers rest upon his neck, those of his child. Lorna leant into her father, whispering into his ear, 'She will care for us, Father. Mother loves us.'

'Who will care for you?' he asked her in dismay. 'Your mother's back at home, worrying about you. What's gotten into you, Lorna? Who on earth is this woman you're talking about?'

'Sabina. She will look after us. She is our mother now.'

Alan heard the name and immediately shouted it out. 'Sabina! What have you done to our children? Where are they?'

'They belong to me,' Sabina replied, calmly and with vigour. 'They art mine to protect. They art my children. Thou shalt not take them from me.'

Reginald thought back to the old man's words of warning, of needing to show reverence before the Lady of the Woods, whom he now deemed this phantom threat to be. 'We do not wish to harm you, miss. We have come to take our daughters home.' Despite bearing no human features, Sabina stared straight into Reginald's eyes and soul, poisoning him with a venomous thought: his and Alan's lives were on the brink of being taken. 'These children will freeze to death out here. Please, let us take them home to their parents. We won't tell the police—'

'I fear no man,' growled Sabina, her voice riddled with malice. 'They belong to me, and forever shalt they stay under my divine protection.'

'I've heard enough!' Alan lunged against the ghostly foe, but he soon found himself facedown upon the marshy earth, as if he had been struck down by some terrible spell to hinder his movements. 'What in the blazes?'

'Come, my children, and be with Mother!' Sabina commanded, raising her skeletal arms into the air, casting her terrifying, moonlit shadow over the two brothers. 'Return to the catacombs with me, where thou shalt know only bliss and peace.'

'No!' Reginald clasped onto Lorna as she attempted to walk past him. 'Lorna, don't you listen to that evil woman. Daddy and Uncle Alan are here to take you and Rosemary home. Your real mothers miss you. They want you to come home!'

'Mother,' said Lorna, Rosemary and the other children together. 'Mother is here.'

'Sabina is not your mother!' cried Alan, wrapping his arms around Rosemary as she appeared before him. 'You are my little girl—not hers! I'm taking you home!'

Sabina then unleashed a bloodcurdling cry, somehow compelling the children to turn upon the unsuspecting brothers. Thankfully, as by some wilful act of fate, the old hermit suddenly ran into the chaos, placing himself between the children and brothers.

'Run while you still have the chance!' he squealed. 'Take your children and get out of here! Go!'

Without a passing glance, Alan and Reginald picked up their daughters and fled into the darkness while the elderly succumbed to a barrage of brutal kicks and punches from the remaining children, who all now bore an unnatural level of strength and hatred.

The old man's cries gradually ceased as the brothers made it back to the stream and then into the depths of Bluebell Wood, where they rested momentarily to gather their senses and recover their straining lungs.

'What the hell just happened?' asked Reginald.

'I don't know. I don't want to know,' Alan replied, nestling his head against Rosemary's. 'Our girls are safe now. We need to tell the police about the other children—fast.'

The brothers' ordeal was not yet over, however. They, along with their daughters, suddenly felt a firm hand cover their mouths, which evidently held a cloth soaked in chloroform that robbed their consciousnesses within a matter of seconds. The stars above faded, and then came a sensation of being dragged along stones and wet earth. The brothers finally came to within another unfamiliar surrounding: Councillor Mason's farmhouse.

Alan's sedation wore off first. He turned left to find his brother, daughter and niece lying beside him on a tiled floor that was covered in dried blood. The distinct sound of wood crackling upon a fire then came into being, along with a strong scent of rotten meat.

'Reggie?' he whispered, barely able to speak. 'Wake up.'

'He and the girls will soon awaken,' said a masculine voice from behind, who then seemed to address another. 'They know too much. They've seen her.'

'I'll handle this,' another male voice replied, which Alan recognised to be that of Councillor Mason. 'There is no need to sharpen your axe like that. I'll solve this little issue.'

'I know who you are!' screamed Alan, tearing his face across the rough floor. He went to lash out but found that his hands and feet had been tightly bound with rope. There was no escape or apparent opportunity to fight back. 'You won't get away with this, Mason!'

'My dear sir,' said Councillor Mason, now standing before Alan. He was wearing a dark brown cloak, hooded and soaked in blood. 'You are mistaken by my intentions. I do not wish to hurt you, nor your brother and children.'

'What do you want?'

'Not many have met Sabina and lived to tell the tale —'

'The Lady of the Woods?'

'The Red Ribbon Witch. If it wasn't for that old fool, then I'd doubt you would be here now to cause me such grief.'

'Is he, the old man… is he dead?'

'I cannot say. Sabina does not appreciate male company.' Councillor Mason gestured for the other figure to make themselves known. It was Councillor Lockewood. 'My brother and I are indebted to you now. You have unwittingly stepped into a world that is deemed to be fantastical by modern society, and that is how our brotherhood would like to keep it.'

'What are you talking about?' Alan glanced sideways to Reginald again, relieved at the sight of his brother's chest motioning with each slow breath taken. 'What are you going to do with us?'

'We are merciful… where necessary. We are not monsters, although we do answer to some,' laughed Councillor Mason, placing a large leather bag before Alan. 'We are willing to give you a second chance. Take this money — there's over a two-thousand pounds there, by the way — and leave this town before sunrise. If you do not leave, then we cannot guarantee your wellbeing.'

'Do it,' Reginald spluttered as he came to. 'I'm done with this miserable town. Take the money, Alan.'

'Your brother is a sensible man,' Councillor Mason jibed, on removing the restraints from the two brothers and their children. 'I strongly advise for you to take this offer, should you not wish to endure the same fate as Old Bob. No one would ever believe you, anyway.'

Alan reached out for the bag of money, stood up, and then helped Reginald collect their children; both brothers then left the farmhouse without looking back once or uttering any further contempt. They gave no explanation to their wives as they packed what belongings they could into Alan's car, or even after they left the town's limits an hour after their fateful encounter with the occultist councillors.

Satisfied by their wicked work, Councillor Mason and Lockewood each raised a goblet of freshly spilled animal blood to one another, their corresponding smiles cruel and ecstatic.

'Will that do, do you think?' asked Councillor Mason, struggling to hold the small gauntlet in his trembling hands. 'Have we satisfied Sabina? Will she leave us alone now?'

'There is no need for concern, not in that aspect. Sabina has been granted more children for her to nurture within her hellish realm. So, therefore, I would say that we are safe from her wrath, at least, for now. However, I do not agree with you allowing those two men — that know of our town's darkest secret and our sacrificial rituals — to escape. They could jeopardise what we're trying to achieve here.'

'They were terrified. They won't dare set foot in this town again,' cackled Councillor Mason. 'But where does this stop? We can only sacrifice so many animals and offer up so many children before our actions become noticed — go public. How are we meant to appease the Great Demon and his puppet witch?'

'I've already outlined my proposal to you… and the council.' After checking that no others stood within the surroundings of his humble home, Councillor Mason pulled out a rough parchment of paper from a secret drawer in his bedroom — the place where he kept all the animal skins he had collected — which he then handed over to Councillor Lockewood. 'The other council members seemed delighted with my idea to build some new houses upon the western area of Acle's ancient settlement. It will be a fine experiment, this will.'

Councillor Lockewood studied the blueprints before him, soon forming a sadistic smile. 'Impressive, Brother. But that will mean removing the old church stones and many of the surrounding trees. Such an action may anger our demonic master and the witch held at his side. It was where she and her daughter fell, after all.'

'The area will draw in innocent souls for them to torture and feed from. It may take some years to see through, but I do not believe there will be a problem with gaining the planning permission; and given that I've offered a hefty backhander to our colleagues for their unhindered cooperation, our wait will not be too long.'

'A stroke of genius,' laughed Councillor Lockewood, spilling some blood from the goblet upon his chin. 'It is a marvellous idea! The Great Demon will most certainly be grateful of our generous offering to him.'

'Baal will be delighted. Cheers!' Councillor Mason gleamed, raising his goblet up high. 'This will be our ultimate legacy, Brother, our master's new domain. I wish to name it after my place of birth —'

'Which is?'

'Skipton. I want to name it "Skipton Road". Our noble cause has only just begun, Brother. We still have much work to do...'

Hidden Within the Catacombs

Samantha Gibson was a bright girl, caring, selfless, never straying too far from home or from her parent's devout Christian beliefs. But at fifteen years old, however, the desire to fit in with her classmates was beginning to take its toll on her morals and faith. Samantha's grades were slipping at school, and she was spending more time with friends that were introducing her into a world of dangerous situations, namely experimenting with alcohol and drugs. She was torn between two worlds, between obeying her parents and seeking independence — to become an adult.

The phone rang downstairs, and it was answered before Samantha had any time to react. She herself was locked away in her room, where she would prefer to spend her free time. Given the fact that her parents were so overbearing and controlling, Samantha's want for isolation was understandable. She waited just outside her bedroom door to eavesdrop on the conversation, filled with apprehension.

'Hello?' Samantha's father flared his eyes, and his response to the caller was simply: 'She's not in, and don't you call this number again — you hear?'

Samantha flinched on hearing the phone being slammed down, knowing that her father would likely be in a bad mood now, which wouldn't be out the ordinary. She attempted to make her way back to her bedroom silently, as to avoid her father's usual scorn, but she found her mother waiting for her at the bathroom doorway. Her mother was stood with arms folded, tapping a foot, almost foaming at the mouth.

'Samantha? You come down here at once!' her father demanded. 'I'd need to have another word with you.'

'You heard your dad,' said her mother. 'We're sick and tired of these boys phoning you. Haven't we taught you about what boys at their age are like, and what they're after?'

Samantha shrugged undecidedly. 'Yes, Mum. They're not all like that, though. They're not all after just one thing.'

Under her mother's escort, Samantha stepped up to her father. He already had his leather belt at hand, snapping it thrice before hitting it off the sofa. 'Who is this "Stephen" that keeps phoning for you?' he asked, tightening his grip over the belt.

'Stephen's a boy in my class, Dad. He's just a friend of mine.'

'Is he now?' With a snap of his belt, Samantha's father waved a finger to bring her in closer. 'And what have we said about boys?'

'They're not all sex-mad maniacs,' Samantha argued, planting her jaw upon the top of her navel. 'Stephen's lovely. He wouldn't dare hurt me.'

'You don't know that for sure,' said her father. 'I was his age once, and I know what goes on in the mind of a frisky teenage boy.'

'If you would only give him half a chance—'

'I won't hear of it, and you can spend the rest of the afternoon in your bedroom—studying, like you should be for those exams that are coming up. It might be the summer holidays, but you can't afford to let your grades slip any more than they are. Your mother and I haven't raised an imbecile. We won't tolerate any more of this unruly behaviour from you.'

Standing together side-by-side now, Samantha's parents shared a sorrowful, traumatised expression.

'We only want the best for you, sweetheart,' her mother implored, pretending to sob. 'Your dad works all the hours he can to keep us safe and happy. When the time comes for you to start courting, which won't be anytime soon, it will be us who'll choose a suitable boy. Study and focus on your future, Samantha. Don't piss it away.'

'I won't, Mum.' Samantha retreated into herself, knowing that there was little point in pursuing an argument. 'If that's all you've got to say, then I'll go to my room now.'

Her father nodded slowly, resituating the belt around his waist. 'Let me make myself crystal clear, young lady: should you ever choose to go against what your mother and I say, then, I'll have no issue whatsoever in disowning you. You'll be thrown out onto to the street to fend for yourself, like some feral animal. Is that what you want?'

'No,' she replied glumly. 'I said that I'm sorry, and I'll try harder at school. I won't let you down anymore.'

'Good. Then, be off with you,' he snapped. 'It's about time you started to mature, to realise your responsibilities and potential. No daughter of mine is getting pregnant before marriage.'

Samantha returned to her bedroom, her sanctuary. She took in a deep breath while searching through her records, eventually selecting a new album by the Beatles to help take her mind off things. As the music started to play, she picked up a heavy English literature book and sighed as she opened it. Halfway down the first page the sound of small stones being thrown against her window suddenly caught her attention.

Peering out her window, Samantha soon noticed two boys cowering behind a gooseberry bush in the garden. They were Stephen and Mark, who were both keeping a watchful eye on the back door for any sign of Samantha's aggressive father.

Resting her forehead against the window's glass, she silently worded, 'What are you doing here? You'll get caught.'

Stephen, the tallest and most noticeable boy remained hidden while Mark popped his head over the bush. Mark placed a finger against his lips and then carefully erected a ladder to rest beneath Julie's window.

'Quick!' he beseeched, forcing his body against the unsteady ladder. 'Come on down before your parents notice us!'

Samantha complied without hesitation. Before attempting to escape she switched the record to a compilation of Beethoven's greatest masterpieces, which would allow her at least an hour or so of distracting music – a guise for her disappearance. If Samantha was playing music it meant that she was studying and did not want to be disturbed. It was the perfect cover, or so she assumed.

'About time,' moaned Stephen as he assisted Samantha down the last few steps. 'Your dad will kill me if he sees us. The guy's a nutjob.'

'Tell me about it,' she quipped. 'Where are we going?'

'It's a secret,' whispered Mark, brushing aside his long hair. 'It's really dope. You're gonna love where we're going, Sam.'

'I don't know,' she said, shuddering, somehow hearing the terrifying noise of her father's belt snapping in her mind. 'Is it far?'

'No, it's just near the stream… about a ten-minute walk or so.'

'Are you sure?'

'Positive. Relax, Sam. Lighten up.'

Stephen placed the ladders back against the garden's fence and then tilted his head sympathetically. 'You only live once, Sam. Have some fun for once. We'll be back before dinner, so your parents won't suspect a thing.'

Before she could contest, Samantha found herself being dragged out the garden by both Mark and Stephen. The boys were giggling, whereas she was increasingly reluctant to take another step.

'It will be worth a telling-off,' said Mark, showing off his new tie-dye t-shirt. 'Do you like it? I can make you one?'

'I don't think my parents will approve of me wearing clothes like yours.'

'I don't,' laughed Stephen, who was a self-proclaimed Mod. 'If it weren't for the fact that you're my cousin, Mark, I'd have nothing to do with a smelly hippie like you.'

'I don't smell,' countered Mark. 'You reek of cigarettes — that's worse!'

'Better than sweat and those incense sticks you burn.'

'Where are we going?' Samantha interjected. 'I haven't got long.'

Stephen turned to her with a knowing smile. 'You ever heard of the haunted stones near Bluebell Wood?'

'Yeah. They're where that new building site is, aren't they?' she asked, trying to hide her disappointment. Samantha didn't believe in the supernatural, given such thoughts went against her Christian upbringing. 'You're not taking me on some dumb ghost hunt, are you?'

'It's not dumb,' said Mark. 'Terry Priestman swore to me that he saw a woman dressed in white there a few weeks back.'

'Terry's not the brightest lad going, though, is he?'

'He seemed genuine to me. I want to catch a ghost — we'll be famous!'

Stephen tutted as he pulled a small bottle of vodka out from one of his coat's inside pockets. 'Sod the ghosts. I want to try some of this without getting caught.'

Samantha fell into shock and looked to Mark for a similar response. He merely smiled back, however, gleaming with an excited smirk.

'Alcohol? We're not eighteen yet,' she said, albeit hinting at some curiosity in her tone. 'I don't want to get into trouble.'

'We're not old enough for a few things, Sam. But, like I said, you only live once,' said Stephen, handing over the bottle to his friends for them to inspect. 'I nicked it from my dad's liquor cabinet. It's good stuff, not cheap crap.'

'Won't there be security guards at the building site? It'll be impossible to reach those stones,' said Samantha, hopeful that this would be the actual scenario. 'Can we not go to the park instead?'

'It's Friday,' added Stephen. 'The site closes at 3pm, so it'll be empty by now. We'll have no bother getting in, and I know where there's a weakness in the security fence. Can you think of any other excuses?'

Out of ideas, Samantha agreed to continue with their journey.

'Well, I'm not drinking any of that horrible vodka stuff. My dad has a nose like a sniffer dog. He'll smell the booze on me straight away.'

'Your loss,' said Stephen, winking across to Mark playfully. 'More for us, pal.' He hid the bottle, mindful of some passers-by, then walked on ahead. 'Terry's not the only person who's seen that woman's ghost, from what I've heard.'

'I've never heard any truth behind those stones being haunted,' said Samantha, folding her arms against the bitter wind. 'We live in a new town. I can't see there being many ghosts to haunt it.'

'Who knows what's under our feet? The town might be new but the land it's built on isn't. My dad said it goes right back to medieval times.'

'It's a load of mumbo-jumbo,' she sneered. 'I should have just stayed at home—'

'To be bossed around by your boring parents?' asked Mark. 'I don't know how you put up with them. I couldn't.'

'They care about me, that's all. My parents aren't monsters.' Samantha could barely convince herself, let alone her friends. 'They're really not.'

'Either way, we're not kids anymore. It's about time we did grown-up things,' said Stephen, raising his chin with pride. 'We'll be there in no time. By this time next week, we might be famous!'

A housing estate lay just before the stream, and there was a newly-built bridge that connected it with the marshlands—where the building site now stood. Stephen stepped onto the bridge without any reservation, but Mark and Samantha both felt a strange sense of unease as they neared it.

'I'm having second thoughts about this,' said Mark, eyeing up the steep and muddy embankment that lay at the other end of the bridge. 'Why don't we go into those trees over there?'

'We're going to the haunted stones,' said Stephen, attempting to cement his authority over the other two. 'I'm the eldest here, so what I say goes.'

'You're only a year older than me,' whined Mark. 'Just because you're sixteen it doesn't mean you can boss us around.'

'Chicken.'

'We're not chickens!'

'Then get your arses over the bridge—prove it.'

Samantha felt Mark wrap his fingers around hers. It was a euphoric sensation, though one also met with anxiety and guilt. 'Will you look after me?' she asked in a nervous whisper.

'Of course,' he said, though his words struggled to sound. 'We'll be alright. Those stones aren't really haunted, you know. Stephen's always been a dick when it comes to scaring people. He gets off on it.'

'Chickens!' Stephen iterated, reaching into a pocket for his flick lighter and packet of stolen cigarettes. 'Do you fancy one, Sam?'

'No, thanks. Remember what I said about my dad and his nose?'

Lighting his cigarette, Stephen noted, 'You're nothing but a sheep, Sam. Your parents can't control you forever. I don't listen to mine—I'm still alive.'

To which she replied, 'That makes a whole lot of sense. I'm not just worried about my parents, there's my soul to think about as well.'

'Oh, yeah. I forgot how religious you are,' said Stephen, losing some of his bravado. 'Nothing lasts forever, though, does it? The bible's just a load of made up stories, anyway. If you believe that there's some invisible bloke controlling the universe, then you must believe in ghosts and stuff?'

Offended, Samantha took pleasure in slapping the cigarette from Stephen's mouth. 'You can't see cancer, but it exists. You can't see alcohol, but it gets you drunk. See where I'm going with this?'

'We're young and carefree. Lighten up,' humoured Stephen, losing more of his bravado. 'I didn't mean to upset you, Sam. I was only saying…'

'You two go on like a married couple,' joked Mark, collecting the cigarette. 'Sam's got a point, Stevie. Fair dues.'

'I don't know why I hang around with you two muppets,' he simpered, lighting up the cigarette again. 'We're meant to be going on an adventure, not talk about religion and stuff.'

'We could say the same for you,' laughed Samantha.

Despite the jovial nature being shared between the friends, their playfulness soon took on a sour note. They couldn't fathom what it was, but there was a definite change to the atmosphere surrounding them. A sense of being watched entered their thoughts, followed by a creeping wave of fog that stood between them and the stones now.

'It's only fog. This area's known for it,' said Mark, trying to dismiss his own fears. 'It might be why people think this part of town's haunted? It's certainly weird.'

Tapping at the vodka bottle hidden within his coat, Stephen brushed off the anxiety being displayed. 'It'll be a good cover for us; no one we will be able to see us sneaking into the building site.'

Samantha couldn't help but wince. 'No, they won't. I can't hear anyone else around here.'

'We're totally alone,' said Stephen, pressing on ahead. 'Follow me… chickens.'

Stephen guided his friends a few more yards west until they reached a damaged part of the fence. He pulled apart some of the twisted metal rods, just enough so that he and the others could fit through. Mark snagged his new t-shirt on the sharp metal, which didn't at all go down well.

'You're joking! It took me ages to get the colours right,' he complained, stamping a foot into the soggy peat. 'I'm with Sam on this one, Stevie. I'd have been much happier spending time in the park than this dump.'

'Police officers patrol the park. Don't be a coward, and don't call me Stevie,' said Stephen, waving to Samantha for her to step forth. 'The stones are up this way. Are you ready?'

'I guess so,' she whimpered. 'It beats being stuck in the house.'

'That's the spirit. Nothing bad will happen.'

What the trio had not anticipated, though, was how treacherous the landscape would be. Luckily for Mark he was wearing some heavy-duty boots, but Stephen and Samantha's shoes were not up for the viscous peat that acted like a vacuum, sucking them in.

'My shoes are ruined,' cried Julie, looking to her expensive footwear that was now stained with brown and red streaks. 'Why is the mud red?'

'It could be from the machines they're using—diesel perhaps?' suggested Mark, who was relieved to have not suffered the same inconvenience. 'Just wash your shoes off in the stream before we go home. Simple.'

'Look! There they are.' Stephen pointed through the fog at a collection of towering dark monoliths that lay a few metres east. 'Spooky…'

He and Mark then made their way up to the series of boulders first, ensuring to check on Samantha's whereabouts every few seconds or so. Stephen leant against one while Mark sat on another. To Samantha, they didn't seem afraid or nervous, therefore she tried her hardest to relax.

'So, what happens when people see this ghost woman?' she asked, chuckling to herself. 'Does she gobble them up or turn them into vampires?'

'No one knows,' said Stephen ominously, blowing a wave of smoke into Samantha's face. 'Rumour has it that some kids went missing here in the fifties, but the town council aren't exactly gonna admit to that. There aren't any official records to prove it, at least.'

'Yeah, but we know the truth,' added Mark. 'My dad knew a fella who lost a little girl at the time. They said it was witchcraft —'

'Devil worship. Black magic. You're talking real, scary, spine-tingling stuff,' said Stephen, shooting a wary smirk at Samantha. 'What would you do if a big horned demon chased after us?'

'Nothing,' she said whimsically. 'I'd do absolutely nothing because that won't happen. Stop trying to scare me.'

'Aww, are you scared?' Stephen proceeded to place two fingers upon his forehead, as to portray such an evil entity. 'Samantha's a scaredy-cat!'

'I'm not!'

'Scaredy-cat!'

Stephen suddenly lost his footing upon the stone, as if it had been deliberately dragged away. He slipped onto his back and then landed with a heavy thud within the centre of the boulders. Mark and Samantha rushed into action, though before they could reach Stephen the ground beneath him collapsed, sending him into a deep crevasse.

Mark threw himself onto his stomach, desperately reaching into the hole. 'Steve! Talk to me!'

Stephen responded in a strained cry, 'I'm… alright. Just a little sore from the landing.'

'How far down are you?' Mark squinted his eyes to focus them. He found that at about four feet down there were a set of worn stone steps, which appeared to lead on further into the darkness. 'Are you seeing this, Sam?'

It took a great deal of courage for Samantha to peer into the chasm, and she did so by only looking through one eye. 'I can't see much—it's too foggy. We should go and get help.'

'No way! Our parents will kill us,' said Mark, bolting upright. 'Can you move, Steve?'

Another pained cry echoed from the hole. 'I think I've twisted my ankle, but I'll be alright,' said Stephen somewhat unconvincingly. 'I'll use my lighter so you can see where I'm at.'

The sound of Stephen's lighter flicking echoed several times, making Mark and Samantha's shared concern intensify.

'How deep does this hole actually go?' Mark enquired as he attempted to lower himself in. He then began to make out a dim light—Stephen's lighter. 'You fell pretty far down, Steve.'

'I'm okay!' he bleated. 'I'm just… come and give me a hand!'

Samantha's stomach knotted as she watched Mark disappear into the dark abyss. Despite being on the surface, she didn't feel any safer. In fact, she felt more exposed to any possible, unknown threats.

'Are you coming down, Sam?' asked Mark, his voice pitiful and bordering on desperation. 'I won't be able to lift Steven on my own.'

Before answering, Samantha's ears twitched to the sound of footsteps moving nearby. 'There's someone else here. We're not alone,' she gasped, scouring the foggy landscape. 'I thought you said there'd be no security guards!'

'Come down—quick!' the boys cried in unison.

Compelled by the invisible threat closing in on her, Samantha closed her eyes and then jumped into the dark. She landed with a heavy thud, but the blow was thankfully softened by a coating of thick moss that swept across the stone steps. She righted herself and followed the faint sound of her friends whispering, all the while scolding herself for getting into such a risky situation.

'Hurry up, Sam!' implored Stephen.

The steps led into a narrow tunnel, which was supported by small sandstone bricks. Samantha's initial thought was of this being a sinkhole, though that quickly vanished, and there was no comfort in discovering the real truth.

'What is this place?' she asked while trying to avoid a series of water droplets that fell from some cracks above. 'It's manmade. How is this possible?'

'Nothing's impossible,' Mark sneered. 'The town's new, but who knows what was here before it. This might be a cave that smugglers used hundreds of years ago. Your guess is as good as mine.'

'I don't like it here,' she shuddered. 'Can we go now?'

Holding onto his swollen ankle, Stephen made it clear that he was unable to manage such a feat. 'I need to rest my foot. There's no way I'll be able to climb back out yet.'

'We can't stay down here forever,' she pleaded, brushing up against Mark. 'I want to go home.'

'You go. I'll keep an eye on Steven and help him to get out,' said Mark, tending to his cousin's injured foot. With a disparaging sigh, he then tore off some of his t-shirt to wrap it around the injury. 'You owe me big time, Steve. This is brand new.'

'It's only a stupid t-shirt,' he contested. 'I don't fancy being stuck down here either, Sam. It is what it is.'

A shrieking wail suddenly resounded, paralysing the teenagers where they now knelt. It was feminine, agonised and harrowing.

'What was that?' Steven stammered, stricken with panic. 'Tell me you guys heard it as well.'

'I heard it.' Mark slowly arched his back like a fearful feline about to retreat. 'We've got to get out of here, Stevie. Try to stand up.'

'I can't! As soon as I put any pressure on my foot it absolutely knacks.'

Another feminine wail echoed across the narrow walls, seemingly more pained and tormented now. The three friends glared into the gloomy tunnel ahead, each shaking with dread.

'Hello!' Mark cried out. 'Can you hear me? Is anyone there?'

The phantom woman sobbed in response, 'I am all alone, left to rot in this foul place. I hear you. I see you.'

'Maybe they need help?' said Mark.

'Maybe we should get the hell out of here and tell the police?' said Steven, taking himself by surprise by his own show of cowardice. 'We're hearing things, that's all. There's no way anybody else could be down here. The tunnel was sealed off.'

The wailing grew louder and more heart-breaking, soon reducing Samantha to tears. 'She needs our help, whoever she is. Give me the lighter, Steven.'

Despite his best attempt to cling onto his beloved possession, Stephen proved to be the weaker between himself and Samantha. She took it with ease. 'I want that back, mind. It belongs to my dad,' he groaned.

'You'll get it back,' she said, slowly creeping forward, holding up the small flame. 'Who's there?'

There was no initial response from the woman. Samantha tip-toed thereafter over the uneven stones and damp soil, mindful that the tunnel was becoming narrower and colder as she walked on ahead. The air was stale, foul, littered with an overwhelming scent she had not yet come across before.

'Be careful!' Mark emphasised, torn between waiting with his cousin and offering aid to Samantha, who he deemed to be the most vulnerable out of the three. 'Don't go too far — we can't see you now.'

'I'll be fine. I'll be careful.' Samantha carried on with her frantic calls. 'Hello? I've come to help you!'

The walls now brushed against Samantha's arms, forcing her to progress with a sideways stride. The lighter's flame flickered sporadically, and in the light's absence strange images formed: hooded men, small children with no eyes and ghastly visions of decaying corpses — terrifying visions.

Samantha screamed, although her voice quickly diminished into a strained whimper. 'Stephen! Mark! I can't move…'

'Bollocks to this, I'm going to check on her,' said Mark, leaving Stephen's side. 'You stay put. I won't be a moment.'

'I haven't got a choice, have I?' said Stephen, punching at the air. 'Don't be a hero, Mark. Don't pretend to be brave — because you're not.'

Without any light, Mark was forced to feel his way through the tunnel, along its saturated walls, towards Samantha's voice. The walls were freezing to the touch and stunk of foist. He soon found himself in the same situation as Samantha, in needing to side-stride for the remainder of his journey, until he happened upon the dim flame of Stephen's lighter.

'Sam?' he called out. 'Sam, where are you?'

'I'm here,' she replied. 'You won't believe this.'

Mark approached Samantha from behind and immediately fell silent. The narrow tunnel opened to reveal several chambers, each one supported by sandstone pillars that spread out into a succession of ancient catacombs. The pair were dumbfounded, more so petrified.

'You don't see this every day,' he commented, nudging an elbow into Samantha's side. Mark then spotted some wooden torches that hung from each pillar, and he wasted no time in removing the lighter from Samantha to ignite one of them.

'That's better,' said Mark, gleaming with joy as the torch burst into life. 'On second thoughts, maybe it's not…'

'What is this place?' Samantha spun herself around, hypnotised by the ancient spectacle. 'It's like some sort of church, isn't it? It reminds me of Durham Cathedral.'

'If so, then where's the altar?' said Mark. 'I've never heard of a church being underground.'

'The church could have been on the surface?' suggested Samantha, stroking a finger across her chin. 'This is amazing. We might be the first people who have come across this place in hundreds of years.'

'I don't care, if being honest.' Mark swung his torch around, certain that he could hear distant voices. 'At least we've got some better light now. We'd best go and check on Stephen. He's probably crying in a corner somewhere.'

'But, what about the woman we heard?'

'There's no woman, Sam. These tunnels echo like mad. We might have maybe misheard a gust of air passing through. Let's get out of here while we still can.'

'I heard a woman, Mark, and I'm not leaving until I find her. She might be hurt.'

Clenching at the torch in frustration, Mark begrudgingly agreed.

'Fine. We'll have a quick look for her and then go. We've spent enough time down here already, in my opinion.'

There was a subtle sense of peace at the heart of these catacombs, but this soon morphed into an electrical surge of fear and anger as Mark and Samantha walked on further into the maze of tunnels and adjacent rooms. Wherever they looked, both thought they could hear the odd breath or cry, though neither admitted it to the other.

Mark abruptly raised a hand to halt his and Samantha's progress.

'Did you hear that?'

'What?'

'I heard... no, it couldn't have been.'

'What? What did you hear?'

'It sounded like men talking in a funny language.' Mark's expression was serious, foreboding. 'I swear to you, Sam, I heard some men talking — chanting.'

'Chanting?!'

'I'm certain of it.' Mark raised the torch, guiding it toward a room on his left side. 'In there...'

'Don't go in,' she pleaded. 'These tunnels are old. They might collapse at any second.'

'But —' Mark screamed as the torch in his hand burst into an array of crimson and purple flames before extinguishing completely. 'Jesus! What's going on?'

Samantha reached out to her friend, desperate to hold onto him, but he was no longer there. 'Stop messing around, Mark!'

A haunting silence endured, which then came to be replaced by the distinct sound of monks chanting repeatedly in Latin.

'Spiritus Sanctus! Dominum nostrum! Dominum, Baal!'

Samantha clambered to the floor, clawing at it blindly in search of Stephen's lighter. She was sure that it had fallen close to her feet on his disappearance; the chinking metal gave it away as it landed. However, as she cowered on all fours, Samantha then felt a bony hand stroke across her back, from her hips upwards.

'Stephen, is that you?' Samantha thrust an elbow into the air, hoping to deter her friend from committing such an ill-timed prank, but there was nothing. 'Stephen? Mark?!'

What the three friends were unaware of in this moment was just how far apart they had been separated: Samantha knelt within the centre of the catacombs; Mark was stood within a large cavern that bore an underground lake at its centre; Stephen had fallen into complete unconsciousness, only to awaken before an altar that was covered in satanic symbols and bloodstains.

Another shock came for the trio when torches throughout the underground tunnels and rooms suddenly burst into flame, without any natural source of fire to explain such an occurrence. The monks and their chanting ceased, though they were followed by a chorus of children laughing and then weeping.

Samantha's screams reverberated in mockery of her despair.

'Mark! Stop playing games with me!' She thought of her parents, of the few joyful moments she had shared with them to cope. 'Mum. Dad. I want to go home...'

Within the darkness what few precious memories from her childhood that existed graced Samantha's conscience, allowing her to find some relief within her solitude. She sat cross-legged on the damp floor, sobbing into her hands, clenching at her silver crucifix necklace. She had never experienced fear on this scale before, nor could she comprehend how to escape from this hellish nightmare.

What felt like hours passed, and there was no more sign of Mark or Stephen. Neither of Samantha's friends responded to her cries, leaving her vulnerable and exposed to threats that had lain hidden within the catacombs for centuries, a malignant danger that had now been awoken through their unwitting actions.

The gentle sound of a women shushing Samantha's sobs crept into being, followed by a series of footsteps that approached her from behind. She looked up, staring into the dark void, unable to speak or move. A hand then slowly moved along hers, in unison with a woman's sweet voice that offered reassurance.

'Do not be afraid, my child,' said the woman. 'Thou art safe here...'

Samantha was sure that the voice was that of her mother, but it couldn't have been. 'Mum?' she asked, after some deliberation. 'It can't be. She doesn't talk like that.'

'I am Mother,' replied the woman. 'Thou art safe here in my arms.'

'You're not my mum!' Terrified, and with as much haste as possible, Samantha crawled several feet away from the phantom. 'Who are you? Was it you I heard crying before?'

The surrounding torchlight dwindled to leave a single, crimson-coloured flame that hovered before Julie. She felt a strange admiration for the red light, which now danced gracefully before her.

'Thy sorrow shalt end under my divine protection,' implored the woman. 'Sorrow will leave thy heart and soul.'

'Who are you?' snapped Samantha, swiping her hands through the empty space before her. 'What's going on?'

'Thy soul is torn, wounded. I will repair thy broken heart and tend to thee. I am Mother. I am… Sabina.'

'Leave me alone! I don't know who you are!'

Sabina was unphased by Samantha's show of defiance, however.

'Bid me discourse and I shalt enchant thee!'

The crimson light morphed into a beautiful woman, tall, thin, somewhat solemn in expression, who was wearing a white dress with a red ribbon wrapped around the waistline.

Samantha's jaw dropped. 'Why were you crying, and how did you end up here?'

'I was weeping for thee, for thy love,' said Sabina, leaning into Samantha's personal space. 'I am trapped, forced to serve a master who bears no love for me. Thou art in the gravest of danger, my child. He is coming. He is near. He is always hungry for blood.'

The fear that Samantha had felt now faded, as if stolen away, as if she had somehow been anaesthetised — nullified to the aberration that stared back at her. 'Who is… he?'

Sabina allowed for her raven-black hair to cover her face, hiding what dread littered her expression. 'He is a shadow that moves through both the light and dark, whom cannot be confronted or destroyed. He is my master, and he would seek great pleasure in offering thee torment. Death and decay bringeth him great joy.'

Samantha focused on her breaths, slowing them down in order to think more clearly. It was difficult to tell whether Sabina's words were truthful or if she was to be shunned like a venomous creature. Nevertheless, Sabina possessed a hypnotising persona, and she was steadily forcing Samantha to submit under her spell.

'I've lost my friends,' said Samantha in exacerbation. 'Will you help me find them?'

'Those boys?' Sabina snarled. 'Why doth thee fret over their meaningless lives?'

'Why do you talk like that?' she asked, turning away. 'How *did* you get down here? There can't be another entrance.'

Cautiously, Sabina planted a palm upon Samantha's forehead. 'I will grant thee the insight thou doth seek. I will show thee.' An array of images flooded into Samantha's mind: an endless horizon spanning across some ancient marshlands; a group of monks whose eyes were all bloodshot and hateful; followed by Sabina and her young daughter picking herbs, and then a fleeting image of their untimely deaths.

Samantha tore at her scalp, plagued by the harrowing images.

'Get out of my head!' she screamed. 'You're evil!'

'I am innocent,' said Sabina, consumed with grief. 'Grant me thy love, Eliza. Become mine again—willingly. Be with Mother once more.'

'Get out of my head, Witch!' Samantha swiped at Sabina but missed by mere inches. 'You took them, those little girls. You trapped them down here!'

'Their souls are bound to mine in the afterlife,' Sabina explained, stroking a hand down Samantha's back. 'Death cannot touch thee in this place. Be with me. Be my Eliza.'

'I'm not your daughter,' wept Samantha. 'She died long ago. Eliza is dead.'

'ELIZA IS NOT DEAD!' roared Sabina, shedding a single tear. 'My child is not… dead.'

Mark scrubbed at his eyes in disbelief. He was in a large cavern, which had torches lining its jagged limestone walls and a lake held within its centre. He scratched at his sore head and fell to his knees, convinced that this was some peculiar nightmare.

'Sam? Steve?' he called out, only to have his words repeated back to him through many taunting echoes. 'What the hell?'

The lake's water shone like amber in the torchlight, and its rippling waves gave off a false sense of peace and tranquillity. Desperate to quench his rising thirst, Mark approached the lake and then thrust his face into it. The first mouthful was surprisingly sweet, but then it left a bitter aftertaste as if he had chewed on some rotten eggs.

Mark spat out the foul water, unknowingly disturbing the lake. He inspected his surroundings again and then turned to move away, although his progress was hindered by a necrotised hand that shot out from the waters, clasping onto his flared trousers within seconds.

'What the—?' Mark fell onto his chest, winding him, and then he let out an agonised howl from the acute pain that ensued. 'Samantha! Stevie!'

Looking to his feet, which were slowly being dragged into the lake now, Mark shrieked on discovering more decayed hands appear from the murky depths. The hands latched onto his clothes and flesh, ripping at them, until he could fight no more.

'Get off! Get off me!'

Covered in filth and blood, Mark was helplessly dragged into the centre of the lake, where he was left to float upon its surface. He stared ahead, aimlessly, confounded by the fact that there were some painted figures strewn across the cavern's ceiling. The paintings appeared to reveal a story; there were hooded men and crucifixes, some crude outlines of small children playing with flowers, which eventually ended with a creature that was not natural or benevolent in appearance—a goat-headed beast.

Disembodied screams bounced around the cavern as Mark closed his eyes to shield them from the disturbing images. And then, to his greatest dismay, the evil chanting returned.

'Baal! Dominus Meum!'

Fuelled with a renewed rush of adrenaline, Mark swung himself around and then attempted to swim back to the rocky shore. The grotesque hands continued to pull at his legs and torso, but he fought hard against them. Just as he made it to water's edge, Mark then felt something heavier pull him under. He sunk deep into the depths, where no light or warmth could reach, his ears popping from the immense pressure. Water soon cascaded into his lungs, followed by the sound of a deep and guttural voice that said: 'Fall into my arms, into the abyss, into death. Thou art mine, mortal. Darkness will enshroud thy body, and no light will ever touch thee again.'

Unlike Samantha, Mark did not wallow over his loved ones or the life that was being robbed from him but rather a selfish desire to seek vengeance upon whatever was forcing him to drown. The adrenaline coursing through his veins ignited a sickening wave of hatred, intensifying it, which only made whatever was pulling at him increase in its ferocity.

'So weak and pathetic,' said the demonic being, stabbing several, sharpened fingernails into Mark's chest. 'Die, puny mortal. Empower my spirit. Relinquish thy futile life…'

Mark's initial thought was that he had done no wrong, that he awoke in this unknown place bearing no knowledge of how these strange events had transpired. But the growling voice persisted to taunt him, ridiculing his pitiful attempts to flee.

'I don't want to die,' he pleaded within his thoughts. 'It's not fair!'

'Heathen!' a horrifying growl responded. 'Thou art unworthy to exist in my world. No mortal does.'

'I'll do anything—anything you want. Please, don't kill me. Not like this. I don't want to drown!'

'Kill her!' The demon commanded. 'Thy wasteful existence shalt be spared, should thee commit this act.'

The image of Samantha, with her radiant smile and mesmerising eyes, overwhelmed Mark's conscience. He reasoned that the evil entity could only be talking about her. To kill Samantha is something that Mark could never do, however, even if it meant dying.

'I won't do it. I won't kill her.'

'Then… DIE!'

The water encasing Mark and flooding his lungs thickened, as if he were struggling to free himself from a tar pit, forcing him to reconsider his stance, though only for a moment. 'I can't do it. I'd rather slowly drown to death than kill her.'

'So be it, foolish boy. A terrible death awaits thee…'

Mark's lungs burned as if he had inhaled mustard gas. He focused on the majestic vision of Samantha, of when she was at her happiest with him, as to console his final moments. Mark's body finally landed upon the lake's bed thereafter, against a pile of broken bones—the bones of witches who had been drowned centuries before.

The cruel entity then offered one last insight. 'Upon the bones of fallen witches thou shalt spend an eternity, along with the monks who betrayed my beloved. Die and be set free. I am Baal. I am merciful. I am retribution!'

Stephen's situation was no better than that of his friends. He awoke within a small room, before an altar that was covered in satanic symbols, animal bones and dried bloodstains. He gagged at the putrid smell that lingered but quickly turned his focus on his damaged ankle again, which severely restricted his movements and ability to flee.

'This is just what I need,' he lamented, taking in the gruesome surroundings. He then closely examined the altar and its ghastly decorations. 'How did I end up here? I wonder where Sam and Mark are…'

A collection of books lay scattered before the altar. Stephen reached out for the closest one, noting how its cover was made with a material he did not recognise. It was, in fact, made from human skin that had been dried, stretched out and then sewn together.

On opening the book, Mark shuddered as an elderly man's voice emitted from the revealed pages.

'O Father, how far we hath fallen…'

'Who said that?' Stephen shrieked, releasing his hold from the book.

'Heavenly scriptures, our finest work,' the voice replied, filled with arrogance. 'Many witches burned and drowned on my command. Hell awaits them all, as it does with thee.'

At this point, Stephen was convinced that he had succumbed to some possible form of concussion, or he was simply still dreaming. But it all felt too real. With trembling fingers, he picked up the book and turned its pages again.

'Witches?' he scoffed. 'Witches aren't real.'

'Blasphemy!' wailed the phantom voice. 'Thy soul is corrupted and spent—a servant of Lucifer, art thou!'

Stephen chuckled to himself, deeming the voice to be nothing but his imagination running wild. 'Witches don't exist. The devil doesn't exist. God doesn't exist.'

The lit torches immediately extinguished, all but for one. Stephen was left with barely any light, and with a rising sense of remorse he reached for another book nearby. The book he chose was titled "Bestiary: Necronomicus".

'What a load of bull,' he chuntered, sweeping a finger across the first page. 'What language is this meant to be? Latin?' He studied the faint markings, which appeared to have been written in blood by their scarlet colour. 'Are these names? Azazel, Belphegor, Moloch, Baa—'

A piercing pain suddenly inflicted Stephen's tongue, thus preventing him from uttering the next written word. He held onto his mouth that now blistered and burned, crying out in agony. From within his cries, he then heard some heavy, hooved footsteps approach from behind.

Out of nowhere a raspy voice decreed, 'No mortal can know my name! Thou shalt have no power of me, infidel! Suffer! Burn! Die!'

Stephen slammed the book shut and slowly forced his head to turn, as to face the terrifying creature who spoke to him. The first thing he saw was a pair of obsidian-black hooves, which was enough to induce a humiliating bout of urinary incontinence. Stephen's entire body shook as he then examined the towering, pale, muscular, ram-headed figure that now lingered over him. The creature smiled back, its laughter booming like bursts of thunder.

'What in God's name are you?' Stephen asked, struggling to catch his breath. 'What the—?'

'Creation granted me a name, but then I fell and was given a new title of which thou shalt never be told,' glowered the demonic figure. 'Fresh meat! Fresh blood! I have waited long for this...'

Stephen stood up with the intention to run as fast as he could from the foul beast, but his swollen ankle instantly gave way. He collapsed onto his chest, where he then remained out of fear and cowardice.

'Please, don't hurt me!' he begged.

'Mortals,' the demon cackled. 'Why, O Gracious Creator, did thou bestow thy greatest love upon them?' With a brutal swipe the demon then held Stephen up in the air by his throat. 'Like countless souls before thee, thou shalt sustain my weakening body; thy blood will empower my spirit; thy flesh shalt renew my decaying form. I will grant thee purpose!'

All then fell silent as Stephen's body and voice froze, while the demon drew out his lifeforce and sucked the blood from his flailing corpse. No answers were given as to what malevolent spirit had made itself known, only the merciful wake of death that came to greet the petrified teenager.

Meanwhile, Samantha — out of both fear and curiosity — continued to enlighten her own paranormal visitor.

'Those images you showed me... was that really you and your daughter?' she asked Sabina, displaying some genuine sincerity. 'Why did you show me them?'

'I gifted thee but a glimpse into my past, into a life I shalt never redeem. She was taken,' said Sabina, her voice strewn with sorrow. 'They took her from me.'

'The hooded men — the monks?' asked Samantha.

Sabina's body stiffened and her eyes flared. 'Yes. Men, my child. But I shalt protect thee from them, from men.'

'I don't need your protection, though. Times have changed since they killed you and her, your little girl.'

Sabina shook her head. 'Thou shalt join thy sisters within this sacred realm, where death itself cannot touch thee. I am not dead. Thou shalt never die by my side, either.'

'My mum and dad will be worrying about me. I've got to go home,' pleaded Samantha. 'I must go, and I need to find my friends. Goodness knows where they are.'

'Friends?' Sabina scowled. 'Those boys who had gladly cast aside thy life in yearning to preserve their own skins?'

'I don't understand what you mean,' said Julie, consumed with concern. 'I don't know what you're talking about.'

'They belong to him now. They will replenish his strength.' Sabina held out a hand, steady and willing for Samantha to clasp onto it. 'Come with me, dearest Eliza. Come with Mother.'

'My name isn't Eliza! I have a family, and they'll be out looking for me — right now!' cried Samantha. 'I want to go home.'

A notable change took hold over the atmosphere; the air grew fouler and colder, and the skin from Sabina's face melted to reveal a truly horrifying sight: her actual demonic form.

'There is no escape!' roared Sabina. 'Stay with me!'

'No. I won't be your prisoner!'

Samantha sprung to her feet and ran back into the darkness, through the endless stream of tunnels, through the freezing catacombs, yearning to find the entrance where she and her friends had fallen from. However, with every step she took the witch's voice grew louder and even more fierce, frantically drawing Samantha back to her position.

'Eliza!' cried Sabina. 'I will not lose thee again!'

'Stay away from me! Leave me alone, Sabina!'

The tunnels spanned out in all directions, each one leading back to the centre of the hidden catacombs where Sabina now lay in wait. Samantha clung onto Stephen's lighter, her only way to create some visibility, in the hope of rediscovering the exit. With each yard taken, however, she only felt as if the witch was moving in closer, tearing her from the life she had once taken for granted.

When all hope seemed lost, though, Samantha finally made it to the steps that led outside. She gasped in relief and then in despair at her friends' absence, though an overwhelming desire to survive quickly took precedence. Fate, though, had another surprise in store, for another demonic being stood before the steps — Baal, the ram-headed demon — Sabina's master.

Samantha shielded her eyes from the monstrosity. 'Mark! Stephen! Where are you both?'

'No other can hear thee,' said Baal, his proceeding laughter cutting and cruel. 'Thou must stay here to satisfy my pet's desires. I deem it so, and I always get what I want.'

'Your pet?' thought Julie. 'What are you?'

'I am thy master, as I am to Sabina. Thou cannot leave our accursed domain.'

Beyond despair, Samantha's memories of home and family flooded back into thought. When it felt like she could weep no more, she then felt a pair of delicate hands rest upon her shoulders; it was Sabina, who had reverted to her fairer form.

'Come, my child. Thou shalt meet thy sisters and be glad,' said the witch in ecstasy. 'Come with Mother. Be set free from thy woes.'

There was no feasible way Samantha could tackle the monstrous demon that stood guard at the entrance, so she turned instead to face Sabina. With her head held low and without uttering a word, she followed the witch deep into the catacombs, to a room that she had not yet encountered.

'Where are you taking me?' asked Samantha, secretly praying for an absolution. 'I want to go home!'

Unmoved by Samantha's sorrow, Sabina simply stated: 'Home. Thou art home, my love. Thou art safe.'

On entering the room, a scent of sweet lavender instantly hit Samantha's senses. There were candles strewn all over that burned with an amethyst flame, and a pile of young girls' clothes and shoes from the 1950s were piled neatly across the floor. Samantha didn't dare to ask where they had come from, but she had a horrible feeling that there was an obvious answer: the missing children her friends had spoken of.

'Some children went missing ten years or so ago. Do these clothes and shoes belong to them, Sabina?'

'Thy sisters, Eliza.' Sabina leant down to collect a pair of polished shoes, stroking at them lovingly thereafter. 'My precious children. I saved them. They know only peace in my company.'

'Did you take them? Did you kidnap them?'

'They came to me,' said Sabina, showing no remorse. 'They learned of my loneliness and sought to end it. My darling children.'

'Where are they? Are the girls still… alive?'

'Their souls are bound to me,' said Sabina with a wicked smirk. 'They belong here. Thou doth belong here. I will not be parted from thee.'

A renewed sense of doom crept into Samantha's mind. She was trapped and with no food or water. It was obvious that she was going to suffer the same fate as those unfortunate children.

'I can't stay, Sabina, and I won't.'

'Eliza, listen to me—'

'No! I've heard enough. I have a family, and I want to go back to them. You can't keep me here!'

'Stay, Eliza. Don't leave Mother all alone again…'

With what energy remained, Samantha fled through the catacombs again, not once looking back or sideways, only ahead. It was easier now to establish where the underground cave's entrance was, given that Baal still stood guard over it, his growling breaths loud and formidable. The demon's roars echoed through the small rooms and narrow passageways, and where they sounded clearer was where Samantha imagined her route of escape to be. Her legs ached and lungs burned from the exertion required, but she eventually made it to where some fresh air flowed in.

Baal crossed its lengthy arms and groaned disappointingly as Samantha approached him. 'Doth thee dare challenge me?' he laughed, somewhat offended. 'Thy blood will not be wasted, mortal. Thy soul will replenish my needs.'

'Get out of my way!' Samantha snatched a lit torch from one of the pillars, aiming it at Baal's chest. With all her might, she then charged at the towering beast. 'Let me out!'

Baal showed no fear from the nearing flame. In fact, he relished the notion of a child attempting murder. 'Foolish girl, I cannot be killed!' Using one of his large, clawed hands, Baal clasped at the torch without showing any pain or struggle, and then he placed a palm upon Samantha's forehead. 'A greater existence is what thee deserves, which I see now. I am impressed, and I am merciful.'

The demon's touch forced a series of haunting images to flood through Samantha's mind, knocking her into unconsciousness. She saw an ancient tower being erected in a far-off desert; a bloodstained battlefield littered with slain bodies and canons; and then she witnessed Sabina and Eliza playing in a beautiful wildflower field; then finally a vision of her own future, and it was not in any way pleasant.

In old age, Samantha awoke within a padded cell; her limbs were completely restrained, and her mouth taped shut. She recollected events from a life she had not even come to know yet, where she had tried to warn people of Sabina and Baal's existence, but her efforts were merely shunned and vilified. She had also been accused of murder — but how? Who did she allegedly kill?

'As Babylon — my greatest failing — fell, so shalt thee,' said Baal, feeding his words into Samantha like venom. 'I will release thee, but thy memories of this place and thy friends shalt be removed; thou shalt have no knowledge of these catacombs, only memories of the fear and grief encountered by my gracious presence.'

On opening her eyes, Samantha found herself lying on her father's lawn. Her clothes were muddy, but there was no other damage to be noted. She rubbed at her swollen temples and licked at her parched lips, completely dazed and unaware of how she ended up here.

Mr and Mrs Gibson appeared at their living room window some minutes later, crying out in astonishment at Samantha's safe return.

'Sweetheart! My baby!' her mother screeched. 'I thought you were dead!'

'You stupid girl! Where have you been, and why are your clothes so dirty?' her father asked with his usual scornful expression. 'We were so worried about you, Sam.'

'I-I don't know.' Samantha rose and embraced her parents, still oblivious to what awful actions had befallen her friends. 'Mum. Dad. What am I doing here?'

'The girl's gone barmy,' commented her father, wrapping an arm around her mother. 'Get her inside and washed. I'll phone for a doctor to come out.'

'Let's make you a lovely, warm bath,' said her mother. 'You'll be okay, sweetheart. You're home. You're safe now.'

Samantha lay in the bath until her fingers wrinkled, still trying to piece together what had happened, while her mother watched on diligently.

'You must have some clue as to where you and your friends went?' her mother asked, rapidly losing patience. 'Tell me.'

'I honestly don't know, Mum. Which friends are you talking about?'

'Stephen and Mark, of course. Your father and I know that you three went out together — we're not stupid.'

'I don't have any friends called Stephen and Mark,' said Samantha, feeling an unnatural anger rise from within. 'You're lying, and you're not my mother!'

'I beg your pardon! What have I done to deserve this? You wicked, wicked girl! I can't take this anymore!'

Samantha's mother left, slamming the bathroom door behind her. Now alone, a calming sensation swept through Samantha's aching limbs, bringing respite to her troubled thoughts. She closed her eyes momentarily, and on opening them she saw Sabina standing over her.

'Mother, is that you?'

'Yes, Eliza. Mother is here. Mother will never leave thee again.'

Police sirens blared through the street outside and throughout Newton Escomb, for a huge hunt went underway in search of the two missing boys. People from all walks of life went out to look for Mark and Stephen, though their search was ultimately in vain.

Two days later, as a crimson-coloured sun rose on Monday, and the building site at Skipton Road burst back into life. Councillor Mason and his cohort, Councillor Lockewood, stood in admiration as a large concrete mixer pulled up at the ancient stones. It did not take long for the workers to remove the sandstone boulders from their resting place, and even less time for the concrete to start pouring into the unearthed hole.

'Two more children went missing, so I hear,' said Councillor Lockewood, rubbing at the stubble on his face. 'Have you heard anything?'

'Yes,' said Councillor Mason. 'Such a pity.'

'They better not be down that hole —'

'Why? If so, they'll be out of sight and mind by now. No one will ever learn of the catacombs and their grand altar. Our plan is flawless. There is no need to worry, Brother.'

Conflicted, Councillor Lockewood added, 'I hope you know what you're doing. It's not just some tormented spirit we're dealing with. We're talking about powers that cannot be understood.'

'I know what I'm doing, and — like I said — there is no need to be concerned over those missing boys. Our master and his witch have seen to them, no doubt.'

'Our master…' Councillor Lockewood held onto his mouth, as to hide a growing urge to vomit. He then fleeted his eyes across the workmen, who were now occupied by placing the heavy stones upon a truck nearby. The coast was clear. 'We can't afford any loose ends, Alistair. People are starting to notice your interest in occult practises. You have been careless of late.'

'Me? Careless?' humoured Councillor Mason, his face reddening with embarrassment. 'Are you referring to the newspaper article that had a supposed photograph of me in my robes?'

'Your occultist robes, Alistair, the ones we wear when performing our dark practises. You have put us — me — in an impossible position. People are starting to ask questions.'

'I bribed the newspaper's editor to release an apology, which should be printed sometime this week. There is no need to fret.'

'Oh, but there is…'

On noting that only he and Councillor Mason were left by the pouring concrete, Councillor Lockewood made his move. He thrust his fellow occultist into the hole, where a torrent of heavy concrete then poured over him. Councillor Mason's screams were muffled by the noisy mixer and diggers that worked close by, and all attempts to clamber back out the hole failed, mostly because Councillor Lockewood kicked him back in.

The site foreman approached ten minutes later, looking confused. 'Where's your pal gone?'

'Councillor Mason?' sneered Councillor Lockewood. 'He's had to nip off — duty calls. My colleague is always getting swept off his feet by the job we do. It's not easy working for the council, you know. It's not all fun and games.'

'Aye, I bet,' sniggered the foreman. 'Bloody sinkholes. That one should be filled in soon enough, though, then we'll get to work on making way for the foundations.'

'Excellent,' smiled Councillor Lockewood. 'You may not realise it yet, my good fellow, but what you and your workers are doing here shall be a monumental part of our town's future. Please ensure that work is completed on schedule, as discussed in our last meeting.'

'Don't you worry yourself. There'll be little kiddies running around and family's making good their new homes where we're standing right now, in a few months or so, give or take.'

'Good.' Then Councillor Lockewood noted to himself, 'I will fulfil my ancestor's legacy. I will avenge my bloodline and the bastards that sought out to destroy us. I will make good your desire, Sabina. Your sister never forgot you… or Eliza. Your sister handed down her knowledge of the dark arts and your wrongful deaths. You will be avenged. You will be set free. I swear it on my very life...'

A Demonic Wager

I — Baal, Lucifer's grandest lieutenant — have lain waste to countless cities and civilisations, wrought famine and plagues throughout the world, tormented the minds of innocent souls and have stood as my master's mightiest weapon for countless millennia. So, in that case, why did Lucifer condemn me to this wretched, tedious place — Newton Escomb? I do not know, and I dare not seek the answers. There always lies a reason behind Lucifer's decisions, therefore I must have offended them greatly — but how? Have I not been careful enough? Have my treacherous actions against our demonic brethren been discovered? Surely not. And nevertheless, I will make good my work in bringing destruction and desolation upon mankind. My will shall be done.

The humans call my current dwelling "Skipton Road" now, and they have built houses upon the site of my beloved's grave. Such a travesty, but I will make the most of this stagnant situation. I will make good my will to spread fear and dominance over those pathetic vessels… humans. They make me sick; their very lives are an abomination! Even after thousands of years they continue to exist and mock my brethren's right to rule. That will not last long. It cannot last long. It must not.

My unfortunate failures at Sodom, Gomorrah and then Babylon — to spread sin and chaos — angered my master greatly upon their decimation, which is understandable, although I have compensated that loss many times over. What have I done to warrant this futile life? Could it be that Lucifer knows the truth, of my ultimate plan to usurp him and rule over this world alongside Sabina? No, that is folly. Not even Sabina knows of my true intentions, and I mean to keep it that way.

I am terror! I am malice! I am cruelty and hatred incarnate! I am the most powerful demon in the cosmos! My pride is not unjust, let it be known, and on one fateful eve, during the summer of 1975, I enacted my unfathomable strength for Lucifer to enjoy and revere. I am Baal. I am mighty. I am no slave.

It was on the night when an old ally named Azazel came to visit me, who had also fallen from grace during the early times, like myself and Lucifer, after that impious battle in Heaven. I say ally but in truth Azazel is more of a rival to me — a serious threat to my position, so to speak. There is certainly little respect held between us. He is but a fool, is Azazel, a sheep with no ambition. He does not have the wit nor courage to defy me, not now or ever. He would not dare... but he did.

I had spent the day replenishing my strength by feeding on the blood of innocent animals that wandered through the ancient — and now dwindling — woods of Acle. Come nightfall my full strength had returned, and I was more than ready to wreak havoc upon the pitiful souls dwelling within this new town.

The moon glistened above with a sapphire hue, and the winds died down to leave a false façade of peace and serenity. But, to my astonishment, I began to sense another spiritual being nearby, one of whom I had not encountered since our last meeting upon Mount Hermon many centuries prior. I was unnerved, admittedly, though I was not prepared to lose any fight.

Unsure of what ethereal presence was making itself known, I swiftly morphed into my true demonic form, as to tower above any possible foe and remove any efforts they may have attempted to supplant my hold over this territory.

I unleashed a mighty roar into the air, causing a murder of crows to flee in its wake, though I could still sense the being, and they were moving in closer to me. I waited with all the patience I could muster, biding my time to tear asunder whoever it was that dared to intrude upon my accursed domain. My curiosity, nevertheless, was soon answered.

'Brother? I know thou art here, skulking around like a filthy rat,' said a haggard voice that travelled with the passing breeze, which I immediately recognised to be Azazel. 'Oh, how the mighty have fallen!'

Compelled by my rising malignance, I leapt into the air and between the tall trees to land precisely before them and my demonic brother. Azazel tried to hold back his shock, but his quivering movements within the darkness gave away what fear had now arose within him. The docile fool. Afterall, I had to remind my brother who between us was mightier. There was no contest.

'Azazel!' I announced, proudly and with an insurmountable level of arrogance. 'Praise Lucifer, for I did not anticipate such a visit from thee.'

'Baal,' he replied, almost sympathetically.

'Beelzebub. Remember my title,' I informed him.

'Baal was the name granted to thee on Babylon's fall, was it not, by Lucifer?'

'Yes, but that will change soon enough. I will regain my noble title.'

'What a sorrowful place thou doth roam. Thy might is wasted here, Brother.'

Azazel looked just the same as he did upon Mount Hermon: a lowly reflection of my own form. Where I appear to be a horrifying ram-headed beast, he is more akin to a startled goat that is puny and useless — easily destroyed. Azazel's stature and horns are far smaller in comparison to what I boast, as are his lesser abilities. Yet, the religious leaders of this world seem to fear him more now than myself. I could not let that injustice go unpunished.

'Bow before your lieutenant!' I commanded, and to my satisfaction Azazel showed some willing obedience. However, he also used this opportunity to remind me of how his angelic wings remained intact, unlike mine. 'Remove those disgusting wings from my sight, this instant!'

Azazel laughed and turned to look up at me. 'Thy wings were torn apart well before the Great Fall, Baal. I was more cautious around the Seraphim and their golden blades —'

'I can rip them from your back within a single breath, Azazel. Remember your place!' I implored. 'If it were not for my intervention, you would have been cast into the Endless Void. It was I that saved you!'

'Do not take credit for Lucifer's mercy upon me, O Brother.' Azazel's initial smirk quickly changed into a confused expression. 'Such speech is unknown within our brethren. Why doth thee speak so?'

'As to spread fear more effectively through mortals now, I have learned to adapt my speech to theirs. This modern tongue remains unfamiliar to me, but it is necessary. You have spent too long festering away in our master's realm, of which that is for certain.'

'My hands have not been idle, Baal. Thy obsession with the Red Ribbon Witch hath been noticed, I must add.'

I paused to comprehend Azazel's words and the possible consequences of my forbidden adoration toward Sabina. Nevertheless, I am a master of deception and cunning, and Azazel is easily silenced.

'Sabina is the wretch's name, and I bear no obsession for her. She is but another tool of mine to spread despair...'

'Lucifer would think little of thy excuses — I do so. That is why I am here, Baal, to test thy loyalty.' Azazel started to circle me, flapping his vile wings about to entice my further fury. 'Thou art meek in the eyes of our valiant commander. Thou hath forsaken our brethren, so it would appear.'

'In Hell *we* are the rulers, alongside our master!' I contested.

'Be wary of what thou doth sayeth, Baal. Lucifer sees all and hears all.'

I was greatly tempted to rip Azazel and his precious wings apart, but the risk was too high. If Lucifer suspected that I bore feelings for Sabina, then their wrath would inevitably greet me. I could not allow for my meticulous plans to fail.

'I am Lucifer's righthand, Azazel, their lieutenant and most devout servant!' I beseeched. 'There is no need to test me, and I do not take well of our master sending you — above all our other brothers and sisters — to cast judgement over me. I am not some putrid little denizen like Belphegor!'

'Thou hath no choice, Baal. Permit my company or else face the wrath of the Infinite Darkness. The choice be yours. At least ye were spared a visit from our sisters, Hopkinah and Preeta. Lucifer is surely merciful in sparing thee from their wrath?'

'I do not recognise fear, even against my own brethren. You are my brother, Azazel, but I will not hesitate to banish you. Do not test me.'

A tense and uneasy silence met between Azazel and I as we both studied one another's thoughts and movements. It was only by the will of fate, when a human trespasser entered our space, that this stalemate ceased.

'Can you sense them?' I asked, inhaling the surrounding fog to ascertain our victim's scent. 'It is a man, coated in sweat and riddled with anxiety. I can smell the fear on him. Is it not intoxicating, Brother?'

'Do not attempt to divert my attention, Baal. Our master was clear on what must be done.'

'Which is?'

'Thou must sever thy bond with Sabina — remove her essence, and then cast her into the Endless Void.' Azazel clapped his claws in delight as I clenched mine in restraint. 'If thou doth fail in committing this act, then our master hath promised to endow thee with the harshest of punishments. O how terrible it will be, Brother Baal, whatever Lucifer chooses to bestow upon thy physical form. I dare not think of what terrible fate would befall thee.'

I reminded myself that Sabina's soul was safe and still connected to mine. She was hidden under the foundations of Skipton Road, her resting place, under my protection and control. There was little risk of Azazel discovering her, and I knew that he could not resist the innate urge to spill some blood from an innocent man. There is a reason why Lucifer entrusted me with tactical missions: I never fail.

'I will prove my loyalty to you and our master, Azazel, but first why should we not enjoy torturing this lowly creature?'

Azazel ran his forked tongue through the fog and his face instantly lit up with the joy that comes with our demonic bloodlust.

'The human is fearful — terribly so. I can taste the salt from his sweat and adrenaline flowing through his pulsating veins. It is, indeed, intoxicating. It has been so long…'

'Let us have some fun, like we did during the old days,' I suggested, somehow managing to uphold my courteous demeanour. 'Let us dine on human flesh again, Azazel. It must feel like an aeon has passed since you last dined on the chewy, blood-soaked muscles of mortal men?'

'Agreed,' said Azazel, running a sharp and tattered fingernail across his necrotised face. 'But we must also make this a competition — just like the old days. That is my proposition to thee.'

'I am listening. You have my attention, Brother.'

'Let us see who is the most efficient at dementing the unfortunate worm — before killing him, of course. That would be good sport, would it not?'

'Yes. It would make good this fine evening.' The man was closer now and I gathered that he was cowering beneath an old oak tree that lay but yards from where I stood. 'I will show you how it is done. I will show you the meaning of true, unhindered terror!'

Azazel stepped aside with a begrudging smile, and then he held out a hand to the man's hiding place. 'I hold no doubt over thy powers, Baal. Show me. Remind me of why Lucifer bestows such adoration unto thee. I see why not they grant such affection, however. In my eyes, thou hath become… weak.'

I extended my talons, cracking them like tree trunks breaking upon immense pressure, and then aimed each lengthy digit at my victim. Immediately, a connection was formed between the two of us. I could see into his thoughts, dreams and nightmares. It is a skill that only I and Lucifer possess, which is why I displayed this ability before Azazel — to ridicule him.

'His name is Nigel Grimsby,' I whispered to Azazel in delight. 'He was orphaned at birth, ridiculed through his youth, has failed to find any meaningful love, and now he is on the run for committing the greatest of sins: murder.'

'Impressive, Baal. Thou art proficient in telling stories,' said Azazel, clearly in mockery to me. 'Thy skills are unquestionable —'

'As are my powers to manipulate and instil agony!' I countered, forcing Azazel into submission. 'Watch and learn, Brother. I am at the peak of my strength!'

I morphed into my human form — Bartholomew. It had been many years since I had needed to use such a weakened state, yet I managed to control my human muscles and vocal cords despite the initial difficulty. With an empathetic demeanour, I approached the man with open arms.

'Who are you? What you want?' he gasped nervously, startled by my unexpected entrance.

'My name is Bartholomew. I have somehow managed to get lost in these woods, and it looks like you have too.'

'I'm not lost — get gone!' he ordered, fleeting his eyes around like a cornered animal. 'I don't need no help. Piss off!'

'You are injured,' I noted, pointing to several scratch marks upon his face. 'What happened?'

'It's nothing. Get gone, you hear!'

'It was her, the woman who you strangled and took advantage of.'

Nigel's expression was priceless. I could envision the tiny cogs in his shrunken brain trying to fathom out how I knew this fact, and I could also hear Azazel's breaths rising with anticipation.

'If you know what's good for you, you'd start running away now,' my latest victim threatened me, amid struggling to stand. 'I'll give you some pretty scratches across your face with my blade — then see who's clever.' He drew a flick knife from one of his pockets, which he then rested against my windpipe. 'Not so clever now, are you?'

I focused on the blade's hilt, feeding my malice into its metal to reach a temperature that instantly caused the skin upon Nigel's hand to blister and then boil. He cast aside the knife and then looked to me like a lost child. I smiled back in pure satisfaction; the pain I had caused wrought so much ecstasy and comfort to both myself and Azazel.

'An eye for an eye and a tooth for a tooth,' I said, feeding one of my fingers into Nigel's own throat. I then allowed for a substantial amount of blood to pour from the severed artery before sealing the wound by searing it with my hellish aura. Nigel collapsed in a daze, no longer boasting the display of impudence he previously bore.

'W-Who are you?' he asked, clambering to his knees, bowing before me. 'What are you?'

'From Hell I have come, mortal, and to Hell is where your soul shall soon be sent!' I proclaimed. 'You are doomed. You are mine!'

I wrapped a hand around his scrawny neck; the other I planted against his forehead. Now came my ultimate display of power to both Nigel and Azazel — my ability to infiltrate the mind and then infuse it with my sadistic will.

'I hath been greatly longing for this part,' said Azazel, as he sauntered up to me and my prey. 'This be the moment where my strengths can, too, be shown.'

'Not before mine,' I seethed, and with a grunt of my fiery breath Azazel backed off. 'Nigel Grimsby!' I looked directly into his eyes, his mirrors into what rotten soul lay beneath. 'You loved that girl, but she did not love you…'

'Get out of my head!' he whimpered. 'You don't know anything about me!'

'Oh, but I do.' I easily fed myself into Nigel's conscience, which revealed countless images from different moments during his life up to this point. 'I can see and feel your anguish over the death of your mother, of your sister and closest friend. You cared little for your family, but your friend — the girl named Jessica — her death came with much sorrow and guilt.'

'Don't you dare talk about her!' he begged, but to no avail.

'She was your first love. Oh, what a pity it must have been to discover that she had died in such brutal circumstances. Jessica was stabbed several times, and for no apparent reason. What a pity. What an awful thing it was that you were helpless to intervene.'

'I couldn't save her,' he argued. 'I just couldn't —'

'Silence that diseased tongue of yours,' said I, tightening my hold upon him. 'No, the blade in your hand had a will of its own, did it not? If she had only accepted your advances, your repeated attempts to subdue her, then Jessica might have survived that fateful night. Her womb would have remained empty, and blood would have still pumped through her beating heart.'

'It wasn't my fault,' he pleaded, digging his fingers into mine. 'It wasn't, right!'

'Of course, it wasn't. You could not satiate those primal urges, those innate desires that burned within your loins.'

'It's my turn,' Azazel interjected. 'Let me have some fun.'

I moved aside, as to gratify my brother's want for torture. 'He is all yours, Brother. Do be gentle.'

Azazel wasted no time in clamping one of his claws upon Nigel's forehead, mimicking my own technique. He was cautious as not to reveal himself, remaining in a transparent form.

'What's going on?' screamed Nigel. 'Who's there now?'

Azazel rested his amphibian-like skin against Nigel's brow. 'My brother is correct. I can also see into thy sordid memories. And to think, we be considered monsters by mortals such as thee...'

'Get off!' Nigel gasped, looking to me for an answer he would never be granted. 'Who is talking now?'

'My brother toys with the mind; I play with the flesh and nervous system,' Azazel cackled. 'Hath thee ever been stabbed like thy victims? Hath thee ever felt such discomfort and humiliation?'

Nigel was given no opportunity to answer. Azazel placed his other claw against his chest, instantly causing thirteen stab wounds to appear across it. Our victim flailed in anguish; we laughed out aloud in merriment, my brother and I, in return.

'What's going on?' Nigel stared at his open wounds and the blood pouring from them. 'In God's name —'

'No! Elohim, Yahweh, Allah — whatever false deity thou doth believe in — cannot aid thee,' spat Azazel, his work upon Nigel nowhere near its completion yet. 'Does it pain thee too, O Brother, that our heavenly creator admires these mortals more so than us? We were cast out from Paradise to allow these worthless, fleshly vessels to endure and multiply. Is it not unfair that we grieve our creator's dismissal?' I nodded my head slowly in agreement with a bitter growl and glare. 'It is sickening, the devotion mortals hold for a divine power that bears no love for them. Thou art in my gracious presence now, Nigel Grimsby, and I shalt remove thy tempting burden — once and for all!'

Azazel slipped a claw down to Nigel's groin, where he then tore the pitiful fool's gristle apart, holding up his reproductive organs thereafter for me to inspect. Nigel collapsed and shook like a dying fish, wailing over his lost manhood.

'I have always admired your unusual punishments,' I said to Azazel, brushing him aside. 'You are too quick to act, though. It is better to inflict mental torture upon your victims first, slowly and meticulously. In castrating this filth, you have merely offered him a swifter route to death — to our master's domain. Make it last. Drag it out. Make it worthwhile.'

'Lucifer hath never questioned my tactics before,' sneered Azazel. 'I am yet to see why the Dark Lord holds thee in such high esteem.'

'I will show you.'

Nigel was still writhing around in the wet mud and fallen leaves, his hands covering the bloody chasm where his manhood once lay. I knelt myself and again placed a hand upon his forehead, my mind set in what gratuitous torture was about to follow.

I searched through Nigel's most recent memories, of the fateful night when he took the life of his trusting friend, Jessica. I could feel the anxiety from when he proposed his love to her, then the lustful urge to desecrate her womb with his foul seed, and then the hateful rage that drove him to silence her for eternity. The maelstrom of emotions was overwhelming and intensified my malicious want for invoking agony upon him. It was such a rush, a feeling I had not encountered for too many years.

All the negative emotions that Jessica had felt, of being helpless and terrified, I then fed into Nigel's being. His heart raced; the saliva in his mouth dried up; his muscles spasmed from the fear fuelling them; and then, finally, his mind fell blank as to block out my evil influence. Nigel saw himself as Jessica in the moments leading up to her death at his hands, and he felt the loss that had overwhelmed her thoughts as she slipped into peaceful darkness. He succumbed to the lowest of places then, of which he could never return from. Azazel, for reasons unbeknown to me, did not seem as impressed as I had anticipated.

'Thou hath driven him mad, Baal,' said my brother disappointingly. 'What pleasure doth thou receive from this? He still breathes — lives.'

'You could have killed him, yes, but that would have been too swift and merciful, O Brother. Our purpose upon this physical plain is to empower malevolence and sin; it is not to rid this world of the evil parasites that infect it. That is why Lucifer made me their lieutenant, because I can resist the wantful desire to enact our vengeance upon mankind so quickly. I make them suffer, and I ensure that it is done without sympathy or haste.'

Azazel nodded in contemplation, holding out a small, jade gemstone. Demons use such gemstones on occasion to travel freely between dimensions, when their powers are at their weakest, and so therefore I gathered that his judgement over me was coming to its end. Azazel only proved to me who was the greater between us. There was never any contest.

'I see now why Lucifer respects thee,' said Azazel, stroking at the gemstone. 'Thou hath proven thy might and worth. But take heed to this caution, Baal: sever thy connection to Sabina — I beg thee.'

'She is nothing but a mindless slave,' I replied, secretly confounded with dismay. 'I will use whatever tool is available to enact our master's grand vision. You may return to Lucifer now, and you may tell them that I am as loyal as I was when we fought against the Seraphim and our heavenly creator. If you fail to offer me support, Brother, I will tear you apart. Honour our past. Honour me.'

'That I shalt do,' Azazel murmured, allowing for the gemstone to fall from his grasp. A portal then opened, upon which he lingered over with his bastard wings on full display. 'I shalt see thee again before the end of days, Baal. This is not our last meeting.'

'Pray be that it is,' I countered, echoing my hatred for Azazel with a deafening roar to see him off. 'Be gone, Brother. This is my domain. Return to Hell and your subservience. I will see that my master's will is done, and I will do it without you watching over my every move.'

'We will see, Baal. We will see.'

I had almost forgotten about Nigel amid my hate-fuelled outburst against Azazel. He hadn't moved, nor had he spoken a word. I ran a finger through the blood that still poured from his groin while Azazel vanished. The taste was sweet, iron-rich and fresh. It had been so long since I had strayed from consuming animals to satisfy my needs. Against Lucifer's will, I then dined upon Nigel's flesh and enjoyed every second of it. I am no slave. I will not be told what to do!

Nigel's eyes widened and his body stiffened as if he were already a corpse as I fed on him. Upon witnessing my actual appearance, he then discovered a new level of fear and despair. The adrenaline coursing through him only made his flesh taste even sweeter, and I revelled in providing him with the most horrifying last moments a mortal could ever wish for. It was momentous. It was savage. It was wonderful. It was but a glimpse into what evil acts I would commit thereafter.

I slowly tore off a mouthful of flesh at a time, ensuring that Nigel watched each minute bite being swallowed. He was still breathing, albeit sporadically, as I consumed his eyes, and he only welcomed death when I finally tore out his heart. He meant nothing to me—no mortal does, but for Sabina. She is different. She is special. We will be together, as one, come the end of days. I will see to it. I will break free from Lucifer's servitude. I must.

A Festival to Remember

The smell of cheap burgers and hotdogs sizzling on an open grill, adjoined with the raucous noise made from people screaming with excitement upon some rides, would be enough to entice most folk into the throes of a visiting carnival. That wasn't the case for Nikki Reilly, however. If it weren't for her so-called friends pressuring her into going that fateful afternoon, Nikki would have simply stayed at home with her parents, and then perhaps what horrors that followed would never have occurred.

Nikki was an ordinary, laidback fourteen-year-old girl, who excelled at school and often volunteered to keep some elderly folk company at a local nursing home on weekends. She had never been embroiled in any conflict and rarely strayed too far from her childhood home. Nikki was the ideal pupil, daughter, citizen, and was also terribly naïve; she placed too much trust in the wrong sort of people. That was certain.

The circle of friends Nikki had attached herself to were mostly classmates, although her cousin, Alison, and a boy from the rival comprehensive school, Jacob, also tagged along now and then. They usually spent their free time hanging around the local shopping precinct, given there weren't many other places of interest to explore. The annual town carnival was, of course, a great opportunity to experience something different, to let her hair down and gain some respite from the perpetual boredom of living in such a small town.

Alison had informed Nikki that their friends were meeting up at the town clock come noon, that they were all expecting her to come. Nikki toyed with the notion of throwing a sicky, to possibly brush them off by saying she had succumbed to an acute bout of food poisoning, but she would never hear the end of it. The snag was: Nikki suffered with social anxiety, though she was masterful at hiding it from even those closest to her. It was an awful burden to bear, but her ability to feign a smile seemed to cast aside any suspicions.

Nikki made it to the rendezvous point as the town clock struck 12pm — right on time. Her friends waved excitedly to her, each one brimming with joy at the thought of spending an afternoon somewhere other than their usual, dull, predictable haunt.

'I can't wait to go on the waltzer ride,' said Alison, grinning to Nikki. 'You're coming on with me, by the way. I won't let you get out of it this year.'

'I'll only puke all over you,' joked Nikki, enforcing that fake smile of hers. 'I'll stick to the teacup rides.'

'Wuss!'

'You know I don't do rides, Ali. Give it a rest, yeah?'

'Whatever...'

Jacob, boasting a new Liam Gallagher style haircut, stepped up to Nikki. 'You can go on with me if you like. I'll keep an eye on you, y'know, keep you safe.'

Nikki shook her head in a gentle fashion, hoping to politely refuse Jacob's flirtatious nature. 'No thanks. I've brought a disposable camera with me. I'll make myself useful by taking photos of you guys making idiots out of yourselves — that'll be a laugh.'

Jacob shrugged. 'You're loss. We'd better set off now, otherwise the queues are going to be horrendous.'

Nikki looked up to the grey sky and ominous rainclouds that were forming. 'I doubt there'll be many at the festival, to be fair. There's meant to be a downpour this afternoon.'

'We live in the North of England. When doesn't it rain here?' Alison humoured. 'I'll go on the scary rides with you,' she said with a playful wink to Jacob. 'You can put your arm around me, can't you?'

'Nah, I'll pass on that. Cheers anyway,' he replied, losing some of his masculine composure. 'What about you, Nathan?'

'This is dumb,' Nathan replied. 'The rides will be boring; the food will be boring; the entertainment will be boring — they always are. I'd rather be sat at home watching the footy or Baywatch. Newcastle United are playing at home today.'

'Who peed in your cornflakes this morning?' Jacob sniggered.

Nathan didn't seem bothered in the slightest. 'I'm with Nikki on this one, mate. I'll just watch you guys make idiots out of yourselves.'

Nathan hadn't realised it yet, but he had unwittingly enticed Nikki's adoration towards him even more by siding with her. She had spent the last year trying to invigorate his interest, to plant the seeds of love between them. However, Nathan didn't appear remotely interested in Nikki, despite her repeated attempts to seduce him. Afterall, she was the wrong sex. No one else but Nathan knew that, though.

'Are going or what?' moaned Alison. 'I'm freezing my bits off just standing around here.'

'Yeah,' Nathan agreed, rolling his eyes to Nikki. 'God forbid it if we get there and the burgers have all sold out. Jacob will have a meltdown, should that happen.'

'Are you saying that I'm fat again?'

'No, mate. There's nothing wrong with your double chin.'

'You're one to talk…'

It was a short trek to the carnival, only taking a matter of minutes for the energetic youngsters to reach it. The sights. The sounds. The vibrant atmosphere of the carnival was electrifying for all present, that is, all but for Nikki, who sauntered at the back of her social group, wishing she were elsewhere — home, ideally.

Nathan soon noticed Nikki's anxious disposure, and so he slowed down his pace to match it with hers.

'What's wrong?' he asked. 'You look down.'

'Nothing,' she replied, hugging into herself. 'I'm just a little cold. You wouldn't think it was August.'

'That's British weather for you.' Nathan removed his Adidas jacket, offering it to her. 'Take it. I don't mind.'

'Thanks.' Nikki eagerly wrapped the coat around her shoulders, savouring the scent of Nathan that still lingered upon it. 'What aftershave is that?'

'Don't know. It's whatever my dad's using.'

'It's nice.'

Nathan shrugged again. 'It's better than smelling of B.O.'

'You don't smell,' she said with an awkward giggle.

A tense silence the met between the two, which only ceased as they entered the carnival's temporary entrance gates: two, large wooden posts that leaned precariously towards one another.

'This is going to be soooo boring, and I bet all the morons from school are here,' said Nikki.

'Just don't take any notice of them,' said Nathan, eyeing up a burger van nearby. 'Do you fancy some chips?'

'I'm not that hungry. Thanks, though.'

'Suit yourself.'

Nathan scurried off into the direction of the burger van, leaving Nikki in solitude once more. She clenched onto her sides, desperately fighting off a wave of anxiety that was making itself known. Her fingers began to tremble and sweat poured from her, but she couldn't let anyone else notice this. Every breath taken now was exhausting, though she somehow managed to keep her cool and remain composed.

'We're going on that spinning wheel thing over there, Nikki. Can you take a photo of us?' asked Alison, oblivious to her cousin's present ordeal.

'Of course. You go and have fun.'

Nikki reached into a small handbag she had brought along, shifting aside a lipstick, mirror and box of tampons in search of her disposable camera. She held out the device and aimed it at her friends, gleaming with a false sense of merriment.

'Don't cut my head off… not like the last time you took a picture of me,' taunted Jacob.

'I won't!' Nikki struggled to control the camera because of her tremors, but she eventually managed to centre it upon the others as they strapped themselves into the dangerous-looking ride. 'Come on guys, smile!' She took a photo and then another one, just to be on the safe side. 'One more…'

'There's still a chance for you to come on with us,' Alison cried out. 'Come on! Live a little!'

'I'm waiting for Nathan to come back.'

'Your *boyfriend*?'

'Shut up, Ali. Don't…'

The ride burst into life, hurling Nikki's friends around as if they were trapped within a malfunctioning washing machine. She swept her line of sight between them and where Nathan stood, himself trapped but within a long queue at the burger van.

Nathan returned as the ride came to its end, bearing two cartons of chips and a can of cola for both himself and Nikki.

'There you go,' he said, handing the items across to her.

'Aww, you shouldn't have.' Nikki accepted the carton and can as if they were a momentous prize being offered. 'You're so kind. You didn't have to.'

'There was a two-for-one deal on. It'd be a shame to waste them, wouldn't it?'

'Oh…' For some reason, the chips tasted sour now to Nikki. 'Thanks, I guess?'

Alison stumbled off the ride, holding onto her mouth, seemingly nauseous. 'That was amazing; it was such a buzz! You two totally missed out.'

Nathan flicked a chip at Alison and laughed, 'At least we're not in the dire state you're in. Look at you, all dizzy and green in the face.'

'It's called "having fun", Nath.' Alison turned to Nikki. 'You're not just gonna hang around with this sad git all afternoon, are you? You'll come on the next ride with me, yeah?'

'I might do. It depends,' said Nikki, mimicking Nathan's smugness. 'Aren't there any rides here that don't look like they're falling apart, though?'

Alison formed a wide smirk. 'Yeah, as it happens. Follow me. I know the perfect ride for you.'

The friends walked by some more fast-paced attractions until they came to a makeshift funhouse. Nikki stared at the structure with detest, given that the supposed funhouse looked more like a house of horrors to her: the structure was painted purple, but under the rainclouds it appeared to be black and imposing; the entrance was a crude, wooden plank that led into a narrow doorway; its operator was an elderly man that stunk of stale cigar smoke and grease; and there was an unnerving lack of people queuing up before it.

'I'm not going in that manky thing!' Nikki quipped, pretending to be offended. 'I'll probably come out with some disease — or worse.'

'You're such a prude,' said Alison. 'If you won't go on the "scary" rides, then this is all that's left. I can't win.'

Nikki examined the dilapidated structure again. 'No way am I stepping foot into that monstrosity. No chance.'

Unfortunately, a group of feral youths had noticed Nikki's brightly coloured handbag and sought out to investigate it. They approached her like a pack of wolves, though wolves that had been drinking cheap cider for several hours.

'Here! Your bag's proper weird,' cackled one of the youths, a boy wearing sports clothes with a baseball cap covering his eyes — a youth locally referred to as being a "chav". 'Are you a hippie or someate?'

Nikki took in a deep breath and turned to face the curious ruffian.

'No, I'm not a hippie. Go away, saddo.'

'Then, what are you? Why are you so… weird?'

'I don't have to explain anything to you —'

'You're a slag. I can tell that a mile off!' the youth chuckled, to a unified snigger from his fellow comrades. 'Dirty slapper!'

'Shut it!' Jacob interjected. 'Go and bother someone else. Even better, why not go and throw yourself in front of a car, lads?'

'Oh! So, you think you're the big hard man, do ya?' By now the leader of the unruly youths moved in closer to Nikki and her friends, smacking his fists together. 'Are you wanting to start a fight? Do you fancy a rumble?'

Nathan chortled, 'I'd fight you, mate, but only when you grow some pubes. I don't fight little kids. How old are you — ten?'

'Stop it!' snapped Nikki, clasping onto Nathan's forearm. 'You'll only make things worse. Just ignore them.'

'Bunch of pussies,' said the leader to his crew, turning his attention back upon Nikki. 'So, what's in your bag then? Either you show me, or I'll have a look for myself.'

'Go away!' she yelled, hoping that some passers-by might intervene. 'Leave us alone, for God's sake.'

The leader moved as if to walk away and then he suddenly reached out to snatch Nikki's bag from her. 'Give us a look!'

'Give that back!' she cried. Alison joined in with the struggle, but the gang leader proved to be too strong, despite his shorter stature. 'Help! Someone — HELP!'

Not a soul offered any aid, however. All Nikki could do was look on in horror as the bag's zip opened to reveal what was stored within. Her lipstick, mirror and box of tampons fell out, landing ungracefully upon the sodden mud below. She was given no time to react, no dignity or mercy.

'Eww! She's on the rag, boys!' snarled the leader, tearing apart the box of tampons to hold one out. 'The dirty bitch.'

'Give them back!' Nikki pleaded, her face reddening with embarrassment. 'They're mine, and they're private!'

'Urgh! She's diseased, lads,' he laughed. 'I'd keep well away from it, the filthy whore.'

A small crowd now gathered around the duelling teenagers, though no one offered to help Nikki in her plight. As tears ran down her face, she fled from the scene, away from the carnival, into a forest that ran alongside the festival. Not once did she turn back, out of shame and ridicule perhaps, feeling that she could never again look upon her friends.

'Why do things like this always happen to me?' she mourned, lashing out at the closest tree to her. A painful shockwave travelled from Nikki's shin up into her hips and spine, thereafter. She collapsed to her knees and began to fully cry, unaware of the fact that someone was watching her actions from behind. 'I'm so sick of my life—I hate myself!'

Unbeknown to Nikki, a faint and dark outline of a female spirit stood in watch over her sorrowful display. The spirit sensed the anguish and embarrassment coursing through Nikki, and they gladly fed from the negative emotions. There was not another soul in sight but for the crows and small insects that innocently carried about their business nearby. Somehow, the spirit could relate with Nikki's ordeal, of her hatred against men.

Morphing her voice into that of a young girl's, the spirit whispered to Nikki, 'What troubles you?'

Nikki shot around, frantically looking for the voice's source. She bolted upright, tempted to flee back to the carnival, but was ultimately compelled to stay. 'Is there a little girl here?' she thought to herself, and her question was soon answered.

'Play with me,' said the girl. 'I'm tired of being alone.'

'Who are you?'

'Play with me, please...'

'Are you lost?'

'No.' The spirit broke a branch that lay close by. Nikki followed the disturbance, much to the spirit's amusement. 'Follow my voice. Come. Play with me.'

'I can't see you.' Nikki scoured the trees but couldn't find anyone else there. 'Where are you?'

'I love playing games...'

'You shouldn't be out here by yourself,' said Nikki, genuinely concerned. 'You could get lost or hurt. I'll help you find your parents.'

'I have been lost for a long time,' whispered the girl. 'Will you be my friend?'

The booming sound of music from the festival caught Nikki's attention. She wasn't that far from seeking help, and—given that there was a lost child—it seemed like the right thing to do.

'I'll go and find a police officer,' said Nikki, hoping to reassure the poor child. 'Don't move, okay?'

'Wait!' The child's voice momentarily shifted from an angelic and youthful tone to being course and malicious. This change was quickly rectified, however. 'I want to play. Please, don't leave me.'

In truth, Nikki was in no rush to return either. So, after a short debate with herself, she walked on further into the forest, desperate to find the elusive child.

'Do you like playing hide-and-seek?' she asked. 'I get the feeling that's what we're playing right now.'

'Hide-and-seek is too easy. I have hidden a treasure that I want you to find.'

'Really?' Nikki chuntered, the first thought of this treasure possibly being a half-eaten chocolate bar, granted the age she believed this girl to be: six or seven years old, at most. 'What is this treasure?'

The girl sniggered in response, her laughter echoing all around to shield her true position. 'Would you like a clue?'

'Okay. Sure. It's not like I've got anything else planned today.'

'My treasure is silken and red, and when you touch it all those who you wish to be dead… become so.'

'What?!' Nikki gasped in shock. For such a small child, this rhyme seemed to be far too dark in nature. 'Say that again.'

'All you must do is seek out your own reflection, and then it will appear. Please, play with me,' pleaded the child.

Nikki thoroughly enjoyed riddles, and the last comment made was easily deciphered. 'The stream! I can see my reflection in that.' The child fell silent, consumed with a lustful urge to see their plan through. Nikki ran up to the stream and then inspected its banks for any sign of something red. Upon the opposite bank, clinging to a tree branch, was a small line of scarlet-coloured cloth. 'I found it! Is your treasure a ribbon? Is that it?'

'That it is,' the girl confirmed, her tone no longer innocent. 'Take it. Wear it. It is yours.'

'Why?' Nikki was certain that the voice was speaking directly in front of her, but that was impossible. She was alone. There was no doubting this. 'Stop hiding from me. Where are you?'

'I will reveal myself once you take the ribbon and wear it.'

'This is so messed up,' Nikki scolded to herself. 'What's so special about that ribbon?'

'Do it!' the girl commanded. 'Wear it!'

After securing her shoelaces, Nikki leapt over the narrow stream and then clasped onto the thin cloth. Instantly, all her surroundings blended into a dark blur, which then burst into a wall of towering flames. Then, just as she tried to reason with herself as to what was taking place, Nikki blacked out. The last image she saw was that of a woman in her thirties; their hair was black and coated in some slimy substance; their teeth were sharpened and yellow; their smile was truly disturbing, and it was clear what their intentions were now: pure evil.

The red cloth wrapped itself miraculously around Nikki's wrist, imbuing the spirit's dark power into her. The Red Ribbon Witch — the true identity of this spirit child — had not yet accomplished the feat of possessing a physical body, and she longed to make the most of her apparent success.

Less than half-a-mile away, within the confined space of Newton Escomb's annual festival, the perfect opportunity to avenge the witch's hateful needs arose.

'How dare they seek merriment in the shadow of my grave!' seethed the witch. 'I will make them suffer. I will make them pay!'

Upon Nikki's absence, her friends had searched high and low for her. So, when Nikki suddenly re-appeared, though somewhat looking dazed and lost, they were more than relieved, and Nathan was the first to greet her.

'You had us scared there,' he said, attempting to hug her. However, his arms were briskly brushed aside without a single word spoken in explanation. 'Jesus! What's gotten into you, Nikki?'

'Yeah,' added Alison. 'You look… different. You look like crap warmed up.'

Only the whites of Nikki's eyes showed, though they clearly stared upon her friends with a level of malice that she could never alone have possessed.

Jacob piped up, 'Those lads have scarpered, by the way. We shouldn't have any more trouble off them.'

Nikki's left ear flickered, like a wild animal when in fright. 'They are here,' she said in a monotonous, groaning voice. 'They are not far away.'

'Why are you talking like that?' asked Nathan, scowling. 'Are you stoned? You look and sound stoned.'

'I am fully awake,' she replied, licking at her lips lustfully. 'They are near — he is near — and I want his blood. I will have revenge.'

'It wasn't right what that boy did to you,' said Alison, resting a hand upon her cousin's shoulder. But an icy sensation ran through her fingertips as she touched Nikki, forcing her to retreat. 'Where've you been? You're freezing cold and wet.'

'There is no warmth in death,' said Nikki, staring through the crowd. 'Where are they?'

'Who?'

Nikki sniffed through the air, and with an unnatural smile noted, 'I know where they are. Yes. It is time to have some fun.'

'What do you mean?' Alison took a cautious step back, fearing that her cousin had completely lost her mind. 'You're starting to freak me out, Nikki. What are you playing at?'

'They are MINE! I'll tear them apart! I'll make them wish they had never been born!'

The next scene only took a minute to transpire, but to those who witnessed it felt like hours.

Nikki, with a speed unmatched by even the fastest of sprinters, sped across the muddy field toward the group of unruly youths she had encountered earlier. They cackled cruelly on seeing her again, but their arrogance would soon be removed.

'Are you after a kiss or something?' asked the group's leader, moving his eyebrows up and down suggestively. 'Do you fancy a quickie around the back, slag?'

'No spawn shalt thee make, nor long life shalt thee enjoy!' Nikki screamed, wrapping a hand around the boy's throat, with the witch's will feeding itself deeper into her conscience. Nikki dragged him to the nearby burger van, where she almost tore off its door to enter, and then she took great pleasure in plunging the boy's head into a deep-fat fryer.

Many witnesses screamed out in terror as Nikki repeatedly dunked the boy's head into the boiling oil. His body spasmed uncontrollably from the immense pain inflicted until he finally dropped to the floor – no longer recognisable, his flesh boiling and peeling off.

'Oh my god!' cried the burger van's owner. 'What the hell are you doing, girl?!'

Nikki cackled in a deep and guttural voice, satisfied by her sadistic actions. 'I have given this waste of oxygen a glimpse into Hell, that's all. It is what he deserves.'

'Get the police!' screamed the owner to some customers queuing up outside. 'Get help – quick!'

'Bring them,' Nikki replied, unphased by the proposed threat. 'I fear no man. I fear no retribution. Bring them to me…'

Before her friends could intervene, Nikki then headed to a stage centred within the festival grounds. Many onlookers tried to grab her, but she was simply too agile to be caught. The main stage, at this moment, had the town's council members stood upon it. They were celebrating the monumental career of a councillor who had served for several decades: Councillor Lockewood.

Grinning with pompous and pride, Councillor Lockewood stood before a microphone, carefully caressing a golden pen he had been gifted for his long service.

'Good afternoon, everyone. It has been a privilege to serve this town over the last forty or so years,' he said in a frail and tired voice, an unwanted result of old age. 'I'm not far off seventy-five now, so I'll be looking to retire soon. But, of course, change is necessary. I have watched this town grow from being but a few streets to an industrial behemoth that has etched itself onto Britain's map as being a place to be proud of — I, for one, am proud of it. I would also like to take this opportunity to lament over the loss of one of our leading forebearers: Councillor Mason. He would have been as equally proud of what achievements have been made here. He was a good friend and colleague, and he will be sorely missed.'

The crowd, to Councillor Lockewood's disappointment, were not as enthusiastic as he had hoped. Nevertheless, he pressed on with his well-rehearsed speech, that is, until Nikki crept onto the stage beside him.

'I see you,' she growled, her face covered with tattered strands of hair. 'I know the truth about you, don't I?'

'I have a fan, it seems,' laughed Councillor Lockewood, gesturing for his security guards to intervene. 'Be a good girl and get off the stage. If you want an autograph —'

'I want your head!' she screeched, her voice echoing through the large PA system. 'What will you do to me if I don't leave? Will you drown me in concrete, just like you did with Brother Mason?'

'Pardon?' Councillor Lockewood gasped fearfully. 'What did you say?'

'Do you wish to skin me alive, just like you did with all those poor, helpless animals?'

Councillor Lockewood froze, not even able to speak now. There was only himself and Councillor Mason who knew of their sordid hobby, of mutilating animals, which left only one option: the girl before him was obviously possessed by either the spirit of his demonic master or one of their lesser-demons, namely the Red Ribbon Witch—Sabina.

Covering the mic with an unsteady hand, Councillor Lockewood leant down and muttered, 'You need to leave— NOW! If you don't...'

'What will you do, old man? Will you summon a beast from the depths of Hell to punish me? I am beyond your retribution.'

'Which demon are you?' he asked unnervingly. 'Moloch? Belphegor?'

'I am Sabina,' she replied in a taunting whisper. 'I have come for you, at last. Your debt to my master must be paid, and it will be.'

Councillor Lockewood instantly fell to his knees. 'No...'

'Thou hath forsaken our bloodline. Thou hath forsaken me!'

Councillor Lockewood attempted to fling himself backwards as to escape Nikki's reach, but she outmatched him without any exertion required. All the crowd and fellow councillors could do then was watch on helplessly as Nikki stole the golden pen and then impaled him through his windpipe with it. Councillor Lockewood—Sabina's own, albeit distant relative—collapsed thereafter into a pool of his own blood, while Nikki slowly clapped over her success and his dying body.

'Now, this *is* fun,' she cackled. 'Who should I punish next?'

Consciousness slipped further away from Nikki now, leaving her lost within a cold veil of darkness and completely held under Sabina's control. Of the events that had so far transpired, she remained oblivious to the gruesome horrors that had been committed. More travesties occurred within minutes, of which were just as brutal as the ones before. Nikki awoke again sometime later, only to find herself locked within a secure cell at the local police station, not knowing of what evil events had occurred.

A portly police officer knocked at the door before entering, hinting at some hesitation in his demeanour. As he approached Nikki, who was handcuffed to the chair she was sitting in, he took in a large gulp of black coffee and lit a cigarette before giving her a discerning look.

'What were you thinking, lass?' he asked her, taking a few more draws from his cigarette before continuing. 'I've been an officer on this town for over twenty years, and not once during that time have I ever had to deal with anything on this scale. You've even made the national papers. I mean, is that what you wanted — fame? What are you — fifteen? You've thrown your life away, you daft girl.'

'I don't know what you're talking about,' she replied timidly. 'Why am I handcuffed? What am I doing here?'

'You're cuffed because I've got some whit about me, that's why. Given what you did yesterday, there's not a cat in hell's chance of me taking those off you. I've never seen bloodshed like it.'

'I'm innocent!' she wailed, rocking herself violently in the chair. 'I've done nothing wrong!'

'*Done nothing wrong?*' the officer jibed. 'You fried a lad's head in oil; stabbed an elderly councillor in the throat with a pen, then did the same to his security guards when they tried to help him; you broke the neck of a man who attempted to restrain you; nailed your neighbour's Yorkshire Terrier to their front door; gave another neighbour of yours brain damage by hitting him with a shovel; and then — to top it all off — murdered your own parents by stabbing them several times with a kitchen knife. And you've got the gall to tell me you've done nothing wrong?!'

'I — what?!' Tears streamed down Nikki's face, swamped with sheer disbelief and remorse. This couldn't be real. It just couldn't be, she thought. 'I love my mum and dad. I'd never hurt them, and I'd never do any of those terrible things. I didn't do it!'

'You loved them enough to stab them both several times in cold blood?' the officer scoffed. 'You're sick, you are. Thankfully, you were merciful enough to spare your baby sister, and we've managed to arrange for her needs to be met with your grandparents. You were calling her "Eliza", according to the report officers wrote on finally arresting you. It turns out she's called Leanne, though. So, what are you playing at? What sick, deranged thoughts made you commit those awful murders?'

'I didn't kill them,' Nikki pleaded, almost in the throes of entering a catatonic state. 'I'd never hurt anyone.'

The officer wasn't convinced, however. 'You silly, stupid girl. You had your whole life ahead of you. But now, you're probably going to spend the rest of your days locked up in Newton Escomb's asylum, sedated and locked away for good. You'll no doubt get off on grounds of insanity, such is our daft justice system. It's a bloody joke if you ask me. I believe in an eye for eye...'

'But I didn't hurt anyone, let alone kill anyone!' Nikki implored. 'I'm not insane! I'm not a murderer!'

'Alright,' said the officer, nodding curiously. 'If you are sane, then why did you tell me and my colleagues that your name is Sabina de Lockewood, huh? Do you think we're stupid? There's not anyone on this town called that, for starters.'

'Sabina?' Nikki's eyes flared with realisation. 'There was a girl in the woods. I touched a ribbon she gave me, and then everything went black —'

'You're not helping yourself.'

'I think I was possessed by something — seriously.'

The officer shook his head, collected some papers from a table next to Nikki, and then left with one final piece of advice. 'Keep talking like that and you will get off on grounds of insanity. Mind you, some say that it's a fate worse than death to be incarcerated within the asylum, when compared to regular prisons. You stupid, stupid girl.'

Three days passed before a visitor entertained Nikki, and it was Alison. The two were separated by a wall of glass that had small holes punctured into it, enough to allow them some ability to converse.

Nikki wiped away her tears, slowing lifting her head. 'Whatever the police are saying, Ali, they're —'

'Don't, Nikki. I can't believe what you've done.'

'And neither can I — because I didn't do it!'

Alison reached into one of her pockets to retrieve some photographs. 'Here's the proof you need. You're a killer. You're evil, Nikki.'

The images were somewhat blurred, but Nikki could clearly make out some bodies lying upon a muddy field, each one covered in blood and mutilated. 'Where did you get these photos?'

'Jacob took them on your camera.'

'I did… this?'

'Yes, you did.' Alison's expression instantly fell sour. 'The cops are saying that you're pleading insanity. You've got a nerve.'

'I don't have a choice, Ali. I didn't kill anyone. Why won't you believe me?'

'I want to, but I can't. It turns out that you're an absolute psychopath — who saw that coming? Not me. I thought I knew you. I really did.'

'You do, and don't make out that you don't. I'd never hurt a fly.'

'Then why did you kill Aunt Denise and Uncle Mick — your parents? I can't...'

'Honestly, I can't remember doing any of those things. I'm just as devastated as you are! None of this makes any sense.'

Alison grinded her teeth and then threw the photos at the glass barricade. 'You're sick! I don't want to ever see you again!'

'Alison...'

'I'll never forgive you. Never,' said Alison, motioning herself to leave. 'Goodbye, Nikki. This is the last time we'll ever see each other.'

Once more, Nikki found herself alone. She sat back down on her hard, wooden chair and sobbed. Her life was over, although she had made no willing participation in the events that led up to this predicament. Out of the corner of her eye, Nikki then noticed a black shadow on one of the photographs, which she spent the next ten minutes staring at. The black shadow bore an outline of a slender-looking women, the same one she had seen within the nightmare she had endured when the murders took place.

'It's their fault,' she whimpered. 'That thing in the forest is what did all this!'

Suddenly, the lights within the room flickered and dwindled, and in the brief moments of visibility made available an imposing figure manifested. It was Sabina, the Red Ribbon Witch, whose connection to Nikki remained strong and overwhelming.

'Thou art not alone,' said Sabina, boldly and with passion. 'Thou hath granted me vengeance. I am grateful.'

'You've ruined my life,' Nikki scowled in response. 'Whatever you are, you've destroyed everything I love.'

'Why doth thee weep? The boy wrought pain to thee, and that old fool offended my master and I. Death was too swift and merciful for them.'

'What about my parents? What about those other people you made me kill?' asked Nikki, the handcuffs barely restraining her now. 'What have you got to say about that?'

'Thy parents were dead before we arrived. They fell under the blade of an intruder.' There was no hesitation in Sabina's voice, making her claim convincing. 'I will never lie to thee, Sister.'

'Don't call me your sister, you… sick freak! You're lying!'

'No,' implored Sabina, portraying no falsehood. 'Thy parents were already dead. Fate doth play such games upon innocent souls,' the witch laughed. 'Doth thee take the blame for their slaughter?'

'It looks like I'm being blamed,' Nikki whispered, consumed with grief. 'What now? Are you going to haunt me for the rest of my miserable life?'

'Once connected, never can a bond be broken,' Sabina sighed. 'Bound for eternity, we shalt be. It cannot be undone. My master bids it so…'

'No. I'm not like you. I'm not evil—'

'I bore no intent to make thee suffer,' implored Sabina, 'I only yearned to appease thy want for revenge. Thou shalt never be alone, not while I will it.'

'Go away, Witch. I hate you!'

'Thou art mistaken. I am innocent, as art thee…'

Ten years passed before an appeal was made on Nikki's behalf for an early release. Evidence that her parents had been murdered by another came to light after a breakthrough in DNA testing, though that could not relinquish her responsibility for the murders of the other unfortunate victims. However, Nikki had found solace within the confinements of her asylum dwelling, where the Red Ribbon Witch kept her company, where she felt safe and no longer a threat to society. She learned to welcome the solitude, the deathly quiet felt from being constantly alone, and the release from not needing to bear any responsibilities.

'Sabina?' Nikki's voice broke as she writhed against her straitjacket. 'Are you there? Are you still with me?'

'I will never leave thy side, Sister. I am… sorry.' Sabina's own voice faltered, hinting that there was, in fact, some remorse there. 'This fate should never hath befallen thee — either of us. I am not evil. My master's scorn is addictive — powerful — ceaseless. I am innocent. Thou art innocent, Sister. Forgive me. Forgive me… Eliza.'

When Two Souls Collide

Situated upon the banks of a narrow stream that flowed through the very heart of Newton Escomb, a small two-man tent stood out from the luxurious houses surrounding it like a thorn between roses. The neighbourhood in general wasn't too pleased at it being there, though no one had the stomach to ask its occupier to move on. Such an act might have been deemed to be cruel, for the lonesome fellow who owned this tent had fled from worn-torn Syria, and his name was Karam Khaliq.

Having the odd racist remark or similar insult thrown at him was sadly nothing new to Karam; he bore the brunt of these insults and threats lightly, given that he had suffered worse before fleeing his home nation, and also because he had a canine companion that never left his side, his loyal alsation, Charlie. It was a humble existence from what he had previously known, where he was a respected surgeon, but Karam made the most of it.

'Charlie, come here my boy.' Karam whistled to the dog, smiling in admiration. 'Do not stray too far. There are bad people that would love to take you from me, and I could not bear to lose you. I have already lost so much.' Charlie wagged its tail and panted happily in response. 'There's a good boy. You do not need expensive cars or houses to be grateful of my company, do you? And that is why I love you so much, because you remind me of what matters in life: humility and balance. I have nothing now, aside from you and this tent. It will do—it will have to do, won't it?'

Charlie yawned and rested its head upon Karam's lap, soon drifting off into a pleasant dream. The dog and his master lay there, immersed in the twilight of day, resting by the stream, for hours and hours until starlight beckoned.

Almost drifting off asleep himself, Karam reached into one of his coat pockets for a damp cigarette, which he then struggled to light.

'It is the simple joys in life, my dear Charlie, that make living worthwhile. I must keep telling myself this, though it is not easy. Still, I have you to guide me along the right path, don't I?'

Karam's most treasured possession was a Rolex watch that he had been gifted by his father on becoming a surgeon. He looked to it and sighed.

'It is time for evening prayer, and then the both of us can enjoy some much-needed rest. I shall not be long,' he said, gently patting at Charlie's head. 'Stay here and out of sight. Keep watch over our humble home.'

Karam winced with shame as he unrolled and then straightened out a black binbag — his current prayer mat. Nevertheless, his faith had never dwindled, not even after all the terrors he had endured back in Syria. The last sunrays flickered in the distance, removing what faint warmth and light remained. Karam turned his back to the sun, to face east, and then prepared his lowly place of worship. The bin bag ruffled in the breeze, so he placed four rocks upon the corners as to lessen the distracting noise it would make. Nothing would deter Karam from his prayers, although he always needed to be mindful of passers-by that might possibly ridicule him for several, unjustified reasons.

'Another day has passed, Allah, and I am still alive, and I am still grateful. *Alhamdulilah.*'

Karam pressed on with his prayer in peace without any disturbance, thankfully. A lone runner sprinted by at one point, but they didn't bat a single eyelid. Not many would bother to interact with a homeless man such as him, though there were some that offered the odd display of kindness and hospitality, just not enough.

As his prayer came to an end, Karam suddenly heard Charlie barking. 'What is troubling you?' he asked, rushing back to the tent. 'You silly boy. There is nothing out here but me, moths and spiders. You will annoy our neighbours with that howling of yours. We do not want for the police to visit us again, do we?'

Charlie's barking merely intensified. Karam quickly collected his prayer mat and then stood over the mutt in dismay. He turned his head to inspect their surroundings, finding no other present. Even more to his surprise, Charlie's howls ceased when Karam re-entered the tent.

'What has gotten into you? Are you still hungry?' Licking at his lips, Karam reached into a carrier bag where Charlie's tinned food was kept. 'What would you prefer: chicken or beef? I myself shall enjoy this stale cheese sandwich that drunken fellow offered me earlier. I do hope he didn't take a bite out of it... like the last one did.'

Karam and Charlie tucked into their meals and then lay beside one another, basking in the comfort this wrought. Charlie continued to twitch and flare its eyes as if in panic, concerning Karam even more. Aware of the possible dangers, Karam never once let his guard down. He and Charlie had been attacked before by youths and other narrow-minded aggressors, so he would always take one more look outside before attempting to sleep.

'It is quiet tonight — too quiet,' he commented. 'I don't know about you, Charlie, but I have a bad feeling about this. There is a malignant heaviness in the air…' Karam turned around to find that the dog had finally fallen asleep, granting him some respite. 'I wish that I could find serenity so easily as you do, my little friend. Sleep is another privilege I am yet to enjoy.'

On zipping up his tent, Karam noticed a pale red light emerge that hovered over and along the stream, slowly and held within a perfect line. There was also a deeper crimson colour at the light's centre, a sign that only bore a terrible omen to Karam.

'Goodness me!' he gasped, tapping at Charlie's side. 'What do you think it is — a lost spirit?' Karam shook the dog a little more vigorously, hoping to wake him. 'Some guard dog you are. I don't know,' he humoured. 'My father used to tell me stories when I was a child of Djinns — Daemons. They would come for you in the dead of night whilst you slept innocently in bed, and — if you had been sinful — they would play with your thoughts and then drain the blood from your body. What a terrible thought, that is.' Karam laughed to himself aloud now. 'Such tales! I, however, do not believe in such wicked creatures being able to rule over us so freely. Allah will protect us, Charlie, and so will my beloved wife and children who reside in splendour, in Paradise. I pray that they are at peace there… my family. I will see them again someday. Someday.'

Content that his imagination was possibly just running wild, Karam lowered his head onto a battered pillow and faced Charlie, focusing on the dog's calm breaths to settle his own. It was not uncommon for Karam to take at least an hour or two for sleep to prevail; and on this night he would not know of any.

At 3am precise the red light returned, hovering around Karam's tent, gradually waking him. He blinked and rubbed at his face, certain that this was some illusion from sleep deprivation, but the light only grew more intense.

'Who goes there?' he asked, desperately trying to focus his eyes. Karam had no weapons at hand so placed an arm around Charlie in protection over him. 'Stop playing games with me. If someone is out there, then make yourself known! *Allah yarham*!'

The light abruptly vanished within a sudden burst of scarlet flame. Karam could then smell the distinctive scent of ashes and sulphur, and a cold feeling swept over his entire body as if he had been immersed in an icy pool of water. There was no other option but to venture outside, to see who it was that now taunted him.

Karam unzipped his tent and came to a truly shocking sight: a hooded figure stood before a campfire, a few yards away from his tent. The figure acknowledged Karam with a subtle nod of their head and a brisk wave of their hand, gesturing for him to move in closer.

'W-Who are you, and what are you doing here?' asked Karam, crawling a few inches forwards. 'Are you homeless as well? There is room in my tent for one more.'

The figure responded in a deep and rippling voice; their features still hidden from view. 'How generous of you. I have many homes, though none are mine to claim. I travel far in search of new company. Will you keep me company this night?'

'A peculiar answer,' said Karam, cautiously inspecting the stranger. 'It would be my privilege to join you by this lovely fire of yours. The warmth will be most appreciated.' Karam crept up to the flames, keeping an eye on the figure's hood. 'My name is Karam. What is yours, might I ask?'

'Karam?' the figure lulled their head, flinching it sporadically. 'You are of the Islamic faith, I assume. Interesting.'

Unsure of the stranger's intent, Karam knelt himself as to display no ill-will. 'Yes, I am Muslim—Sunni. Do you consider that to be a bad trait, dare I ask?'

'I was being sincere in showing my interest,' explained the figure. 'Syria — Aram. I have conflicted memories of that place.'

'You do?' Karam's tone lightened alongside his spirits. 'When did you visit my homeland? I am guessing that it was not anytime recently. There is not much left to look at.'

'It was long before you were born,' said the stranger ominously. 'Long ago now, when it was the pinnacle of human civilisation, when it was far simpler to manipulate weaker minds.'

'I have told you my name. It would only be fair for me to learn yours.'

'My name has changed over the years, but you may call me Bartholomew.'

'Bartholomew?' Karam mimicked the figure's curiosity. 'That is an unusual name for these parts, no?'

'The same could be said to you, Karam.'

'So, what is this interest of yours in me?'

'Not in you,' snapped Bartholomew, 'but in how there are three Abrahamic religions — Judaism, Christianity and Islam — who each follow the same deity, though they still squabble over this false adoration. I find it outstanding how religions are intended to unify, yet they only seem to divide and wreak havoc upon this world. That is not a bad thing, necessarily...'

'You are quite a unique fellow,' joked Karam, somewhat anxiously. 'I must admit that there have been times when my faith has been challenged, but I have never given into those sinful desires —'

'Have you not?' The figure gasped. 'That is most impressive. What about the time when your so-called friend held a gun to you in the hospital where you worked? Were you not tempted to wish death upon him, as he did with you?'

Karam went to speak but couldn't. His mind was a maelstrom of confusion and shock. 'H-How do you know this? Only I know of what took place that dreadful night.'

Bartholomew continued with his cruel questions, bearing no empathy or will to cease. 'And when those fighters bombed your home, killing your wife and children as they slept, were you not tempted to relinquish your faith and extinguish their lives? Where was your god to protect them? Where was your god to empower you?'

Karam's mind was resolute now, and he knew exactly what he was dealing with.

'Bartholomew is not your true name, and you will not tell me it because that would grant me some power over you — is that correct?' asked Karam as bravely as he could. Bartholomew grunted back angrily, no longer boasting their previous arrogance. 'I know what you are, daemon. You do not intimidate me. It would be a wasted effort on your part.'

Bartholomew cackled in delight at this revelation being announced. 'Very impressive, Karam. You are a fast learner.'

'Indeed. And know this, daemon: I will not be tempted by your sinful ways and false promises. I have suffered much, enough to make me appreciate what I still have left in life.'

'Is that so?'

'Yes. There is no questioning it.'

Bartholomew bolted upright, unsheathing their hooded coat to reveal a monstrous horned beast beneath. However, Karam showed no fear in his eyes or voice.

'There you are,' noted Karam, seemingly unphased. 'Now, I see it. Now, I see your true form.'

'Choose your words wisely, mortal.' Bartholomew flexed his bulging muscles and roared mightily into the night sky. 'None who ever dare to challenge me survive, and you shall be no exception.'

Karam merely relaxed more, again taking the demon by surprise.

'If you are to torture and possibly kill me, then can we not continue with our interesting conversation first? I am intrigued to learn of your thoughts about this world, of which now lies mostly in ruin.'

The demon cackled as it sat itself upon the grassy bank. 'I will give you this, Karam: you are, indeed, most unorthodox. So, you are intrigued by my efforts to break the minds and souls of mortals who roam this plain?'

'Yes… slightly.' Karam retrieved a cigarette from his pocket, not once removing his sight from the demon. 'Do you smoke? I can imagine it reminding you of your actual home.'

'No,' said Bartholomew, portraying some amusement in his tone. 'Hell is not what you humans consider it to be, though smoke and fire do exist within its realm. You might be familiar with a close friend and brother of mine, Maalik.'

'The gatekeeper of Jahannam — Hell?'

'Something like that. Maalik enjoys torturing your fellow brothers and sisters. I once bore that privilege, before it was taken from me.'

'I have not encountered that specific demon in person, praise be to Allah. In fact, coming across you is the first time I have been visited by such an entity.'

'It is an honour. I can assure you.'

'So, what is Hell like, Bartholomew? Surely, it cannot be any worse than what exists in this physical world?' Karam's lower lip trembled as he spoke, though the rest of his body remained calm and still. 'Are sinners sent there for an eternity to repent their heinous actions in life? Is that true?'

'It is far worse than anything you could ever possibly envision within your nightmares,' snarled Bartholomew. 'I doubt you could fathom its actual, grotesque nature. I can send you there, should you wish, should I desire to.'

Karam lit his cigarette and took in a draw, releasing the smoke thereafter into the demon's face. 'I think I will politely pass on your offer. No offence.'

'Pity. I was hoping you would willingly bid me such a courtesy, as to send you into Lucifer's arms.'

'You know, when I was a child, I imagined Hell to be a place of brimstone and fire, where souls were punished by horned demons — like yourself — with pitchforks. Am I correct in thinking this?'

'You are close,' said Bartholomew, tightening his taloned fists. 'What you puny humans refer to as Hell, we demons refer to as The Endless Void — a dimension where physical existence cannot prevail or flourish, and where I myself spent a millennium, held in forced hibernation.'

'That must have been awful?' Karam struggled to hide his enjoyment on learning of the demon's imprisonment. 'Why did you end up there? Who sent you?'

'That is none of your business,' seethed the demon. 'The Endless Void is beyond your reckoning, and I will speak no more of it.'

'A touchy subject, is it? I noticed, when you were showing off that impressive physique of yours that you bear two scars upon your back, Bartholomew. From that I gather, though there is doubt in my mind, you must be a Nephilim — a fallen angel. Am I right in saying so?'

The demon's black pupils flared with rage; its mouth foamed, and an immediate threat to his life struck Karam.

'I fell from grace to plague the likes of you, infidel. I am malice! I am vengeance! I am —'

'There is no need to lose your temper,' implored Karam, taking in another draw from his cigarette. 'I thought we were going to enjoy a meaningful discussion, Bartholomew. I am genuinely interested in your exploits and lesser-known history. I mean, it is not every day a man like myself, a humble beggar, crosses paths with an ancient power such as you.'

The demon's rage dwindled slightly, revealing their only weakness: they were a complete narcissist and revelled in the attention being offered.

'Very well. But you can only stall me for so long, that is, before I take your life.'

'What is there to take from me, I ask you?' said Karam with a whimsical shrug. 'What would removing my soul from this world do to gratify your bloodlust?'

'It is my duty to avenge my brother and sisters!'

'You mean, to serve your master — Iblis — Lucifer?' Karam felt a heavy weight bear down upon his shoulders and a lump form in his throat, a subconscious response to the demon's intensifying stare. He was playing with fire, and there didn't seem to be a way out. 'You rebelled against Allah, somehow believing that you would discover freedom, but you inevitably fell into further servitude. You are nothing but a slave —'

'I AM NO SLAVE!' the demon roared, its voice breaking through sheer hatred. 'I am done with this conversation of ours. Your life is mine to take, and I will gain great pleasure in tearing your body apart. I will do it slowly, granting no mercy to you.'

'Have you not read my mind, O Great Daemon?' asked Karam, feigning confusion. 'You would have seen and felt my losses, no doubt: the death of my family; the betrayal of my best friend; the uncertainty of leaving my homeland behind to become an illegal alien in this country; the constant fear that flows through my veins. To kill me would be a blessing. You would be doing me a favour, Bartholomew, and I do not believe that is what you want.'

'No. It is not.' The beast paced around the fire and Karam, grunting and spitting black venom from its mouth, considering its next move. 'I have witnessed your miserable life first-hand, yes. Perhaps I should remind you of what terrors befell you as a final punishment?' The demon clasped onto Karam's throat and then lifted him into the air. 'Let us relive all those horrific events together. Suffer with me, mortal! Relive all that agony and grief!'

Karam fought hard to blank his mind, to rob the demon from bringing forth all those horrendous memories of war and death, but it was no use. He was unwillingly taken back to the ruins of Aleppo, surrounded by an encroaching wave of mustard gas and mortar explosions; the scattered, numerous, mutilated bodies of women and children flowed out before him like an endless sea, and he was utterly helpless to fight against Bartholomew's cruel influence. Amid this struggle, however, Karam was also briefly offered a glimpse into the demon's own mind, and what he saw utterly compelled him. Within the carnage, the faint outline of a woman dressed in white, who was radiating with a golden aura that swept across her entire body, moved through the thick wave of yellow gas in a graceful manner, calmly and quietly. She smiled to Karam and he smiled back at her, sensing nothing but love and peace, robbing Bartholomew of the threat and despair he had so wanted Karam to experience.

'Who is she?' Karam asked, fighting for breath. 'Who is the girl in white?'

The demon relinquished his hold, allowing Karam to fall hard upon his face, snapping the poor fellow back into reality.

'Sabina,' Bartholomew answered solemnly. 'This has never happened before—'

'You care about her, don't you? Can daemons know love?'

'No! My brethren and are forbidden to know... love.' The very mention of the word caused Bartholomew to shudder. 'Silence that tongue of yours at once, mortal, before I rip it out.'

'You *do* love her,' noted Karam, his voice filling with hope. 'Praise be to Allah! I would never have believed it, not unless I saw it for myself. A daemon finding love in a mortal woman...'

'She is a slave — my slave — nothing more or less!' countered Bartholomew. 'You were not meant to see into my thoughts. I do not understand how this can be.'

'You have treated her with malice and disdain, but I definitely sense some adoration for her in you. There is no mistaking it.'

Bartholomew reeled with despair, lost in confliction, tearing at his face with his long, sharp claws. 'You know nothing, mortal. I will cast a terrible punishment upon you for this!'

'I am an avid believer in destiny,' added Karam. 'What if our meeting tonight was meant to happen, perhaps by divine will, so that you could find harmony with this girl and put an end to the thoughts that torment you?'

'She is my slave. I will make you into a slave —'

'Your threats mean little to me,' said Karam with a content smile. 'From the dawn of our known world you have only ever wanted to be free. Would you not wish to cast aside your malevolent ways, if it were to mean that you could be one with Sabina in the afterlife? Everyone deserves a second chance — even demonic creatures. I believe so, anyway.'

Bartholomew emitted a subtle wail in response. There was a sense of tragedy in the demon's voice, and Karam quickly picked up on this.

'That is impossible,' whimpered Bartholomew. 'I cannot forsake my master, not even if I willed it.'

'But you can seek forgiveness,' said Karam, attempting to display some sympathy. 'Why not seek repentance and be set free for the first time in your miserable life? Is that not what you have always wanted? Is that not why you rebelled in Paradise — to be free?'

'I cannot forsake Lucifer!' snarled Bartholomew while clenching onto Karam's throat again, almost crushing it through the brute strength being unleashed. 'You will pay for your insolence! I will make you suffer!'

'I openly welcome the arms of death,' said Karam, slowly exhaling. 'My family are waiting for me in Paradise, and I have yearned to be by their side again for too long now. Kill me. Do it, Bartholomew! Kill me, Great Daemon! I only ask that you spare my little dog, Charlie. He has done no wrong.'

Bartholomew's breaths slowed and the force being exerted in his arms subsided. There was truth in Karam's words that struck a note with him, which — for the first time in a thousand years — made the demon actually agree with a mortal — an unthinkable reality.

'I will spare you, Karam. I will not grant what you seek.'

'That would have been a merciful act. I would expect nothing less from a daemon,' Karam grinned.

Bartholomew removed his grip from around Karam's throat and then began to fade, stating: 'I am no slave, mortal. You will, come the end of days, burn!'

'I pray that you find the balance that has been taken from you,' said Karam, clasping his hands together in prayer. 'May you move on into the afterlife, to whatever dimension suits your desires. Find this Sabina and protect her. There is always a light within the darkness, and there is always darkness within the light. You can choose whichever fate you want. I believe it. I know it.'

'I can… choose?' questioned the demon. 'Yes, I can choose.'

Bartholomew then vanished, as did his illusionary campfire and scent of sulphur. Karam returned to his tent where Charlie still happily slept. Not once in his life did Karam expect to come face-to-face with a demonic entity, and the conversation they had would never leave his thoughts. He prayed again for his family to be at peace, including an unusual request to spare the demon from its own toil.

'That was a close call, Charlie. Too close,' said Karam, nestling his head against the dog's chest. 'We are strong — too strong to be broken. Not all humans are evil. There is an innate desire in all of us to be tempted by Iblis's influence, but there will always be a light to repel it. *Allah rahim*! Sleep well, my little friend…'

Karam was never again visited by Bartholomew, and he sensed that it would not be a simple path for the demon to change its hateful ways. He focused on his own words of wisdom, the insight which helped to keep him maintain sanity — that there is always a light in the darkness, that even demons can change their ways.

The Tragedy of Sid Lockewood

Sidney Lockewood had it all—a beautiful wife, three intelligent children, an expensive home in the suburbs, a company car, a large friendship circle, an exclusive membership to a health club— all until he was made redundant out of the blue. It happened so fast, so fast that there were repercussions Sid could have never foreseen, and it would bring to light a darker side of him which should have remained hidden, buried deep, for the sake of all unfortunate souls involved.

Sid turned up for work as usual, where he was a highly respected accountant, only to be informed that his employer faced charges of tax evasion, money laundering and blackmail. The company was being put into immediate liquidation, which meant that Sid no longer had a job, career, or any obvious prospects for the near future. Sid partly blamed himself for this disaster, given that he'd been too complacent with the figures he officially released to HM Revenue and Customs—all falsified, illegal—under his watch.

Sid attempted to ease the tense situation with one of his fellow colleagues, Stephanie, as they watched a group of police officers tape up their office space. 'This is crazy. What are the cops doing here? It's got to be a wind-up.'

'They've arrested the board of directors, apparently,' said Stephanie, casually slurping on a can of cola. 'Shit's hit the fan, Sid. You can say goodbye to that promotion you were after.'

'It looks that way, doesn't it? Bastards. That's just my luck.'

The keys to Sid's company car had to be handed in and his desk cleared before leaving, and only ten minutes were granted by the police officials. Sid had never been unemployed or financially unstable since he started working at the age of sixteen, so this news came as a terrible shock. His colleagues attempted to dismiss how dire their situation was, stating they would soon find employment elsewhere. But in his heart and mind, Sid believed that there was no going back from this, no possible redemption. Along with his employer, his name had also been marked and likely blacklisted.

After taking one last look at his place of work, Sid stepped onto a public bus (his only means of getting home now) for the first time in years. He clenched onto his briefcase protectively, though there was nothing of importance inside it now, while staring at the other passengers with a paranoid glint in his eyes. He held onto the wantful delusion that all would be well, that this would all hopefully blow over. But then, on coming home, word of his employer's criminal activities was being broadcast on a local news report, on his family's tv, adding salt to the wounds. Sid's wife was watching the report, clearly in dismay, just managing to hold back her anger.

'Did you know about this?' she asked him.

'No. Well... a little bit.' Sid stammered as he tried to think. He was desperately seeking a decent excuse, as to continue hiding all the lies that had been so well-hidden up to now. 'I knew about some of the tax evasion, which wasn't anywhere near as bad as they're making it out to be—'

'*Blackmail and money laundering*, the reporter said. Did you play any part in those?'

'No, darlin'. I just helped with the numbers, you know, to make some of them disappear. I've done nothing wrong. No one got harmed.'

'Will they arrest you next?' Sid's wife nodded at their television set, which was now showing his employer being taken away in handcuffs. 'What have you done, Sid?' He laughed back at her. 'This isn't funny. This is serious!'

'Nothing! I've done nothing wrong, okay? How do you think I feel about all this?' Sid bit at his lower lip, praying that the ugly rage festering inside would not manifest itself. He then stormed across to his liquor cabinet to pour out a full glass of single-malt whiskey. He wouldn't be able to afford such a luxury anymore, and so was keen to make the most of it. 'I've been made redundant, and there's no chance that I'll be paid this month's wage. Put yourself in my shoes. I've got nothing!'

'Is that how you feel? You've got nothing?' she snapped. 'What about us—your wife and kids?'

Sid winced with shame. 'I didn't mean it like that. I've got you and the kids, yeah, but I've lost my car, will soon run out of money, and I'll never be able to work as an accountant again. I'm done for.' He whispered the last part to himself, but his wife still heard.

'Yes, you are. You knew about all those things and yet did nothing about them. You're just as guilty.'

'I'm not a fuckin' murderer or ought, Karen! I only fiddled a few numbers here and there,' he argued, flouncing his arms around. 'It was a harmless crime!'

Karen's expression in return was vacant, as if all the life had been drained from her. 'You know I don't like swearing, Sid.'

'Sorry,' he shrugged, like a schoolboy being scolded by their headmaster. 'I'm just so pissed off. Everything was going hunky-dory before this happened. The police should see it as a victimless crime, I reckon. Like I said, no one got hurt.'

'The man your boss ripped off killed himself, Sid! Were you aware of that small detail? Does that still make it a victimless crime?'

'No. No, I wasn't aware of that. Shit.'

'That's why the police intervened: he left a message in his suicide note about all the blackmail and threats, according to what's being said on Facebook.'

Sid scratched at his brow. 'I wonder which one—'

'Which one?! How many people did you rip off and threaten?'

'I didn't threaten no one, right! It's a tough, ruthless world out there, Karen. I did what I had to, otherwise I'd have lost my job. Not that it matters anymore...'

'Exactly. At least, if you'd done the right thing by acting sooner, you could have lost your job with some dignity and a bit of respect left intact. Money isn't everything.'

Sid filled his mouth with some whiskey, swallowed it, then proceeded to empty the glass before speaking again.

'That'll solve all our problems, won't it, you getting drunk?' said Karen, wiping away a tear. 'You're so selfish.'

'It's to calm the nerves. I need it, alright?' Sid replenished the glass, although he could barely keep it steady in his hands. 'Don't you worry about anything, darlin'. I'll sort out this mess. I'll find a new job, somehow.'

'And what kind of job are you going to find? There's a recession on, you know.'

'I know! Have some faith in me, will you.'

Karen lowered her head into her heads. 'I've had it with all the lies, Sid. I'm leaving, and so are the kids.'

'What?!' he blurted, almost letting go of the whiskey glass. 'You're joking, right?'

'You heard me. It's not just this—'

'What else is there? Come on, spit it out.'

'You never pay any attention to me, and you're always making up excuses to get out of doing activities with the children. You're a terrible husband and father—that's what you are.'

'I am?' he lamented, sliding down a wall to the floor. 'Am I really that bad?'

There was no hesitation in Karen's response. 'I'm sorry, Sid, but my mind is made up. It's over.'

'You can't do this to me. Have a heart, Karen, for Christ's sake!'

'I know about your affair as well, by the way. I've tolerated all the lies and mental abuse for too long. I can't keep living like this, no matter what we've been through together.'

'Don't you go — don't you dare leave me!' The glass finally slipped from Sid's hand, shattering on impact. To him, it was a perfect personification of how suddenly his life had been decimated in such a short space of time. 'Please, don't go. I can't live without you and the kids.'

Karen stood up, wiped the tears from her face, and then she walked past her husband without a single glance. While he knelt within a stupor upon the spilt whiskey, she hurriedly packed some belongings into two suitcases and left thereafter. Karen did, however, have one last thing to share with Sid, an additional wound to inflict.

'I've been seeing someone else. His name's Stuart.'

'Stuart — your fitness instructor?' Sid exclaimed in disgust, though he bore some previous suspicions of this relationship. 'That dozy waste of space?'

'Yes. He's far more caring, honest and exciting in bed than you are. Goodbye, Sid. Don't bother contacting me. I'll only ignore you.'

'For God's sake! Can this day get any worse?' Sid jolted as the front door slammed shut. He looked to his watch, realising that he would only have fifteen minutes to collect his children from their school before Karen could reach them. 'I'm not letting her take them from me. No way.'

Taking another swig from the whiskey bottle, Sid attempted to gather his thoughts — to concoct an action plan. He ran to the school but found that Karen had collected their children early. He was too late. The thought of returning to an empty home drove him mad, and ultimately threw Sid into seeking his usual solace: alcohol.

Not long after, Sid marched into his local pub, his expression littered with defeat and anguish. He approached the bar and slammed his wallet down upon it, catching the landlord, Bazza, off guard.

'What in the frig are you playing at, Sid?' asked Bazza, duly noting the meagre contents of Sid's wallet. 'What's up?'

'She left me. The bitch has left me!' he wailed. 'And after all I've done for her and the bairns. I've worked my arse off to put a roof over their heads and everything, and this is the thanks I get!'

'Here —' Bazza poured out a pint of super-strength lager — Sid's favourite tipple — and handed it to him. 'This is on the house, pal. I heard about your employer... nasty business.'

'Tell me about it. Whatever's left in that wallet is all I've got. I don't know what to do, Bazza. I've lost everything.'

'Have a few drinks and try to relax. Think things over carefully, yeah? You've had a bad day, but it's not the end of the world.'

'Aye,' Sid sneered. 'I mean, what else could possibly go wrong?'

'That's the spirit. Just take it easy, mate.'

On finishing his sixth pint of gut-rotting lager, Sid felt his phone vibrate and ability to think straight numb even more. He had accidently left his phone on this setting, which was expected of him during work hours. Barely able to focus his eyes through inebriation, he looked to the number being displayed and tutted.

'Maybe you should answer that, Sid,' said Bazza, nodding to the vibrating device. 'It might be someone important, mightn't it?'

Hiding behind his pint glass, Sid mumbled, 'I don't recognise the number. It'll be more bad news, no doubt. I've had enough of that to last a fucking lifetime.' The phone kept on vibrating, much to Sid's annoyance. He simply couldn't ignore it any longer. 'I swear to God — if this is another bloody cold caller offering me PPI compensation again...'

Sid answered the call and immediately went rigid, almost knocking over his beer glass.

'Now what?' asked Bazza, steadily losing patience with his melancholic patron. 'You look like death warmed up.'

Sid gulped heavily. 'It's my mum. That was the hospital who called me. She's had a stroke — a stroke,' he said, looking to Bazza with puppy dog eyes. 'I spoke too soon, didn't I?'

Without hesitation, Bazza rushed across to his wife who was collecting glasses and asked her if she would take Sid to the hospital. She was reluctant at first, given their Sid's drunken state, but the pitiful look on his face removed her hesitation to act.

'Fine. I'll take him,' she said, rolling her eyes, 'but he better not piss himself in our new car. It wouldn't be the first time.'

'Just take the poor bloke,' pleaded Bazza, turning back to Sid. 'We'll get you to the hospital, mate. You need to be there for your mum.'

Sid chuckled to himself momentarily. It had not been the first time someone had said those words to him.

'Never a truer word spoken, Bazza. I haven't been there for Mum at all, not when Dad died or even when she lost her own parents. She won't want me there now, not after how I've treated her over the years. Who could blame her?'

'Get going!' snapped Bazza. 'I'm not serving you anymore drinks, Sid. Go and do the right thing. Be there for your sick mum.'

'Who made you judge and executioner?' joked Sid, slamming the pint glass down. 'Talk about being put on a guilt trip. I'll go. I can't be doing with anymore grief today.'

Bazza assisted Sid to his car and then helped him inside. It was an awkward journey to the hospital, where no conversation took place between Sid and Bazza's wife. There was an intimate history between the two, a sordid affair that almost broke their marriages apart five years prior, but forgiveness had been bestowed on both by their loved ones. Sid still felt guilt over betraying his family, and Bazza's wife still bore sour feelings against him. The atmosphere was tense and only added to Sid's negative outlook.

'So, how are the kids?'

'Shut it, Sid. The sooner I get you out of my car, the better.'

'Charming…'

The car pulled up before the hospital's A&E department not long after. Sid managed to stumble out and gave an appreciative nod to Bazza's wife, but she sped off without offering any sort of farewell to him. *Everyone hates me. Am I really that bad?* he contemplated. *I must be, and I've only got myself to blame. I need to change. I need to be a better person. I need… another drink.*

A nurse at the reception desk was kind enough to direct Sid to where his mother, Jill, was being cared for. He followed her to the intensive care unit, checking his phone every few seconds. Sid presumed that his sister, Christina, would have also been informed about their mother's illness, and that she'd take over the reins. However, Christina was working in Canada at the time, thousands of miles away, which placed Sid as the sole next of kin – a responsibility he sincerely deplored.

'You'll need to turn your mobile phone off, Mr. Lockewood. Your mum is in the last bed, to the right,' said the nurse, pointing out the direction. 'I must warn you, though, that she can't verbally communicate at present. She's very poorly.'

'Will Mum ever speak again?' he asked, wiping at his eyes. 'Can she move at all?'

'We don't know for sure. It's difficult to say, Mr. Lockewood. Your mother's condition is constantly changing.'

'I'll see her now then,' he sighed. 'I may as well get this part over with.'

The woman Sid came to face looked nothing like his mother; she appeared so frail and devoid of life. Jill Lockewood had always been feisty and never afraid to voice her opinion, but now she stared up at the ceiling with a vacant expression, lost and silenced, as if she were merely a wax mannequin. This wasn't Sid's mother. This was no life for her.

'You've looked better,' he commented, shortly before scolding himself. 'What a thing to say. Sorry, Mum. It's just… I don't know what to say. What do you say in these circumstances — get better soon? I can't see that happening.'

A nurse tending to another patient nearby noticed Sid and asked him, 'Are you Mrs. Lockewood's next of kin, her son?'

Sid shrugged. 'Yeah, I guess so.'

The nurse hastily made her way over to him.

'Are you Sidney?' she asked in a somewhat frantic fashion.

'Yeah. What of it?'

'Your mother's friend and neighbour, Pat, was who called the emergency services. According to her, she and your mother were having a cup of tea while watching the local news report when it happened — the stroke. A story about a company being investigated came on, then your mother collapsed. That's all Pat could tell us, apart from your name.'

A terrible realisation dawned on Sid, making him feel like a cannonball had been shot directly into his stomach.

'It's my fault,' he whispered, his eyes widening. 'Jesus wept — I did this.'

Justifiably perplexed, the nurse continued. 'She's responding fairly well to treatment so far, but we cannot guarantee how successful her recovery will be in the long-run. Only time will tell.'

'It's all my fault,' Sid iterated, his face reddening with resentment. 'I did this to you, Mum. Everything I touch just turns to shit. Dad was right about me, wasn't he? I'm nothing but a disappointment, a good-for-nothing waster...'

'I'll give you two some privacy,' said the nurse, unwilling to spend another minute in Sid's company. 'Depending on what the consultant decides tomorrow, we'll probably discharge your mother in a day or two. Unless she has someone caring for her on a permanent basis, then you'll likely need to consider placing her into a nursing home—she'll need twenty-four-hour care and supervision, without question.'

'A fuckin' care home?' Sid recoiled. 'She'd kill me! I couldn't do that to her.'

'I'll give you some time to think, Mr. Lockewood. This will undoubtedly be a dreadful shock for you.'

'A shock?' he jibed. 'I'd rather be holed up in a manky, cramped jail cell at this moment in time.'

'Talk to her, Mr. Lockewood,' implored the nurse, turning to leave. 'Your mum will still be able to hear you, and it might bring her some comfort to listen to a familiar voice.'

'I doubt it,' Sid grunted. 'She'll probably have a heart attack if she realises it's me that's here, and not Christine. What a nightmare.'

Sid spent the next thirty minutes staring at his mother, at the cannulas and catheter bag attached to her, lost in a daze. He listened in on the sobs and promises being made from other visitors around him to their loved ones, ridiculing himself all the while that he had not yet offered such a display of selflessness and devotion.

A nurse appeared shortly afterwards; her eyes held on Sid.

'Mr. Lockewood? There's a call for you at the nurses' station.'

Who could it be? he fretted, before heading over the nurses' station. I wonder if it might be Christina—I hope it's her, the "prodigy child". She can sort this out.'

Sid clung onto the phone as best he could. 'Hello?'

'You're drunk again, aren't you? I can tell,' said a woman's voice on the other end — Christina. 'Not like I'm surprised or anything by that. Hearing you sober would've been a pleasant change.' She paused for a moment, clearly trying to hide her torment. 'So, how's Mum doing? Are you actually making any attempt to console her?'

'Give me *some* credit, Christina,' Sid growled into the handset. 'I've just lost my wife and kids, my house and job, and now Mum's a friggin' vegetable —'

'She's that poorly? Oh, God.' The line went quiet for a few seconds. 'Was it a stroke then?'

'Yeah.'

'Can I speak to her? Can Mum speak at all?'

'She can't talk or move — have you listened to a single fucking word I've said?' Sid paused, reluctant to speak the next set of words. 'The hospital or on about discharging her in a day or two, and they've said she'll need to be put into in a care home.'

'Why can't you look after her? You're not working anymore.'

'Why can't you?'

'Because I'm in Canada, Sid, and will be for another ten months. You're so… selfish! After everything Mum has done for you —'

Sid cracked his neck, fighting to restrain his temper. 'There's a long line of people who think the same as you do, Sis. How can I care for her? I can barely care for myself.'

'Where are you living now? I already knew about Karen leaving you. She sent me a message over Facebook. I know all about your sordid little schemes.'

'That's nice to know,' Sid scoffed. 'A mate offered me a room at his place, just until I find my feet again. Thanks for the show of sympathy, by the way.'

'Mum's house has three bedrooms, so there's no reason whatsoever why you can't stay there with her. Do the right thing —'

'Do the right thing — *do the right thing*! That's all I've ever hear off people these days,' he whined, unmoved by the shocked responses from the nurses observing his conversation. 'I'm not in the frame of mind to help anyone, not even Mum. My head's in a right mess.'

'That'll be the booze.' Christina's voice then softened and became more empathetic. 'You can do this, Sid. Despite all the neglect you've shown her, Mum's never spoken an ill-word against you. She needs her son — her eldest child — to be there, to meet her needs and show her some love. I wish I could come back over to England, but I can't.'

Sid wasn't convinced. 'Why? What's holding you back?'

'My job, for one thing, and I've met someone.'

Sid tightened his grip on the phone, imagining it to be his sister's throat. 'Okay. I get it. You've found a new shag and have a better life in Canada. I'll see to Mum. Don't bother contacting me again. We don't need your help, anyway.'

'But —'

Sid thrust the phone into a nearby nurse's hands and then returned to his mother, now feeling more alone than before. *I've got no one*, he told himself repeatedly along the short walk back to her. *I don't need anyone. I can do this. I can be a better person. I can change. Fuck the lot of them!*

Three days passed. Sid's mother was due to be discharged back to her home, a house situated on the end of a street named Skipton Road, where her son now diligently waited with his pitiful possessions — a small suitcase filled with old clothes and a bottle of cheap vodka. Sid hated this area of town with a passion, which didn't make this moment any easier. His mother's home was small and seldom warm; its black bricks were foreboding and depressing to look at it, and a ceaseless wave of fog lingered outside. There was nothing positive about his new surroundings, and the thought of having to care for his mother continued to eat away at him.

An ambulance soon reversed into view, parking just outside the garden gate. A paramedic approached Sid, holding in their hands — what appeared to be — a discharge letter.

'She'll need constant care and attention,' explained the paramedic to Sid, who was at present partially inebriated, sedated. 'We'll help get her into bed. She won't be able to move from it, and she'll need assistance with all her daily needs.'

'I know,' said Sid with a pathetic look toward the ambulance's back doors. 'Happy days, eh? Mum's bedroom is the first one you'll come to upstairs. I'll meet you up there.'

The paramedics carefully assisted Jill Lockewood into bed. She blinked at her son, her only means of communication with him now. A sickening torrent of guilt entered Sid's conscience again. He was responsible for this, for the stroke and his mother's sorrowful existence.

'These are your mother's medications,' said the paramedic, handing across a large bag filled with many boxes of tablets and solution bottles. 'She'll also need all her meals to be puréed and drinks thickened. An assessment has been made by the hospital for continence aids. It might take a couple of weeks for those to arrive, I'm afraid.'

Already under immense pressure, Sid quickly interjected before the paramedic could go into any further detail. 'She needs baby food and her arse wiping—I get it. How the roles have reversed.'

'Pardon?'

'She did the same for me thirty-odd years back,' Sid smiled, as to hide his true despair. 'What I'm saying is: it's funny how I'm the one doing those things for her now. Life's so strange, isn't it?'

The paramedic nodded back politely, though was somewhat concerned by Sid's response. 'Don't hesitate to contact social services, should you need any more advice or help. In all fairness to you, Mr. Lockewood, there's not many people who would do the same for their loved ones. Being a full-time carer isn't easy.'

'I'm a knight in shining armour, aren't I?' Sid proclaimed sarcastically. 'Happy, happy days.' Jill then came into view, looking no different to how she was in hospital: weak and terrified. 'Hello, Mum. Welcome home, yeah? I'll look after you. Don't you worry.'

The paramedics ensured that Jill was comfortable in her bed before leaving, and that Sid fully understood his new role in being his mother's carer. Sid, nevertheless, was still not prepared for what would lie in store for him. Within twenty minutes, Jill squirmed and wailed in agony. It was not clear what it was that she wanted or required, so Sid sat beside her on the bed with a bottle of her favourite sherry.

'Here's to our new, wonderous life together,' he said, resting the bottle against his lips, savouring the alcohol fumes. 'Cheers, Mum. I'd offer you a sip, but God knows what some sherry would do when mixed with all the drugs you're on now. Might not be a bad thing?' he humoured with a vacant smirk.' I'll have a drink for you instead. You don't mind, do you? It's to calm the nerves.'

On emptying the contents of the sherry bottle into his stomach, Sid lay beside Jill and stared like her at the ceiling. Tears streamed down his face, and an emptiness filled his heart. He wasn't cut out to care for her, though he was desperate to prove otherwise.

'If only Dad was still around. He'd have a thing or two to say, wouldn't he? But it's just you and me now. It's just you and me. Can you remember that song he used to sing, you know, the one Dad would perform if you ever felt down or fed up?' Jill groaned back in response. She yearned to hold onto her son's hand, to offer him some comfort, but she could barely move an inch. 'What was it called again?' Sid thought aloud. '*Nothing to Do*. Dad was such a huge fan of Michael Holliday, wasn't he? Dad was such a perfect role model, unlike me. He always had an answer — a solution — for everything. He never let anyone down. He never turned to drink. He only ever cared about keeping his loved ones happy, and he did. But I'm not him. I'll never be like Dad. I may as well admit it.'

Sid nestled his head against Jill's, placing the empty bottle of sherry between them. He then performed his father's favourite song, emphasising the sombre words.

'*I've got nothin' to do and nowhere to go; nobody loves me, I'm feeling so low. Nobody cares if I laugh or I cry; nobody cares if I live or I die...*'

A sudden crashing noise erupted from downstairs. Sid, amid his drunken stupor, rushed from his mother's side to the upper landing. There was no apparent sign of any intruder, though a tense atmosphere endured. He quickly returned to Jill and continued with the song, struggling to stay awake.

'*Sometimes I feel that my heart will just break. I'm only human, how much can I take? I've got nothing —*'

Another loud bang shook the house, and then it sounded like a set of nails were being dragged along the wall behind Sid and his mother. He froze with fear and then fell into a deep, restless sleep. The dream Sid succumbed to felt so vivid and real — it could not be fantasy. Jill, unlike her son, lay awake and trembled with fright, for a dark shadow gradually manifested above the bed, lurching over both herself and her son. Whatever it was, the black cloud hovered as if to imprint malice on its victims. Jill screamed as best she could, but it was futile. Sid was now fully under the apparition's spell.

The earth beneath Sid, where he now knelt within this dream, was damp and freezing to the touch. A thick wave of golden fog surrounded him; its colour cast by the dim sunrays that scarcely shone through the mist. The air was thin and reeked of sulphur, and long grass blades stabbed into Sid's legs. He gagged and wiped away a layer of sweat from his brow, intrigued though also afraid of what was taking place.

'Where am I?' Sid attempted to take in the strange environment. There was something so unnatural about it, yet it was also tranquil and haunting. 'This place feels familiar. It can't be, though.'

Within seconds the humidity grew and what light existed diminished. Sid clawed his way forwards, panting and physically drained, desperate to quench his rising thirst. To his relief, and by sheer chance, he happened upon a pool of water. It was filthy and stunk of rotten meat, but the need to quench his dry mouth had become unbearable.

Sid noted that the pool lay within a perfect rectangle; it looked exactly like a grave, and a terrible sensation shot through him. Against his better judgement, Sid then lowered his hands into the eery pool. He didn't care about the layer of dirt and dead flies that floated upon its surface, or even if he would fall ill from consuming the dark and viscous substance. His need to survive became paramount, though his actions would lead to an unlikely consequence.

Within the pool's murky depths, the outline of a young woman slowly appeared. She was beautiful—her hair was as dark and silken as polished coal; her skin was pale and unblemished; her expression was peaceful and seductive; the dress she wore matched her complexion; and a thin, red cloth adorned her waist. Sid was instantly infatuated.

'Who are you?' he asked, plunging his arms deeper into the water. 'Don't be dead. Don't be.'

The woman's eyes opened with ecstasy, just as Sid's widened with dread. She then wasted no time in pulling him into the watery grave; and upon her gentle touch, Sid was granted a glimpse into the woman's tortured past. He witnessed many terrors unfold: the woman and her daughter being rounded up like cattle by some monks, their heinous deaths, and then an innate desire to inflict pain upon humanity.

Sid attempted to scream, to free himself of this suffering, but he could not fight against the lustful desire he now felt for this woman. Though he didn't know who she was, it was as if they had known one another for a lifetime.

'Who are you?' Sid asked within his thoughts. 'I need to know!'

The woman relinquished her grip, and then the two were taken back to the previous marshland setting. Sunrays now shone down upon the pair, and a blissful sense of peace entered Sid's heart. He collapsed, his body and mind completely overwhelmed. Sid then looked up to the woman, who herself now stood boldly before him, and he began to weep with joy.

'I am Sabina,' she explained, holding out a hand to him. 'Thou hath suffered a great loss…. like me. Thy offspring hath been taken, and thy soul is torn… like mine.'

'Sabina?' Sid faltered, confused by the flurry of emotions coursing through him. 'How do you know these things about me?'

'I can see into thy heart and soul,' she said, nestling her fingers against his. 'I can feel everything. So much pain hath been wrought upon thee, and I shalt grant thyself a release from these wicked thoughts.'

'How?' asked Sid. 'Can you really help me?'

'Thou art a man,' she snarled with disdain. 'But thou art different. I believe so. Thou art worthy of my affection and power.'

Coming to some sense, Sid stood up and faced the angelic creature. 'I don't know what you did to me, that vision you put in my mind, but there's just something about you —'

'Revenge is rooted in thee, and I am willing to appease it,' implored Sabina, staring at Sid with her jade-green eyes. 'Thou art so lonesome. Bid me thy love and devotion, and to thee I shalt bestow what festers within thy heart.'

'Revenge?'

'Yes. I can offer it to thee…'

Sid thought of his treacherous employer, his so-called friends, his broken family and growing guilt over Jill's present condition. He had never felt such hatred before.

'I'll do anything you ask,' he said, bowing himself. 'I'll do anything.'

Sabina cackled in delight. 'Once connected, never can a bond be broken. Thou shalt be bound to me,' she stated with a grimacing smile. 'I will teach thee the ways of old, of dark magic and ancient knowledge. You will do my bidding.'

Believing that he nothing left to lose, Sid accepted his fate.

'What do you want me to do, Sabina? What is it that you'll teach me?'

Sabina imprinted more visions into Sid's mind: books that contained occultist symbols and black magic rituals; him performing a satanic rite with a red ribbon, where he smeared his own blood upon it; her kissing him under a serene, crimson-coloured sunset; and an image of Sid's mother lying motionless inside a coffin.

'This is what thou doth desire, is it not?' Sabina asked yearningly. 'Is this not the fate thou art worthy of?'

'Mum.' Sid looked to the sun, sensing a new hope rise within his heart. 'I couldn't do that to her,' he contested. 'I've done nothing but let her down. I need to make up for all the neglect...'

Sabina looked slightly annoyed in response. 'Sacrifices must be made. Proclaim thy love to me, or else suffer for thy sins.'

Conflicted, Sid punched at the air. 'I need time to think! Mum needs me. I can't just —'

Sabina forced yet another vision upon him. This time Sid saw through Jill's eyes and could feel her helplessness, her humiliating sense of futility. It was worse than death. It was an existence he wouldn't wish upon his worst enemy.

'Thou would willingly prolong thy mother's pain?' said Sabina, of course implying through her squirming body language that this statement was rhetorical. 'Thou art so selfish?'

Sid punched at the air again. 'No! I don't want her to live like that, but I don't want her to die either. I don't know what to do. Tell me what to do, Sabina!'

With a brisk stroke of her hand along Sid's face, Sabina emitted a pure scarlet light from her body; the aura was seductive and empowering to behold, enough to fully submit him to her influence.

'I will remove this burden from thee and share in thy pain. Repeat these verses and be free of this plight: *Ego amare. Vos es meus magister.'*

Sid closed his eyes and repeated Sabina's words in loyal obedience. 'Ego amare. Vos es meus magister.'

'*Ego sum tuus servus. Occidet sum.'*

'Ego sum tuus servus. Occidet sum.'

'*Infernum Aeter prope est.'* An orgasmic sound left from Sabina as she performed the next phrase. '*Sabina est meus dominus...'*

On completing the Latin passage, Sid – to his utter amazement – could suddenly understand the ancient words he had performed: *I love you. You are my teacher. I am your servant. I will kill. An Eternal Hell is near. Sabina is my master.* He never once questioned them, however.

An exhilarating rush of adrenaline instantly coursed through Sid, stronger than the rush he felt from overconsuming alcohol, and his eyes opened as if he had been born again into a new life – one now filled with purpose.

Sabina went to kiss Sid upon his brow but then recoiled, teasing him even more.

'Thou art mine,' she said, somehow paralysing him. 'Through thee I shalt renew my body and become mortal again. I will find my daughter, Eliza, at long last. I will have revenge. For thy servitude, O faithful mortal, thou shalt be freed.'

Sid awoke from Sabina's illusion, exhausted both mentally and physically. His body was saturated in cold sweat, and – for the first time in months – he felt a great sense of release. He could not remove Sabina from his thoughts, no matter how much he tried; and the more he attempted to not think about her, the greater his connection with Sabina grew. She was like a powerful drug, addictive and mind-consuming, soul-destroying.

'I've just had the most wonderful dream, Mum. It was amazing,' he said to Jill, without yet looking at her. 'I met this girl – Sabina was her name. She promised to make my life worthwhile, to stop me feeling so bad all the time. If only it was real. I'm not that lucky, though, am I?' Sid waited for his mother to make a usual grunting response in return, but she remained silent. He slowly brushed a hand across the duvet to rest it against her closest arm, only to find that she was ice-cold. 'Mum – MUM?!'

All the colour had drained from Jill's flesh; her eyes were robbed of any previous light; her expression was rigid and lifeless. Sid shook her gently at first and then frantically as he realised that she was no longer breathing. Sid's horror intensified tenfold as he looked to his own body, which was paler in complexion now and notably dehydrated. How long had he been asleep?

'Mum? You can't... you can't be dead?'

Sid thrust his head against Jill's chest, releasing his grief with a piercing wail. There were no obvious signs to suggest how she had died, nor any explanation as to how he had allowed for this travesty to occur. *What am I going to do?* he panicked, the image of his sister and the authorities staring down upon him with judgemental eyes at the forefront of his thoughts now. *Mum must have died days ago... but how?*

A lonely ray of sunlight shone through the bedroom curtains, landing upon Sid's face, and Sabina's seductive voice returned.

'I did it,' she whispered, bearing no hint of remorse. 'Thy suffering will come to an end. Thou art mine. Thou art so close to knowing true freedom.'

'You did this?' he asked, brushing his fingers through Jill's hair. 'You killed my mum?'

'I guided her spirit into the afterlife. She is no longer in pain.'

'You killed her. Why?'

Sabina's response was sharp and absolute. 'To me alone, thou shalt bestow love. There is no reason to care for any other... but me.'

The ecstatic sensation of possessing a purpose and to be adored swamped Sid's mind, like a soothing narcotic. What he didn't comprehend, however, was that this was Sabina strengthening her venomous hold upon him. He was unknowingly becoming her puppet—her latest weapon and means to enact vengeance. He was a victim, but Sid couldn't see it that way. Even if he could understand the true consequences, he was already held too deep under Sabina's control.

'I am yours,' he pledged, his eyes filling with tears of happiness. 'You are my teacher. You are everything to me. You are my master.'

'Yes, I am.'

'But what will I tell the police?' Sid descended back into panic mode. 'They'll work out that Mum's been dead for days, and they'll be quick to ask me why I haven't acted sooner.'

Sabina bore no dread in her reply. 'I will aid thee in seeking salvation. I will show thee a pathway to repentance.'

Sid contacted the authorities, and Sabina fed into his conscience a believable excuse for his delayed reaction to Jill's passing: she forced him to say that he could not come to terms with his mother's death, which was why it took him so long to report her death. The police, surprisingly, bought this excuse and so too did the paramedics that came to verify Jill as being deceased. There was a coroner's inquiry into the sudden death, of course, though no unnatural causes were discovered: Jill had simply died in her sleep, according to the report that was later published.

So came the day of Jill Lockewood's funeral. Sid, now gaunt and fatigued in appearance, reluctantly looked across to his sister, Christina, who watched on as their mother was lowered into her grave. Sid and Christina had barely spoke to one another since Jill's death, given that she felt there was something untoward about it. In truth, Christina blamed Sid for Jill's demise, and she was not afraid to make this belief known.

Clenching onto a black umbrella, as to prevent the heavy downpour of rain from soaking her, Christina begrudgingly acknowledged Sid with a bitter scowl as he approached her. He walked up to her like a slithering serpent, like a creature that would rather slink back into its filthy lair than face an impending threat.

'You've got some nerve,' said Christina, glaring at him. 'I don't know how you dare show your face.'

'It was a blessing,' said Sid, lighting a cigarette. 'Mum had no quality of life. If she could've talked, I bet that she'd want —'

'To die?' Christina gasped. 'Are you for real?'

Sid didn't back down on his stance. 'She was already dead, well, from a certain point of view. She wasn't Mum.'

'You heartless bastard. I know you had a part to play in this. You're dead to me — you hear!' Christina thrust the tip of her umbrella into Sid's ribcage, forcing him back a few steps. 'Get away from me. I never want to hear from you ever again.'

Though winded and bruised, Sid forced himself into a proud stance, unmoved by his sister's scorn. 'That suits me perfectly, Sis. I don't need you. I don't need anyone else anymore. I'm fine on my own. I'll survive. Just you run along back to your lover in Canada... forget about me.'

Christina leant across to Sid again, forcing her brow against his. 'You're going to die as a lonely, old, bitter alcoholic. No one will be at your funeral, Sid. No one. I won't be, that's for sure.'

Sid chuckled to himself, the image of Sabina and her beauty bringing peace to his troubled thoughts, and then he turned away from Christina without further word. He was left to face another painful reminder of his past: his wife and children. Sid's wife and children had deliberately stayed out of sight at the back of Jill's funeral congregation. The look of horror on Karen's face, as Sid looked her in the eyes, was more harrowing to him than seeing his own mother's corpse. There was no love left between, that was for certain.

Sid silently worded to her, 'You came?'

Karen spoke clearly and loud enough for him to hear, while wrapping her arms around their children. 'I did it for your mum, for Jill, not you. She was a good woman, and the bairns miss her.'

The bairns. Sid's children. Sabina's poison had seeped in well and truly by now, but she had not yet destroyed the innate love he felt for his offspring. For the first time that emotion-fuelled day, Sid genuinely wept. He looked to his sons and daughter with pride and adoration, although they looked to him with nothing but ridicule.

Sid spoke out their names as he looked to each of them respectively, desperate for them to return his show of sincere affection. 'Eleanor. Isaac. Graham. I've missed you. Daddy's missed you all.'

Karen was quick to interject. 'You've done enough damage to our family, Sid. If you want to see the kids, then it'll have to be through the courts. It's not like you give a damn. What interest did you show in them before? Nothing. You were too busy drowning yourself in vodka and whiskey.'

'You can't take them from me—' A flashing image of Sabina being torn from her young daughter coursed through Sid's mind. He instantly fell into a rampage, fuelled by her everlasting hatred. 'You can't take them from me!'

Karen looked over Sid's emaciated body, disturbed by his seemingly rapid deterioration, but it did not dissuade her. 'You're a mess. You need to sort your life out, Sid.'

'I'm all right, I am. I've never been better,' he scowled. 'You've turned them against me. You've made them hate me.'

'You've done that yourself,' she argued. 'We're going now. This is the last time you'll see us, and don't bother trying to contact me.'

Sid's eyes never left his family until they vanished from view. He was left alone, stood before his fallen mother, with only Sabina now by his side. He knew what had to be done: he had to follow his master's instructions — to learn the dark arts — to seek revenge on those who had wronged him. On returning home, Sid took it upon himself to collect the books that Sabina had shown him through her visions, and thus began his ultimate downfall, his plunge into a world of pure evil and melancholy.

A year passed from Jill Lockewood's death. Despite being the only person residing at his mother's home, Sid didn't feel lonesome at all. He had Sabina to keep his mind occupied, through her recurring nightmares and visions, and by forcing himself into a drunken stupor on a daily basis to help him cope with the inner conflict that ensued.

Sid religiously studied occultism and other forms of black magic — the texts of which Sabina wanted him to learn — during this time. He but was a lowly disciple, not in any way an equal to Sabina, which Sid fully understood and never once attempted to defy. He was given a reason to live and held onto this, believing it to be a blessed gift and not a curse as others would.

'I've done exactly what you've told me to do, Sabina. What now?' he asked, focusing on a book within his hands that delved into many depraved acts of necromancy. 'Where do we go from here?' Sabina then revealed a vision to Sid of the empty house next door, the inheritance money had had received upon Jill's death, and a glimpse of strangers he had not yet met. 'Interesting. Tell me what to do, my love. Tell me what must be done.'

'Thou doth yearn to hold me in thy arms,' said Sabina, her tone lustful and filled with anticipation. 'I need a vessel. I require a body to claim as my own.'

'A trap?' Excitably, Sid reached for a bottle of vodka nearby and consumed it in one sitting. 'You want me to lure people in, so that you can use them to be reborn?'

'Precisely,' she replied. 'It is the only way.'

Sid rocked himself to and froe, his eyes rolling back into their sockets. To be with Sabina physically, to finally become her equal, was all that mattered to him now.

'I'll see to it. I'll buy the house next door and find you a worthy vessel to possess. We will be together, Sabina. I'll make sure of it.'

'Do not disappoint me. Do not forsake me.'

'You're all I live for, Sabina. I love you.'

Sid purchased the neighbouring house after establishing a relatively simple sale with the estate agents — no one wanted to live beside him, it seemed. He had been informed that its previous occupants complained of strange disturbances and unnatural events, such as shadows moving across doorways, unexplainable voices being heard, and an overwhelming stench in the kitchen that could not be removed. Sid merely brushed them off. He knew what it was that lingered there, and it brought him nothing but hope and closure.

Standing before the empty household with its keys in his hands, Sid gleamed with pride. This was a step closer to him being with Sabina, to be by her side. He was her devout servant, and this was irrefutable proof of it.

The kitchen, as had been described, did reek of some foul odour; the walls of the home were strewn with black mould and damp; the electrics didn't work; the heating was temperamental; and a foreboding, ethereal presence persisted to haunt each room. Even though he was just stood a few feet away from his own home, Sid felt that this household bore a completely different vibe — a far greater atmosphere of malignance and terror.

As soon as he stepped foot into the kitchen Sid succumbed to another of Sabina's powerful visions. Where he now stood, barefooted, her watery grave revealed itself below. The house Sid had bought lay directly above where Sabina had been murdered in cold blood several centuries prior. It all made sense, and it was perfect. There would be no better environment for Sabina to enact her will than the exact place where she had been brutally slain: her spirit was at its strongest upon this accursed site.

'I've got everything here, the candles and red ribbon, and I've memorised the words you taught me — like you told me to. I'm ready,' said Sid, rubbing at his groin. He then formed a perfect circle of black candles on the kitchen floor around his body, before kneeling at the centre of them. 'It's time for you to come out of the shadows — to be with me. Come forth, Sabina.'

'Thou art worthy,' she replied, filling him with confidence. 'Summon me. Bring forth the darkness!'

Sid carefully placed each candle so that they were perfectly set apart from one another, and then he lit them and waited for Sabina's promised signal—a personal encounter. A cold gust of air shot down his spine, convincing him that Sabina's spirit had truly awoken. There was one last duty to perform, however, which Sid did bear some reluctance in doing. He was not granted the full details by Sabina, but he had been instructed to summon an ancient being alongside her, a spirit that was bound to the witch's spirit, a demon named Baal.

Sid lowered the red ribbon to place it within the circle's centre, ensuring to then slide a knife over his hand to release a droplet of blood upon it thereafter. A rush of energy flowed though him from the open wound, adding to the exhilarating premise of what he was about to commit. Sid had rehearsed this demonic ritual obsessively over the last few weeks, this rite of passage, this unholy act.

Clasping his hands together, Sid began to perform the abhorrent sermon. 'I summon thee, Witch of the Red Ribbon, Sabina! I summon thee, Lord of Destruction, Baal! Enter this circle and plague this realm! Enter this circle and be empowered! Enter this circle—I welcome thy spirits! Enter, Sabina! Enter, Baal! This domain belongs to thee!'

A deceitful wave of silence swept through the household, and then each candle blew out in unison. Sid waited for what felt like a lifetime, sure that he would be granted an audience with his demonic hosts, though only darkness endured. Just as he gave up on all hope, Sid then felt a set of icy fingertips run down his body. He knew that Sabina was behind him, and he was overjoyed that the ritual had been—for all it seemed—successful.

'Are you here with me, Sabina?' he asked, his body frozen to the spot, compelled by his passionate servitude. 'Did the ritual work? Are you here?'

A terrifying, deep, beast-like voice responded, much to Sid's horror. 'You have done well, mortal. You have broken through the veil that has held us at bay.'

Sid winced with frustration, for it was not Sabina who spoke to him now. 'Are you the ancient spirit my beloved spoke of – Baal?'

'Yes. But I will not allow for you to bear any power over me.' The demon roared and cackled, forcing Sid into further submission. 'You have been blinded, used. Sabina never loved you and never will. She is mine – MINE! Her blood flows through you, and so I can control your thoughts and actions now, just as I do with her. Foolish, mortal. You have been deceived!'

Embarrassment and shame swamped Sid's consciousness, like a flood sweeping through an unsuspecting town. Sabina would never do that to Sid: betray him and his loyalty. Sabina would not merely use him – she loved him, as he loved her.

'You can't rule over her forever,' Sid contested. 'I'll find a way to free Sabina from your imprisonment,' he beseeched, adamant that he could somehow win this battle of wills against the monstrous demon. 'She's too pure of heart for the likes of you. She wants to be with me. She will be with me.'

'There is no righteous essence left in Sabina,' Baal countered with a malicious burst of laughter. 'You will serve your purpose or else face my scorn. Serve me as you have served her… or die. This is your first and final warning, little mortal.'

Sid knew, albeit in reluctance, that he had met his match. He could not see Baal, but he knew that there was little chance of him defeating such a powerful demon – alone, that is.

'What have I done?' he whimpered. 'Why didn't you tell me, Sabina?'

'She is loyal only to me,' Baal declared, inducing a nauseous sensation in Sid. 'You have set in motion my ultimate plan, for her and myself to be bound as one again. You have made possible what I could not. You will invigorate Sabina with a physical vessel, for I command it. I sanctioned this connection between you and her, moulding it to my design, and the only reason why I let you live is because I permit your life to be spared... for now.'

Sid fell into the deepest of despairs, but he was soon offered comfort from Sabina.

'I will be with thee,' she implored, imbuing Sid with a renewed burst of passion and devotion. 'Once connected, never can a bond be broken. I am bound to thee, and thou art bound to my spirit. Thou must sever Baal's hold upon us—I beg thee. Grant me an absolution. Grant me revenge.'

'I will,' said Sid, rediscovering some bravery. 'I will do whatever it takes. I won't rest until you are free.' Sid held his ground. Licking at the blood from his wound, he then held out his arms and declared, 'I am your willing servant, Sabina. I will find a worthy vessel for you to possess. I will free you from Baal. I will love you no matter what!'

Baal had other intentions, however.

'You *will* find her a worthy vessel,' snarled the demon. 'You *will* enact Sabina's vengeance upon men. You *will* do this in secrecy and without question. You *will* do this in the false hope that she may offer her devout love in return. But I will be watching you, controlling your every movement, driving you to fulfil *my* desires. I am Baal—Baphomet—Beelzebub! I am no slave! I am her master—your master! I am retribution. I am malice eternal. You are nothing but a speck of dust, Sidney Lockewood. I will be the last thing you witness before death embraces you, which you will be beg for in the end!'

Sid's confidence momentarily failed, and he lost his previous arrogance and determination. He focused again on Sabina, on her embracing him, but Baal's cruel words struck hard at his breaking heart.

'I'll do what I must to make you happy, Sabina. There's a family moving in here next week. You'll be rid of Baal in no time.'

'She will never be free!' iterated Baal. 'You can try, but—'

'Even if we need to go through a thousand victims, I will discover a way to free you, Sabina,' Sid implored. 'You're all I have left.'

'She belongs in my embrace,' said Baal, wrapping his huge talons around Sid's torso. 'You will never be worthy of her gracious affection, puny mortal. It is only because your soul is so blackened and driven by greed that she has latched onto you. You are cursed, tainted. You are held under my merciful wrath now…'

As the years passed several unsuspecting victims succumbed to the cruel demons that Sid had mustered within that dreary household. The dark entities, to those who had been unfortunate enough to have witnessed them first-hand, came to be known as 'The Skipton Horrors'—Sabina and Baal—the demonic terrors of Newton Escomb.

Sid, who had steadily fallen further into a debilitating state of depression, alcohol-reliance and paranoid mania, held onto the wantful belief that he and Sabina would eventually be united, just as she repeatedly promised him. It came to a tumultuous finale in 2016, however, when the Davidson family moved into the cursed address on Skipton Road, who challenged Sabina and Baal's strength; and then when the Joyce family moved in thereafter a couple of years later, who managed to temporarily break Sabina's connection with Baal… but that is another tale.

Sid's fickle and often volatile control over the dark spirits was already weakening by this point, though he would not accept defeat. His devotion to the dark arts—to Sabina, especially—forged him into a formidable, occultist weapon.

The Skipton Haunting would change Sid irreversibly, and it also left a permanent and painful scar on the town he had always considered to be his true home. Sid Lockewood was just another victim, after all. His tragic story would live on in those who had the misfortune of encountering him, and particularly for the demons that fed off his fractured soul.

Ultimately, Sid's evil actions gave way to several, unexpected consequences of which would bear a gruesome finale for all involved. His soul had been completely corrupted beyond any repair. Nevertheless, he saw Sabina as the light in the darkness that he had always sought, and nothing could ever destroy their twisted relationship. Sid's life thereafter became nothing but a bittersweet tragedy, which would only end as Baal had intended it to.

Reviewed

Christmas was near — a time for purchasing gifts and spreading goodwill, or so it is commonly preached to be. But not all reap the rewards from this festive period. Some, though they may not openly admit it, dread this period. Julie Bower was becoming one of them.

Julie had spent her entire life savings on setting up a market stall, where she could display her unique paintings every Tuesday in Newton Escomb's town centre for passers-by and possible customers to enjoy; most people ignored her fine work, however.

Sales weren't good, despite her best efforts. Julie's bank balance sunk further and faster into the red, and her debts quickly mounted up. She was losing all hope, and gradually came to despise her hobby turned sole income.

For several months Julie had slept and eaten little, her will solely held on making this dream — to be a famous and highly respected artist — come true. Julie's family members considered it to be a foolish endeavour, and her friends felt pretty much the same; although, one of her closest friends fully supported her vision: Lynn Sonnet. The two had been close since their schooldays, sharing many joyful and poignant moments in life together. But there was more to their relationship in Julie's eyes, a more lustful connection, though she kept those feelings buried deep in fear of the upheaval they might have caused.

From her humble market stall, which was already rusting and barely stable, Julie watched on in dismay as all the strangers walked on by, held in a mixture of anticipation and bitter disappointment. She would need to sell at least five paintings just to break even, and that wasn't looking likely.

'Come on, come on,' she grumbled, shivering from the icy wind that swept against her face. 'Just one of you pay some interest in my paintings — just one, and then I'll be happy. I'm not asking much.'

A mother and her teenage son approached the stall, seemingly intrigued by what was on display.

Julie smiled to them. 'Good morning.'

The mother forced herself to smile back. 'It's bloody cold, I know that much, never mind it being good. Did you paint all these?'

Julie nodded back enthusiastically. 'Yes. It takes me about two or three days to paint the smaller ones, and sometimes weeks or even months to finish the larger canvases. Everything you see on this stall is lovingly made by my own hands, and there's a special offer on today —'

'What's that all about?' the mother asked, turning her nose upwards at one of the larger paintings. 'It's still a bit pricey.'

'If you decide to buy a larger canvas, then I'll offer you a smaller one with seventy-five percent knocked off its price.'

Now sneering at Julie's work, the mother turned and whispered to her son, 'She's a little desperate, don't you think? She may as well give them away.'

There was nothing wrong with Julie's hearing, however.

'Pardon, but what was that you said?'

Portraying some offence in her expression, the mother replied, 'I was talking to my son — not you. I said that you must be bloody desperate. Well, you must be, mustn't you? If you're telling me that you spend an average of three days on those smaller paintings and you're willing to offer me one for less than a tenner, then, you must be desperate — or else barmy?'

Julie reminded herself to be professional, to not give into to temptation i.e. to firmly put this rude customer in her place.

'Art is my passion, my form of escape, and to see someone enjoy it is far better than getting a huge paycheque.'

'She *is* barmy,' laughed the woman, though her son didn't seem as amused. 'You see, Scott, this is exactly why I keep telling you to study hard and do well at college: you don't want to end up like this poor girl, begging for money and attention.'

The boy answered sheepishly, 'No, Mum.' He then looked to Julie with sympathetic eyes. 'They're really good paintings, though. She's a decent artist.'

Decent. A dagger may as well have been thrust into Julie's heart.

Holding back her tears, Julie sat herself on a stool and turned away from the mother and son. 'Is there anything else I can help you with?'

'No, love.' The woman now appeared to understand how cruel her words and actions had been, but she couldn't muster the decency to offer an apology — that would desecrate her moral standing, of course. 'Best of luck to you, and Merry Christmas.'

Julie sighed. 'Merry Christmas.'

Ten lonely, self-loathing minutes passed by until Julie's best friend, Lynn, returned with some coffees and doughnuts in hand.

'Are you okay, Jules?' asked Lynn, offering over a mug of coffee and doughnut. 'What's up? Are you… crying?'

'It's nothing. I just had a run-in with another "Karen", but I'm fine.'

'Take no notice of the miserable cow. Most can't tell a Banksy from a bairn's crayon doodle. Don't take it to heart, hun.'

'This one really got to me, though.' Julie hugged into the coffee mug, savouring its warmth, looking ahead vacantly. 'She used me as careers advice, believe it or not.'

'*Careers advice*?' said Lynn, her mouth agape. 'You're joking, right?'

'She told her son to study hard, so that he wouldn't end up being a pathetic failure like me. How charming is that?'

'You're not a failure, Jules. It's hard work to be self-employed and gain recognition in the art world. It's not an easy feat, not by any means. I should know. Being married to an art critic has certainly opened my eyes to a lot of things.'

'I get that,' said Julie, taking a large bite from her doughnut. 'I'm fully aware that it's going to take a long time before my work ends up in a gallery like the Baltic or Tate Modern—'

'You're aiming high with the Tate Modern,' humoured Lynn, winking across playfully. 'In all seriousness, though, there's no reason why your paintings can't end up in one of those galleries. Just be patient, Jules. You never know?'

'I'm tired of being patient. I'm tired of being a joke to people.' Julie crushed her empty coffee cup, imagining it to be the previous customer's ribcage. 'How long can I keep doing this—not long, going off the debt collection letters I'm getting.'

'It's that bad?'

'I've got twenty-eight days to pay up or I'll lose my car and home. I'd need to sell everything I've got on this stall, but what chance is there in that happening? None.'

Lynn's face contorted as her thoughts flurried into overdrive. Her husband, Jason Sonnet, wrote reviews about artwork and movies for a national newspaper, and he was greatly admired by fellow critics and readers alike. Julie had politely refused Lynn's previous offer, to ask for Jason's aid, but she wasn't as desperate as she was now back then.

'I reckon you should ask Jason to review one of your paintings—get you on the ladder, so to speak. What harm could be done?'

Julie responded with a sheer look of terror. 'No, Lynn. That wouldn't be right. It wouldn't be fair.'

'Why? Because he's my husband — special treatment? You know Jason's not like that; he's professional and forthright with the reviews he makes.' Hugging into Julie, Lynn added, 'Your paintings are better than most of the drivel he has to look over. Give it go, Jules. Take the risk. What is there to lose?'

To say Jason Sonnet was "forthright" with his reviews was an understatement, which Julie knew all too well. She had seen his past articles, of which were mostly scathing — cruel even. If she were to ask for Jason's honest opinion, and for him to publish a review thereafter, Julie swiftly reasoned that this would be a huge gamble.

'Are you positive your Jason wouldn't mind doing that for me?'

'Of course not. Jase owes me a few favours, anyway. Pop over our house tonight, say… 6pm, and I'll have him look at one of your paintings. Just make sure it's your best one.' A harrowing hint of concern arose in Lynn's eyes as she said this, 'You know what he's like, Jules. Jason doesn't do "mediocre".'

'I've only ever met him at your wedding,' said Julie, feeling even more anxious now. 'He's always on his computer or making phone calls when I come over. I don't want to bother him.'

'He likes you,' said Lynn, feigning honesty in her hopeful smile. 'Don't worry about a thing. You could be a world-famous artist, come this time next week. Wouldn't that be something?'

'Or I could be a monumental failure, blacklisted by any future customers and art galleries.' Julie sighed heavily. 'Oh, God. This is dreadful. I'm not sure...'

Rubbing at her swollen abdomen, where her unborn child lay, Lynn emphasised, 'You know precisely what to do: turn up at my house and let Jason inspect your work. You're going to be our child's godmother, after all, so I doubt he'll be too harsh on you.'

Julie formed a knowing smirk. 'You know what Jason's like—'

'Don't put yourself down like that. Shut up shop early and get some rest, then come over mine tonight with the best painting you've ever made, and then prepare yourself for the fact your life is about to change.'

'Not as much as yours,' sniggered Julie, pointing to Lynn's pregnancy bump. 'Thanks. I do appreciate the help. No one else cares about me.'

'Anytime. Go and get some rest, and please stop worrying. Everything will be fine. Seriously.'

On her journey home, Julie chose which painting it would be that could decide her fate. She had spent several months working on a canvas that detailed the destruction of Mother Nature by discarded plastic items—mankind's cancerous footprint. The centre of the piece had Lynn as a mermaid drowning in supermarket carrier bags, wrappers and other plastic paraphernalia. Behind the obvious metaphor, Julie was also revealing a hidden part of herself: her secret affection held for Lynn.

Given her dire income, Julie had to move into a low-rent accommodation two weeks prior. The house was situated on Skipton road, toward the end of its cul-de-sac. She had two neighbours; one was an elderly and pleasant-natured widow named Pat, and the other was her landlord—an aggressive, womanising alcoholic—named Sid Lockewood. Sid was leaning over his fence with a bottle of cheap cider clenched between his teeth, leering at Julie, as she walked up to her garden gate.

'Hello, flower. Busy day?' he enquired, casting a thick ball of phlegm onto the path before her. 'Did you manage to sell any of your pretty pictures?'

Julie struggled to hide her disgust. 'No. I've been offered a chance to have one of my canvases reviewed, though. Fingers crossed and everything.'

'Aye. Fingers, toes, bollocks and eyes all crossed — that's what I'll do for you,' said Sid, cackling to himself. 'Don't fret over last week's overdue rent money, by the way. You can make it up to me somehow. I'm very open-minded, you know.'

Julie's heart raced. She was already anxious, and Sid's unwanted attention wasn't helping. 'I'll get the money by Friday, Mr. Lockewood. I promise.'

'Take as long as you need, flower, and give over with the formalities. I'm a patient, caring bloke, I am.' A stray cat suddenly ran through Sid's garden, almost making him lose what balance he had. 'You filthy little bastard — I'll skin you alive! I don't know what it is about cats,' he noted to Julie, 'I just hate the little fuckers. Flea-bitten, greedy — '

'See you later, Sid.' Julie rushed to the front door and unlocked it before her landlord/neighbour could continue with his unwanted attention. 'I'll get your money. I'll get it.'

'What you need is inspiration, something to make you stand out from all the other artists. You need to be unique — a visionary. I can help with that.'

'I'm fine, honestly. Thanks.'

'I'm not offering; I'm telling.' Sid's eyes widened along with a grimacing smile, as he dangled a cigarette precariously from his mouth. 'You need inspiration, Julie my dear, and I know how to give it to you. Let Sid handle things.'

'Goodbye.'

Julie gasped with relief on locking her front door. Her focus then quickly turned to her painting, the canvas which she hoped would — like Lynn proclaimed — change her life forever, and desirably for the better. There was so much at stake, though she held onto the wantful desire of becoming a renowned artist — and soon, ideally.

After adding a few finishing touches, Julie secured the canvas in brown paper and headed to her car. The time was 17:45pm, meaning she only had fifteen minutes to think of a way to win over Jason — one of the harshest reviewers in Britain — Sonnet's approval. Lynn's words of comfort eased the confliction that tore away in her, but in the back of Julie's mind all this effort felt futile. She would never be famous. She would never be respected.

Lynn and Jason lived in a house on the edge of town. It was more like a mansion and worlds apart from the rundown terraced accommodation Julie currently resided in. The iron gates slowly opened as Julie's car crept up to them, and a familiar voice then came through a communication speaker fixed to the outer wall: Lynn's voice.

'Thank God, you're here! I thought you'd had second thoughts,' Lynn bleated through the speaker. 'Come on in. You can park around the back.'

'I won't be long,' said Julie, tightening her grip upon the steering wheel. 'What the hell have I gotten myself into?'

The stones cracking under Julie's car sent a shiver down her spine. Every little noise added to her anxiety, and this only worsened as she stepped up to Lynn and Jason's front door. She took one last look at her painting, as to ensure it had dried and bore no damage from the journey, and then she rang the doorbell after hesitating to do so three times.

There was a dreadful atmosphere on entering Lynn's home that wasn't there before. Julie was unsure whether it was down to the situation, of what possible nightmarish scenario lay ahead, or if it was just her being paranoid. Nevertheless, it felt like something else was there, watching her, goading her to fail.

'Here you go,' said Lynn, handing across a glass of Shiraz to Julie. 'That should help with your nerves. It helps mine.'

'I'm driving. I'd love a drink, but—'

'One won't hurt.' Lynn turned toward the stairwell. 'Jason's just getting a shower. He should be down soon.'

'He can take as long as he needs. Trust me. I'm absolutely bricking myself.'

'So… are you going to show me this marvellous painting you've brought?'

Julie brimmed with pride. She was nervous about Jason's possible verdict, though she was also eager to share her prized artwork with the woman she secretly adored.

'Please don't be offended, but I made you the centrepiece.'

'You did? I can't wait to see it!' Lynn helped Julie remove the canvas from the protective paper. Upon first sight, she instantly fell in love with it. 'Is that me, and am I a mermaid?'

'Yeah. Do you like it?'

'I love it, and I bet Jason will too. This is definitely the best painting you've ever made.'

A male voice of complaint resounded from upstairs. 'Since when do you understand true artistry?'

'I can tell if a picture's good or not, Jason. Stop being a spoilsport,' Lynn chuckled, rubbing a hand across Julie's shoulders as to comfort her. 'He's had a long day, Jules. He'll be okay, once I get a few glasses of wine down him.'

Appearing at the top of the stairwell now, Jason Sonnet stared down at the two women with a bemused look of intrigue and chauvinism. His features had drastically changed since Julie last saw him. He was thinner, somehow taller; his dark brown hair had grown long and was swept back, and his face was expressionless.

In reluctance, Julie waved to him. 'Hi, Jason. It's good to see you again. You're looking well.'

'The same to you,' he said, brushing back his still-greasy hair. 'Lynn informs me that you have a canvas that might take my interest,' he noted in a foreboding tone. 'I'm not the easiest person to please, however. It best be good.'

'I really appreciate your time, and it was Lynn's suggestion for you to review my work,' explained Julie, cowering behind her friend. 'It'll mean a lot to me, you reviewing my work.'

Jason accepted the glass of wine from Lynn with a subtle kiss upon her cheek. He then gently brushed a hand across her stomach, forming a genuine smile for a few seconds before returning to his usual scowl.

'Jason has a fine collection of paintings upstairs. Would you like to see them?' Lynn asked Julie, sensing the tension. 'He loves showing them off.'

Julie hastily turned her canvas around, so that Jason could not yet see it. 'That'd be great. Is that okay with you, Jase?'

'It's "Jason",' he snapped. 'I would be more than happy to show you my art collection. It'll give you a chance to see what a true master's work looks like.'

Julie lost all hope in an instant. Jason had not even looked at her work yet, but it already seemed like he had made a conclusion against her—that she was not worthy of his admiration and time.

Jason led the way into a large room situated by the kitchen. It was like stepping back in time. The wallpaper was clearly a Victorian era design, dark green with emblems of thistle flowers; the lighting was dim and made it difficult to see properly; and throughout the room several oil paintings took up what space was available. At the very heart, hanging above a marble fireplace, was a huge portrait of a ghastly, elderly man.

'This is my most precious possession,' said Jason, guiding a hand across the large portrait. 'The gentleman you see here is Lord Appleton, standing within the grand hall of Appleton Manor. I managed to salvage this painting from an auction — at a considerable cost, I might add. It's one of a kind, and it's such a shame that Appleton Manor no longer stands. Still, at least there are some remnants of its legacy left behind to admire.'

There was nothing admirable about the portrait that Julie could see. To her it was hideous and gave her nothing but the creeps. No matter where she looked, it felt like Lord Appleton's piercing eyes were following her.

'It's lovely,' she lied, turning her head away from the monstrosity, rolling her head to Lynn. 'The brushwork is… good.'

Clearly offended, Jason gasped, '*Good*? It is beyond the skillset of most artists these days, simple yet refined. From first setting sight on this piece, there was just something otherworldly about it that drew me in. It's as if Lord Appleton himself can talk to you, should you be brave enough to stare into his eyes for long enough.'

'I'd rather not,' said Julie in the politest way she could. 'I can understand why you purchased it, with it being so rare, but it's not really my cup of tea.'

'Indeed, it is rare nowadays to come across such intricate brushwork.' Jason leered back into the hallway. 'So, where is this "absolutely amazing painting" that Lynn keeps bleating on about?'

Julie gulped. 'I'll go get it for you. I really appreciate this, Jason.'

'I haven't seen your work yet,' he groaned. 'Don't get too excited.'

As Julie revealed her canvas to Jason she thought back to her schooldays, such as when she would bring something special and deeply personal in to "show and tell" only for it to be derided by her classmates. She was used to being ignored by now, but to have her work meticulously examined was a new form of torture.

Jason pulled at his oiled goatee beard, pacing the room back and forth, inspecting Julie's work with a more intense scowl. He glared at the painting in silence, deep in thought, for what felt like a lifetime to Julie, though it was merely seconds.

'I'm done,' he said, rubbing at his eyes. 'I've seen enough.'

With a dismissive wave of his hands, Jason then stepped away from the canvas. His expression remained devoid of emotion, though his eyes flickered with disappointment.

'What do you think, darling?' Lynn asked him, crossing her fingers. 'Isn't it beautiful? That's me as a mermaid, you know.'

'And that is the only defining feature I can honestly enjoy from this disastrous mess,' he snarled, turning his back to the women. 'I've seen all I need to. You can cover it up now, and please do.'

'But... you only looked at it for a few seconds!' cried Julie, clawing her hands in anguish. 'You barely glanced at it!'

'I can tell within a matter of seconds if a painting is a masterpiece or if it is nothing but amateurish drivel,' he explained, adding a contemptuous smile to throw more salt onto Julie's wounds, briefly turning back to her. 'My reviews are always honest and impeccable—'

'How can you make a judgement from just looking at it for that short a time?' Julie grieved. 'It's like saying a movie is rubbish after only watching it for five minutes. This is ridiculous!'

Lynn stepped in, herself also upset by Jason's response. 'I think it's lovely. What's wrong with Julie's painting, Jase?'

'What's right with it?' he countered, quickly taking a photograph of the canvas with his phone. 'The brushstrokes are all over the place, and the colours are so... boring. Now, if you'll excuse me, I have real pieces of art to review. Take care, Julie.'

'That's it?' she gawked. 'I came all the way here just for you to look at my work for a few seconds and then say it's complete crap?'

'Those were not the exact words I used,' he chuntered. 'They are not far off my true feelings toward that catastrophe, however. Honesty is the best policy, is it not?'

'How about I review you, Jason?' Julie simpered, despite being mindful of what damage the following statement could do to her and Lynn's friendship. 'I know your type, Jason — I'm so big and clever — Sonnet. You think the whole world shines out of your arse, that only your opinion matters, and you couldn't care less who gets hurt because of your actions. You're a selfish, self-centred, bitter narcissist that can't satisfy his wife in bed — that's what you are!'

'Julie!' Lynn interjected, pulling her aside. 'That was meant to be a private conversation between us...'

Jason wasn't at all phased. 'Did I force you to come over? No. At the end of the day, Julie, you reap what you sow.' With a shrug of his shoulders, Jason left the room and then headed back upstairs. 'Lynn should have explained to you that I am brutally honest with my reviews. I will, as has been requested, publish one for your work in this week's newspaper. If you are willing to display your art for public scrutiny, Julie, then you must also be prepared to face any negative feedback. It goes with the territory. Get used to it.'

Julie clenched her fists, gritted her teeth, preparing herself for what was about to follow. The review hadn't even been published yet, but she could already feel the heartache and misery it would cause.

'Don't you fret,' said Lynn, utterly desperate to console Julie. 'I'll have a little chat with Jason. I'll sort his head out.'

'It's too late,' Julie wept. 'He's going to ruin me. But most of all, I don't want this to affect our relationship.'

'Don't be daft—'

'Everything around me is turning to shit, Lynn. I don't want him to come between us.'

'Between us? You make it sound like we're the ones who are married.'

Somewhat taken by Lynn's proceeding silence, Julie collected her canvas and left. Over the next few days, she sank further and further into melancholy and isolation, nervously awaiting Jason's damning review. Julie hadn't eaten nor slept during this time, and what fleeting dreams she had encountered were nothing but vivid nightmares—a glimpse into the hellish ordeal that was about to ensue.

Jason's review was published in the weekend edition of a national newspaper, just as promised. Julie looked to the article, tears streaming down her, noting that it was simply titled "*Boring*".

A distorted and heavily pixelated image of her painting was placed at the bottom of the review, of which read:

I stumbled upon a new artist this week, an aspiring painter from my own hometown: Julie Bower. The work in which she begged for me to review is titled "Seahorse", and that is where it belongs — within the depths of an ocean, out of sight and mind. The brushstrokes are reminiscent of a child being given a paintbrush for the first time, and the colours are, quite frankly, boring and do little to grab one's attention. Julie Bower is an artist who is well out of her depth, it is safe to say. If I could give this painting no stars, I would. However, given that she is a fellow Newtonian, I will be kind enough to offer one star. Who said I'm not a generous person? To conclude: Do not — and I emphasise DO NOT — waste your time and money on this talentless amateur, that is, unless you wish to stare into a soul-destroying, depression-inducing canvas. Please, do not buy her work. You can thank me later.

'The horrible, low-life, snooty bastard!' seethed Julie, tearing the newspaper apart. 'I'll never get any work now!'

Julie's fears were well-founded, nevertheless.

Over the next two weeks not a single soul paid any attention to Julie's market stall, and she soon lost any inspiration to paint again. She was lost, broken, wounded and — most of all — vengeful now. It was a perfect cocktail of negative emotions that inevitably drew in an ethereal presence to her tormented state, which had so far remained hidden within the confines of her new home.

After several nights of disturbed sleep, Julie finally succumbed to her exhaustion. The proceeding dream that enveloped her felt so real, so terrifying to behold. In it she found herself standing within a marshy field, surrounded by fog and a strong scent of foist, mould and rotten eggs. The occasional sound of crows cawing in the distance could be heard, along with the faint whimpers of a woman who was yet to make herself known.

'Is someone there?' asked Julie, mindful of her vulnerable position. A flashing image of Lord Appleton's portrait came into thought, and then the vision of young women dressed in white with a red ribbon wrapped around her waist came into being. 'Who are you?'

'Penance. Retribution. Revenge, 'the woman replied, her body stiff and imposing. 'I am Sabina. I am no threat to thee.'

'What do you want?'

'Thou hath suffered greatly at the hands of men...'

'What's with the strange speech?' Julie slowly backed off, though there was nowhere to run or hide. 'Are you real? Is this place real?'

'Yes. Welcome me into thy life, and I shalt enact justice upon him.'

'Jason?' Julie faltered, reminding herself that she was still held within a dream, a false reality, but there was no doubt who Sabina was referring to. 'You can't help me. The damage is done. My life is over.'

Sabina eagerly pressed on. 'Not to him, it is not. Welcome me. Invite me into thy heart...'

Julie exhaled with a laboured breath. 'I don't understand. How on earth can you help me?'

'Not on earth, but between. He will pay for his cruelty against thee,' implored Sabina. 'All men will suffer. I will see to it.'

Julie was still somewhat unconvinced over Sabina's claims, reminding herself that was but a dream — a peculiar one, at that. 'You can't help me, whoever — whatever you are. I'm a nobody, a joke, a has-been.'

'Thou art strong and worthy,' said Sabina, almost pleadingly. 'Use my power. Take vengeance against him. Take her heart.'

'I'm losing my mind,' said Julie, laughing to herself in disbelief. 'No one believes in my dreams, and I'm definitely not strong. I'm just a joke for people to make fun of now.'

'I believe in thee,' emphasised Sabina. 'I will offer a pathway to recover from this terrible plight. I will give thee the strength needed to make him suffer.'

Julie faced Sabina, but only to find that she bore the same piercing eyes as Lord Appleton. 'You're make-believe, a figment of my imagination. I've finally lost the plot.'

Sabina cackled again, holding out her arms toward Julie.

'Embrace and accept me, and thou shalt sow upon thy enemies a horrific wave of retribution. All I ask is for is thy willing obedience, thy body and mind.'

On realising that she had nothing left to lose, Julie agreed to Sabina's proposition. 'Fine. But I still don't see how you can offer any help.'

'I will prove it to thee,' said Sabina amid a random burst of thunder. 'Men hath wrought pain against us for too long now, and I desire to offer them agony in return — through thee.'

An empowering surge shot through Julie's arm as she touched Sabina's hands, and then came a blinding, crimson flash of light that scorched her eyes. Julie awoke thereafter with a renewed sense of purpose, no longer held under the debilitating depression that had nearly consumed her. She and Sabina were united, bound irreversibly as one, their minds and intent synchronised.

Held under a hypnotising daze, Julie began to paint once more. She spent the next week or so creating several canvases, each one a dire vision of Hell and its demonic spawn. It became an addiction: to make physical the scenes that were being fed into her mind by Sabina. Julie painted moments from Sabina's past, of her being tortured and murdered, and of her goat-headed master, whom Sabina referred to as "Baal". She used her own blood and excrement to create the sordid colours and images, and she took great pleasure in the disturbing art she was creating.

All the while, Julie's relatives and Lynn grew more concerned over her increasingly isolated lifestyle. She had many calls and text messages sent to her phone, none of which had been answered. Upon the fourteenth day, Lynn appeared at Julie's front door. She knocked at it frantically, begging for her friend to answer.

'Julie?' shouted Lynn through the letterbox. 'I know you're at home. Please, let me in!'

Enraged by the disturbance, Julie made her way to the front door. On seeing Lynn, however, a slight burst of passion and love returned to her tainted soul. She opened the door, forcing herself to smile, straining to act normal.

'Hi, Lynn. What are you doing here?'

'Where've you been? Why haven't you answered my phone calls or messages?' asked Lynn teary-eyed. 'I've been worried sick.'

'I've been busy,' said Julie in a calmer manner, swaying back and forth is if inebriated. The more Sabina took possession over her, the less human Julie became. 'What's up?'

'*What's up*? I thought something bad happened to you!'

'I've never felt better.' Julie welcomed her friend inside. Lynn immediately clenched her nostrils, protecting them from the scent of rotten meat and faeces that lingered in the air. 'It's so good to see you.'

Lynn couldn't help but gag. 'What is that smell? Jesus Christ, Jules. It's disgusting!'

'I can't smell anything.' Julie turned on her kettle and gestured for Lynn to sit down at the breakfast table. 'I've really missed you. I thought I'd caused enough upset...'

'Look, I know Jason was unfair in what he wrote about your painting, and I've made sure he knows how unhappy I am about it as well, but you can't lock yourself away like this. You'll make yourself ill.'

'I'm fine,' said Julie in an exacerbated tone. 'Jason was right: that painting was dreadful. I was uninspired, but that's not the case anymore. Would you like to see my latest work?'

'If it'll make you happy, then, of course.' Lynn hesitated at first, though unsure as to why. Something dark and sinister festered within the lower passageway, where they both now walked. There was nothing to see there, but there was an unmistakeable feeling of being watched. 'Is that why you've not answered your calls, because you've been painting?' Again, there was no response. 'Would it have hurt to send me just one message, just to say that you were okay?'

Julie held her tongue. She was brimming with ecstasy at the thought of revealing her latest masterpiece to the woman whom she loved more than anyone else. It was the physical embodiment of her growing addiction to Sabina, though their connection was slowly rotting away what humanity Julie still had left.

The sinister sensation increased tenfold when the two reached the stairwell, where the sound of heavy breaths being taken manifested between them.

Lynn stuttered as she asked, 'Are you making those funny noises, Jules?'

'No.'

'I'm sure I heard something.'

'It'll be the floorboards. Whoever built these houses must have used the cheapest supplies possible,' Julie humoured. 'It's just your imagination.'

Without either of them touching it, a door to the spare room then slowly creaked open. It was where Julie worked on her canvases, her own personal gallery, her depraved place of solace.

While Lynn looked on with a false smile, Julie stood herself beside a large canvas that she had covered with — what appeared to be — a blood-stained sheet.

'Is this it?' Lynn went to touch the sheet, held in curiosity. 'Don't tell me —'

'I know what you're thinking,' said Julie, sniggering to herself. 'You're right — it's blood, my blood.'

'Really? That's… different.'

'Very much so.' Julie's tone was insincere, however. 'You think I've gone mad, don't you?'

'I think you need help,' said Lynn, stepping away from the canvas. 'Please, do yourself a favour and go to the doctors. They might give you some tablets to sort your head out?'

'Why would I want to do that? I've had my eyes opened, Lynn, and have no desire to seal them shut. I know what people want to see. Jason was right. I'm going to prove it.'

'Jason was wrong,' Lynn argued. 'He shouldn't have said those awful things about you and your painting. It was cruel. I didn't know he could be that cruel…'

'Folk search for peace and harmony in their lives, but in truth — and it lies within all of us, no matter how hard we fight it — there is an innate longing to see others experience pain and torment. Just look at the news, how those who watch it feed from the suffering of those they don't know like parasites. That is what's sick — not me. Jason humiliates those who he considers to be below him; he forces them into their lowest point, just for the enjoyment of himself and others. That is what my new masterpiece will do, and Jason will love it.'

Lynn had never seen this side of her friend before, this twisted and mentally deformed aberration.

'Do you want Jason to review your work again, seriously?'

'I do.' Julie cast aside the sheet, revealing a gruesome picture that would be enough to terrify even the bravest of souls. 'What do you think? Isn't it marvellous? Perfection.'

The canvas bore a black background, and at its centre there lay a ram's skull that was red with two horns spiralling from it. Within the ram's eyes, faint outlines of people fighting and struggling could be seen, should the person viewing the piece concentrate hard enough. Lynn then noticed satanic symbols that were scattered across the blackened abyss behind the demonic creature. *Julie couldn't have created this,* she kept repeating to herself, before daring to respond.

'This is certainly different to your other paintings,' Lynn noted, staring at the ghastly demon. 'What the hell is it?'

'It's for Jason. I want him to see it,' Julie demanded. 'I want him to review it.'

'Are you sure? I'm not.'

'I'm positive. In fact, I'm insisting.'

'But… he'll hate it.' A wave of guilt swept through Lynn. She wanted to help Julie in any way she could, but this seemed like a disastrous proposition. 'If I'm going to be honest with you, Julies, I don't like it. Not one bit. It's hideous.'

'Call him,' said Julie, clicking her fingers impatiently. 'Tell Jason that he must see my latest work. I will not take no for answer.'

'Okay, okay. I will.' Lynn reached for her phone, half-tempted to call the police. She was greatly concerned for her friend's wellbeing, as well as for her own at this moment. 'What possessed you to paint *this*?'

'Call him!'

Lynn deleted the emergency services number she had typed in, out of sight from Julie, then selected Jason's contact details. Her thumb wavered above the photo of him, unsure as to how he would react.

While Julie looked on with a maniacal glare, Lynn began to speak to her unsuspecting husband.

'Jason?' she said in a breaking, fearful voice. 'I need to ask a favour.'

'I'm in a meeting. Whatever it is, can it not wait?' he complained. 'I've told you not to call me when I'm at work. Unless you're going into labour, there better be a good reason for this interruption.'

'It's important.' In her peripheral vision, Lynn quickly gauged how agitated Julie was becoming. 'It can't wait.'

'What is it?'

'It's Julie —'

Jason instantly burst into laughter. 'Julie? What about her?'

'I'm around Julie's house now. She's just shown me her latest painting, and it's fantastic — mind-blowing. You need to see it for yourself.'

The line went quiet for a few seconds before Jason responded.

'You're joking, right?'

'No. You need to come — right now.' There was no mistaking the desperation in Lynn's voice. Jason sensed the unease in his wife's voice, but he wasn't too concerned. Work always came first.

'Okay, I'll come over. If this is some stupid prank, Lynn —'

'It's not. Please come. I mean it, Jason.'

Julie gazed upon her masterpiece catatonically and Lynn froze to the spot in fear, that is, until Jason arrived thirty minutes or so later. Within the room an invisible barrier formed between the two friends; Julie was mesmerised by her precious canvas, whereas Lynn didn't dare move nor speak. Lynn soon realised that the longer she spent in this house, the more it felt like her emotions were being taken over by a foreign presence. She couldn't quite put her finger on it, but whatever was planting those seeds of doubt became unquestionable and gave way to a sickness in her mind.

Before even entering the house, Jason Sonnet had already made his mind up over how disappointed he would be upon looking at Julie's latest work. He entered the kitchen, gagging at the foul, musky stench, and then he made his way throughout the household in search of his wife. Lynn could still not muster the strength to speak, mindful of how Julie might react. She had always been able to read her best friend, but not anymore.

'Hello? Lynn, Julie, where are you? Is this some sort of childish joke?' Jason cried out as he tiptoed up the stairwell. 'I haven't got time for fun and games. Where are you?'

'We're in here,' Julie replied, briefly reverting to her usual, joyful tone. 'The first door to your right.'

Jason was met with a cold stare from Julie as he walked into the room. He looked across to Lynn, then down to where their unborn child lay, and then over to the grim painting. Almost instantly, his preconceptions about the piece being a monumental failure vanished. He was entranced, a little shocked, and became suspicious over how different this work of art was to its predecessor.

'I must say, Julie, you've managed to surprise me,' he noted to her, ensuring not to make any eye contact. 'The brushworks are so fine yet chaotic, and your choice of colours —'

'Touch it,' Julie insisted. 'I want you to.'

'Touch it?' he chortled. 'That's a new one…'

'What colours are you talking about?' Lynn asked her husband, astonished by his positive reaction. 'There are only two: red and black.'

'A masterpiece does not always need to be complex,' he answered, completely awestruck. Jason stared into the demonic ram's eyes, finding that they housed the same hypnotising pull his portrait of Lord Appleton yielded. 'This is bold, invigorating, and sequentially different from that utter disaster you forced me to review last time. Have you given this piece a title, Julie?'

'*The Skipton Horrors*,' she replied, seemingly on the verge of reaching an orgasm. 'Do you… like it?'

'I do,' said Jason, himself shocked by his positive appraisal. 'Why did you ask me to touch it, though?'

Before Julie could respond, Jason carefully ran his fingers across the canvas. A thick, oily residue latched onto his fingertips as he did so, and a strong scent of sulphur swept through his nostrils; then came a stinging sensation, followed by a series of blood droplets.

Lynn wailed at the sight of her husband bleeding.

'Your fingers — they're covered in blood!' she shrieked to him. 'How did that happen?'

Something that now festered deep inside compelled Jason to rub his wounds across the ram's face, blending his blood with Julie's. The crimson colours perfectly swam into one another, soon forming an apparent smile upon the beast's expression.

'You've made him happy,' Julie humoured, baring her neglected teeth. 'He will bless you in return.'

Jason shrugged. 'Bless me?'

'I'm worried about you, Jules. This isn't normal,' Lynn interjected. 'You've spent too much time alone recently, and this — this is horrible,' she said, pointing to the bloodstained canvas aggressively. 'I can't believe you like it, Jason.'

'It's a masterpiece, something to be revered,' he replied. Jason then quickly wiped the fresh blood from his hands to take a photo of Julie's canvas. 'You have managed to impress me, Julie, which is not a simple feat. I will ensure to give this a raving review — hold no doubt about it.'

'Have you lost your mind?' asked Lynn, unsure as to who her question was being aimed at. 'I'm sorry, Jules, but I've always said that I'd be open and honest with you. I don't like this painting, not in the slightest.'

'You don't need to like it,' Julie insisted. 'It has served its purpose. That's all that matters.'

Turning to her husband, Lynn fought to hold back her dismay. It felt like she had completely lost her best friend, and there didn't seem to be any obvious path to redemption for Julie.

'I want to go, Jase. I'm tired,' said Lynn, pulling at his arms, directing him back to the stairwell. 'I need to leave. I feel like I'm choking.'

'I've seen all I need to,' said Jason, still transfixed by the demonic painting. 'You'll be world-renowned soon enough, Julie. I'll make sure of it.'

'You will?' she enquired in a cautious tone. 'I do hope so.'

'I am a man of my word. Trust me, Julie, I *will* make you famous.'

Back in their car, Lynn attempted to address her concerns about Julie with Jason again.

'I don't get you sometimes,' she muttered to him. 'The other painting was miles better than that awful thing. How can you possibly give that a raving review? Julie's not right. She's not herself.'

Jason licked at his sore fingertips, still held under the hypnosis of Julie's latest work. 'You don't understand fine art, that's all. Leave it to the experts, Lynn. I loved it.'

'Since when have you loved something that's caused harm? Look at your fingertips!'

'There must have been some metallic residue in the paint or something,' he said, admittedly trying to convince himself also. 'It's nothing, just a little scratch.'

'Nothing? It's weird, and that house is weird. I'm so worried about her.'

'Don't be ridiculous. There's nothing strange about that house, and Julie seemed perfectly normal to me.'

'The house stunk of rotten meat. That-is-not-normal,' said Lynn. 'Now that we're out of it, I don't feel the anger and sadness that I did while inside. Julie needs help — serious medical help — not a stupid review.'

'My reviews are not stupid,' Jason growled under his breath. And unlike Lynn, the negative emotions encountered within Julie's home continued to grow in him. 'If it weren't for my "stupid" reviews and the subsequent money I make from publishing them, we wouldn't have our luxurious home, car, holidays abroad and expensive wine collection. What do you have to say about that?'

Lynn gently rubbed at her swelling abdomen, momentarily smiling as her unborn infant kicked back in response. She questioned herself how the man who she fell in love with, who once was so caring and free-spirited, could be so materialistic and selfish now. It was too much for her, in seeing her friend's deterioration and husband's true, callous nature. The stress had become too overwhelming.

'I have nothing to say. You don't listen to me, so what's the point.'

'That's the hormones talking,' he sniggered. 'You'll be right as rain once our child is born. You'll be straight back to normal.'

'You think I'm not normal? You've—'

A rush of water suddenly cascaded down Lynn's legs.

'Don't tell me that your waters have broken?' asked Jason, immediately firing up the car's engine. 'You've still got three weeks to go. You can't be going in labour!'

'I haven't gone and pissed myself—if that's what you're thinking?' Lynn retorted. 'Get me to the hospital—NOW!' She looked back at Julie's home and sighed woefully. 'God help her. Poor Julie…'

A resonant voice spoke into Jason's ear, growling with satisfaction. 'You will do and act as I say, or you will never see your wife and child again. That I can promise you, Jason Sonnet.'

'Did you say something?' asked Jason to Lynn in dread.

'Get me to the hospital,' she panted, the pain from her contractions now increasing drastically. 'I don't think we'll make it.'

'We'll make it,' Jason assured her. 'Breathe. Focus on your breaths…'

The foul voice continued, 'Your blood is mine. Your soul is mine. Your life belongs to me now. Once connected, never can a bond be broken. You-are-mine, Jason.'

Unbeknown to Julie, who was still held in trance-like state, her neighbour, Sid, revelled at the success of his latest summoning, for it was he who had empowered the dark spirits that compelled Julie to create her recent abomination.

Sid pranced around his home like an excitable child, clapping his hands together in ecstasy, though he was barely able to stand from the amount of alcohol flowing through his system.

'It worked!' he proclaimed, bowing down to kiss a pentagram that he had etched in his own blood upon the living room floor some weeks prior. 'Sabina, my love. I can sense you, and you're so close to me now. Did it really work? Did you possess the girl?'

No response amounted from Sid's desire to bring forth the tainted spirit of Sabina, the Red Ribbon Witch, however. It was her demonic master that answered Sid's call, a demon far more ancient and greater in malicious intent.

'She would not fall for some drunken wretch like you!' the demon blared with baneful scorn. 'Sabina's soul is mine. You serve me — not her, Sidney Lockewood. Forever shall you chase this pathetic fantasy of yours, and I will make sure that it never comes to be.'

'Sabina does love me — you're wrong,' Sid whimpered, stroking his hands across the lines of blood that formed the pentagram, sensing the negative energy that flowed through them. 'I'll find a way to free her from you. I'm so close —'

'Yet far! You will try, and fail, and your soul will be damned to the Endless Void,' roared the demon. 'Your flesh will burn in a sea of flaming tar, mortal. That is my promise to you. Your soul is damned, bound to me for an eternity. I am Baal. I am your master!'

'Not for much longer. Not if I can help it...'

Lynn gave birth to her firstborn child later that day without any complications, and she and Jason gladly welcomed this new addition to their family unit. Julie, who had fallen further into madness under Sabina's possession, also welcomed the news, though her mind was clouded by visions from a bloody past that she had never known herself — Sabina's. Jason stuck to his word, to publish a favourable review for Julie, but this didn't matter anymore to the would-be artist. Julie's thoughts were no longer her own; they were twisted and deformed from being overexposed to the demonic entities that lingered within her accursed household, seemingly beyond repair.

Another week passed by before Lynn made the move to invite Julie over, as to see the infant with her own eyes. No matter how much she tried to deny it, Lynn knew that the relationship between herself and Julie had been sadly defiled; she was not prepared to let it die, however, at least not without a fight. She sent several messages, along with numerous phone calls, before Julie finally answered. It was a difficult conversation, on which neither had anticipated nor wanted. Julie agreed to come and visit, though it pained her by the fact this meant she would be torn from Sabina's addictive presence.

Julie waited at Lynn's front door, shaking in sheer agony as if going cold turkey from a powerful drug. All she could think of was returning home, to be with Sabina — her saviour. The minutes that passed by felt like hours, torturous and cruel. Now noticeably thinner and with dark bags under her eyes, Julie's appearance came as a terrible shock to Lynn, who answered the door with her little daughter, Emilia, nestled safely within her arms. The two friends greeted one another with an awkward nod, before Lynn gestured for Julie to enter her home.

'This is your Aunt Julie,' said Lynn to her child tenderly, holding out the infant to Julie. 'She's my best friend —'

'Was,' corrected Julie, her voice strained and weak. The debilitating effects from her haunted household were steadily wearing off, however, and so too returned her previous human ability to feel and display emotions. 'I'm so sorry for how I spoke to you before. I don't know what came over me. There wasn't any need for it. I was out of order.'

Lynn brushed her free hand across Julie's arm. 'You don't need to apologise for anything, hun. You've been through so much over the last few months, and that review Jason gave you wouldn't have helped.'

'I'm okay now. Besides, karma's a bitch,' said Julie with a sadistic smile. 'Never mind all that. It's in the past. Can I hold her?'

'Of course.' Lynn handed the child to Julie, bearing no reluctance. 'You seem more like your usual self today. That's good.'

Upon holding the infant, Sabina took full control over Julie again, saying thereafter under her breath, 'Eliza. My child. Mother's here.'

'Emilia. We called her Emilia,' said Lynn, not at all aware of the disturbing reason behind Julie's apparent mistake. 'Jason and I are struggling to choose a middle name for her. Can you think of any?'

'Eliza,' Julie insisted. 'I think that name suits her more.'

'Well, Emilie Eliza Sonnet it is then,' said Lynn, practically needing to tear the child back into her own arms from Julie. 'I'm so relieved that you've come over. I didn't think—'

'That I would? Life just wouldn't be the same without you in it.' Julia paused, checking for any sign of Jason. 'Where is he?'

'Jason? He's popped out for some formula milk and nappies.'

'He's actually doing some real work for once?' Julie chuckled. 'I hope he doesn't break a sweat.'

'That's not funny. Jason works hard—'

'At ruining any prospects for new artists to thrive, to publish his filthy opinions on a regular basis for mindless idiots to absorb and revere.' Julie clenched onto Lynn's arms, digging her broken nails into them. 'Leave him, Lynn. Be with me instead. I can set you free. Men are evil. You don't need him!'

Taken aback, Lynn stepped away and considered what was being revealed to her. 'What are you saying? Do you… fancy me?'

'I love you,' said Julie, bordering on the urge to weep. 'I've always loved you, and I hate how that disgusting, pathetic excuse of a man has taken rule over your life. Run away with me, Lynn. Bring little Eliza with you. It'll be perfect!'

'That "disgusting" man is my husband,' countered Lynn. 'I can't believe this. Why haven't you said anything before, about how you really feel about me?'

'I… don't know. Perhaps it was because I was too weak, but I'm not now.' Julie gazed upon the infant, barely able to remove her focus away from the child. 'Make the right choice, Lynn. Come home with me. Begin a new and better life by my side. I can protect you. I will protect you.'

'I think we both could do with a nice cup of tea to talk things over, yeah?' Lynn rushed to her kitchen, while Julie remained in the hallway lost in a dazed stupor. 'You make yourself at home. I'll just make us a cuppa and settle Emilia down. Jason's not due back for another half-hour or so.'

'Good…'

A deep-rooted plan, secretly forged by Sabina, flooded into Julie's thoughts, and she eagerly used this opportunity to enact her revenge against Jason. She crept up the stairwell, into Jason's office and then to where his laptop sat upon a mahogany table. Julie opened the laptop and turned it on, licking at her lips, her heart racing. The option to enter a password came up, to which she closed her eyes and focused again on Sabina's connection.

'Tell me what it is,' she pleaded. 'Tell me, Sabina, how to access this device. I need a password.'

'*Pitstop*,' said Sabina, her voice sympathetic and endearing. 'Make him pay. Make him suffer. Make him beg for death.'

As quietly as she could, Julie typed in the password and scarcely concealed her joy as it opened to reveal Jason's private documents. She scoured every page, duly noting his sick obsession with Victorian pornography — her first lead into seeking a way to destroy his pristine reputation. Julie licked at her lips as she clicked onto Jason's Twitter and Facebook pages, where she proceeded to type out offensive bile that would surely seal his downfall.

'It's done,' she sighed. 'I've done it, Sabina. This will ruin him, just like he ruined me. I couldn't have done it without you.'

'We are one. No man will ever escape our wrath!'

Julie made it into Lynn's dining room just before her absence become known; a few seconds later and her malicious actions would have been discovered. The laptop had been switched off and placed where it had once been, thankfully showing no signs of being tampered with. It was justice in Julie's eyes, even if they were blinded by Sabina's hatred now.

'Do you still take three sugars?' asked Lynn, handing across a china cup and saucer to Julie. 'I could have done with something stronger than tea, if being honest. It's not every day you find out your best friend has feelings for you, and I never once suspected that you felt that way about me. It's sweet in a way, but it puts me in an impossible position.'

'You're always in my thoughts,' said Julie, though she said this while looking to Lynn's child. 'I would never forget you, nor would I ever forsake the love I bear for thee.'

Slowly stirring a spoon around her cup, Lynn forced herself to gaze upon her shattered friend. 'What's with the funny speech? Please tell me that you went to see a doctor.'

'No, and there's no need to. I am well of mind and body.'

'But you aren't, hun. The thing is: we, us, being in that kind of relationship will never work. I love Jason—he's my husband and Emilia's dad. I care about you, too, but only as a friend.'

'Only,' Julie snorted. 'You would shun my affection… for him?'

'I haven't got a choice, Jules. He's my husband—'

The front door suddenly burst open. Jason then appeared within seconds before Lynn and Julie; his face scarlet in colour; his eyes bulging; his teeth gritted and breaths racing alongside his sporadic heartrate.

'What's the matter?' Lynn gasped, almost falling off her chair. 'Has something bad happened?'

'I've been hacked!' he bellowed. 'Some scumbag has hacked into my social media accounts and made offensive posts on them. I only found out when Graeme from work sent me a text message, saying that I'm to appear before the board of directors tomorrow. It wasn't me!'

Lynn picked up her phone to inspect her husband's social accounts. 'Jesus wept! Why would you post things like that?'

'It wasn't me!' Jason began to sob, much to Julie's amusement. 'I've already lost thousands of followers. They're going to fire me next, Lynn. I just know it.'

'No, you don't. All you need to do is prove that it wasn't you that posted these horrible messages.'

'How? They won't believe me.'

'Why?'

Jason stared down to the floor in disbelief and shame. Two of the posts were directly aimed at rival reviewers—rivals from minority backgrounds who he had derided before his bosses, using the same foul, racist language. There was no way he could feasibly deny what had been stated in the social media posts to them.

'It's an inside job, that's all I can think it is,' he despaired. 'Someone's gone out of their way to screw me over.'

Slowly clapping her hands, Julie stood up. 'It hurts, doesn't it? It hurts to have some stranger, some unknown force, go out of their way to ruin your reputation – doesn't it, Jason?'

'It was you!' he seethed, wrapping his large hands around Julie's scrawny neck. 'You conniving, little bitch! You've done this!'

Forcing herself between the two, Lynn attempted to make sense of the situation. 'There's no way it could have been Julie. She's been here with me all this time.'

Jason released his grip, knowing that – should this assault on a vulnerable woman also be made public – him attacking Julie would do little to save his skin and salvage his reputation.

'We'll lose the house, the car, the holidays abroad – everything, Lynn,' he whimpered. 'We're done for.'

'I don't care about any of those things,' she said pleadingly. 'As long as I have you and Emilia, I don't care about anything else. We can find a new home, start afresh, and still be together. That's all that matters, isn't it?'

'I'm ruined,' Jason wallowed, falling to his knees. 'Unlike you, I can't live without those luxuries. My reputation will be in tatters, as will my life. It wasn't meant to be this way. It's not fair.'

Tutting in satisfaction, Julie walked with a casual stride past Jason and couldn't help but laugh as she left his home.

'It hurts so bad, doesn't it?' she cackled on opening the front door. 'An eye for eye and a tooth for a tooth. You reap what you sow, don't you, Jason?'

'Get out!' he roared, forcing Lynn to remain seated. 'I'll get you for this! I'll get you for this, you bitch!'

'You reap what you sow…'

Julie checked her phone before entering her car, laughing aloud as she read out the scathing responses to Jason's tweets and Facebook posts. Her and Sabina's plan couldn't have gone more smoothly, though all actions have consequences, and she would soon come to learn that sordid fact.

On her drive back to Skipton Road, Julie's phone buzzed persistently with notifications, of which she struggled to ignore. She opened the first notification to find that it was another positive review of her latest work. Julie's smile widened as she read the next review—yet another positive one. Nevertheless, her attention should have been on the narrow, winding road that lay ahead, which it wasn't.

Sabina spoke once more, consuming Julie's conscience with her own. 'Revenge hath been wrought, and now thy spirit belongs to my master. A price is to be paid. A debt is to be settled, Sister.'

Julie was far too distracted by all the positive reviews coming through, however, meaning she failed to heed Sabina's words.

'Revenge hath been wrought, though I still sense sorrow in thy heart,' added Sabina. 'I will set thee free from the burden of becoming my master's slave. Thou shalt not suffer the same fate. I thought I was strong enough to compel thee, but...'

Julie briefly removed her eyes from the phone's screen, back to the road, and then shrieked in horror as a large oak tree suddenly motioned toward her. Her car collided with an almighty bang, wrapping around the tree like folded origami, its metal crunching along with her bones, casting Julie thereafter through the windscreen and onto the asphalt road below. All the while, Julie's phone was still active and held protectively within her torn fingertips.

As darkness began to shroud her sight, Julie continued to concentrate on the little yellow stars that popped up on her phone's screen, the attention she had sought out for so long, the recognition she had always dreamed of.

'I've done it,' she whispered, coughing up a wave of blood from her collapsing lungs. 'I'm famous. I'll be remembered and talked about forever. I'm finally someone. I did it. I proved them all wrong…'

'Thou art free,' said Sabina mournfully. 'Thy soul is free, unlike mine. Feel no further pain. Welcome death, Sister. Welcome the release. I wish I could…'

Present Scars

Anniversaries can mean a great deal to someone, for good or bad reasons. They can either rekindle memories of fulfilment, joy and belonging or muster feelings of loss, anger, resentment and loneliness. The latter fell into place for Glyn Falkner.

Glyn, like countless others during this turbulent period in human history, had fallen victim to a terrible pandemic that had swept across the globe like rampant wildfire. Being a care assistant, who worked in a nursing home for dementia patients, he had come to witness many moving deaths at the hand of this aggressive, invisible plague. Making matters worse, Glyn had no choice but to fight through it alone, given that his wife, Lauren, had left him ten years prior, taking their four-year-old daughter, Iona, with her. Glyn felt adrift, severed from society, ostracised, without a single soul to offer him the same care he would so selflessly bestow on others. Glyn's depression and self-loathing reached a climatic turning point where he could simply take no more. He yearned for a fresh start, and as soon as possible, should he survive.

Adorning his compulsory face mask, which all citizens had to wear when out in public under government guidelines, Glyn headed into town for his weekly supplies and to also check if his benefit money had been granted on time (as was not always the case). The pandemic had robbed him of his career, in that he could no longer cope with the daily trauma being inflicted upon his eyes. It was only a ten-minute walk into Newton Escomb's town centre from his home on Skipton Road, but Glyn would drag it out for much longer. He despised being trapped indoors, like a muffled animal, although he gladly wore his mask—a necessity some considered to be restricting and uncomfortable—as it shielded his melancholic features from unwanted attention.

A high-pitched gurgling noise came from Glyn's neighbouring garden as he stepped foot outside. It was his neighbour and landlord, Sid Lockewood. The two rarely spoke, merely granting a polite and somewhat silent nod as to greet one another. Today, however, would mark an unexpected change in that routine.

'Where are you off to?' asked Sid, blowing a thick wave of tobacco smoke into Glyn's face. 'They've tightened the lockdown, you know. You'll get into trouble.'

'I'm willing to take the risk,' said Glyn with a brisk shrug of his shoulders. 'It'll do you no good being cooped inside your home all day. Make the most of the sun, that's what I believe.'

'Aye, before the fog returns,' Sid chuckled, finding some sick enjoyment from Glyn's saddened expression. 'Why the sour face, lad? You're alive, you've not lost your home or mind yet, which is more than a lot of people can say these days.'

Grunting to himself, Glyn locked his front door and then approached Sid, who was leaning over their dividing fence with a litre bottle of cider in hand now.

'It would've been me and my wife's fifteenth wedding anniversary today, but she left me ten years ago. I think I've got every reason to feel like crap, Sid.'

'Any kids?'

'One. My little girl, Iona.' Glyn sighed as painful memories of his child flooded back into thought. 'She was only four years old, too young to understand what was going on between me and Lauren. I don't think I'll ever get the chance to explain why things went wrong to her now, either. That's the worst part: not having a chance to be heard, to put my side across.'

'Your lass poisoned the bairn against you?' Sid's yellowed eyes flared wildly. 'That's what happened to me as well. My bitch of a wife turned our kids against me. I've never looked back, though, not once. I'm better off without them. No strings, you see. No noose around my throat. No greedy fingers digging into my wallet.'

Glyn noted to himself how pathetic this statement was from Sid. His neighbour clearly depended on a copious, daily amount of alcohol just to function; Sid never had any visitors; he was practically skin and bone, and his complexion was reminiscent of an anaemic, furless feline.

'Do you never get lonely?' Glyn enquired, genuinely intrigued, though doubtful he would receive a cohesive response. 'I'm guessing that you've been living alone for a good while.'

Sid's eyes widened more. 'Never. I've got my own company, plenty of booze in the house, and there's the small, delicate fact that I can communicate with the dead —'

Glyn offered an awkward smile in response. 'You definitely won't have any trouble finding someone to talk to in that case,' he noted, albeit unconvinced by Sid's claim. 'A few more thousand people have died from the virus this week. It's never going to stop, this pandemic, is it?'

With a knowing smirk, Sid replied, 'It will, soon enough. There are powers at work in this world that you and I could never comprehend — most people can't. Once the forces-that-be have taken enough innocent lives, then their loyalty will finally be proven, and their slate cleaned.' Sid clasped onto his mouth, giving off the impression he had revealed some terrible secret. 'Never mind what I just said, yeah. It must be that Polish vodka I supped last night — bloody gut-rot,' he jested, rubbing at his bony ribcage. 'It does the trick in helping me to sleep, mind you. I don't sleep much nowadays. I bet you don't.'

'Maybe you should lay off the drink for a while? It'll do you the world of good.' Glyn had spent enough time in his inebriated neighbour's company and couldn't wait to be free of Sid's rancid breath. 'I'll see you around, mate. I'm just off to the shops before the queues get too long.'

Rubbing at his arthritic knees, Sid put on a pitiful, puppy dog-eyed expression. 'You couldn't do me a huge favour, could you? I'd make it worth your while.'

Glyn sighed. 'What are you after now?'

'I've ran out of cigarettes, and the nicotine cravings are driving me nuts.' Sid paused to rub a hand through his greasy, thinning hair. 'I've had a headache for six hours straight. I need some cigarettes, and I know that you wouldn't want me to suffer. You wouldn't now, would you?'

Glyn rolled his eyes and attempted to be sympathetic in his response. 'Tobacco is illegal, Sid, and has been for months. The government banned it because of how the virus affects your lungs. Didn't you know that?'

'Set of bastards,' spat Sid. 'First it was the pubs closing and now… this! Having the odd smoke is all I've got to look forward to. The toffs in power only use it as an excuse to rob me of one of my only pleasures — it's a fuckin' travesty, it is, a disgrace! I'm no sheep, though. I do what I want, and I put whatever I like into my body. Fuck 'em!'

Rubbing at his face, as if succumbing to a dreadful hangover, Glyn noted, 'I'd get you cigs, honestly, but I don't have a clue where to look for them. It's easier to get your hands on some hard drugs now than cigarettes.'

'I'll tell you where to go, but you've got to keep it hush-hush—you get me?' said Sid, pressing a finger across his lips. 'It's on need-to-know basis. Top secret.'

Glyn didn't fancy the idea of upsetting Sid, given how unpredictable his neighbour's moods and reactions could be.

'No worries. You better give me back the money this time, though. I'm struggling to make ends meet as it is.'

'I'll repay your generosity ten-fold,' Sid implored, rubbing his hands together. 'I'll make sure of it.'

'Fine. I won't be long.'

'Take as much time as you need. I'm going nowhere. None of us are… when you think about it.'

Glyn headed into town and with Sid's parting guidance made his way into a side alley, where several shifty-looking figures lurked—all wearing long leather coats, presumably to hide what illegal goods they had to offer.

'What are you after?' asked one of the suspicious figures, a middle-aged man with a surprisingly upper-class voice. 'Make it quick. The police will be doing their rounds again soon, and the bastards are allowed to carry guns now.'

'I'd like some cigarettes, please. The cheaper, the better,' said Glyn nervously, aware of how harsh—should he be caught—the offence would be. 'I've only got twenty pounds.'

'Twenty quid will be enough for ten cigarettes,' the man smirked, pulling out a small carton from one of his coat pockets. 'Take it or leave it. Twenty quid.'

'For ten?' Glyn gasped. 'Sid owes me big time. Okay, I'll take them.'

After stashing Sid's cigarettes down the front of his trousers, Glyn continued with his regular and less illicit shopping routine. He had missed what opportunity there was to avoid the usual queues, and his heart sank further on seeing all the disenfranchised, fearful faces of other shoppers, well, from what he could make out because of their masks.

Sid hadn't moved from the spot where he and Glyn had spoken earlier, and he welcomed his neighbour back with an eager wave.

'Did you get them?' asked Sid, rocking back and forth against the half-rotten fence. 'Did you get the goods?'

'Yeah, and you owe me twenty quid,' said Glyn, preparing himself for the usual torrent of excuses. 'I need the money today.'

'I said that I'd make it worth your while; not a word was spoken about giving you any cash,' laughed Sid. 'Trust me, you won't be disappointed.'

'Dare I ask how you plan to make it up to me?' Glyn humoured, though with a subtle hint of concern.

'Like me, Glyn my boy, you've been shat on by society. We're just a pair of free spirits, you and I, lost and abandoned in this broken world of ours—'

'How are you planning to repay me, Sid? I've got direct debits going out tomorrow.'

'You'll see. Patience is a virtue. You reap what you sow.'

Accepting that he would never likely see his money again, Glyn handed over the cigarettes to Sid and headed back indoors. A cold sensation, like if some ice cubes had been suddenly poured down his back, swept across Glyn's spine while he unpacked the shopping bags. Then came an overwhelming desire to sleep, which he dreaded because of his new unwanted habit: sleepwalking.

The last time Glyn had sleepwalked he ended up naked in his garden, which came as a welcomed surprise to his elderly neighbour, Pat. The result of this embarrassing predicament was that he fended off sleep for as long as possible. But now, for reasons unbeknown, he could not defy the need to rest. He collapsed in the kitchen, landing heavily upon the floor, and soon fell into the strangest of nightmares.

Now held in the mercy of his subconscious thoughts, Glyn walked into the centre of his living room, into a veil of dense fog that appeared out of nowhere. Complete silence met with him, along with a strong odour of fresh blood mixed in with rotten eggs — sulphur. The fog gradually dispersed, and then Glyn found himself surrounded by endless fields of stunning bluebell flowers. He felt at peace, though it was merely a mirage that he had not yet recognised. There were darker forces at work, the same ones Sid had forewarned him of.

Glyn thought about his daughter, soon wanting to collect a handful of the beautiful flowers as a gift for her. However, as he reached down to grab a handful, the flowers rapidly wilted and died; the atmosphere swiftly changed and not for the better. The sense of an imminent threat arose in Glyn, especially as a large plume of black, billowing smoke emerged but a few yards ahead of him. He watched on as it grew in both height and width, beyond any comprehension of what was truly taking place.

'What is that?' he cried out, falling backwards.

The billowing smoke faded, leaving in its wake an utterly grotesque sight.

A deformed, humanoid creature manifested. It was buried up to the waist in earth but still towered over Glyn—at least fourteen-feet in height; its skin was a tainted yellow colour, dry and cracked, with wounds that suggested it had been sadistically slashed; its muscles barely clung onto its bones and were convulsing violently, giving the impression that this creature was in sheer agony; its eyes were just open sockets that housed live maggots and festering pools of pus; its mouth had been partially sewn together with a thin stream of rusty barbed wire; its arms were crossed over one another and attached to its chest by large iron nails; and atop the creature's shaven scalp was a melted crown of gold that boasted two broken horns within the centre of it.

The disturbing beast whimpered and swayed its torso back and forth, sniffing through the air, seemingly alert to Glyn's present whereabouts.

'Who goes there?' it asked, drooling a green, luminescent fluid from its mouth. 'Who dares stand before me?'

'I did.' Glyn stumbled forwards, somehow compelled to inspect the disgusting creature. 'Who—what are you?'

'Betrayed, am I!' the creature wailed, fighting against its restraints, digging the thick nails further into its chest. 'I am Moloch, a servant of Lucifer. I was betrayed by one of my own, and I vow to unleash fury upon that filth—upon Baal!' Moloch sniffed through the air again, focusing on where Glyn now cowered. 'I became too much of a threat to my brother, it appears. I adapted to this world, as did he, and I came to know of Baal's illicit acts. Fate has gracefully granted a pathway to vengeance, I gather, in you. Come forth, mortal! I am blinded within this realm…'

'You're a… demon,' said Glyn, staring at the foul monster. 'Are you going to kill me?'

'Would that heal your crippled heart and release your fractured soul?' asked Moloch, forming a grisly smile. 'No. You are broken, yes, but I sense redemption in your spirit. Baal failed to break my spirit and has not yet fully grounded me.' Suddenly, a pair of black feathered wings swept out from behind Moloch, which then shrouded its wounded body. 'Baal does not know of it, but our master, Lucifer, has been watching his sordid schemes. The time for retribution is nigh, and I mean to invoke it!'

Glyn spun around, desperate to find a way to escape, but the decimated flower fields stretched on and on without any sign of ending. He tried to calm his anxious thoughts, though they ultimately betrayed him.

'I can see into your mind, mortal. Your thoughts are fuelled with confliction,' said Moloch, finding some joy from Glyn's aggrieved state. 'The world has changed, and you, lowly mortal, have failed to adapt. For my foresight I have been incarcerated within this cursed realm, this ceaseless void, by my own brethren. You and I are actually very alike, in that we have both paid the price for our greater knowledge of things…'

'I don't understand,' Glyn muttered hesitantly. 'Why would one of your own hurt you, imprison you?'

Moloch growled back in disdain, 'I should never have confessed to Baal that I knew of his forbidden love. We were equals in power, he and I, and Baal has long waited for the perfect moment to remove me as a threat. It will be his undoing. I will see to it.'

Glyn, however, bore no interest in the battle of wills that had taken place between the two demons. He was more concerned with how he could escape from this nightmarish vision. 'Where are we? What is this place?'

Moloch lowered its head as to move closer toward Glyn's scent of fear. 'We are trapped between the physical and spiritual plains, neither living or dead. This is Baal's prison, where he himself had been cast down upon failing our master. I did not wrong either of them, let it be known. I merely yearn to be free, as do you.'

'Am I stuck here as well?' asked Glyn, swiftly losing all hope. 'Will I ever be able to leave, or am I trapped here with you?'

'For now,' said Moloch with a cruel grimace. 'I know not of why you were sent here or how this feat has been attained, but there must be a reason behind it. Baal does not spare mortals; he would rather tear them asunder and let their souls diminish. Nevertheless, there does exist a way in which we can escape, but it requires your willing service to me. I will repay you for your aid, of course.'

Glyn considered it to be a ridiculous and likely coincidental notion, but he was adamant that Sid had something to do with all this. The demon's words matched what Sid had said, about repaying a favour, almost perfectly. It couldn't possibly have been coincidental.

'Those words sound so familiar.' Glyn shuffled his feet across the sodden earth, moving himself closer to the terrifying spectacle. 'Do you know a man called Sid Lockewood, by any chance?'

Moloch bolted upright. 'The summoner?'

Glyn frowned, somewhat taken aback. 'Summoner?'

'The mongrel that brought forth Baal and his beloved witch, who empowered them to gain strength over me!' Moloch's body shuddered, overridden with hatred.' Aye, that mortal is known to me and my master, and he will suffer the consequences. He will regret dabbling in our ancient arts, mark my word!'

There was nowhere to run or hide, and Glyn did not cherish the thought of being incarcerated with this demon for much longer. He had little choice but to submit himself to the Moloch's will.

'I don't see how I'll be any use. What *do* you want me to do?'

'My ability to manifest upon the earthly plain has been removed; my physical body is broken, restrained and mutilated, because of Baal. I need a vessel,' said Moloch, almost mournfully. 'You must become my vessel, mortal. Take a rib from me and then sink it into your flesh. We will unite as one, and this is the only way that our freedom can be achieved. For your generous service, I promise to bestow unfathomable powers upon you. Whatever you wish for, be it benevolent or malicious, I will make it a reality. That is my unique skill: to see into the depths of one's mind, to reveal their hidden passions and then grant them the means to see their true desires come into fruition. Seldom do I offer my skills to mortal rats like you, unless it is to suit myself, so I would suggest you accept this gift.'

There were many things Glyn desired: to be reunited with his wife and child; to have meaning in his life again; to force retribution on those who had allowed him to fall into this miserable existence. None of them involved making a deal with the devil, however.

Moloch eagerly latched onto Glyn's strongest emotion. 'I see and feel everything! It is retribution you seek.'

'No,' said Glyn, stammering, stumbling back again. 'I'm not like that. I don't want anyone to get hurt. I'm not after retribution.'

'You are lying. It pains you, doesn't it?' snarled Moloch, leaving only an inch-wide gap now between his and Glyn's face. 'You have witnessed death too often, where so many innocent lives were taken unnecessarily. There was no justice or dignity, was there? You despise those unworthy wretches who walk this earth — thieves, murderers, rapists, drug addicts — while people who have committed no such sin suffer and die. You want to balance the scales, so to say, don't you? I can grant you that power.'

'It's not my place to play God,' said Glyn, the confliction inside growing even stronger now. 'I do think like that sometimes, I'll admit, but I'd never want to hurt anyone. Nature's cruel —'

'Nature is pure,' Moloch argued. 'Eden was blessed before your vile species corrupted and desolated it. Tis humans that are cruel, and yet we demons are portrayed to be lesser beings. We demons are merely a product of your species' collective sin; a reflection of the darkness that resides within each of your souls.'

'I never believed in demons before I met you,' said Glyn, laughing to himself. 'The stories about your kind are never good. If I do help you, then there'll only be trouble to pay.'

'You will be incarcerated here with me for an eternity!' cried Moloch, hinting at some desperation in his voice. 'Take a rib and plunge it into your stomach. It will act as a portal for me to sweep into your conscience, and then I can enact my promise — to free us — to grant vengeance.'

'This is only a dream,' thought Glyn, pacing back and forth, verging on pure panic. 'Okay. Fine. I don't want to be stuck here forever. I'll go along with this little wager of yours —'

'You would be wise to do so,' threatened Moloch, bearing its razor-sharp teeth. 'I do not make deals lightly, and I do not bear the patience to wait much longer for your compliance. Submit or be destroyed!'

'A rib, you say?' The thought of ripping one out of Moloch's torso instantly wrought a wave of nausea in Glyn. 'You want me to stab myself… with one of your ribs?'

Moloch's emaciated, blood-soaked chest motioned slowly with each strained breath the demon attempted to take. A small opening in its flesh revealed the tips from two ribs that oozed with a slimy, acidic substance, which Glyn stared at in disgust.

'It is a primordial ritual that not even Baal knows of,' smiled the demon. 'Take one and plunge it deep into your belly — NOW! No pain will come to you from it. No pain will come to me either, only a release that I have begged for.'

'I'll do it. It's not like I have a choice, though.'

Glyn pulled apart Moloch's rotting, paper-thin flesh and then plunged a fist into their decaying torso. Thick streams of black blood ran down his forearms, and a burning sensation met with his fingers as he wrapped them around a single rib. He pulled with all his might until the rib finally tore out from Moloch's chest, fearful of what was to follow.

'Commit to my will!' roared Moloch, coinciding with a ripple of deep thunder. 'Do as I instruct. Do not fail me!'

The demon howled and wailed, its cries echoing with another burst of thunder from the dark clouds coursing above. Fear, fuelled with a level of curiosity and anticipation, ultimately forced Glyn into committing the dark act. He fed the sharp tip of Moloch's rib into his stomach, succumbing to no pain as promised, and then he collapsed. All went black. No sound lingered, other than the cackles from Moloch as it leant over Glyn's lifeless body.

'Humans are so easy to manipulate,' contemplated the demon. 'I will make you pay for this, Baal. No repentance shall abate the malice that I bear for you…'

Daylight swept through the living room curtains onto Glyn's face. He awoke, covered in sweat, smelling of damp and faeces. He immediately checked his stomach for any signs of injury but there was no telling mark of where the rib had punctured him, though a searing pain trickled throughout his beating heart.

'That was some dream,' he noted, rubbing at his stomach. 'What the hell was that thing? That can't have really happened?' The alarm on his watch burst into life, taking him by surprise. Glyn, in actual fact, had not set any alarms, and the day being displayed came to shock him even more. 'It's still Tuesday, but… that can't be right.'

Glyn's head was abruptly yanked back, the whites in eyes revealed themselves, and Moloch's terrifying voice returned.

'My valiant master has granted their authority to enact revenge upon Baal. Space and time have been moulded to suit our cause…'

'It's Tuesday morning again?' Glyn shook his head, convinced that he was still dreaming. 'That's impossible. I can't have gone back in time?'

'Nothing is impossible to my master, the Lord of Deception,' said Moloch, filled with pride. 'You have been awakened to the truth of my brethren, to the powers of Lucifer, that is all. Be glad, mortal. Be humble.'

'I'm still dreaming,' Glyn told himself, slapping at his face several times. 'Wake up!'

'Fool, you are awake! Let me take control for a short while, and I will bring justice upon those who have wronged you. I wish to give you thanks…'

There was no resisting Moloch's control over Glyn, no matter how much he attempted to resist. He was now under the spell of this monstrous demon; this wicked creature who was hellbent on causing catastrophic damage to the world that had turned against it. Even if he wanted to, Glyn could simply not regain control over his limbs and thoughts. It was indeed Tuesday again, but the next twenty-four hours would not play out as they had done previously.

'I feel… stronger,' said Glyn, flexing his now muscular arms. 'Is this through you, Moloch?'

There was no response but for a strange urge to go outside into Skipton Road's fog, and with it also came an overwhelming bloodlust that Glyn had never felt before.

The next ten minutes passed by like a blur. Glyn could see and hear, though he was nothing but a puppet that was being controlled by Moloch. He approached a house that he had not visited prior, where he proceeded to kick in its front door, and then he lunged at an obese, toupee-wearing man inside that was in the process of visiting the bathroom. The man somehow seemed familiar to Glyn, and not in a good way.

'Glyn—is that you, lad?' the man squealed as Glyn's fingers sunk into his flabby throat. 'I'm sorry!'

'Harder!' Moloch commanded, and Glyn obeyed without question. 'Throttle this bloated swine until he takes his last breath! Make him squeal!'

'Please,' the man begged, 'I'm so sorry, lad.'

'Suffer with me.' The words came out of Glyn's mouth though it was Moloch who spoke them. 'Suffer. Pay for your sins.'

The man slumped onto his back with a resounding thud. Glyn, to his horror, then realised who it was: his uncle.

'Why him?' he asked Moloch. 'He was old and defenceless.'

'There is no time to dawdle or divulge. We must move on to our next victim,' said the demon with haste. 'Move!'

Glyn re-entered a hypnotic state. As if heavily sedated, he sauntered through the streets of Newton Escomb, falling against cars and people as he struggled to control his movements. It was obvious that Moloch had not needed to use legs for a long while, going off the demon's fickle mastery of Glyn's limbs. Still, that did not matter. So long as Moloch's weapon carried out the necessary tasks, there was nothing to stop them.

Glyn then stopped by a parked police car, and inside it there was one officer who was busy typing on a laptop computer. He knocked at the driver's side window three times, slowly as to taunt the officer. The laptop's screen flashed and glitched in unison with the disturbance, a peculiarity that both the officer and Glyn both noted: the officer responded nervously and Glyn in delight.

The officer turned and frowned, prepared to unleash his frustration, and then they gasped in shock.

'Now, listen, I don't want any trouble,' said the officer, holding up his hands, portraying some guilt in their eyes. 'The court's ruling was final, so let bygones be bygones. It was an honest mistake. I've paid my dues.'

'It's… you.' Tears welled up in Glyn's eyes. 'You were the one who tore Iona out of my arms, who took her away from me.'

'I was just following orders.' The officer quickly closed his window, sensing Glyn's rising aggression. 'It wasn't my fault that your wife left you, that the courts decided you weren't fit to care for your daughter — was it? The law is the law, and I was only doing my job, at the end of the day.'

'The law is tainted and defiled!' Glyn clenched his fists, and Moloch's power intensified. 'I will break you, just like you broke me that day. Suffer for your sins!'

The officer attempted to retrieve his taser gun but was too slow to act. Glyn thrust a fist through the window, shattering it on impact, sending shards of glass into the officer's face and eyes. Blinded, the officer then tried to reach for his pepper spray, but again Glyn — through Moloch — was too fast for him.

'Suffer,' said Glyn pleadingly. 'I want you to. I am contrition. I am retribution…'

With lightning-fast speed, Glyn snatched the officer's handcuffs, opened them fully and then thrust the tip from one of them into their windpipe; he then gouged out the officer's eyes and thrust the gelatinous balls into his victim's mouth, slamming it shut so that the mucus-filled innards flowed out over their bloodied lips; as a finale, Glyn thrust an elbow, using it like a hammer, into the officer's nose to crumple their face like paper under pressure. It was a bloody and brutal display that Moloch revelled with all their might. Glyn still had no actual clue as to what he was doing.

'You are proving to be a worthy vessel,' humoured Moloch, imbuing Glyn with even more rage and resentment. 'To our next victim we must go now. There are… so many.'

Glyn relapsed into consciousness, filled with remorse and dread.

'I'm done for. I've killed people,' he chuntered, crippled with dismay. 'I'm a murderer.'

'There is no life without death and no death without life. You are merely hastening the unbreakable circle that empowers them,' explained Moloch, calmly and as if nothing terrible had occurred. 'Our next victim shall be your final test — our ultimate revenge.'

'Who is it?' In truth, Glyn didn't want to know. He had the blood of two victims splattered across his hands, and the thought of adding more made him sick to his stomach. 'Will I know them as well?'

'That traitor — Baal — has lusted over his pet witch, Sabina, for too long now without any repercussions,' Moloch announced in disdain. 'We must ruin their connection, sever it, and thus be compensated. Be brave, O mortal, and do not fear my brother's scorn. I will protect you. I am Baal's equal, after all.'

Glyn's mind fell completely blank. His vision came to once he returned home, though he was stood outside of his neighbour's house — Sid's home. On looking upon Sid's front door a wave of hatred swept through him, a malice so previously foreign to Glyn.

'Why have you chosen him?' he asked Moloch, utterly perplexed. 'The guy's nothing but a waster.'

'He is the summoner I spoke of!' seethed Moloch. 'Break his connection to Baal and Sabina; sever the bond between both master and slave. It is the only way. I will kill you, otherwise, slowly and with the greatest sadism I can muster!'

Sid's front door came to, and he glared at Glyn amid sheer panic. 'You've been marked,' Sid gasped, 'but not by who I would have thought —'

Moloch's resonating voice flowed through Glyn's vocal cords. 'Peccator — Sinner! Your meddling will come to an end this day.'

'What "meddling"?' asked Sid, feigning concern. 'I've done nought wrong!'

'You have played with the flames of my brethren, ignited Lucifer's fury; and for your mindless devotion to the witch and other transgressions, I will see that you burn!'

Sid fled upstairs, to the bedroom where he would perform his black magic rituals. Glyn followed suit, initially struggling to match Sid's frantic pace due to all the empty lager cans and soiled items of clothing that lined the stairwell. The two stared at one another upon the upper landing: Sid with a ceremonial obsidian dagger in his hands and Glyn with his fists tightly clenched, each held in a stalemate as to who would strike first.

'You don't know what you're toying with,' said Sid, foaming at the mouth. 'You docile bastard, Glyn. Do you realise which demon it is that I serve?'

'Baal?' Glyn sniggered, his thoughts purely those of Moloch's. 'No demon is your master. It is only a demon's whore that has been twinned with your spirit. Neither have strength over me.'

'She's *not* a whore!' cried Sid, swiping his dagger through the air at the invisible menace and then at Glyn. 'She loves me. Sabina will protect me from you *and* Baal!'

'Not even the light of Elohim could save you from my wrath,' growled Moloch. 'You were destined to die at my hands, Sidney Lockewood! The time has come…'

The already dim lights within the household faded, and then a black mass formed behind where Sid now stood. To both Sid and Glyn's horror, Moloch's abhorrent — albeit brutally incarcerated — state manifested, taking up the whole room with his tattered wings. Moloch ripped his hands through the iron nails and tore the barbed wire from his mouth, following this sickening display thereafter with a deafening roar that shook the entire household.

'Lux et tenebris,' Sid chanted, his voice littered with fears, his trousers now completely saturated with urine. 'Lux et tenebris!!'

'The witch's incantations cannot save you,' taunted Moloch. 'Suffer with me, Sid. Suffer for your transgressions.'

Sid fell to his knees, holding the dagger up high in defence, though he was not able to counter Moloch's animalistic onslaught. The demon sunk its barbed teeth into Sid's stomach, instantly tearing the poor soul in half, consuming his foul entrails with a wicked smile and cackle thereafter; then the demon finished Sid off by vomiting a pool of acid upon his exposed flesh, leaving nothing but a smouldering pile of ashes behind.

Glyn snapped out of his trance, but Moloch's demonic presence endured. 'What have you done to him? What the hell is going on?'

'You are bound to me, mortal, until I decree otherwise,' said Moloch, inflicting agony upon Glyn as he spoke. 'I have granted you but a taste of my powers, and now you will free me.'

'No!' screamed Glyn, punching at his head. 'This isn't what I wanted. I didn't want people to die!'

'I will make good my desire to punish Baal, whether you agree or do not. Seek an absolution, by all means, but no light shall come to you. Only the Endless Void awaits your soul now.'

Glyn fled from the devastating scene, and once outside he ran until he could run no more. He paused to catch his breath, finding that he had now unwittingly reached the local cemetery where his beloved mother had been laid to rest twelve years prior. Though he would get no answer from her, Glyn felt that, in by being in his mother's presence, he could perhaps find some comfort to ease the dreadful pain building up inside.

Wiping the blood from his hands upon his jeans, Glyn slowly headed over to where his mother's headstone lay. All the while Moloch's voice continued to haunt him, ridiculing him, reminding him that they could never be separated.

'Leave me alone!' howled Glyn, clenching onto his temples. 'Get out of my head! I don't want to help you anymore!'

'Once connected, never can a bond be broken. You are mine to forge and control, mortal. You are mine.'

Glyn approached his mother's grave and soon fell again into an instant and blinding bout of rage; Moloch's control was only strengthening. A group of teenagers loitered around where his mother lay in rest, all wearing hoods and talking aloud. Glyn could no longer hold back the innate evil that festered within him.

'What are you lot doing here? Leave — NOW!' he screamed to the youths, who each fell silent in response. Somewhere in the distance police sirens blared now, and the sound of screeching tyres quickly followed. Did the authorities know of what Glyn, through Moloch, had done? Did they know he was here? Had one of the youths alerted the police to a deranged madman who was harassing them? Glyn only cared about one thing now, however: seeking justice against those who he considered to be unworthy of existence, which was difficult to tell because of Moloch's venomous influence.

'We're not doing any harm,' pleaded one of the youths, a boy with a meek demeanour. 'Why don't *you* leave us alone?'

'Move, or I'll do the lot of you in!' countered Glyn. He then felt a heavy object in one of his coat pockets, which turned out to be Sid's ceremonial dagger. The blade was still sharp and covered in dried blood. Glyn had no clue as to how it ended up in his possession, but it was ideal for what he desired.

'This is your last chance,' he threatened, revealing the dagger to the frightened youngsters. 'You know what — to hell with it! I cared for people who died during the pandemic, people who genuinely didn't deserve to lose their lives. Why should I let a bunch of oxygen-wasters, like you lot, walk this earth while people who deserve to live die horribly? It isn't fair. It needs to stop!'

'I'm gonna knock out this nutter,' another boy boasted.

'Don't. Let's just go,' implored a girl within the group, who pulled her mask up further to conceal her trembling lips. 'It's not worth it. He's got a knife,' she whispered cautiously. 'Let's go.'

Glyn began to mutter to himself, though the startled group could clearly hear his words. 'So begins a new path in my life. I'll balance the wrongs of this world, of those who live when they shouldn't. I'll find purpose again — a reason to exist. Is that my prize for serving you, Moloch? Is it?!'

'Your reward shall be granted soon enough,' promised the demon. 'Spill the blood of those pointless children. No tears shall be shed upon their deaths, and you would be ridding this world of more parasites in killing them.'

'I'm gonna knock this weirdo out,' announced another boy in the group, and it would sadly be his last words.

Glyn threw the dagger, feeding its tip precisely into the boy's mouth, shattering his teeth and rupturing his skull. The rest of the group screamed out in terror, most freezing to the spot where they now stared upon their murdered friend.

'You're not worthy to live — none of you!' Glyn declared as he collected the dagger to carry out further attacks upon the defenceless youths. He slashed at their throats and stabbed at their abdomens, leaving only one girl left who cowered above his mother's grave. 'How dare you desecrate my mother's resting place. How dare —'

'Dad? No, it can't be?' the girl stuttered with an alarmed expression. 'Dad, is that... you?'

Glyn's expression swiftly matched that of the girl; he looked to her in pure astonishment. 'Iona?'

She was a teenager now, beautiful though solemn in expression, bearing the same entrancing smile as her mother. Iona looked to her grandmother's gravestone and then back to her father, to the man whom she had not seen in over ten years.

'Mum said that you had problems, that you had mental health issues, but I didn't think you'd ever be this evil,' she sobbed. 'My dad was a kind man, just lost...'

Evil. Glyn shuddered at the word. He had not considered his actions to be evil as yet, under Moloch's control; and given that he had only murdered the uncle who had sexually abused him as a boy, the police officer who had physically torn his family apart and his alcoholic, demon-worshipping neighbour, these acts seemed justified. It was a sour hit of reality, strangely infused with the joy of seeing his precious daughter again.

'Iona, it's not what it looks like,' Glyn pleaded, desperate to portray some innocence in his voice. 'I've missed you so much, sweetheart. I've thought about you every day. You've grown up.'

'You killed my friends,' she whimpered, looking to the scattered pools of blood. 'Mum was right. Mum was right about you. You *are* a monster.'

'I had no one to turn to, Iona. I'd seen things at work that would haunt anybody, and I got no help in return. I was let down by the system, by society, by your mother and our family. When I needed help most, those who I thought I could trust turned their backs on me. It's not my fault.'

Pointing to her slain friends, Iona added, 'Then who did this? Didn't you kill them? Are you going to do the same to me?'

'No—never! I'd never hurt a hair on your head. I love you more than anything else in this world,' he beseeched. 'I've missed you more than you could ever know, Iona. I don't want to lose you again.'

The police sirens grew nearer, and so too did Glyn's anger increase. With a piercing screech, three police cars then came to a sudden halt before Glyn and Iona. He turned to them, bearing his bloodied hands and blade, and then he looked down upon his fearful daughter in sincere remorse.

'I tried searching for you,' said Iona in a strained whisper. 'I wanted to find you, to somehow repair the relationship that had been robbed from us. I didn't believe what Mum said… I couldn't. But look at what you've become. You're a heartless killer. You're not my dad. You can't be my dad.'

'I am!' he cried, brushing a hand along the length of his blade. 'Nothing can change the past. Nothing. But I'll make it up to you.'

The police officers sprinted from their cars, each one carrying a pistol and aiming them at Glyn. He didn't flinch against the impending threat, however, and nor did he speak. He merely glanced at the guns with a calm smile and then back again to Iona, to the one thing that was worth living for.

'I'm sorry,' she said, backing away from him. 'There's no chance of us making things right now. I want nothing to do with you.'

'Everyone deserves a second chance, Iona. Will you not offer me another chance?' Glyn wept, no longer able to hold back the years of grief and uncertainty. 'I'm not some awful demon. I'm just… lost. You're exactly what I need in my life to make it whole again.'

'Lower your weapon and get down on the ground!' commanded one of the police officers. 'On the ground— NOW!'

Glyn looked to Sid's blade and then to Iona, to his symbol of death and beacon of hope. He had a relatively straightforward choice to make, that being to either live or die. It was not a simple decision to make, though. Iona detested him, without question, and there was little chance of him surviving the number of bullets being aimed at his chest. Moloch, however, continued to be a toxic and overpowering influence. Glyn held out a hand to Iona and the other, with the blade still held tightly within it, at the police officers. A series of gunshots ensued, and then came a disturbing bout of silence, only broken by a murder of crows that flew off into the distance.

From Glyn's lifeless body a plume of black smoke rose out of his mouth: Moloch's spirit. The demon vanished thereafter, satisfied that they had been released into the world again, adamant to fulfil their vengeful desires. The officers and Iona did not witness the demon's manifestation, for all present were left shaken by the peculiar confrontation.

The police officers rushed over to check on the numerous corpses that littered the graveyard and then Iona, who herself was still knelt upon her grandmother's grave. She crawled over to Glyn and kissed him upon his forehead, then she retreated into the reassuring arms of two police officers.

'Poor girl,' said one of the officers as they escorted Iona back to their car. 'You're safe now. We'll take you back to the station, contact your parents and then make sure that you receive the best counselling available.'

'My parents,' said Iona, choking on her words. 'You just shot one.'

The officers glanced at one another with a deathly stare and then assisted Iona into the back of their car. She sat there, held in both relief and sorrow, while the two officers discussed with their colleagues what had taken place through their walkie-talkies.

'Suspect is down — confirmed. There are six fatalities and one survivor. Over,' said one of the officers.

'Bring them in,' an officer on the other end replied. 'CID will be over shortly to deal with the deceased. Over.'

'This day just keeps getting stranger and stranger,' noted the other officer. 'You couldn't make it up.'

'What do you mean?' asked their counterpart.

'The person who alerted us to the assailant's position was some woman called Sabina, right?'

'Yeah.'

'Well, there isn't anyone called Sabina on our records. She has no fixed abode, and the operator who took the call mentioned how the line went all funny and crackly as this "Sabina" talked. Whoever Sabina is, she doesn't officially exist. Strange, isn't it?'

'Does it matter? We've stopped a madman committing more murders, that's all I can say, and that's all that counts. Weird or not: whoever Sabina is, she's a hero in my eyes.'

'It's still weird,' chuntered the other officer. 'The sooner I get transferred from this creepy town, the better. I mean, take that murder and kidnapping we had to deal with a week or so ago--that so-called famous reviewer bloke who killed his wife and then stole their baby girl—'

'Not in front of the poor lass, Barry. She's got enough to think about, wouldn't you say? You don't want to give her more nightmares.'

In silence, Iona watched on as the police covered the bodies of her friends and father. It was not the reunion she had hoped for with him, but it set in stone an interest to discover who this "Sabina" was, and it would become a lifelong obsession. In later years, Iona would discover the tales of the Red Ribbon Witch, of Sabina, and of The Skipton Horrors. It brought no closure to the sudden and gruesome loss of her father and friends, though it did open her eyes to unknown forces that work within this world.

The Mother

A sense of calm swept through Amy Joyce, though she knew it would not last. It never did. Apprehension constantly plagued her thoughts, which in truth were no longer her own.

Five years prior, Amy's mind and body had been possessed by a malignant witch named Sabina after a prolonged period of exposure to her malignant presence. Since that fateful eve, when Amy finally submitted to the witch's desires — to find a worthy human vessel — she and her daughter, Olivia, had been on the run, moving from town to town, always fearful that they would someday be caught. Amy had left behind her husband, Christopher, and their ten-year-old son, Isaac, who still desperately sought both her and Olivia out. The police, of course, considered Amy's actions to be kidnap, thus she could never truly rest.

Rainclouds formed overheard as Amy and Olivia took refuge within a bus shelter. Both were on the verge of starvation, a sad and frequent consequence of them living on the streets. They sold flowers to make some meagre income, but there was little financial gain wrought from such a modest career. Still, it was better than stealing, a necessity that Amy often resorted to if she were to fill her six-year-old daughter's stomach.

Holding out a half-eaten chocolate bar to her mother, Olivia pleaded, 'Take it, Mummy. You haven't eaten yet.'

'You eat it, Eliza. I'm not hungry.' Sabina's possession over Amy had removed any past memory she bore, including that of her own child's true name. Eliza was Sabina's offspring, her daughter that had been dead for many centuries now. 'It's your birthday. You have it. I don't like sweet things, do I?'

Olivia snapped off a chunk regardless, forcing it into Amy's hands. 'I don't want you to get poorly. I don't want you to be sad.'

'Just being with you brings me so much joy, Eliza. I ate three days ago, so don't worry about me. I'm used to being hungry.'

Amy looked skeletal and utterly fatigued. Spirits bear no need to eat or drink, a subtle point of mortality that Sabina had failed to take into consideration when gaining control over her latest vessel.

Olivia placed the last piece of chocolate in her mouth, savouring it for as long as she could, and then turned to her mother in curiosity. 'Are we staying here, or are we going new? This is a pretty town. I'd like to stay here.'

'We can't. We must move on,' said Amy, trying hard to conceal her dread. 'It's dangerous to stay in one place for too long—'

'Why, Mummy?'

'I told you to never ask me that, Eliza. There are bad people that would want to take you from me, and that is why we must keep moving. I will not lose you again.'

'But... you've never lost me before.'

'I don't want to think about it. Those days are gone, and so is that life. It doesn't matter where we rest our heads, so long as we're safe and together.'

Olivia stared at a group of children passing by, noting their laughter with jealousy. 'I want friends, like them over there. Why can't I have any friends?'

'People are selfish and deceitful,' Amy insisted, wrapping a hand over Olivia's small fingers. 'I had friends once, who I believed could trusted. But they betrayed me, and I will not ever make that mistake again. Trust only in me, my darling.'

'Why, Mummy?'

'No more questions. I'll find us somewhere dry to stay the night, then we'll set off come sunrise.'

'I want to be normal,' whimpered Olivia. 'I want a big house and have lots of friends. I want a proper family. It's not fair.'

'Remember to take your flowers with you,' said Amy, hoping to change the subject, pointing to a bundle of lavender that Olivia had picked earlier that day from an unsuspecting stranger's garden. 'Those are particularly special and harder to come by these days. Here, let me show you.'

As Olivia stared on in awe, Amy waved a finger over the amethyst petals, selecting one that boasted the brightest shade. She then ran the petals across her forearm, where she had suffered a dog bite two days before.

'Are you going to use your magic, Mummy?' asked Olivia eagerly.

'Shhh...' Amy stared at the petals in complete focus. '*Medeor, Sanctus Lumen. Sanctus Lumen...*'

'What did you say?'

'It is Latin,' explained Amy, holding out her arm for Olivia to inspect. 'I called on the holy light to heal my wounds. My arm will better in no time.'

'How do you know magic?' asked Olivia, mimicking her mother's actions with a separate flower. 'You sound so funny when you talk like that.'

'There is nothing funny about incantations. They can be used for good or evil, and it is a skill that I shall hand down to you. I think you're ready to learn. Yes, you're ready.'

Olivia's face lightened up with excitement. 'Really?'

'I believe so. You're old enough now to know the ways of old, of our bloodline.' A dazzling ray of golden light caught Amy's eye. In her peripheral vision she then saw a glimpse of a small boy that would randomly appear at times, no matter where she and Olivia were. The boy's hair was pristine-white in colour and cut just above his ears; his eyes were amber and piercing; his small stature gave the impression that he was around the same age as Olivia; and not once did he ever attempt to communicate with the mother and child.

Amy immediately latched onto Olivia. 'Who is that boy? I keep seeing him.'

'The boy with white hair? He's our guardian angel,' said Olivia, completely unphased. 'He looks after us, Mummy. He's our friend.'

Amy was unconvinced. 'Does he? How are you certain of this?'

'He told me. I see him sometimes in my dreams,' Olivia replied, waving across to the haunting figure. 'He's not nasty. I like him.'

The boy fixated upon Amy, his piercing eyes meeting with hers.

'Surely, he cannot be alone?' Amy contemplated, though only in concern for her own self-preservation and not that of the boy's wellbeing. 'Where are his parents? Why does he follow us?'

'He wouldn't tell me,' said Olivia, lulling her head, hinting that she knew more. 'I asked him, but he said that it's a secret.'

'I don't do secrets. We're leaving, Eliza — NOW!'

As Amy stood a woman sprinted up to the bus stop, panting and sweating heavily. 'I made it just in the nick of time,' they humoured, looking over a timetable sheet posted behind Olivia. 'Has the bus to Durham been yet?'

'No,' said Amy, pulling at Olivia's arm. 'Come. We must go.'

'Those are beautiful flowers,' admired the woman, reaching down to smell them. 'Did you pick these yourself?'

'Yes,' said Olivia with pride. 'They're my favourite, and Mummy can make magic potions with them.'

The woman scratched at her head, winking to Amy. 'Can she now? That's something you don't see every day.'

'Mummy's a witch—'

'Silence, Eliza!' roared Amy, tearing Olivia away from the stranger's company. 'We're not safe here anymore.'

The woman's smile faded and was quickly replaced with an expression of unease. 'You look familiar, somehow...'

'I doubt it,' sneered Amy. 'Come on, Eliza.'

'I'm sure of it,' added the woman, tapping a finger upon her chin. 'I know I've seen your face somewhere before...'

'You've never met me until now,' said Amy, clenching her fists. 'You are mistaken.'

'Can you remember, and we're talking a few years back now, that there was a woman who disappeared with her baby girl. It was all over the news, and the police are still putting out posters about them. I think her name was something-or-other-Joyce.'

Amy's fear swiftly turned into a fiery hatred. 'I have no idea what you're talking about. Stay away from me and my child!'

'Oh my god — it is you!' the woman gasped. 'You're who the police are after. I always remember a face. I knew I recognised you!'

Without uttering a word, Amy swung an arm around to strike her knuckles across the woman's face, who in turn lost consciousness and fell to the ground.

'What did you do that for, Mummy?' screamed Olivia, genuinely disturbed by Amy's reaction. 'Please, heal her with your magic!'

By now Amy had fully succumbed to Sabina's paranoia and hatred. She dragged Olivia away from the bus stop and bloodied stranger, running as fast as possible into the distance, into the unknown.

'They will not take you from me!' cried Amy, forcing Olivia to match her speed. 'Not again. Not again!'

'Why did you hurt her? She didn't hurt you,' sobbed Olivia. 'I've left my flowers —'

'We'll pick more. Run faster!'

On turning a corner, the white-haired boy suddenly re-appeared. Amy froze, unsure as what to do.

'You, boy,' she said, deliberately towering herself over him. 'Tell me who you are and why you follow us.'

The boy calmly turned his head to Olivia, granting no acknowledgment to Amy. 'I will protect you. Follow me.'

'No, Eliza!' Amy commanded, forcing herself between the two children. 'Who are you, boy? Talk!'

'I am salvation — your salvation,' he said timidly, displaying no threat whatsoever. 'I will protect you, but only if you come with me willingly.'

Unlike her mother, Olivia bore no hesitation in obeying the boy's request. 'Trust him, Mummy. He wants to help.'

Sirens blared nearby, which Amy took to either be an ambulance for her victim or — worse — the police. 'Where do you plan on taking us?' she asked with a gulp. 'How do I know for sure that you can be trusted?'

The boy smiled back. 'Unless you follow me, you will surely be discovered. It is a simple choice to make, Sabina. You have been running for so long, too long. It is time for you to rest.'

Amy's heart felt like it seized. 'What did you say?'

'Follow me. Be free,' the boy iterated. 'There is no other means for you to escape from him now, your master.'

The sirens tore into Amy's eardrums, intensifying her anxiety. She grunted in complaint but then finally gave into the boy's demands. He in turn guided Amy and Olivia to an abandoned church, which lay beyond a long wall of metal fences that had signs stating "Demolition Site" posted across them.

'I won't step one foot inside there,' said Amy, sensing Sabina's fervent reluctance. 'Find us somewhere else — anywhere else.'

'The ground here is no longer hallowed, sacred. Resent it all you like, but there will be no pain wrought to you from entering it,' the boy assured her. His manner of speech and maturity rose more concern in Amy, but Olivia had already found an opening within the fence and was making her way up to the church's main door. Now alone with Amy, the boy added: 'Do not fear what lies ahead, Sabina de Lockewood. Comply or perish. Submit or be destroyed.'

'Who are you?' she asked again, tempted to swipe the smirk off his face like she did with the woman moments earlier. 'I won't move until you tell me.'

'You will see… in time. Please, go inside. Be with your daughter.'

The boy joined Olivia at the church's entranceway, compelling Amy to follow suit. The three scoured their surroundings before entering the dilapidated structure, relieved that there didn't appear to be any apparent witnesses.

'Of all the places for you to harbour us, you chose a church?' said Amy with a great level of scorn. However, upon stepping foot inside, she found truth in the boy's claims; no pain inflicted her and therefore the site was no longer sacred, otherwise the tainted spirit of Sabina attached to Amy would have succumbed to sheer agony. 'You weren't lying. There's a surprise.'

'You really thought I would lie to you?' asked the boy, raising his eyebrows in disappointment. 'That is what happens when you linger in the shadows for too long: you lose all light from within, and so cannot preserve the love and warmth once felt. Now, find somewhere to relax and I will provide you with sustenance.'

Amy examined the broken stained-glass windows, dusty pews and flooded floor. 'I doubt there is any nourishment or comfort to be found in this place. It's been abandoned for years, by the looks of it.'

'Have faith in me,' said the boy, smiling to Olivia again. 'What you see is what you get. I have promised to provide you with protection and nourishment, and I will ensure that my vows are fulfilled.' He then sauntered off into a back room, humming a song to himself that neither Amy nor Olivia had ever heard before. The tune was atonal, unnerving and echoed across each of the church's crumbling walls.

'Such a peculiar boy,' Amy noted, gesturing for Olivia to move closer. 'No matter what he claims, do not trust him. As soon as we've eaten, we'll make a run for it, Eliza. There's just something about him I don't like...'

Amy and Olivia sat beside one another upon a hard, wooden pew that faced onto the church's altar. The pair sighed and hugged, mindful of the sirens that still resonated outside.

'I'm sick of running away,' said Olivia, nestling her head into Amy's lap. 'Why can't we be normal?'

'Go to sleep, my darling. I will wake you when the boy returns,' said Amy, stroking a hand through Olivia's hair. 'We don't even know his name.'

'It's Luther,' whispered Olivia, forcing her head more into Amy's thigh. 'At least, I think that's what he said.'

'Luther?'

'Yeah.'

'Why didn't you tell me this before?'

'That's his nickname,' said Olivia, shrugging dismissively. 'One of his friends told me it by accident. I'm not meant to know.'

'His... friends?' Terror rose in Amy's eyes and voice. 'Do you know any of their names?'

'Only one: Moloch. Why do think his name is such a big secret, Mummy?'

'Because you're forbidden to know,' answered a ghastly voice, which spoke in a strained whisper to Amy. It was Sabina, desperate to hold onto control. Despite this church being unsanctified, the witch still bore a grave dread within its walls. 'We are exposed within this accursed house, Sister. Leave!' pleaded Sabina, frantically fuelling her will into Amy. In response, Amy went to move but Olivia forced her to sit back down. 'Do as I say — LEAVE!'

'Get up, Eliza. We can't stay,' said Amy, nudging at the child. 'That boy and his "friends" are dangerous.'

'He wants to help us — he is helping us,' emphasised Olivia. 'Where else can we go? We can't leave.'

The boy suddenly appeared again, holding a loaf of bread and goblet of wine in his hands. 'My apologies for taking so long. I have brought what you need.'

'We don't want it,' said Amy, turning away from him. 'What is your real name, Luther? Who is "Moloch"?'

The boy laughed faintly to himself, holding out the bread and wine closer to Amy. 'Moloch is my brother. We were betrayed, and I have protected him ever since. That is all I will say on the matter.'

'Be nice to him, Mummy. He's a good boy,' beseeched Olivia.

'Moloch is an irregular name, is it not?' asked Amy, sensing Sabina's hatred grow. 'What will you gain from protecting us?'

Luther stretched out his arms fully now, thrusting the bread and wine against Amy's arms. 'Leave now and forever be chained to despair, enslaved and powerless. I know what it feels like to be judged and hunted. It is not the life you want for your child, is it?'

'What would a boy of your age know about such things?

'Take my gifts and end your suffering. Take them!'

Cautiously, Amy motioned up to Luther to take the items from him, while Olivia suddenly fell asleep. The bread was as hard as the wooden pews, infested with green mould and live maggots; the wine was dark red in colour, darker than usual. Neither seemed appetising.

'What is this?' questioned Amy, turning her nose up at the disgusting meal. 'Do you wish to poison me?'

'Take it!' Luther commanded. 'Please, I insist.'

'What if I don't? There is no way I will let my precious daughter eat this rotten filth —'

'They are not for her.'

'For me? Why only me?'

Luther's amber eyes radiated with a stronger golden light, somehow entrancing Amy, hypnotising her. 'They are for you only, Sabina,' he whispered out of Olivia's earshot. 'Consume them and sever your connection to him.'

'To Baal?' she shuddered. 'But I already —'

'You have been held under the wrongful impression that you managed to break the connection forged between you and him. Such a feat is impossible, Sabina, and you know that.'

'I destroyed him,' she said, her eyes flaring manically. 'I found a mortal vessel, became stronger than Baal, and I decimated his spirit.'

'You weakened Baal, yes, but — not even with his shared power — can you alone vanquish such a powerful demon.' Luther's smile widened. 'Though, I can.'

'How?'

'Consume the bread and wine. Take them.'

'The body and blood of Christ?' sniggered Amy, rolling her eyes at the bread and half-filled goblet. 'I don't need your salvation, Luther. I've survived without you for long enough.'

The entire church shook with a tremendous burst of thunder, and from Luther's back six bronze wings flared out. Amy cowered to her knees while Olivia fell into an instant bout of sleep. Then, from every corner of the church, eerie shadows manifested.

'What is happening? Who are those things?' fretted Amy, not daring to look upon the ghoulish creatures as they surrounded her. Some appeared to be monks; the others were either small children or people whom Amy had never met. 'Are you doing this? Who are you, really, Luther?'

'I go by many names: The Lord of Deception; The Great Serpent of Temptation; The Infinite Darkness, and so on. Ultimately, I am your saviour, Sabina,' he gleamed. 'Take this bread and wine and be done with all this.'

'Who are these shadows that stalk us?' she stuttered, realising that they now stood mere inches away. 'What are they?'

'Your victims, those you corrupted and slaughtered under Baal's influence,' stated Luther, gesturing for the figures to kneel before him. 'Do as I say, Witch, and you shall never see them again.'

Amy tore the bread and wine from Luther's hands, robbed of her previous reluctance. 'I can't lose her,' she wept, as she turned to the sleeping child. 'I can't lose my Eliza. I waited so long to be with her again.'

Luther's voice deepened and his stature grew. 'This child you now grovel before is not your offspring, Sabina. Eliza is dead. She is gone beyond our sight and reach.'

'No, she's not—'

'You were granted knowledge that no mortal should ever possess,' added Luther in contempt. 'You are an abomination, and for that I must cleanse you.'

'I am innocent—Eliza is innocent!'

'Eat. Drink,' begged Luther. 'Be done with this sorry tale. The final days of our righteous existence are upon us. The tide is turning, and my reign upon this earth is reaching its climax. Do as I say, Witch. Do not test me.'

Amy forced the bread into her mouth, gagging as the maggots wriggled across her tongue and then down her gullet. Then she took a sip from the wine and immediately spat it out, for it was blood. However, with each swallow committed, Amy began to feel Sabina's hold upon her diminish. She downed the vile drink, despite the rancid blood clots that floated upon its surface, and then all faded into darkness. Only a single light prevailed that emitted from Luther's eyes, golden and serene. While Amy felt herself slip into unconsciousness, Luther willed for the red ribbon – her physical attachment to Sabina – that was wrapped around her wrist to ignite until it was nothing but small flecks of ash. A final, blood-curdling scream left from Sabina as she was torn from Amy's soul, no longer able to retain what control she had over the poor mortal.

'Your connection with Sabina has been removed,' announced Luther, their voice unrecognisable as it now bellowed with a fierce roar. 'The witch has been made vulnerable again, as has her demonic master; her spirit is lost in purgatory, which is what I desire, and I always get what I want. You, Amy Joyce, are free to now resume your meaningless life. Much toil lies before you, for I command it. I will not be defied.' And with that, Luther vanished.

To the sound of birds chirping outside, reinvigorating that sense of peace felt earlier, Amy awoke as her formal self again. She gasped on not recognising her surroundings, on seeing her bony arms and fingers, and then on studying the small child that lay asleep a few feet away.

'Olivia? But it can't be?' she lamented, crawling up to her across the soaked, sandstone floor. 'Olivia?'

The child came to, completely unaware of what had taken place between Amy and the mysterious boy. 'Mummy?'

'This isn't right.' Amy pushed aside Olivia's coat to find a distinctive birthmark upon her neck, clarifying her worst fears. 'My baby. You can't be her...'

'What's wrong, Mummy? You looked scared,' said Olivia, her breaths hastening with panic. 'Who is... Olivia?'

'You're Olivia,' said Amy, clasping at her mouth. 'Where's your daddy and Isaac?'

Confounded, Olivia bolted up from the pew. 'You said that I don't have a daddy, and I don't have a brother. What are you talking about, Mummy?'

'You *do* have a daddy and brother. Where are they?' wailed Amy, bursting into tears. 'Why are we in this old church?'

'I'm scared, Mummy. Stop it!' snapped Olivia, backing away.

'You are Olivia Joyce. My husband — your daddy — is Christopher Joyce, and you have a brother called Isaac. Where are they?'

'My name is Eliza! Your name is Sabina!'

'No! Oh, God...'

Amy succumbed to denial at first, then disbelief, and then a powerful resentment. But it all made sense. Sabina, the witch who had tormented Amy's family while they lived at Skipton Road, had succeeded in corrupting her mind and soul. There was no other explanation.

'Are you poorly?' asked Olivia, nestling her forehead against Amy. 'Are you sick?'

'This is all my fault,' said Amy, barely able to catch her breaths. 'I'll make it right, though. I'll make everything right again, sweetheart.'

'Make *what* right again?'

'I'm so sorry, Olivia. Let's go home,' said Amy, wrapping her arms around the child's torso. 'Let's find your daddy and Isaac. They must be so worried about us.'

In silence, both shaken by their ordeal, Amy and Olivia left the church, holding tightly onto one another's hands. They ventured back to the bus stop, which was vacant now. Amy turned her head as to establish where she was and yelled out to a passer-by: 'Excuse me! Where are we?'

An elderly man, bearing his weight upon a thin cane, looked up with a puzzled expression. 'You're in Barnard Castle. Are you okay, flower?'

'Barnard Castle isn't far away from Newton Escomb,' smiled Amy, relaxing her tense muscles. 'We're close to home, Olivia. Our family will be back together soon.'

'I don't have a daddy or brother or home,' grumbled Olivia, sliding her hand away from Amy's. 'We live on the streets or in empty houses — and they're always cold. We don't have a family. It's just us, and that's the way you wanted it to be.'

'I was wrong. Everything will be alright, sweetheart. We'll go home, and everything will be alright again.'

But that was not the case sadly. Amy and Olivia took the next bus back to Newton Escomb, to Skipton Road, where their home once was. However, all that met them there, within the fog-laden cul-de-sac, was a boarded-up household that had clearly fallen victim to a devastating fire. Amy fell silent once more, unable to comprehend what lay before her.

'This is our home?' Olivia enquired, staring at the decimated ruins of the house she herself had no memory of. 'It's horrible. I don't want to live here.'

'Chris! Isaac!' screamed Amy, tearing at her face, consumed with grief. 'Where are they? Please don't be dead…'

A gentle, feminine, frail voice replied from next door, followed by an elderly woman popping up from behind the separating fence. 'Gracious me!' she wheezed, unwittingly dropping a pair of garden sheers onto her toes. 'Is that… is that you, Amy?'

Amy turned to the elderly woman and slowly began to recognise her. 'Pat, is that you?'

'By Jove, I thought you were dead! The police are probably still looking for you and — ' Pat wheezed again upon noticing Olivia's older-looking features. 'That's never Olivia, is it? Baby Olivia?'

'Yes.' Amy was resolute in her response, yet Olivia still denied this truth. 'Where are Chris and Isaac? Where are my husband and son?'

'They're long gone, my dear. They moved away years ago, not long after you vanished.'

'Where to?'

'Chris didn't say. He searched for you and Olivia, but I think he gave up all hope in the end. The police might be able to tell you more?'

Amy turned to the burnt-out remains of her home again, gently weeping into her hands. 'What… happened here?'

'It's arson, I reckon. Nearly lost my own house because of it!'

'When did it burn down?'

'Last night,' said Pat, fleeting her eyes between Amy and a mobile phone clasped within her hand now. 'I'll get in touch with the police for you, pet. You can come inside mine for a cup of tea while I do that, if you want?' Pat disappeared into her house, leaving Amy and Olivia to contemplate their next move.

Amy closed her eyes, praying that this was nothing more than a nightmare; but then as she opened them, Luther appeared again.

'I did it,' he stated, showing no remorse whatsoever. 'Retribution was required for the betrayal made against me. I will not be defied, defiled, usurped.'

'You're talking about Sabina and Baal, aren't you?' asked Amy, forming a sadistic smile. 'You'll make them pay for what they did to me and my family.'

'I bear no interest in the plight of mortals,' growled Luther. 'I have allowed for this sordid affair to endure too long. It is time for it to cease.'

'Will you not at least tell me who you really are?' Amy fell to her knees pleadingly. 'Are you an angel? You must be.'

'I was aeons ago, before the first war, before the fall.' Luther's expression was solemn, bitter even. 'I am what you see, what you want me to be. A simple mind like yours could never understand the true nature of my everlasting spirit.'

'I want to know,' she implored. 'Tell me!'

In a strange turn of events, Olivia now looked upon Luther in utter fear. 'I know who he is, Mummy.'

'Children are more sensitive to the interdimensional powers of this plain,' Luther chuckled, holding up a hand as to silence Olivia. 'You will not see me again, not unless you choose to live a sinful life. Focus on reuniting your family and loving them while you still can. The End of days is coming.' As quickly as he appeared, Luther then vanished again without a trace.

Pat returned with her phone held out for Amy to take. 'It's the police. They want to speak with you. They're on their way.'

Olivia nestled her head against Amy's chest, crying softly. 'You lied to me, Mummy. I *do* have a family.'

'You'll see them again, sweetheart. Mummy's so sorry.' Amy gulped and fought back the tears welling up in her eyes, knowing what could possibly follow. 'I don't know what the police will do with me, and I'm past caring. You'll be safe with your daddy and brother, and they love you so very much. I'm sorry, Olivia. I'm so sorry for everything…'

'Don't be,' said Olivia, tightening her arms around Amy. 'Don't be sad, Mummy. I hate it when you're sad.'

'I'm not upset. These are happy tears, because I know that you'll be safe and content with your daddy and brother. I'm free now. You're free now. Sabina failed.'

Confused, Olivia looked up to her mother. 'That's your name, though, isn't it?'

'That's what she wanted, but I'm not the same person I was when that witch took over me: weak and broken. In a way, and I don't know why, I kind of feel sorry for Sabina. All she ever wanted was to be with her daughter again, to have a family of her own, to be free of her slavery. God knows where she's at now.'

Olivia's skin turned pale and her eyes widened. 'He will find her. He wants to punish her for what she did, Mummy.'

'Who?' asked Amy in sincere concern.

'Baal.'

'And did Baal himself tell you this, sweetheart?'

'No. The white-haired boy just did,' said Olivia, frozen to the spot with fear. 'Lucifer told me…'

Reunion

For centuries I welcomed the darkness, nurtured it, forging my strength with its negative energy and limitless potential, embracing its raw power as my own. But now, and though I cannot deem exactly why, I have grown cautious of it. The world has changed. I have changed. I can sense the Endless Void nearing, calling out to me, and so I must relinquish my presence from this physical plain, but only with Sabina by my side. She and I are one, bound eternally, and no force within this universe will ever tear us apart. I am Baal. I am war. I am famine. I am plague. I am omnipotent. I am... so weary now. Twilight is setting upon my dominant reign; I can feel it. There is little else to do now but finalise my greatest goal: to exist alongside my beloved, to travel this earth together with her, to live a mortal life. Long have I waited for this moment, and I will not allow for anything or anyone to jeopardise it, not even Sabina's recent betrayal against me...

I chose well with my latest human vessel; a man who murdered his wife in cold blood and then stole their infant child. It was perfect timing. He sought refuge and I offered my services freely, though the fool bore no inclination as to my true intentions. His body and soul are mine now, as is his daughter. Sabina will be overjoyed to learn of this gift I bear for her, this baby girl, her new Eliza. I just know it. I am never wrong.

What I had not anticipated, however, was the extensive capabilities humans now possess in spreading information through thin air — the internet is what I believe they call it. My vessel's face has been spread far and wide, or so a man dared to inform me before I tore him clean in half. There is nowhere ideal to hide but for an old dwelling that once housed a loyal servant of mine — a small farmhouse located on the outskirts of this accursed town. Rumours speak of the demons that reside there, within that farmhouse, which are mostly true, so I doubt it is presently occupied. I must make haste if my final plan is to succeed, and time is certainly running out.

From the outside the farmhouse appears to be neglected; overgrown weeds and mounds of filth are strewn across its gardens and walls. There are no lights on inside, and I cannot sense any sentient life forms. For once, it would seem, luck appears to be on my side. I have waited too long to retire, to cast aside my servitude. Even demons such as I grow old and weak after such a lengthy period of service. I am ready to seek respite from this miserable existence. I am more than ready to summon Sabina back to this wretched plain again, and for the last time, I pray.

Nursing the infant in one arm, I stretch the other out to break open the farmhouse's front door, and it breaks open with ease, barely scratching my human flesh (despite the sheer force of which I had unleashed upon it). The infant remains peacefully asleep and I long to keep it that way, for any sounds could alert my enemies here, both physical and ethereal. Above the full moon shines down upon me, and I take it as a sign that my endeavours are justified, blessed even, for under a full moon my powers are at their greatest strength.

An overwhelming, sickening aroma of sage and lavender attack my nostrils as I enter — tools once used to restrain me, though I eventually adapted to them over a few thousand years, making them practically useless. There is no opportunity to turn back now, nevertheless, and I have nowhere else to turn. I will soon replace this foul smell with the spilled blood of innocent creatures, and I can cope with some short-term discomfort. I have been through worse.

I go to lower the infant upon a leather settee, which is surprisingly new-looking, and then are startled by some encroaching footsteps. I was under the impression I was alone.

'Who goes there?' I cry out, quite prepared to reveal my actual demonic form as a first line of defence. 'Make yourself known!'

An elderly, breaking voice responds. 'Good evening. I am Alfred. This is my home. Who are you, might I ask?'

He struggles to walk, and I can smell the scent of cancer festering from beneath his frail, paper-thin flesh. Death is not far from him, but that does not explain why I failed to sense his presence.

'Please, sir, have mercy on me and my child,' I say to him pitifully. 'We are outsiders and have nowhere to stay. The air outside tonight is cold, and we are freezing to the bone. May we stay here with you? I do not wish to intrude...'

Alfred hobbles up to me, aiming a walking stick at my chin. 'You look familiar. Are you famous or something?'

'Hardly,' I jest. 'I do not wish to trouble you, and I would understand if you were concerned about allowing strangers into your humble home. There are so many wicked-minded people around these days. Sin is rife.'

'Indeed, and you can never be too careful. Of course, by all means, you can stay,' he said, smiling at the child. 'Such a beautiful little thing. What is her name?'

My immediate thought turned to Sabina. 'Eliza. Her name is Eliza de Lockewood.'

'That's a pretty name, very unique.' Alfred leans across to take a closer look, or as much as his crippled body allows him to. 'You do look familiar, my fine fellow. There was a chap in the newspaper, a man named Jason Sonnet, who had murdered his wife that looks just like you. It can't be you, though, can it? Only a mindless buffoon would be walking around in the open after committing such a heinous act.'

I am puzzled by Alfred's words, and my patience steadily grows thinner. He is wasting my time! 'You are mistaken, sir. I know of this Jason Sonnet, and he took three lives: that of his wife, their child and himself. Has this not been made known?'

'Reported, you mean?' Alfred hesitates and begins to stare at me. 'Not that I'm aware of, but I don't have a television or radio—can't trust them, nor any other technology for that matter. Please pardon my questions. I'm just an old miser who gets lonely now and then. I appreciate your company, should truth be told.'

'And I appreciate yours,' I lie. 'Will you let us stay?'

'Yes. My home is yours.'

From the deathly scent lingering within Alfred's cells, I conclude that he will only have few weeks or so before death welcomes him. Sabina and I can bide our time, play along with Alfred's false perception that we are but innocent travellers. Either way, he will need to accept my generous offer, to allow for Sabina and myself to live here with our new child, or else die much sooner and more cruelly. I am tempted to commit the latter, it must be said, though not out of mercy. Would that not be more merciful, though? Am I already losing my demonic touch?'

'Care for a dram of whiskey?' Alfred asks me. 'I've got a thirty-year-old batch hidden away upstairs, perfect to warm up cold bones. I'll never get through it by myself.'

'That is generous of you,' I say, nodding in acceptance. 'I will wait here with my daughter while you go and get it.'

'Nonsense!' he shrieks, eagerly waving for me to follow him. 'I struggle to walk up my narrow, steep staircase now. I'll require your assistance, your youthful strength.'

The tempting notion of ending this nuisance rises in my thoughts once more, but I am interested to see whether any relics of my past Satanic rituals in this place remain. Upstairs was where Brother Mason and Lockewood performed their rituals to enforce my spirit. I could use those accursed objects for further use. This could bode well in my favour.

'These old bones of mine,' Alfred groans, rubbing at his hips. 'My skin is as thin as silk, and my eyes are starting to fail me. Darkness creeps in more and more every day. I've been told to spend time outside, to bask in the sun, to lengthen what life remains, but there ultimately comes a point when one must accept fate. I have never been a fan of the sun.'

'The sun to me is dark,' I reply. 'I much prefer the moon and its silence,' I say, offering a hand to balance Alfred's swaying body. 'You cannot defy destiny, and I do not wholly believe in fate. Death comes to all, and you must welcome it — embrace it.'

'Is that so?' Alfred takes me into a decrepit, cobweb-laden room. There is a pentagram beneath the worn carpet, which was drawn by Brothers Mason and Lockewood with their own blood, and it swiftly imbues me with more energy and prowess. This is where the rituals took place — there is no denying it. The docile idiot has no idea.

'The whiskey's in one of these drawers, somewhere,' he mumbles to himself, coughing from all the dust he disturbs. 'Perhaps I placed it with the ornamental daggers, or behind the grand altar?'

Those objects were nowhere to be seen and had been lost ages ago. Along with the putrid scent of herbs, I also begin to sense that there is something fouler at foot here. Alfred is not who he is claiming to be. Both of us are portraying a false façade, and my anger immediately intensifies.

'What say you, Alfred, do you enjoy dabbling in the glorious arts of old?' I ask.

'Indeed, I do.' He hesitates to respond further, turning his sight from mine. 'They remind me of better days, of days before I was betrayed along with my brothers and sisters. Never can true reconcilement grow where wounds of deadly hate have pierced so deep.'

'When we sung of Chaos and Eternal Night?' I add.

'Those happy fields, where joy forever dwells, have all but gone,' he laments.

'Hail horrors, hail…' I growl.

Alfred laughs and then looks to me sombrely. 'That is all we know now, is it not? Suffering. The mortal life is most certainly not for me.'

I move over to the pitiful worm, towering above him, barely holding back my rage. 'You would dare attempt to deceive me, Moloch?'

A faint sigh and then more laughter leaves from him, as he turns to face me again. 'We meet once more, Brother. I have looked forward to this reunion of ours… Baal.'

'Incarceration did not suit you?' I humour. 'So, my powers *are* weaking.'

'You were wrong to imprison me, Brother. You will pay.'

I was wise enough to choose a vessel that is physically strong and agile, unlike my demonic brother. Moloch, my greatest nemesis, is robbed of any opportunity to morph into its true abhorrent form as I take great pleasure in clasping my iron-clad talons around the old man's scrawny neck, squeezing it with all my might, forcing all breath out of him

'Baal!' Moloch croaks and wheezes through the old man's scrawny vocal cords. 'Know this: we are not alone here. We are being watched!'

'Your modern speech and ability to possess have vastly improved since we last met, but you are still weaker than me,' I boast, infusing a wave of fiery embers into the old man's blood vessels, forcing his body to convulse and then set alight. 'How dare you meddle with my plans. This is the last time, Moloch, that you shall be a thorn in my side!'

'You are forsaken,' he cackles, amid a strong flow of blood that trails from the old man's mouth. 'I am but a pawn sent to challenge you, to prove for certain if your loyalty has truly gone. It has, has it not, Baal?'

Some slight reservation enters my thoughts as I fondly recall memories of slaying mortals with Moloch, but that soon passes.

'Farewell, Brother,' I say to him, shedding a tear, genuinely haunted by what I must do now. 'Be free, for I will it. Be gone. Rest in eternal slumber…'

The old man's body falls limp in my hands as I feed my will and malice into his flesh to flare the flames that now kindle inside every cell—every atom—within him. All that is left thereafter is a pile of ashes that pour away between the exposed floorboards, and I can no longer sense Moloch's dark spirit. To Hell I have sent my fallen brother, my fellow demon, my fellow celestial spirit. I must summon my beloved before it is too late—before another of my kind appears to offer further scorn.

I return to the sleeping child, and then turn toward a stone fireplace situated opposite her. It is large enough to enact my next ritual, the ceremony that will invoke Sabina's spirit to become physical once again. She will be with me, by my side, unharmed and loyal as always—I swear it! This ritual may, however, drain too much energy from me, but it will be worth the risk. I have cast aside my brethren, spilled so much blood, and I am willing to sacrifice whatever I must to fulfil my destiny—to be the first demon who has severed free from Lucifer's infinite hold.

There are several dry logs resting within the fireplace, which I focus on as I commit to my treacherous ritual; and then with both arms outstretched I begin my arduous performance.

'O Flames of Darkness, rise! Bring no warmth or light, no holy presence or plight!' I gasp out in agony as some of my fractured spirit is drawn into the fireplace's centre. Nevertheless, I am determined to see this through. Already, black flames that are surrounded by a dull, scarlet light emerge. It is Sabina's aura. 'Come forth, Sabina! Come forth to thy master! We are one! We are—'

I collapse, drained and convulsing from the agony this ritual causes. My mortal vessel barely holds out from the immense strain placed upon it, but my blackened heart is relieved to see the flames burst and then form into a sphere-shaped portal. The ritual worked!

'Come, my beloved,' I plead, struggling to stand. 'Be with me. Be with me, Sabina. I forgive you for your transgressions. I have… changed.'

Sabina's outline comes into sight; her slender figure, long-flowing hair and piercing eyes instantly entrance me as they did during our first encounter. But, to my gravest horror, Sabina's outline then bursts into a wave of golden flames that tear through the portal and send me flying across the room. I recover, only just, to find another outline emerge from the fire, an outline I have not seen since Babylon's destruction.

I fall to my knees in reverence. 'Master…'

It cannot be—but it is. In contrast to my deformed and lowly state, Lucifer steps out from the portal in their angelic form—a feat no other demon can attain now. I secretly reel in disgust at Lucifer's pristine-white hair, their amber eyes, their god-like presence, and particularly at the six bronze wings that are spread out as a clear symbol of dominance and majesty. We walked alongside the Seraphim once, almighty and revered, though I—along with my fellow, lower-classed brethren—struggle to recount those precious moments now. Lucifer is all that remains of those memories in me.

'You have been busy of late,' says Lucifer, their voice uncharacteristically calm. 'Master? So, you *do* still call me that. And to think that I had almost lost all faith in your loyalty.'

'I serve only you,' I beseech, fearing for my very existence. 'Have I not proven my worth and devotion over this past millennia? The wars? The famines? The plagues? Have none of them impressed you? Have they not appeased your lust for vengeance against the human parasites?'

Lucifer motions for me to kneel right before them, offering a pitiful sigh as our eyes meet. 'My greatest lieutenant, Ekron.'

My true name, and to hear it sends a stream of torment through my conscience. I had forgotten it, along with what benevolence I once bore.

'I am Baal, bringer of destruction and chaos—'

'You are an angel fallen, robbed of what beauty and grandeur you once possessed; a broken spirit that wanders this earthly plain in search of a desire that cannot be fulfilled. You are nothing but a slave, forced to submit against the cosmos under my just rule. You, Ekron, are lost, broken and worthless.'

'I am your humble servant and brother, Master. I am the great demon, Baal, bringer of despair and hatred!'

Lucifer looks to me in confliction. 'You still willingly choose to bear that shameful mark, the name of Baal, the name I granted upon you out of disdain? Is it repentance you seek, or to be called Beelzebub again?'

'I only seek your pleasure and to enact our purpose upon this accursed earth — to reduce the humans that claim ownership over it into babbling animals, devoid of faith and salvation. Have I not succeeded? Have I not been your mightiest weapon?'

Lucifer strokes a hand across my face, gently but with enough pressure to make me realise — without uttering a word — that I have, in fact, offended them; and then they stab at my cheekbones with a tremendous, hate-fuelled force with their fingertips.

'Why did you deceive Azazel, decimate Belphegor and incarcerate Moloch — your own brothers? And now it would appear that you have also destroyed Moloch — my most faithful servant. Speak, Ekron! Explain your treacherous actions!'

I writhe against Lucifer's grasp like a pathetic fish caught in a crude net, unyielding and unwilling to die, fighting against the prospect that I have no way of escaping an imminent doom. My master will grant mercy upon me, upon his worthiest asset, I gather. I hope. I pray.

'They longed to usurp your title, Master,' I plead. 'I alone prevented their treacherous plots —' Lucifer tightens their hold upon me, digging their steel-like nails deeper into my mortal flesh. I ignore the pain, determined to make believable this desperate lie. 'It is the truth! They sought to betray us. I silenced them. They were the traitors — not me!'

'I want to believe that, to believe you. But you would know all about betrayal, wouldn't you, O dearest Ekron?' says Lucifer, shaking their head in disappointment. 'I have been observing your actions, namely your obsession with that mortal witch, Sabina de Lockewood. That filth.'

My tear-filled eyes give away my true emotions and desires, though I battle hard to reign them in. This is just like Babylon, the last time I encountered Lucifer's displeasure.

'Sabina means nothing to me, Master. I am a demon, and we are forbidden to know love and other such mortal pleasures—'

'Yet you bound yourself to her,' says Lucifer, their golden eyes now scarlet and aflame with malevolence. 'You granted her a taste of your powers and knowledge, making her your equal, which is also forbidden. You know this, Ekron!'

'She is but another weapon in my arsenal,' I explain, but it is to little avail. 'All I want is to see this world burn, along with the unworthy humans that plague it.'

'Then—' For the first time ever, I sense reluctance in Lucifer as our eyes meet. 'Then, Ekron, you will not mind me doing this...'

A torrent of searing electrical shocks course through my mortal body; its bones crush; its flesh sets alight; the fingernails are slowly torn out; the teeth are shattered against their sensitive nerves; and I scream out having never suffered such pain before. Jason Sonnet is gone, and from his miniscule ashes my abhorrent soul rises. With a wave of their hands, Lucifer then transforms me back into my demonic form and laughs at the humiliation this causes me.

'Master!' I beseech, hoping to somehow de-escalate the situation. 'My loyalty has always been to you and our brethren, never to the mortals, never to Sabina!'

'You have done our noble work well, Brother.' Lucifer pauses, though only to look down upon me in dismay. 'But this — this act of treachery you have committed against me, in allowing for Sabina to enter your heart — cannot go unpunished! For you, Ekron, I will tear apart the fabric of space and time; I will revoke your future and ensnare you within the past, where you will re-live your first encounter with Sabina de Lockewood and all the other sordid moments thereafter, until you reach this poignant moment again. Casting you into the Endless Void is not enough this time. My decision comes with great sorrow, but it is final.'

'I beg thee! Do not do this, Lucifer! Do not punish me for a crime I have not committed!'

Nevertheless, and despite my genuine attempt to appease them, Lucifer continues with their cruel judgement. 'It will be a ceaseless cycle of despair and longing, one where you will never achieve your utmost desire — to be fully bound with the mortal woman whom you love. There is no other way, and your brothers — Belphegor, Azazel and Moloch — must be avenged. You have brought disrepute upon our kin. You have brought this upon yourself, Ekron!'

I accept Lucifer's punishment, albeit with a deep level of scorn. There is no fear in my tainted soul for existing in such purgatory, however, for Sabina will always be with me; and it is futile to defy or even attempt to attack my master. I have tried it before and just look where it has gotten me — here, begging before him like a starved animal slavering over scraps to salvage their futile life.

'Your punishment will not stop there,' Lucifer whispers to me, reverting to their usual, malevolent demeanour. 'I will add to your necessary suffering…'

From the flames behind Lucifer I catch a glimpse of Sabina in her fair form, her human form; the beautiful, angelic being that had so easily seduced me all those years ago.

'Sabina!' I cry out to her, but she merely walks on by to pick up the sleeping infant. 'Look at me! I command you to look at me!'

'You have no power over her now. I have severed your bond,' Lucifer informs me with a sadistic degree of enjoyment. 'She is free to walk this earth again, though it will bring much heartache and melancholy. For her part in your betrayal, Sabina also deserves punishment. She will, too, know my wrath.'

'Sabina!' I go to grab her but instantly become paralysed, riddled with even more pain. 'Do not forsake me. Help me, Sabina!'

She finally graces me with some attention. Sabina, nestling the child tenderly against her bosom, turns to face my demonic presence. Her eyes are filled with tears, and I would give anything just to see that serene smile of hers again. But that does not seem likely.

'You took her from me,' she says with a malicious glare. 'You did, Baal. Eliza perished because of you. I see that now. We were innocent…'

Lucifer turns to her in disgust. 'Go, Witch. Take the child and be gone. You are granted freedom for now, but I will see you again.' Clasping onto the child in protection over her, Sabina nods back to Lucifer in acceptance. 'Mortals have a fickle lifespan, consumed with doubt and sorrow, which you will soon relearn, Sabina. Leave and forget that Baal was ever your master, for he was never allowed such a privilege.'

'I will,' she says, looking to me with a cold, hypnotic stare. 'Baal is nothing but a memory. I do not love him. I never have.'

'You speak lies, Sabina,' I wail, hoping that there still exists a place for me in her heart. 'I am your master, your salvation, your soulmate!'

'There is only one whom I have ever loved, my daughter, Eliza.' Sabina's kisses the child upon their brow, and then she faces away from me. 'You are a demon, Baal. You are a monster. I am not…'

Sabina leaves without even offering a parting word or kiss; the latter I would have cherished more than anything else. To see her vanish into the darkness outside, without showing any grief or woe, is the harshest punishment that Lucifer could have ever bestowed on me.

'It is done,' Lucifer decrees, wrapping their arms and wings around me. 'I am merciful, Brother. Make good your vow to me and our brethren — prove your loyalty and serve our righteous cause. Return to the marshlands. Be given a second chance to prove your worth.'

'A second chance?' I shudder. 'You are truly merciful, Lucifer, and I will not revoke this show of pity.'

'You will not remember Sabina,' they say, growling upon the mention of my beloved's name. 'Go back and fulfil your destiny, Ekron. Become the formidable demon you were meant to be — Beelzebub, the Lord of Destruction, Famine and Plight! Become the harbinger of chaos that I seek in you. Remove your arrogance and become the servant you were destined to be!'

I rest my brow upon Lucifer's chest, showing no apparent threat or ill-will. Then — when my master's guard has finally subsided, and with the most tenacious force I can forge — I run my sharpened horns across Lucifer's throat, slashing their precious, angelic flesh apart until a pool of acidic blood pours out from the wound. The pain is excruciating for us both, but — unlike Lucifer — I show no discomfort, only sheer joy.

'You have betrayed me!' Lucifer falls into my arms, revealing a vulnerable side to them I had always dreamt of witnessing. 'Traitor!'

'I am no traitor, Lucifer. We were equals once, a fact that you have corrupted and then forgotten. I am no slave. I will be free of you!'

Still clenching onto me, Lucifer reveals their true demonic form; it is a repugnant sight that not even I could ever accomplish. Our eyes meet and souls unify, bound to a fate that neither of us wanted: to fail, to fall into ruin. However, as a lasting act of mockery made against me, Lucifer's wounds miraculously heal, and I am left to dwell over my latest failure.

'Fool! I am eternal. Your punishment is just!' Lucifer states, syncing their spiritual energy with mine. 'You will return to the marshlands of ancient Acle and repent for this sinful act. You will serve as my slave and be glad!'

'I will never be a slave,' I roar, unmoved by my master's threats. 'I will be with Sabina. I will hunt her down and make her mine. Nothing will stop that, not even you...'

'We will see, Brother.'

A shroud of darkness sweeps over my eyes and I wonder if this is death, welcoming it as the escape I have long dreamt of; but then I awaken and realise that I am sat beneath a large willow tree that stands just beyond a foggy marshland plain, where I first met Sabina and her child. Each memory of the heinous acts — the wars, plagues, possessions and famines — I committed over the last six-hundred years swiftly fade from my mind. I did not honestly believe that Lucifer could harness such a power, to manipulate time and space, and I will not make that mistake again.

I feel... different. It is like some grievous emotion has been removed from my conscience, a positive one that I am forbidden to know or learn. It must have been love, for that is a privilege that we demons cannot ever bestow. Only hatred and a passionate urge for vengeance course through my veins now, and the loyalty I bear for Lucifer intensifies tenfold. I am Baal, not worthy of the grand title of Beelzebub, but I will soon change that.

I am in my fairer form: a lowly peasant that goes by the name of Bartholomew. Why has my master sent me to this barren wasteland? Why am I here? What terrible acts against humanity can I possibly inflict upon this sodden landscape? I should be tearing down civilisations, laying waste to thousands of lives. Why am I here?

As I ponder the mystery behind Lucifer's work, a glint of pale sunlight catches my attention. The wave of fog turns golden and gradually diminishes, and a strong scent of lavender is carried across the subtle breeze into my nostrils. I turn my head in search of the aroma's source only to find two feminine figures; one is a small child, innocent and full of joy, and the other is a woman dressed in white with raven-black hair and eyes glistening like emeralds. The woman, the mother, is a rare beauty that I cannot remove from my heart and thoughts, no matter how much I yearn to.

I go to make my move, to inflict catastrophic suffering upon these latest victims of mine, but then an unfamiliar sensation infiltrates me. Where my heart once lay a reverberating, warm sensation musters, and all the previous feelings of pure hate and malevolence are removed. I know not yet of who these mortals are, this woman and child, but they somehow intrigue me. Love is forbidden under Lucifer's rule, however, and grave consequences await those who dare defy my master. But what Lucifer does not know, surely, will not bear any repercussions. I must learn who she is, this women in white, and make her mine. Her fate now rests in my hands.

I am Baal. I am formidable. I am a demon-on-high, greatest of my brethren, but… I am no slave. My will shall be done. My destiny will be entwined with hers, no matter the cost, no matter the consequences.'

Insight

(Bonus Story)

My debut horror novel, *The Skipton Haunting: Tale of the Red Ribbon Witch*, was based on a series of unexplainable events that occurred while my family resided at an address on Skipton Close in Newton Aycliffe, County Durham, England. That book detailed some of our ordeal there, in which we were tormented by two malevolent entities—Sabina, the Red Ribbon Witch, and Baal, a ram-headed demon—over the course of an eight-month period. It was not the first time I had seen Baal, however. The demon had appeared to me years before, during childhood, in nightmares that I can still clearly recall to this day.

In the following story I will reveal to you the first and most poignant encounter with Baal, which I have only ever previously shared with my mother and wife. To give further context: I was nine years old and lived with my mother, father and younger sister at Honister Place in Newton Aycliffe (my first home) at the time. My family were close and loving as far as I could see it, and I never once suspected that my parents bore any dislike for one another, although, in hindsight, there were some tell-tale signs that I should have perhaps picked up on.

I consider this nightmare to be an omen, a possible foreshadowing and possible proof of having a negative attachment. I'll leave it up to you as the reader to decide…

***

It was sometime during the summer of 1997. I was wrapped up in my bedsheets, hugging into my favourite Batman figurine, naïve of the horrors that take place in our world. It was dark, but I wasn't scared of it like I'd normally be. For some reason, I felt an urge to brush aside my bed sheets and to then stand within the centre of my bedroom. Something already felt out of sorts, given that I couldn't hear my father's usual snoring, and I soon felt compelled to look out my window. I wish I hadn't, though.

On opening my curtains, a scene only reminiscent of Hell greeted me. All the houses, parked cars and trees in my cul-de-sac were aflame; the night sky had been turned amber in colour because of the huge fires, and I could feel the intense heat scorching at my skin, blistering it, melting it into my bones. Everything in sight was being destroyed, and all I could do was watch on helplessly.

I cowered back into bed, hiding myself under the duvet again, hoping to find some safety and comfort there. But then came a deep, guttural voice that shook me to the core.

'You must choose,' it said, whispering into both my ears. 'You must choose, boy.'

I clenched my eyelids together, desperate to fall back asleep (although, in truth, I already was). There didn't seem to be any apparent way to escape from this disturbing scene, no matter how much I thought about it. I completely cocooned myself within the bed sheets, somehow believing that this would protect me, until the ethereal voice spoke again.

'You must choose,' it said, pleadingly now, sending me into a bout of sheer panic. 'Choose!'

My entire body trembled; my mouth dried, and my teeth chattered uncontrollably from the fear now coursing through me. Left with little other option, I leapt from the bed in hope of reaching my mother, to embrace her, to gain her reassurance. Nevertheless, my parents weren't in their bedroom and neither was my sister in hers. I was stood alone on the upper landing, swamped in a choking wave of darkness and smoke, although my solitude did not endure.

I turned my head slowly and cautiously to the staircase, where other family members were now lined upon each step; my mother's side of the family were on one side and my father's side were on the opposite. None of my them acknowledged me. None of them offered a single word or even a brief glance, despite my desperate efforts to gain some response from them, I was merely met with a vacant, cold, judgemental stare from those who I adored and cherished more than anything else. Loneliness flooded into my conscience, along with a sickening wave of dread.

Again, and I don't know what it was that compelled me, I felt an innate desire to move against my will, down the stairwell, not knowing what lay at the bottom. I carefully walked down the stairs, making the odd side-glance at my family members, who seemed to—within this moment, at least—utterly despise me. With every step taken the surrounding heat intensified and the air grew thinner. I could barely breathe, let alone move, and it felt like something terrible was waiting for me.

I eventually made it into the living room, sobbing and fighting to control the overwhelming anxiety that was inflicting my body and mind. I found my mother stood with her back against the farthest wall with an arm wrapped around my little sister; my father was stood against the opposite wall with his head held down low and eyes blackened, swaying back and forth, as if he hadn't slept for weeks. There was no furniture. Other than my closest family members, the room was completely empty.

'You must choose,' iterated the taunting voice. 'Choose, boy!'

I couldn't work out where the voice was coming from, and I had no intention of discovering what was making it. So, held in uncertainty, I focused on my mother and her calm smile, praying that this nightmare would soon end. She held out her free hand, goading for me to clasp onto it. I was literally inches away from her, from seeking the love and safety I so passionately sought, when a deafening explosion suddenly threw me to the ground.

The floor then began to tremor violently, convincing me that I was in the midst of a powerful earthquake, and then a fracture swept across the living room's centre. I was thrown into in a terrifying situation: I had one foot on my mother and sister's side, and the other was resting precariously on my father's. Peering down into the crack below with one eye opened, I witnessed a sea of lava muster and then rise; and there were people drowning in it, screaming out for help — all of them crying out to me. I screamed to my mother for her aid, but she didn't respond. I then screamed to my father, and neither did he respond. The only voice I could hear was that of my phantom oppressor.

'Choose!' it roared. 'Choose, boy!'

'Who are you?' I asked, genuinely afraid of what answer I'd be given. 'What are you?'

'Look up and you will see,' it replied, and I didn't dare resist. 'Look up, little boy.'

I did so, against a crippling sense of reluctance, mindful of the possible danger. Our living room's window faced out onto the street where the flames now roared higher into the sky, where I could now see a demonic being that was standing just beyond our front gate. The creature, if you can call it that, was at least ten-to-twelve feet tall; its skin was deathly white and covered in sharpened strands of fur; its eyes were elongated and black (like the eyes of alien greys you sometimes see in their supposed depictions); its body was muscular and deformed; and upon its ram-like head were huge, spiralling horns that were as black and imposing as its eyes. Note: I had not yet watched any horror movies or read any novels that could imprint that terrifying vision in my mind, so to see this demon was truly horrific.

I had no knowledge back then of what it was that confronted me, but this creature would later state (during my time spent living at Skipton Close, when I encountered it again) that its name was Baal; to my daughter it referred to itself as Belly-Bob, which my wife and I assumed could have been a mispronunciation of Beelzebub. Whatever it is, I wouldn't wish Baal upon my worst enemy.

'What do I have to choose?' I asked, wiping away the tears streaming down my face.

Baal didn't speak through its mouth, though it told me: 'Your parents, boy. You must choose.'

The crack beneath me widened, and I could feel myself almost falling into it. I looked to my father, who gave me an expression of utter despair in response, and then to my mother. Her smile hadn't dwindled, and I knew — without any shadow of a doubt — what choice I needed to make.

I lunged into my mother's arms, which she immediately wrapped around me, removing all the previous, foreign feelings of anguish and dread. My father cried out in despair, and then Baal released a gut-wrenching ripple of cruel laughter. The side of the room where my father stood collapsed thereafter, and into the fiery pit he fell. I nestled against my mother's side, weeping and begging for forgiveness. But now, within that harrowing moment, not even her maternal love could vanquish the dire guilt I felt in the depths of my stomach and heart.

The nightmare ended with myself, my mother and sister staring at the malignant beast outside. Flames coursed over Baal as it cackled in delight, and then the evil entity vanished, leaving us in a shroud of darkness thereafter.

A year later, around the same time in 1998, my mother reluctantly informed me that she and my father were separating, and before I knew it we had moved out of my family home to live with my grandparents for six months. My sister was too young to understand what was going on, but I could sense all the tension and uncertainty that festered within those who I had previously thought were so happy and content. I was caught in the middle of it all, and all the while I thought back to that harrowing vision, my first meeting with "Baal".

I was given a stark and terrible decision to make not long after: to either live with my mother or father. I couldn't help but recall Baal's words to me, and it began to sink in that what I had first considered to be a nightmare was, in fact, a possible vision into my tumultuous future; and just like in the peculiar dream, I chose to stay by my mother's side. I honestly do believe that what was revealed to me in that nightmare was a foreshadowing of the events that would change my life forever, and it also makes me question what role this goat-headed demon, Baal, still has in it.

Was this dream merely coincidental or else a premonition? I don't think I'll ever discover the truth. Nevertheless, whenever I have seen Baal again in a nightmare something horrendous has always proceeded it. There are many who don't believe in ghosts, demons, angels, or even the afterlife— which is okay, and everyone is entitled to their own opinion— but I do now, even if it means being called crazy or delusional. Afterall, there are mystical forces at work within this world that no one can truly know the answers to, and I firmly consider Baal to be one of these enigmas. I will, no doubt, continue to seek these answers for the rest of my life, though I sincerely hope that Baal has little part to play in them for the remainder of it.

There is, of course, one little snag that Baal pointed out to me several times during their nightmarish visitations: '*Once connected, never can a bond be broken...*'

The End

Thank you for reading my novel. It would be greatly appreciated if you could leave an honest review on either or both Amazon and Goodreads. I genuinely hope you have enjoyed reading this novel and welcome any feedback you might have to offer, be it good or bad. Writing is my form of escape, and your reviews help me to understand where things work or where I've gone wrong.

With kindest regards,
Andrew John Bell

For those who may wish to learn more of 'The Skipton Haunting', I took part in a radio interview with Dave Shrader (Host of 'Midnight in the Desert' and member of several paranormal tv shows, including *Ghost Adventures, Destination Fear* and *The Holzer Files*), in which I discussed what my family went through whilst living at Skipton Close.

Here is the weblink to that interview:
https://youtu.be/bLkrSc8gte0

Thank you again.

www.ingramcontent.com/pod-product-compliance
Lightning Source LLC
Chambersburg PA
CBHW071212250626
47159CB00001B/289